Praise for Joyce Gee and The Altira Series

"A wonderful epic fantasy, which offers enough familiarity for fans of the genre while crafting a unique story. With a great plot, characters who truly shine, and a brilliant world." —*Starred Review, 5/5*

"A compelling, well thought out story which leaves you wanting more."
—*Early Reader Review*

"*Magic of Lies* is fast-paced, witty, and was instantly my new favorite fantasy series. Joyce Gee built a beautifully rich and diverse world. *The Altira Series* deserves a home on any fantasy lovers' bookshelf alongside George R.R. Martin, J.R.R. Tolkien, and Sarah J. Maas. With so many enchanting characters, you'll be rooting for them all. I highly recommend reading it!" —*Alex Williams, editor*

"I loved Joyce Gee's debut, *Magic of Lies*. Princess Eirian is sent away after her birth and returns to her father's kingdom twenty years later with the expectation that she will become queen. But she is a magic user in a kingdom that does not like magic users, and her father Nolan suffers from a terrible disease that is robbing him of his memory. I loved the tension in this fantasy novel, with war looming, with the questions about King Nolan, about Eirian's magic and her worries about ascending the throne. I also really liked the friend group, and the tension with the various romantic leads, Aidan the captain of the guard and Celian. I am looking forward to book two!" —*Starred Review, 5/5*

"Magical and exciting! I can't wait for the rest of the series!"
—*Cori Nevruz, thriller and suspense author*

About the author Joyce Gee

Joyce Gee is an Australian author based in Mandurah, Western Australia. Growing up among the rainforests of Far North Queensland, she loved to vanish into the other worlds hidden within the trees. When she isn't writing, she enjoys drinking tea, pottering around the garden with husband and their two children, or escaping with her camera to capture the beautiful landscape of Western Australia.

Her latest release is *The Altira Series*, composed by *Magic of Lies*, *Blood of Husks*, *Grave of Dandelions*, *Shadows of Life*, *Game of Gods*, and *Fires of Unmaking*.

The Altira Series

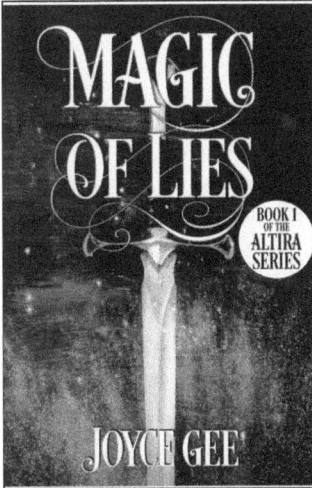

MAGIC OF LIES

BOOK 1 OF THE ALTIRA SERIES

JOYCE GEE

When Princess Eirian returned home after decades away, she thought it would be a fresh start. Born with magic, she struggles to balance her ability to give life with the desire to kill. Raised a mage in a distant city, she struggles to adjust to life as a princess in a court where magic is undesired.

With assassination attempts and rumors of war, Eirian proves to those around her that she is not one to hide from confrontation. Even when it risks her life.

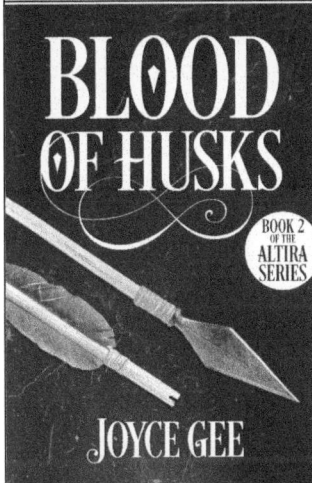

BLOOD OF HUSKS

BOOK 2 OF THE ALTIRA SERIES

JOYCE GEE

The Kingdom of Endara is at war and Eirian refuses to be the soft-hearted queen the enemy expects. Among her growing collection of secrets is one that can help turn the tide of battle, even if it means that her people might turn on her.

She knows she can buy the precious time needed for reinforcements to arrive, but she will have to break her promises to the ones closest to her.

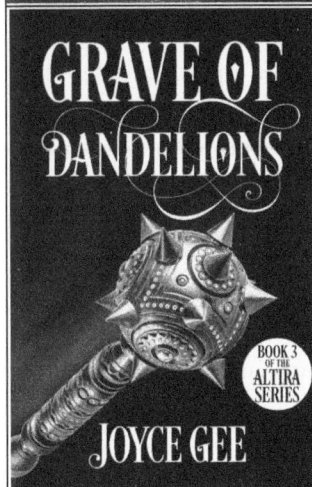

GRAVE OF DANDELIONS

BOOK 3 OF THE ALTIRA SERIES

JOYCE GEE

With nightmares clawing at her fragile mind, Eirian embraces the whispers that have followed her for as long as she can remember. In the aftermath of the real enemy revealing herself, Eirian retreats from the allied armies to seek answers.

Accompanied by Aiden, Celiaen, and Galameyvin, they are determined to confront the spirit of the last mage and face the dark god seeking their destruction. The price for victory is one that Eirian is willing to pay, even if her friends are not.

The Altira Series (continued)

SHADOWS OF LIFE

BOOK 4 OF THE ALTIRA SERIES

JOYCE GEE

Tormented by her mother's memories, Eirian fears what she will become if she accepts her duty. The gods of Death and War have waited patiently for Eirian to make her move. Willing to do whatever they must to ensure the enemy is destroyed and reborn, the gods of War and Death must risk Eirian turning Tir into dust to keep her on their path.

GAME OF GODS

BOOK 5 OF THE ALTIRA SERIES

JOYCE GEE

There is a thin line between saving the world or destroying it, and Eirian finds staying on the right side harder with each passing day. Determined to bring down Annawyn, Eirian returns to where she grew up. No longer hiding the truth, she knows her presence will cause disruption across the land.

But with increasing attacks from the Unseelie army, Eirian cannot stand by while innocent lives are destroyed because of her mistakes.

FIRES OF UNMAKING

BOOK 6 OF THE ALTIRA SERIES

JOYCE GEE

Faced with distrust, Eirian tries to protect the ones she loves with the help of War and Death. All she needs to do is find a way to force the mad god to pass over before her manipulations destroy Endara. But unraveling the darkness woven throughout the people she once ruled is not an easy task.

They know that if they do not stop the enemy's forces, countless innocent lives will be lost.

GRAVE OF DANDELIONS

BOOK 3 OF THE ALTIRA SERIES

JOYCE GEE

GRAVE OF DANDELIONS

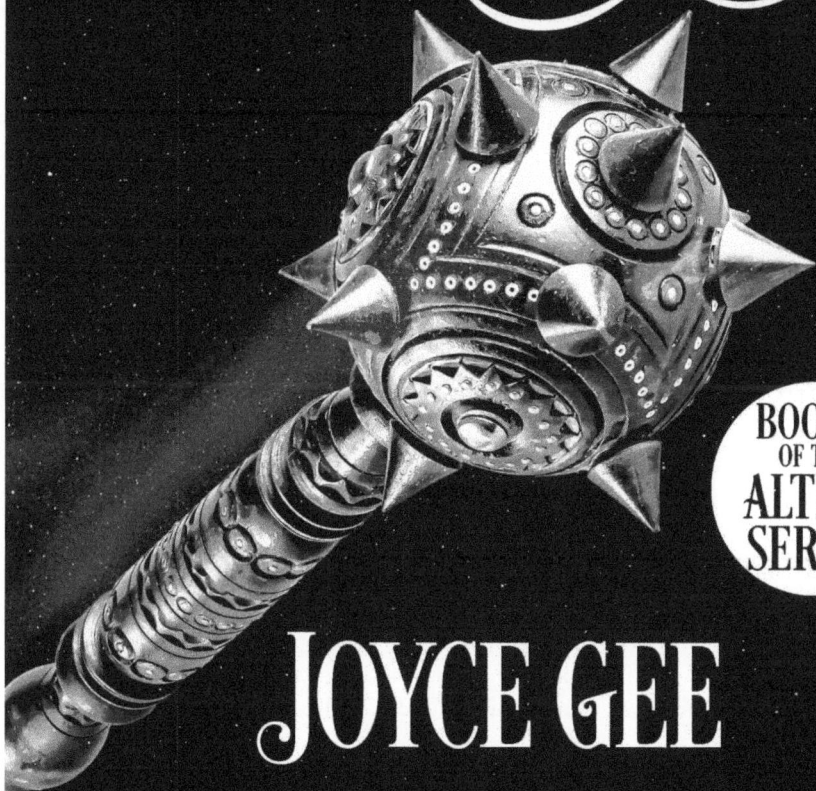

BOOK 3 OF THE ALTIRA SERIES

JOYCE GEE

5310
PUBLISHING

Published by
5310 Publishing Company
Go to 5310publishing.com for more great books!

SCAN ME

Our books may be purchased in bulk for promotional, educational, or business purposes. Please contact your local bookseller or 5310 Publishing at sales@5310publishing.com or refer to our website at 5310PUBLISHING.COM.

GRAVE OF DANDELIONS (1st Edition) - ISBNs:
Hardcover: 9781998839216
Paperback: 9781998839223
Ebook/Kindle: 9781998839209

Author: Joyce Gee
Editor: Alex Williams
Cover Design: Eric Williams
Map Illustrator: Dewi Hargreaves

GRAVE OF DANDELIONS (1st Edition) was released in June 2024.

ADULT FICTION (with Young Adult interest; it can be categorized as New Adult 16+)
Fantasy / Epic
Fantasy / Action & Adventure
Fantasy / General

Themes explored include: Epic fantasy; Adventure fiction; Love and relationships; Coming of age; Death, grief, loss; Interior life; Identity / belonging; Politics; Narrative theme: Social issues; Mythical creatures: elves.

In the aftermath of the real enemy revealing itself, Eirian is determined to confront the spirit of the last mage and face the dark god seeking their destruction. The price for victory is one she is willing to pay, even if her friends are not.

For Beau

You are my forever and always.

Acknowledgements

I'd like to begin by acknowledging the Traditional Owners of Australia and pay my respects to Elders past and present.

To my wonderful, patient, and always encouraging husband, Beau. I couldn't have done this without you. You are my rock, my sanctuary, the one I can always rely on, and I will always choose you. For my two children, keep dreaming of the stars, and I will keep holding you up to reach them. To Kyle, your enthusiasm to read this series means the world to me. And to the rest of my family, thank you for your support!

To Freya, I hope you're watching on and laughing at me. Every story I write is for you. Always. I miss you every day. And I hope you love every piece of art I've had commissioned for these characters that you loved. To Barbara, I still hope you're proud of me.

As always, I could not have done this without the support of Anita and Meghan, my fabulous alpha readers. Especially Anita; your support is everything. I love knowing I can throw a first draft at you, and you'll read it. As for you, Callai, thank you for being one of my best friends. You keep me sane, and I love you. Please never stop sending me funny bird videos at random hours. To Grace, and Dana: thank you for cheering me on.

To the ladies of the TMT. You always know who you are. Thank you for being incredible.

—Joyce Gee, author

CAST OF CHARACTERS

Kingdom of Endara
Eirian Altira: Princess of Endara, purple mage
Duke Everett Altira: Eirian's cousin, next in line to the throne, Duke of Tamantal
Duke Marcellus: Nolan's cousin, Duke of Raellwynt
Duchess Brenna: Marcellus's wife, chief of Eirian's ladies in waiting
Earl Gallagher: Earl of Jurien
Earl Kendall: Kathleen's husband
General Cameron: Endaran small council, commander of the Endaran military
Lady Isabella: Eirian's lady in waiting, daughter of Countess Kathleen
Captain Gunter: Captain of Everett's guard

Kingdom of Endara – Eirian's guards
Captain Aiden Cathasaigh: Captain of Eirian's guard
Merle: Aiden's second in command
Devin: Merle's squad
Fox: Merle's squad
John: Merle's squad
Sid: Merle's squad
Tobin: Merle's squad

Fionn: Squad leader
Kyson: Fionn's squad
Paxton: Fionn's squad
Zack: Fionn's squad
Tyler: Fionn's squad

Fisk: Aiden's squad
Gram: Aiden's squad
Lyle: Aiden's squad
Randolph: Aiden's squad
David: Aiden's squad
Mac: Aiden's squad

Gabe: Squad leader
Jack: Gabe's squad
Kip: Gabe's squad
Wade: Gabe's squad
Kane: Gabe's squad

Kingdom of Ensaycal
King Paienven Kaetiel: King of Ensaycal, red mage
Queen Sannaeh Zarthein: Paienven's wife, sister of Archmage Baenlin Zarthein, red mage

Kingdom of Ensaycal – Princes of Ensaycal
Prince Galameyvin Kaetiel: Prince of Ensaycal, Celiaen's cousin, blue mage
Prince Celiaen Kaetiel: Crown Prince of Ensaycal, son of Paienven and Sannaeh, red mage

Kingdom of Ensaycal – Celiaen's companions
Tara: Red mage in charge
Alyse: Tara's assigned blue
Tynan: Blue assigned to Celiaen
Kenna: Red mage
Ianto: Blue mage assigned to Kenna
Lydia: Green mage
Harlow: Yellow mage
Link: Yellow mage
Rosemary: Yellow mage
Kelsea: Green mage
Tully: Red mage
Cai: Blue mage assigned to Tully
Owen: Red mage
Lachlan: Blue mage assigned to Owen
Amy: Green mage
Tyrone: Red mage
Caitir: Blue mage assigned to Tyrone
Imogen: Red mage
Darcie: Blue mage assigned to Imogen
Mabel: Red mage
Osric: Blue mage assigned to Mabel

Mages of Riane
Archmage Baenlin Zarthein: First red archmage of the high council
Tessa Valkera: Future grand mage, purple mage, Jaren's sister
Fayleen: Yellow mage, Eirian's best friend
Soren: Blue mage assigned to Baenlin
Jaren Valkera: Red mage, friend of Eirian
Zack: Blue mage assigned to Jaren
Rylee: Red mage, friend of Eirian
Luke: Blue mage assigned to Rylee

Kingdom of Telmia

King Neriwyn: King of Telmia
Lord Vartan: Telmian general
Lord Faolan: Telmian envoy to Eirian
Lady Saoirse: Faolan's twin sister, part of Telmian delegation
Lord Tharen: Part of Telmian delegation
Ilar: Part of the Telmian delegation
Muireann: Part of the Telmian delegation
Slaine: Part of the Telmian delegation
Kearney: Part of delegation, Kiernan's twin
Kiernan: Part of delegation

Kingdom of Athnaral

King Aeyren: King of Athnaral
General Tomas: Athnaralan general

Other characters

Ona: Child Eirian rescues
Lieutenant Todd: Commander of an Endaran company

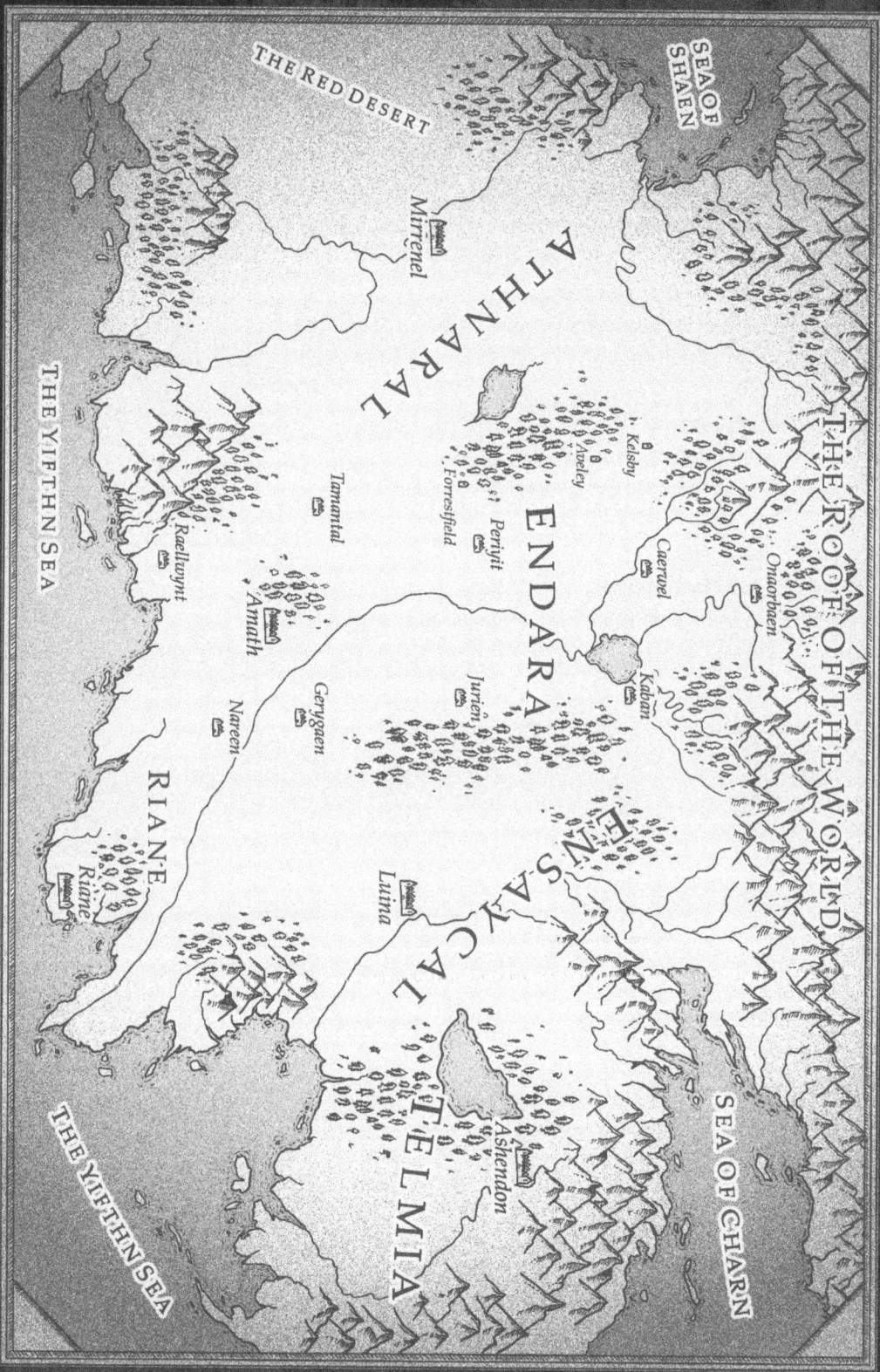

THE RED DESERT

SEA OF SHAEN

ATHNAARAL

Mirrenel

THE YIFTHN SEA

Kelsby

Aveley

Forrestfield

Tamantal

Periyit

ENDARA

Caervael

Omaorbaen

Raelliwynt

Amrath

Jurien

Kaban

THE ROOF OF THE WORLD

Gerygaen

Nareen

ENSAXCAL

RIANE

Riane

Luina

TELMIA

SEA OF CHARN

Asherndon

THE YIFTHN SEA

ONE

"I thought I'd find you here."

Not turning, Eirian gazed out at the sea of tents. "Yes, I'm very predictable, Gal."

He chuckled, walking over to join her at the edge. It was understandable why Eirian preferred the rooftop. The view of the allied forces was impressive, and Galameyvin suspected she was watching the ripple of wards protecting the camp. Between the daoine and the mages of the Ensaycalan legion, they had blanketed Kelsby with magic, hoping to keep the darkness out.

"You're troubled."

"That's what you're going with?"

Galameyvin smiled faintly. "Too obvious?"

Waving at the view, Eirian said, "We leave for Cynwrig Tor tomorrow. I don't know how long we'll be gone, and I suspect Darragh and others will use my absence to attack Aeyren."

"Ree—"

"No, no, I haven't finished. There's a good chance I'll lose my throne while I'm off doing whatever I'm going to do after questioning the previous Eirian Altira. I think I'll go down in Endaran history as the shortest reigning monarch. Not that it matters when I'm probably going to die, anyway."

Rolling his eyes, Galameyvin sighed. Tempted to argue, he reminded himself that when Eirian was in a mood, bashing his head against a wall was less painful. It was one of those times when shoving her in a training square with Celiaen was the best solution. Unfortunately, he could not do that. They had sent him to fetch her for a strategic meeting before she left Kelsby.

"At least you'll make a stubborn corpse," he muttered. "By the way, you're wanted downstairs."

"Really?"

"No, I just thought I'd say it for no reason."

Eirian huffed. "No need to be an ass, Gal."

Arching a brow, Galameyvin craned to look over his shoulder at his backside. "I thought you liked my ass."

Groaning, she covered her face. Memories and whispers warred in her head. They were a racket Eirian could not silence. It was getting worse with each passing day, but she dared not tell anyone. When they thought she would not notice, their expressions confirmed they already suspected something was going on. There was no need to provide them with evidence to suggest the darkness affected her.

"I suppose Celi will be at this meeting?"

"He sent me to get you."

"Well then, better not keep my future husband waiting." Eirian turned, adding, "I'm not sure why we're continuing with the pretense."

Following her, Galameyvin answered, "We don't know for sure you're going to die or lose your throne. Better to keep Paienven happy and avoid him turning on Endara."

In the stairway, guards waited for her. They were more relaxed than Eirian expected, and she directed a suspicious look at Galameyvin. Lurking in the shadow of a bend, Gabe was fiddling with the silver quaternary knot he wore, and the sight of it caused her to halt. Staring at him, she waved for the others to keep going.

"Gabe, I need to ask you something."

Tucking the pendant beneath his armor, Gabe replied, "Yes, I can."

"What?"

"You weren't going to ask me to kill Aeyren?"

Arching a brow, Eirian muttered, "No, I wasn't. At least not today."

"I'd like to do it for you."

"And I'd like to do it myself."

"We could do it together," he suggested.

Inhaling sharply, Eirian struggled to push away the whispers crowding in on her thoughts. Shadows danced at the edge of her vision, taunting with suggestions of what she could do to Aeyren. Watching closely, Gabe did not move from his spot against the wall. He saw the flicker of power in her eyes, but did not fear it or what it meant. The others were far enough down the stairs that he felt confident to speak freely.

"I can tell you're tempted, ma'am."

"This isn't what I wanted to talk about."

Smiling faintly, Gabe asked, "What did you want to discuss?"

Rubbing her face, Eirian attempted to remember why she had stopped him. Going back over what had happened leading up to that moment, she remembered the necklace.

"Your necklace. The knot. Where did you get it?"

"What necklace?"

She felt a flicker of doubt, but the laughter of the whispers mocking her inability to remember drove Eirian to push the feeling aside. "The quaternary knot. You know exactly what I'm talking about."

Surprised, Gabe said, "It's just something I found years ago in a market."

"I kept meaning to ask you about it, but then I'd forget until the next time I saw you playing with it. Vartan said my—"

"I'm sure it's nothing to worry about."

"What?"

"It's just some random symbol, ma'am. Pretty, decorative, meaningless." Gabe gestured dismissively.

Disagreeing, Eirian shook her head. "No, it's not. My mother wore it."

"Well, it's meaningless to me."

"Then why wear it?"

"Because it's an excellent distraction." Staring at her impassively, Gabe explained, "I toy with it when I'm bored. Better I fiddle with a piece of silver on a cord around my neck than stick a knife in some passing person."

Sighing, Eirian could not find a reason to counter his explanation. Her mind continued to cling to the symbol, and taking a step closer to Gabe, she extended her hand, palm upward, and crooked her fingers.

"I want a closer look."

"I'm not sure—"

"Are you arguing with your queen, Gabe?"

Grunting, he fished the pendant out from beneath his armor and stared up at the ceiling. Leaning in, Eirian studied the twist of silver, her eyes following the endless loops entwined by a circle. Tracing a fingertip over the pattern, she frowned and cocked her head to the side, listening to the whispers in her mind.

"It's four loops. Why would she tell him it symbolized her bond with the others? What others?"

Listening to Eirian's muttering, Gabe asked, "What are you talking about?"

"There are three bloodlines, not four." Pressing her fingertips into her eyes, Eirian growled, "No, that's not right. It doesn't feel right."

"Perhaps you should stop thinking about it."

"Why that symbol? Why four endless loops?"

Tucking the necklace away, Gabe watched with concern. Magic swirled around Eirian, betraying her agitation, and it left him uncomfortable. Reaching out, he wrapped his hands around her wrists, pulling them down. Eyes opening, she stared at him with a mixture of confusion and recognition.

"It's time to go to your meeting, ma'am," he told her.

She frowned. "What meeting?"

"The one with the generals and other important people. Like King Neriwyn. Prince Celiaen."

"I think I see it in my dreams."

"No, you don't."

"I almost remember it. It's like they drew inky black lines across my skin. Four endless loops entwined that are drawn together and forced apart constantly."

Gabe shifted his grip on her wrists, forcing Eirian to step closer. Meeting her eyes, he held her gaze, and she thought she saw a flash of blue. There was a name on the tip of her tongue, the whispers coaxing her to say it.

"Stop thinking about it, Eirian," Gabe commanded. "You're working yourself up over nothing. It's just decoration and means nothing."

The whispers fell silent while she stared at him, and Eirian replied, "I can't."

"Yes, you can. Now, we better hurry before the others come back up looking for us. I don't fancy arguing with anyone for the moment."

"You're right."

He winked, letting go of her wrists. There was still a troubled look in her eyes, but it was clear Eirian was attempting to bring her magic under control again. Gabe knew it was important she kept quiet and contained whatever was bothering her. They could not afford to have people questioning Eirian's sanity in the middle of a war. Sensing Galameyvin's magic coming back toward them, he nodded at the stairs and waved for her to go first.

"Gabe."

"Yes, ma'am?"

Eirian kept her eyes on the stairs, careful not to miss a step and slip as she said, "I'm not sure I can do this."

"That's okay. You don't have to be sure. All you have to do is put one foot after another and head in a forward direction. I've seen you heal. If you fall face-first down the stairs, you'll be fine," Gabe replied cheerfully

Glancing back at him to argue it was not what she meant, Eirian did precisely what she was trying to avoid. Misjudging her step down, her boot slid on the edge of the stone, but rather than hitting the ground, she found herself clinging to Galameyvin. Holding her steady, he chuckled at the flustered look on her face as Gabe did his best not to laugh.

"I told you, if you fall, you'll be fine."

Resting her head on Galameyvin's chest, Eirian embraced his calming power and felt his heartbeat echoing in her mind. It was easy to count. She knew its beat as well as she knew her own. It was more effective at soothing her agitation than his magic was. Inhaling his scent, she ignored Gabe's presence behind her. Wrapping his arms around Eirian, Galameyvin kissed the top of her head before looking at the guard expectantly.

"She's just a little flustered," Gabe said dismissively.

"What's wrong, Ree? Please tell me, I want to help you."

Mumbling something they did not catch, Eirian did not move from her spot. Watching concern appear on Gabe's face, Galameyvin wondered what they had discussed. He wanted to ask, but he worried bringing it up again would further agitate Eirian. Holding her tight, he wished he could communicate with Celiaen like the daoine did. Mind to mind. She was an emotional mess, and he did not think a military meeting was the right place for Eirian to be.

"Ree, sweetie, I need you to focus." Pulling her away from his chest, Galameyvin commanded, "Look at me, and listen to my voice."

Lifting her gaze to his, Eirian sighed. "I'm tired, Gal. So tired of not knowing what to do."

"I know. We'll get some answers tomorrow. It'll do you good to be away from all these people and the tension of a battlefront. Don't you agree, Captain?"

Standing on her toes to peer over Galameyvin's shoulder at Aiden, Eirian suspected Celiaen had also sent him to make sure she attended the meeting. She felt like an errant novice being fetched for class. The thought made her chuckle and step sideways to slip around him.

"I better hurry before anyone else is sent to escort me."

Aiden arched a brow. "They didn't send me to get you."

"You weren't?" She paused beside him. "Then why are you here?"

"I had a feeling you might need me."

Grunting, Eirian shot a look at Galameyvin before continuing down the stairs while the three men remained where she left them. Pointing at Gabe, Galameyvin directed Aiden's attention to him.

"What were you talking about?" Galameyvin inquired. "Because she wasn't as bad when we left the roof."

"Nothing much. I actually thought she was going to ask me to kill Aeyren."

"Her nightmares were bad last night," Aiden commented.

Focus shifted to him, and shrugging, the Captain waved at Gabe. Nodding, he hurried down the stairs after Eirian. Left alone with Galameyvin, Aiden leaned against the wall, rubbing his chin in concern.

"I had trouble calming her."

"Did she?"

"No, she didn't lose control of her magic. They're getting worse."

Galameyvin understood Aiden's concern and glanced down the stairs. The nightmares had always bothered him. He had tried to glimpse what Eirian was dreaming in the past and failed. During the dreams, something blocked him from her mind, but Galameyvin had never told anyone. He feared what they might say if they found out. About both his attempts and the fact Eirian's mind could not be accessed.

"Don't take this the wrong way, but did you sleep with her?"

"It didn't make a difference. She was talking in her sleep," Aiden replied. Frowning, he murmured, "Ree doesn't normally talk."

"I heard Neriwyn's name."

"He told Ree about her mother. Maybe she was dreaming about that?"

Arching a brow, Aiden said pointedly, "Do you believe that?"

"No, but I want to."

"Do you trust him?"

It was a troubling question to answer, and Galameyvin shook his head. Turning, he started down the stairs, but Aiden grabbed his arm and stopped him. Clamping down on his magic, he resisted the urge to force the other man to release him.

"You didn't answer my question."

"I expected you to work it out." Galameyvin muttered, "Silence is telling."

"How do we help her?"

Running a hand through his curls, the prince shrugged. He did not know, and the worried expression on Aiden's face made him feel guilty. It was the same look Celiaen wore when asking the same question. Reminded of the other prince and his mixed feelings toward Aiden, Galameyvin took a moment to study him. He understood the confused emotions Celiaen experienced. Something about Aiden drew him as well.

"I think getting her away from Kelsby will be a good start. Seeing an army every day won't be making Ree feel any better about what's going on."

Nodding, he agreed. "It just makes her feel more responsible. Tell me, will your cousin fight our trying to do whatever we can to help her?"

"No. Celi's working on his jealousy. He knows Ree needs all of us to support her. It's our job to hold her together, and that means working as a team even if the two of you can't decide if you want to kill each other or...."

"Or what?" Aiden demanded.

Smirking, Galameyvin moved up to stand on the same step as Aiden and replied, "You know what. The three of you are so fucking obvious. Well, to me anyway. I know Celi and Ree better than they know themselves, and you're just like them."

"You're wrong."

"Oh, Captain, I know what you felt when you watched the two of them spar yesterday. It's okay, I understand. Celi has that effect. Luckily, it wouldn't take much effort on your part to have him where you want him."

Nose flaring, Aiden struggled to push aside the thoughts stirring in his mind. He wanted to blame the magic, but the blue mage had it under control. If he tried to deny it, his words would come across as hollow. Arching a brow, Galameyvin enjoyed the conflicting emotions rolling off the younger man. They left him tempted to push him against the wall. He wanted to kiss Aiden to find out how he would respond.

"It'd be so easy for you to make Celi beg."

"Why are—"

"Because we're all in love with the same woman, and most of us are mages."

Frustrated, Aiden argued, "That's hardly relevant at the moment."

"Well, while you follow me down the stairs with your eyes on my ass—"

"Don't flatter yourself."

Laughing at him, Galameyvin turned and started downward. He did not want to miss the whole meeting, and suspected it would be better if they were there to monitor Eirian. Muttering curses, Aiden followed, trying to avoid looking at Galameyvin. Every time his gaze dropped, he quickly redirected his thoughts.

"I feel you looking, Captain. Such delightful emotions."

"Keep telling yourself that," Aiden snapped.

Knowing Aiden could not see his smile, Galameyvin replied, "I don't mind. You're not a mage, but I'd make an exception. I'd make many exceptions for you."

Seeing the opportunity presented, Aiden asked a question that had bothered him since he learned about the bond between Celiaen and Eirian. "Why does their bond need to be consummated? I mean, it's a bond between their powers, right?"

"Oh, Captain, you have no idea. When two mages are intimate, their magic is involved." Glancing back at him, Galameyvin added, "We're at our most vulnerable."

"I see."

"No, I don't think you do."

"If there's one thing I've learned about magic, it's that there's a strong emotional connection."

They reached the bottom of the stairs and made their way through the corridors toward the main hall, walking side by side. People did not pay them much attention. Without Eirian's presence, they dismissed Aiden as just another soldier. Galameyvin received a second glance from some, but there were enough elves around that most ignored him. Watching out of the corner of his eye, Aiden decided Galameyvin was much easier to get along with than Celiaen.

"Do you think we're going to get anything out of this trip?" he asked quietly.

"I don't know, but I hope so. What do you think of Ree's request to go north?"

He had discussed the request with Everett, and Aiden was in two minds over the matter. Removing Eirian from the battlefront was something he had tried to do repeatedly. But he worried about what could happen to the people at Kelsby if she was not there to protect them from the darkness.

"She's never seen mountains," Aiden answered.

"No, we never ventured near mountains. They'd be something entirely new to Ree, and maybe that look she gets will make it worthwhile."

Knowing precisely what look Galameyvin was talking about, Aiden smiled. People flowed in both directions through the open doors of the hall, busy with their duties. Magic was thick in the air, and Aiden struggled to pick the daoine from the elven mages. Over the top of it all, he detected the sweet scent of flowers and spotted Eirian standing at the furthest end of the table arrangement. She looked up, gaze settling on them while Celiaen spoke.

Hands landed on their shoulders, and the familiar jolt Galameyvin felt informed him of who it was before he glanced at Neriwyn. Aiden clenched his jaw, eyes darting to look at the man holding them back. Slinging his arms over their shoulders, Neriwyn smirked and nodded at Eirian and Celiaen.

"Aren't they pretty together?" he asked with a chuckle.

Galameyvin did not know what game Neriwyn was playing. "How can we help you, sire?"

"It occurred to me, sweet prince, you haven't asked my permission to go off with our dear little queen tomorrow."

"I thought you intended to come as well."

Cocking his head, Neriwyn gazed at Eirian sadly. "I've been convinced otherwise."

Biting his tongue, Aiden said nothing. Noticing Gabe staring at them blankly, he gave a slight shake of his head to confirm they were fine. There was no need to draw attention, and the worried looks Eirian kept giving them were enough.

"Have you told Her Majesty?"

"I'm sure she knows. Lord Faolan will come, and that's all. The rest is up to the four of you to figure out for yourselves." Neriwyn squeezed their shoulders. "One link alone is not as strong as the whole chain together."

Screwing up his face, Aiden asked, "Is this some attempt to impart wisdom?"

"No, this is me saying the view would be so much prettier if the two of you were standing with them where you belong."

"So I take it I've got your permission to go?" Galameyvin inquired, trying to hide his amusement.

Watching Neriwyn gently tuck a stray curl behind Galameyvin's ear, Aiden arched his brows in surprise. There was a tenderness to the action and the king's expression that he did not expect to see.

"Of course, sweet prince. I know who you belong to. Now, they need the two of you. You make each other stronger, even if some of you are too stubborn to see it. Such a typical Altira trait," Neriwyn commented, looking at Aiden pointedly.

Feeling a flare of Eirian's power, they shifted their attention to where she was arguing with Darragh. Slipping his arm off Aiden's shoulders, Neriwyn moved into a crowd of officers. Galameyvin sighed in relief at his departure, exchanging a look with Aiden.

"Did you sleep with him?" Aiden muttered, startled by the pang of jealousy he felt.

"Not for lack of trying."

"Why?"

"King Neriwyn was a challenge I wanted to overcome. Blame my ego. I'm not used to being told no. Especially by overconfident warriors." Galameyvin chuckled. "I'm not sorry I failed. Something tells me it would've been a bad idea to sleep with him."

Dropping his gaze to the swords hanging from Galameyvin's belt, Aiden said, "Overconfident warriors?"

"They're my favorites. Would you like me to show you why?"

"No, not today. But Neriwyn had a point. We should join them. Powers know, someone needs to keep them from doing something stupid."

Galameyvin agreed, and they started moving again. "It's a full-time task. Honestly, the two of them feed off each other's recklessness. I mean, I love them both dearly, but...."

"You just want to strangle them. Frequently."

"It would only encourage them more."

Laughing, Aiden said, "Yes, it would."

When they slipped in to join the group with Eirian, Celiaen stepped back to stand with them. His dark eyes darted from one to the other, narrowing at the amusement he saw on their faces. Winking at Aiden, Galameyvin did not hide his pleasure at the flustered expression that appeared on Celiaen.

"I don't think I want to know," he muttered.

"Are you sure about that?" Aiden leaned in closer to murmur, "Gal was giving me advice on how to handle you."

Covering his mouth to stop his laughter, Galameyvin enjoyed the conflicting emotions rolling off Celiaen. Moving closer, he smiled knowingly and cocked his head to the side, eyes roaming over Aiden while Celiaen watched. Unamused, Gabe cleared his throat, staring blankly at them before looking at Eirian's back. Shaking his head, Celiaen took a deep breath before he bothered to speak to them.

"Ree told them we'll be gone for a few weeks."

"We knew she wanted to go north," Galameyvin replied.

"She's refusing an escort."

Mouth twisting, Aiden shot a glare at her back. "Are you surprised? If it's just our two groups, we'll cover the distance quicker."

Celiaen waved at the Telmian group. "But what about the daoine contingent?"

"Neriwyn said they will not accompany us. I suppose it would be unwise to remove the Queen of Endara, the Prince of Ensaycal, and the King of Telmia from the negotiations. Better he remain here," Galameyvin replied.

Agreeing with Galameyvin, Aiden said, "He has more authority than the generals or Everett. Aeyren might respect him more. You know, king to king."

"That's true. Neriwyn certainly commands more authority than some people here."

Eyes darting between Aiden and Galameyvin, Celiaen grumbled, "I don't like this. The two of you getting along? No. Just no. It's weird."

"Poor Celi, are you jealous the Captain likes me more than you?"

Clicking his tongue, Aiden said to Galameyvin, "Is it so inconceivable that we could like each other?"

"We all want the same thing."

"That's right."

Pinching the bridge of his nose, Gabe muttered, "This is insane."

"So it'll just be us?" Celiaen confirmed. "No daoine, no company of Endaran soldiers, and no gaggle of nobles?"

Galameyvin replied, "Yes, Celi, just us. Like it used to be. Except with twenty-odd human guards included."

"Normally, I'd be the first to argue we should have at least a company of soldiers accompanying us, but I've got a feeling it's better we don't. Eirian will relax without them," Aiden informed them, keeping his voice low.

Following the slide of Aiden's gaze, Celiaen's mouth twisted. "Nightmares?"

"They've gotten worse since the encounter."

"Have you been able to calm her?"

"No. You can have your turn once we're away."

Surprised by Aiden's comment, Celiaen asked, "You're going to let me?"

"She needs us to work together. We achieve nothing by fighting. Personally, I'd rather not condemn the people of our kingdoms to endless wars because I couldn't get over my jealousy."

Gazing at Aiden, Galameyvin remembered all the comments Neriwyn had made to him about setting aside jealousy. It had seemed like they were about Celiaen, but he could not help wondering if Neriwyn had known about Aiden. Shifting his focus to Eirian, Galameyvin saw her glance at them while Cameron argued with Vartan. A faint smile tugged at her lips, accompanied by a sense of relief and a wave of desire. Her face flushed, meeting his gaze.

"Aiden's right. This isn't about us. It's about defeating the darkness and making sure Ree doesn't die."

Celiaen murmured, "We can't just stop arguing. It doesn't work like that."

"Why, princeling, do you enjoy fighting with me that much?" Aiden chuckled. "Does it get you as hot and bothered as it gets her?"

"I'm just saying that we can't turn off our emotions."

Snorting, Galameyvin said, "No, we can't. It's okay to feel these things, but we mustn't let them dictate our decisions. We're stronger if we work together. Besides, Ree is too fucking powerful for any one of us to deal with alone. She can't deny all three of us."

"True. We might be the only thing standing between Ree and her doing something truly reprehensible," Celiaen replied.

Shaking his head at the three of them, Gabe stated, "She won't buy it."

Glancing at him, Galameyvin asked, "Have you been listening to us the entire time?"

"Yes."

"Gabe is frequently overlooked." Aiden inclined his head. "He notices things others don't."

"Look, you're right about being stronger as a team." Gabe pulled a face. "But she expects you to fight with each other. So keep that in mind."

Sweeping his gaze around the room, Celiaen felt the tug at his bond. It was a mixture of relief and concern, with a dash of fear. He had seen the way her eyes darted to watch them and the tilt of her head as she attempted to catch their quiet words. While Gabe had a point, Celiaen suspected she wanted them to get along. Remembering the way she had clung to him and Galameyvin, he shrugged at the other men.

"She'll get over her suspicions. Whatever Ree needs from us, we give it to her. It won't be easy. I know I'll still have moments where I want to kill you both to keep you away from her. But let's get rid of the darkness before we fight it out between us."

"Darkness first," Aiden declared.

TWO

"Well now," Tessa muttered. "That's an interesting development."

Watching Baenlin clench his jaw and direct a furious look at Sannaeh, Tessa leaned forward in the saddle. She rested her arms on the pommel and continued to observe the siblings. Beside her, Fayleen and Jaren argued over something trivial she had not bothered to pay attention to. Whatever it was, it was nothing compared to the sight in front of them.

They had reached the tail end of at least a legion of the Ensaycalan army. Banners fluttered in the breeze, the triple sword emblem making it clear who the soldiers answered to. Everyone knew King Paienven was on his way north to Kelsby, but Tessa had overheard multiple arguments between Baenlin and Sannaeh over the prospect. The apparent hate Baenlin felt for Paienven rivetted her.

"What did you say?" Rylee asked, shifting her attention from the gathering officers to Tessa. "Did you say something?"

"I said I'm planning to kill the king."

Rolling her eyes, Rylee expressed her doubts. "Sure you are."

"What are the chances he'll summon me to his side?" Tessa pondered.

Mouth twisting, Jaren hoped the chances were slim. He did not like the way his sister tried to attract Baenlin's attention. Nor did he appreciate the calculating looks the archmage directed her way when she was not paying attention. As much as he wanted Tessa to find her confidence and take command of her position as the future grand mage, Jaren did not want her to do so by making deals with Baenlin.

"You want to avoid Paienven," Fayleen told her.

Tessa disagreed. "Don't think I do. I'm going to be the grand mage."

"Paienven is an ass, and I don't think gaining his attention is a good idea."

"Using inside information?" Jaren chuckled.

Fayleen rubbed her face. "Celi isn't the biggest fan of his father, even if he's always trying to earn his approval."

Amused by their conversation, Zack commented, "Everyone knows Paienven pulls the strings of the high council."

"All the more reason for Tessa to avoid meeting him." Rylee glanced at the sky, mouth twisting. "Her charming personality will go down oh so well with him."

Giving Tessa a knowing look, Fayleen joked, "Maybe it will impress the archmage."

Scratching her cheek, Tessa continued to watch the gathering. In the time since Baenlin discovered her presence, he had barely let her out of his sight. He avoided speaking to her as much as possible, leaving Tessa perplexed by the situation. Yet, as much as it bothered her, she was thankful to continue her work without distraction.

"We'll be at Kelsby soon. Once we're there, you can side with Ree for support against Paienven without risking yourself," Zack stated. "There's no fucking chance she'll like him."

"That's a given," Rylee muttered.

A cloud drifted over the sun to cast shadows across the area. It was warm, almost unbearably so, with a hint of humidity in the air. Reports had told of the storms battering the northern region of Endara, slowing down the movement of troops and the progress of Athnaral's invasion. Fayleen wondered if Eirian had been enjoying herself in them. She found something reassuring about her memories of her friend walking through lightning, illuminated by magic.

It was difficult to tell if the Ensaycalan forces had stopped progressing forward, but the mages had halted behind them. Moving armies was a slow business. While stuck in Baenlin's shadow, Tessa had been taking the chance presented to learn. She watched quietly while he discussed the logistics with the masters each evening. Occasionally, she risked a question to be answered with condescending amusement. Those answers reminded her why Mayve had spent decades doing little more than playing in her gardens and appearing only when required.

She had no intention of doing the same. Tessa was uncertain how she would balance her drive to experiment and create with her desire to lead the high council properly. But she was determined to find a way, even if it meant sacrificing some plans. Glancing at Jaren, Zack, and Fayleen, Tessa was thankful for their support. Fayleen, in particular. Her cheerful nature and fierce attitude easily withstood Tessa's moods to push her forward.

"Don't worry, I won't force anything to happen. Besides, something tells me our dear friend will do his best to make sure I'm kept away from Paienven," Tessa said.

Running a hand through her hair, Rylee played with the earring at the tip of her ear. She watched the fluctuating number of people surrounding Baenlin and Sannaeh, observing the looks directed their way by Soren. It was likely Baenlin would task him with ensuring Tessa remained precisely where he wanted her. They all knew Soren was one of the few people Baenlin trusted.

"Ten silver on Soren joining our merry company," Rylee said and chuckled, nodding in his direction. "He's got eyes on us."

Luke muttered, "You mean, eyes on Tessa."

"True. The rest of us are meaningless."

"No, we're just less likely to cause a scene!" Jaren said in amusement.

Fayleen dismissed the group of masters and archmages in favor of watching the Ensaycalans. She suspected Paienven would come to them once he knew of Sannaeh's presence. The Queen of Ensaycal was a fearsome woman, but she had seen her softer side whenever Celiaen was around.

"I'll take your wager, Rylee, and counter it with Baenlin will have Soren drag Tessa over there. He'll want to parade the future grand mage as his as a threat to Paienven," Fayleen said, her tone serious. "Baenlin hates Paienven. I've heard Celi mention it enough."

"If Fay's right—"

"I'm not wrong."

Huffing, Zack continued, "If Fay's right, Soren will have a few choice threats for Tessa. Baenlin wouldn't want to risk Tessa showing him up."

Scrunching her nose, Tessa pulled her braid over her shoulder and toyed with the yellow ribbon attached to the end. She suspected Fayleen and Zack were correct about the situation. Glancing at Jaren, Tessa met his gaze and inclined her head to where Baenlin presided. From the look on his face, it was easy to determine he was concerned by what might happen.

"Don't worry, I won't misbehave if Fay's right. I'm not interested in being a tool for Paienven." Tessa assured her companions.

Eyebrows rising in surprise, Rylee asked, "You'll play along with whatever Baenlin might decide to do?"

"Better to dance with the partner you know than the one who'll stab you in the back."

"That doesn't make sense."

Chuckling, Fayleen said, "It does a little. I think what she means is that she knows what Baenlin expects, but Paienven is likely to try killing her if she doesn't step to his tune."

"Well, why didn't you just say that?" Rylee grumbled.

Looking her over, Tessa muttered, "Remind me again what Ree saw in you?"

"I'm not fucking stupid, Valkera, so don't act like I am."

"Don't act like you are, and I won't!"

"At least I'm not drooling over a man who only sees me as a tool to use."

"You don't know what you're talking about," Tessa snarled.

Jaren groaned when he felt the shift in the surrounding air. It carried a bite, warning him that Tessa was close to losing her temper with Rylee. They could not risk her making a demonstration of her abilities with Paienven so close. With the stories of what Eirian had done at Kelsby running riot, there was concern over what other purples were hiding. Anything else Tessa might reveal would threaten the entire order and destabilize the power structure of Riane.

"That's enough!" Jaren snarled, ending their argument. "Just shut the fuck up."

"What an excellent suggestion," Soren said behind them. "You're worse than children. And while I'm sure Archmage Baenlin would enjoy Tessa on her knees for him, Rylee, I think he'd rather she behaves like the future grand mage. That is, with self-control and modicum of dignity."

Eyes widening, Rylee stared at Soren fearfully and apologized while Fayleen regarded them in boredom. Crossing her arms, Tessa glared at him briefly before glancing away to gather her emotions. A hand loosely clasped the reins of his horse, the other resting on the pommel of the saddle as he studied the woman they had sent him to fetch. The depth of her anger intrigued Soren, causing him to wonder if Baenlin knew what he was up against. Tessa was not like Eirian. There was no hot, fiery rage to be cooled with a good fight. Instead, hers was a slow-burning fire, a thousand tiny cuts they would not notice until it was too late.

Exchanging looks, Zack and Luke remained silent. Soren was their superior, a master who served an archmage. Neither wanted to risk his ire. They had seen the results of what happened when he was let loose on someone. The council dedicated rooms to those who had suffered at the hands of a blue. Most were the result of punishments sanctioned by the council, with Soren frequently chosen to deliver them.

"He requires your presence," Soren informed Tessa.

Nose flaring, Tessa glanced at Fayleen for reassurance. "Surprising."

"I don't recommend it."

"Answering his summons?"

"No, playing games."

Gazing at Soren as docilely as she could manage, Tessa murmured, "I'd never deign to do such a thing."

Snorting, he said, "And I'd never deign to render you speechless for a day."

Jaren arched a brow, leaning forward in his saddle. "Are you threatening the future grand mage?"

"Careful, we're a long way away from your father. I might be a blue, but I don't answer to Archmage Hugh."

"I don't need my father to fight any battles for me."

Sighing loudly, Tessa gave Jaren a silencing look. "And I don't need my brother to fight my battles."

"Tessa—" he started, but she cut him off.

"I can take care of my own battles, thank you." Looking at Soren, Tessa said, "Don't worry, I'll behave."

Arms stretched above her head, Fayleen chuckled, "What about the rest of us? Are we expected to come along quietly as Tessa's protection?"

Soren waved a hand in her direction dismissively. "Your services aren't needed. Tessa won't be leaving his side. She'll have the personal protection of the greatest warrior alive."

"But is he?" Fayleen drawled.

Pressing her lips together, Rylee tried not to laugh at the bewildered look on Soren's face. She had to admire Fayleen's courage in daring to ask the question. The others stared at Fayleen in horror, receiving a smile in response.

"It's a fair question. Archmage Baenlin isn't young, and others could be better. Like Prince Celiaen, for example."

"I don't know if your audacity is amusing. You'd best be careful not to say such things where he can hear them," Soren stated.

Looking over at where Baenlin and Sannaeh held court, Tessa spotted him turning in their direction. It prompted her to roll her shoulders and nod to Soren. His eyes narrowed, suspicious of what she might have planned. If he could have it his way, he would not let her anywhere near Paienven.

"We'd best join him. I wouldn't want to make Baenlin angry before he deals with King Paienven," she kept her voice soft.

"Then you'd best keep your mouth shut unless directly spoken to."

Smiling faintly, Tessa said, "I'm well aware of what he wants from me. The king is to believe I'm a puppet, and Baenlin is my master."

Grunting, Soren turned his mount around. Winking at her companions, Tessa followed in silence. They watched her go, exchanging concerned looks and unspoken hopes that she would follow through with her assurances. Humming as they crossed the short distance to the other group, Tessa forced a smile, doing her best to appear cheerful before joining Baenlin.

"Don't do that."

"Do what?" Tessa inquired.

Eyeing her warily, Soren answered, "That fake smile. All it does is give away the fact you're planning something."

"I'm not planning anything other than doing as required of me."

"The day you willingly do what you're told is the day I'll retire from my position."

She met Baenlin's perturbed gaze and said, "You're in for a surprise, Soren. I'm not planning anything. Whatever is between Baenlin and Paienven, I know whose side I'm on."

Remaining dubious, Soren scoffed. "I'll believe it when I see it. Let me warn you, though, crossing him is not in your best interest."

"I'm sure it's not."

Falling silent, they joined the group, and the mages surrounding Baenlin and Sannaeh parted to let the duo through. Tessa kept her mouth shut, determined to follow through with her promise from the start. If she was going to prove her worth to Baenlin, she had to demonstrate her willingness to cooperate. Dark eyes glanced over her before settling on Soren.

"We're going to continue the march. No point wasting the day sitting here waiting for His Majesty," Baenlin informed Soren.

"Good idea. It's still early enough to cover the distance you planned on. The Fifth Legion has kept going, so we won't be too far up their asses."

Yawning, Sannaeh commented, "The land isn't too bad. No reason we couldn't divert along the side of the infantry."

Baenlin grumbled, "In a hurry to join the insufferable man you call a husband?"

"We're mounted. There's always the possibility of overtaking my husband's forces and reaching Kelsby first." Knowing Baenlin well, Sannaeh added, "I'm sure you'd like to dig your claws into the young queen before he gets a chance."

It was hard to resist saying anything in response when Tessa knew Celiaen was already in Kelsby with Eirian. Her lips twitched, but glancing away, she tried to hide her amusement. Winking at Tessa, Sannaeh reached up to fix one of the thin knives holding her braids in a bun. Catching their exchange, Baenlin muttered under his breath and shook his head at Soren.

"I know what you're doing, Sannaeh."

"Excellent. I shouldn't have to stick my foot too far up your ass to make you see sense. Unlike the performance you put on in Riane. Honestly, Baenlin."

Leaning toward Tessa, Soren whispered, "If you laugh, you'll regret it."

She smiled tensely, but could not hide the mirth in her eyes. Whatever Baenlin might do to her was worth watching Sannaeh scold him like a child. It would become a memory for Tessa to hold close and recall whenever he irritated her. Making a show of looking at the sky and shading her face, she remained silent.

"A good observation, Grand Mage," Sannaeh said. "Give the order, little brother. We'll go around the Fifth rather than get stuck in their dust."

Grinding his teeth, Baenlin kept his temper under control. She was trying to annoy him. It was her way of showing affection, and Sannaeh derived enjoyment from the reactions of those around them. Knowing it was impossible to argue with her, Baenlin turned to his officers, issuing the orders to divert the mage army to go around the Ensaycalans.

"We're likely to encounter Paienven, and, Tessa, you will remain by my side."

"As you wish, Archmage," Tessa replied quietly.

Giving her a second look, Baenlin sneered at the bright-yellow bow adorning her braid. He did not know where she found the colorful ribbons, but Tessa had refused his attempts to dissuade her from wearing them. Soren had quietly suggested ignoring it, but he hoped to keep Tessa focused on defying him about the ribbons. It was his theory that it would distract her from fighting him over everything else. Something within Baenlin enjoyed the exchange with Tessa and the defiant gleam in her eye whenever he brought up the ribbons.

He snapped, "Get rid of that ridiculous bow before we do. It makes you look like a child, not the future grand mage."

"Don't listen to him, Tessa." Sannaeh laughed. "He's jealous. Maybe you should lend him one to tie back his hair."

Dragging her braid over her shoulder, Tessa deliberately twisted it through her fingers while staring at Baenlin with a faint smile. Beside her, Soren rolled his eyes, focusing on Baenlin for a sign of how he wanted to respond. Giving Sannaeh an unimpressed look, he nudged his horse to follow the line of mages. Laughter sounded from the two women, but they trailed after him.

Maneuvering in beside him, Soren glanced back and muttered, "Just say the word."

"Don't worry. If she makes a fool of me in front of Paienven, I will."

"I'm not so sure about that."

Baenlin arched a brow, grumbling, "What's that supposed to mean?"

"She's got more… fire than Mayve. You want Tessa to go head-to-head with Paienven."

"Does that sound like something I'd do?"

"Yes. Honestly, she's a far better option for grand mage than Eirian. One of them is an unyielding mountain, and it isn't Tessa. Maybe you should let her make an enemy of Paienven. There are alliances you could make with her if you can get past the derangement," Soren said.

"Fucking blue, there's no need to keep pointing it out."

"It might surprise you what positive reinforcement will do for your plans."

Rubbing the hilt of a sword, Baenlin shifted in his saddle to assess the movement of his army. They were approaching the tail of the Ensaycalan legion, alert officers keeping a close eye on the mages. He had received enough reports on the Athnaralans to appreciate their wariness. Whatever was driving the enemy twisted the mind. Yaernan had informed him that the blues in his forces had investigated prisoners, finding traces of something, but they did not know where it came from.

People whispered of darkness and nightmares, coaxing old stories from long-forgotten memories. Baenlin did not want to believe it. He remembered his grandmother telling him what she had learned from her grandparents. The darkness that drove the mage wars. As a child, he had dismissed the tales as fantasy. Those words repeated at his bedside spoke of their family coming from faraway lands beyond the Red Desert. His grandmother had told Baenlin and Sannaeh how the Zarthein family had a link to the Altira line.

But he had never forgotten them, and now Baenlin questioned their truth. Sannaeh had smiled knowingly when he mentioned them, making him suspect she knew something he did not. It had never seemed right that she encouraged Paienven to name the united elven kingdoms after the destroyed city in their grandmother's stories. Especially when Endara already bore the name of the second city.

"I've got some advice for you, Grand Mage," Sannaeh murmured, keeping her gaze on Baenlin's back.

Maintaining a blank expression, Tessa asked, "And what is that?"

"Keep doing what you're doing. My brother likes things to make sense. He thrives on organization, and from what I've gathered, you're the opposite."

"I'm not sure where you're going with this."

"You're more than familiar with the state of the high council."

"And the involvement of your husband," Tessa remarked.

Shrugging, Sannaeh tugged at a bracer. "It takes a strong person to temper the ambitions of a king."

Frowning, Tessa was not sure what to think of the comment. Gazing at the Endaran landscape, she relaxed her hold over her magic to feel the vibrations between particles in the air. They calmed her, serving as a reminder that she was not defenseless or weak. Jaren had said to make the best of every opportunity. No matter how loudly her parents' voices echoed in her mind, Tessa intended to try. She would prove them wrong and show everyone she was not crazy or useless.

They had passed through a forest the day before, ancient eucalypts and scrub giving way to a landscape that looked like the gods had thrown a tantrum. Tessa thought it resembled a giant creature with the spine ripped out. Passage through the forest had been slow, but Forrestfield had forewarned the garrison on the other side to expect them. She had attended the meeting with the Endaran officers and Baenlin, watching in fascination as they discussed the best options.

Keeping to the main road in this region, the mages followed the same route Eirian had taken. The Endarans had informed them of Paienven's forces and his decision to take an inwards road to avoid the hilly region. Tessa had to wonder if that would change. She doubted it. Paienven marched with roughly fifteen-thousand elves, by all estimates. Taking them by the road through Aveley would be slower.

"You're familiar with the Endaran queen," Sannaeh said. "What do you think she did to stop Aeyren's legion?"

Tessa's gaze slid in her direction as she replied, "I don't know."

"My son loves her dearly, and as his mother, I'll do whatever I must to protect him. However, should Eirian's actions be a cause for concern, I'd appreciate you doing whatever you can to keep her alive."

"What exactly do you think I can do?"

"The Telmians claim she's the Altira mage. Our light in the darkness to come. If Paienven or the high council decide Eirian is too dangerous to be left alive, you'll protect her. We can't afford for her to be killed."

"Why do I get the feeling you know more than you're letting on?" Tessa muttered, giving her a knowing look.

Smiling, Sannaeh arched a brow. "Probably for the same reason I suspect you do. I'm a wise queen, Tessa Valkera. I won't say old, as it's not true, but I know things. I've seen a lot, heard many stories."

"You'd have made a better archmage than your brother."

"Probably, but I doubt you'd look at me the way you look at him. Not that I'd complain if you did. I'd be flattered. It's a pity he's too caught up in his schemes to see what's in front of him."

Turning her face away to hide her blush, Tessa muttered, "I'm not—"

"Ah, Tessa, don't protest. Besides, Nadinna told me all about it."

Huffing, Tessa told herself to kill her friend the next time they saw each other. Nadinna was one of the few people she had ever called a friend, and Tessa wished she could make her archmage instead of Hugh. Glancing back, she searched for Fayleen's familiar straw-colored hair and gave thanks she had her support.

"My husband isn't far off, so I'll give you some quick words of advice," Sannaeh said, cocking her head to the side.

"How do you know that?"

"Never mind how. You're going to want to throw your weight around, but I suggest you don't. Baenlin expects you to do something foolish, surprise him. Keep silent, lurk in the shadows, watch how they interact with each other. Learn your opponent."

The suggestion made Tessa nod in agreement. Her plan had been to do precisely what Sannaeh advised, and it was reassuring to have it confirmed. Eyes narrowing, Sannaeh studied Tessa before smiling confidently.

"You'll do good, Tessa. I've got confidence in your ability to learn and adapt. Unlike my husband and brother, you'll play the game instead of forcing it."

Tessa allowed herself a faint smirk. "If I wanted to, I could force it."

"We're women, Tessa, and we have the advantage. They think they're in charge, but if you play your cards right, you can have them believing it was their idea all along. Behave the way Baenlin wants, rather than how he expects, and you'll make him amiable. Think of him as a stubborn pet in need of treats."

Laughing at the picture conjured by Sannaeh's description, Tessa covered her mouth when Baenlin turned to look back at them. Horns announcing the approach of riders recalled his focus to the front of the line. When she saw the triple sword emblem on its background of midnight blue, Sannaeh shook her head at Tessa and nudged her horse to move forward.

Keeping back, it did not surprise Tessa when Soren made his way to her side. His expression was severe, and she felt the influence of his magic escaping from his grasp. Reeling her own back with a bored smile, she brought her horse to a halt in response to the riders ahead stopping. There was no point getting too close to where Baenlin and Sannaeh were facing another group led by the King of Ensaycal.

She had seen Paienven before, but Tessa would recognize the golden Kaetiel curls anywhere, even if she had not. Celiaen was the only member of the family who did not possess them, which she had always thought odd. The sun continued to shine down on them, the summer warmth leaving dark patches on their horses. Shading her eyes, Tessa leaned forward in the saddle, trying to appear unimportant while listening to the exchange.

"Greetings, Your Majesty," Sannaeh said. "Well met!"

Sneering, Paienven gave Baenlin a dismissive look and replied, "I'd heard you went to fetch your useless brother. You should go home, Archmage, you've missed most of the fun. I've taken care of the Athnaralan dogs without your help."

Baenlin chuckled. "And I heard Queen Eirian took care of a legion with half the numbers. Seems like Endara might not need either of us."

"Just because she has her mother's army at her back doesn't mean she has the numbers to deal with Athnaral."

Sharing a look with Soren, Tessa saw his surprise. They were not the only ones thrown by Paienven's words. Baenlin was befuddled, though Sannaeh did not bat an eyelid. Her expression remained blank as she regarded her husband.

"What are you talking about?"

Gloating, Paienven said, "Oh, haven't you heard? Turns out our dear Queen of Endara is actually the daughter of Queen Shianeni Malfaer."

"By the powers," Tessa whispered to Soren. "It all makes sense. No wonder she's so powerful. She's half duine."

Equally stunned, he murmured, "How could we've missed it?"

"Are you sure? What purpose would the Queen of Telmia have to lie about her identity and marry the King of Endara?" Baenlin scoffed.

"General Darragh was present when the truth came out. Athnaral has an ally in the form of a long-forgotten enemy. You know of whom I speak. Queen Shianeni orchestrated the existence of a powerful Altira mage to fight it."

"The darkness," Sannaeh commented.

Waving at her, Baenlin replied, "The darkness is nothing more than a children's story told to make us fear the consequences of our decisions. It doesn't exist."

"Darragh saw it. Or her, to be specific. She's a god, one of those who created us," Paienven stated, all signs of pleasure over the exchange fading.

"You want me to believe we're going to be fighting a god and that little Eirian Altira is our salvation? I think you've lost what little you had left of your mind, Paienven."

From the way Soren's hands clenched, Tessa suspected he thought there would be an argument between Paienven and Baenlin. Eyes drifting over the crowd of mages, Paienven shook his head slowly.

"I understand your skepticism, Archmage, but I trust Darragh's report. The Endarans are scrambling to decide what to do. At the time of his report, she had the support of her army and several of the most influential nobles of the Endaran small council."

Clicking his tongue, Baenlin cast a look at Tessa thoughtfully. If the information about Eirian was correct, his plans had to change. He knew the laws of Riane. A duine, even a half blood, could not serve on the high council because of the treaty with Telmia.

"Well then, it's a good thing I'm on my way to Kelsby. Endara will benefit from the involvement of the high council in this matter. After the war, we'll deal with the legalities of Eirian reigning as queen of Endara—"

"She'll be remaining queen. I'll see to that. After all, she'll be my daughter soon. Once the marriage contracts between Eirian and Celiaen have been completed," Paienven said, his smugness returning. "It'll be the start of a wonderful new alliance between Endara and Ensaycal."

THREE

The icy waters of the Arianell trickled over his fingers as Celiaen crouched at the edge, watching Eirian balance on a rock with her arms outstretched. Behind her, water tumbled down the moss-covered rock face in multiple places. It was easy to picture the waterfall in spring when the snow melted. Further down, a secondary smaller drop leveled out into a wider stretch of water. Grass grew to the bank, broken only by sections of rough pebbles. The sunlight caught the spray from the falls, casting glittering rainbows of color.

Banishing the images his mind conjured of Eirian naked beneath the waterfall, Celiaen said, "If you're not careful, Ree, you're going to end up going for a swim."

Tossing him a look, Eirian grinned. "When have you known me to slip and fall, Celi? I'm a mountain goat."

"You're cocky, and I'll enjoy watching you land with a splash. What do you say, Captain?" Looking at Aiden, Celiaen chuckled. "Think she's going to end up ass first?"

He observed Eirian confidently hopping to the next rock and muttered, "I'd say it's about equal either way."

"I don't like equal odds."

Balancing on one foot, Eirian stretched out the other behind her carefully with a broad grin. The look on Celiaen's face was worth the risk of getting wet.

"If I get wet, I'll do my best shag on a rock impression. Besides, Celi, you're jealous because you'd trade your grace dancing for my grace as a goat."

Cocking his head to the side, Aiden blinked in surprise when she reached back and caught her foot. Her balance did not falter.

"Now you're just showing off, darling."

Scrambling down the bank, Fox let out a low whistle when he saw Eirian. "You raised by a mountain goat?"

Letting go of her foot and bringing it in beside the other on the rock, she laughed. "You're my new favorite, Fox."

"That's wonderful, ma'am, but I thought I already was?" Glancing between Celiaen and Aiden, he added, "The camp is ready."

"Thank you, Fox," Aiden replied, keeping a close eye as Eirian stepped from rock to rock toward dry land.

"It feels strange to be back here," she told them.

Making a last jump from the stone to the shore, Eirian turned her gaze toward the hill that loomed off to the side. Following her stare, Celiaen could not help but agree that it was a forbidding sight. Something about the place made his skin crawl, and Galameyvin had told him the same thing.

"I'm worried about the weather. We might need to do this and return to Kelsby."

Shaking her head, Eirian said, "You can if you're worried about getting a little wet. I knew we were facing a weather change, but I'm not worried. Are you worried, Aiden?"

"Yes." He gave her a look that said he was not interested in getting caught in a storm.

"Well then, you can all go back to the nice cozy town, and I'll go on my own. It would be faster not having to worry about all you slow people holding me back."

Fox grunted, "I'm not worried."

Looking at him, Eirian smiled. "You want to set eyes on your mountains again just in case you don't make it through this war."

"Or maybe I think you could get me closer to the Roof so I can go fuck this, it's not my problem, and run off to avoid the war."

He intended it as a joke, but the words sat uncomfortably for Eirian, her mind lingering on the lives of so many who did not know they were in danger. Recognizing her expression, Celiaen and Aiden glanced at each other in concern.

"There's no avoiding this war, Fox. Now, if you said you'd go warn all those living up there, that'd be different. You'd have my blessing to go."

"No one's stupid enough to take an army into the Roof," Fox replied with a shrug.

"The darkness doesn't need an army. She can whisper into the minds of anyone, anywhere, anytime. No one is safe."

Dwelling on their task, Celiaen sighed. "Come on, we should get this done. It's going to be disconcerting enough talking to a dead person without doing it in the pelting rain."

Swiping a hand over his brow, Aiden agreed. "It's very humid."

Following her up the bank toward their camp, Celiaen caught her hand.

Aiden had quietly mentioned her nightmares during the ride. He wanted to make sure Eirian could handle what they were about to do. She frowned, eyes dropping to his hand entwined in hers.

"Are you alright, Ree?"

"Why do you keep asking me that?"

"Because I'm worried about you. I can feel your turmoil through the bond, and I can see the sadness that crosses your face when you're not paying attention. We know about the nightmares. So, I'm going to keep asking you, and if it annoys you, then good, at least it's something." Releasing her hand, he nodded at the small collection of tents. "I know you probably didn't want those, but there's no guarantee we'll leave tomorrow."

Remaining still, Eirian watched their companions move around in the camp and spotted Faolan sitting in his wolf form with his back to them. Sensing her, he jumped up and trotted over with his ears pricked forward. Chuckling, Celiaen shook his head when the wolf rubbed his head against Eirian's leg before licking her hand.

"How come he gets to rub himself all over you like that? If I tried, you'd break my nose, crack a rib, and probably cut off my balls."

Moving past them, Aiden snorted. "Because he's covered in fur, and she likes fur."

Sharing a look with Faolan, Eirian saw the amusement in his green eyes. She was glad for his company.

"Oh, both of you shush. Faolan gets to because he's such an adorable puppy. I mean, just look at him and tell me how such a sweet thing could frighten anyone?" Ruffling his fur, Eirian grinned when Faolan pulled away with a growl.

"Yes, so adorable. Sweet is definitely what I'd think while watching him tear out the throat of an enemy with those teeth," Aiden responded.

Faolan slinked over to rub his head against his leg, and Aiden gave Eirian a horrified look. Pressing his lips together, Celiaen did his best not to laugh.

"That was not an invitation, Lord Faolan."

Laughing, Eirian started walking toward the tor, ignoring the horses staked out. The sunlight took away some deep green of the land and washed out the gray of the rocks that broke through the dirt. Picturing the gently rolling hills and flatter lands to the south, she wondered how the land could be so different. Stopping again, she shaded her eyes and turned to follow the flow of the Arianell. The water gleamed like a moving pool of silver. A flash of white downstream caught her attention, and watching it move, Eirian realized it was a tall bird.

Standing beside her, Fox peered in the same direction, muttering, "Probably an egret."

"Thank you," she replied, returning her focus to the towering hill ahead.

Hearing a shout, they looked back at the camp and watched Galameyvin jogging toward them with a mix of guards. He had all his weapons, and Eirian glanced at her waist, reminding herself she had her knives. She had left her swords and bow in the camp. After exchanging nods with Celiaen and Aiden, Galameyvin looked at her with a raised brow before pointing at the tor.

"Are you sure you don't want to leave it until tomorrow?"

"Yes, I'm sure," Eirian answered, resuming her stride across the land.

They had camped closer than the last time, and she was thankful. She had no desire to go near the farm where Ona's family had died, even though the girl was safe with Brenna. The images of dead children plagued her dreams without the help of the darkness. At least, the dreams she could remember.

Approaching Cynwrig Tor with her magic wrapped closely around her, Eirian instinctively sought the cairn of her ancestor. Without the worry of horses, the guards did not remain a distance back and followed. Celiaen felt like the rocks were trying to deter them and frowned at Eirian and Aiden walking with the wolf leaping along between them. Glancing at Galameyvin, he saw frustration.

"Stop." He lifted a hand, halting them to ask, "Don't you feel it?"

Cocking her head, Eirian blinked. The whispers mocked Celiaen's question, demanding she continue without him.

"What do you mean?"

"We're not welcome here," Merle muttered, casting a wary look at the peak.

"I feel nothing different to last time." She shrugged. "Aiden?"

Shaking his head, Aiden gave each of his men a concerned look. It was clear they were uncomfortable with the situation, but like Eirian, he felt nothing felt different.

"None of you came this close last time. If you want to go back, that's fine."

"But, Cap'n, why don't you feel anything?" Kip asked. "Because it feels like I'm trying to walk with a weight chained to my feet."

Staring at the wolf sitting beside her, Eirian watched him point his nose at Aiden before looking up at her expectantly "Because of his blood. This is an Altira grave, and they only intended it for someone with Altira blood."

Exchanging looks, the guards waited for Aiden to speak again. "Just head back, wait where you feel comfortable, and take some of these elves with you."

Kenna sneered. "You don't speak for us."

Agreeing with Aiden, Celiaen said, "No, he's right. We don't know if Eirian can call forth her ancestor again. Adding more people may lessen the chances."

"Maybe I should try on my own," Eirian suggested.

"We'll try together, Ree." Seeing her prepare to protest, Galameyvin emphasized, "Together."

Huffing, she continued up the slope with Faolan at her heels. "Fine, but we haven't got all day."

"She gets funny when she doesn't get her way," Celiaen chuckled and braced himself to push against the wards trying to deter them.

"Keep an eye out for threats." Aiden reminded his men.

Saluting, Merle said, "You know we will."

Lingering in place while the rest of the group turned back, Aiden watched the two princes struggle after Eirian. Then, smirking, he came up behind them and slung an arm over their shoulders, positioning himself in the middle. They gave Aiden annoyed looks, making him grin.

"How does it feel? For a change, I'm the one who gets to go prancing after her."

Letting go of them, Aiden shoved through and hurried after Eirian. If their difficulties were not obvious, he would have taken more time to mock them.

"Yeah, there's something wrong with that. He doesn't have magic, and these wards ignore him," Celiaen grumbled, glaring at Aiden's back.

Galameyvin sighed. "Remember, we're working together to support Ree."

"I know."

Keeping herself a short distance from the cairn, Eirian rubbed her arms to chase away the chill. Less bothered, Faolan circled the pile of stones, sniffing to see if anyone had been there recently. His ears constantly flicked as he listened to the three men approaching. Glancing at Aiden when he came to a halt beside her, Eirian noticed the lines of worry around his eyes.

"Check the ground before you do any kneeling this time. Remember your knee." Aiden cautioned, nodding at the ground.

"It's only a little blood, Aiden. Would you like to offer yours instead?"

Catching her comment, Celiaen laughed. "I'd be more than happy to assist you in offering your blood, Captain."

Lip curling in a sneer, he muttered, "I doubt I have the right blood. But I can still give a little if you think the extra Altira would help."

"He may have a point." Able to see the logic in the suggestion, Galameyvin added, "I think it's worth a shot. You were already thinking of it, weren't you, Ree? Otherwise, you'd have insisted he remained with the others."

Her lips twitched, resisting the urge to smile. "Would I do that?"

"Yes," they all replied.

Offering her hand to Aiden, Eirian nodded at the stones. "I won't ask you to get naked before I take your blood."

"Well, that's boring," Celiaen commented in disappointment.

Giving him a cocky smile, Aiden took Eirian's hand. "I prefer my lovers not to be covered in blood when I get naked with them."

Faolan yipped, amusement in his eyes. His magic swirled, leaving him crouching on the stony ground, watching Eirian and Aiden. The emotions rolling off the four of them were undeniable, and he wished Saoirse was there to make off-hand comments to point it out.

"I don't know, little queen. I think it might work better if you're all naked."

"Faolan, this is not the time for personal gratification. You want to see Aiden naked, do it some other time," Eirian scolded.

Once they were all standing around the cairn, Eirian drew a knife free. Keeping his eyes on the blade in her free hand, Aiden swallowed anxiously. If there was a time to use banter to distract himself, it was while waiting to surrender blood for magical purposes.

"You'll never see me naked, wolf."

"Promises, promises, Captain," he quipped back.

Winking at Aiden to quell his anxiousness, Eirian slid the flat of the blade between their hands. It was cool against their skin, and without warning, she turned it on its side and drew it back out. Grunting at the sudden pain, Aiden did not let go as she pressed their hands to the top of the pile of stones. He watched the trickle of blood in fascination, barely noticing Eirian's magic as she forced the wards to respond. The knife remained tightly clasped in her other hand, blood coating the edges.

"By the powers," Celiaen whispered, stepping closer to the cairn, eyes wide as a misty figure appeared on the other side of the stones.

"I didn't expect to see you again." The long-dead woman stared at Eirian, ignoring the others. "I don't know if I'm amused by your audacity or angered by it."

Slightly apologetic, Eirian flickered a glance at Aiden to make sure he was alright. He was staring at the ghostly figure in amazement, hand forgotten.

"I'm sorry for disturbing you again, but we need to know what you did to win the war."

"I defeated the mad god and bound her in her cage."

"What do you mean in her cage?" Faolan asked.

Recognizing his voice, the spirit turned toward him. "Faolan? If you're here, then Shianeni can't be far."

"My queen is dead, Eirian. I serve another now."

"No! No, she can't be dead. You lie, wolf. You stand there and lie." There was anger in her tone that made her descendants recoil.

He shook his head. "No, old friend, I'm not lying. She's dead, but she left behind our only hope. With your help, our hope can prevail."

Squeezing Eirian's hand tightly, Aiden read the worry in her eyes as she released the knife to clatter to the ground. He was not sure she had noticed her action.

"Eirian," Aiden murmured.

Hearing their name spoken, the spirit refocused on the Queen. "I see it now. The last time I said looking at you was like looking at a mix of my daughter and my greatest friend. You're her child, and yet you're an Altira."

"Yes, that's true. Shianeni married the King of Endara and bore me, giving her life. But we need your help, please," Eirian pleaded.

Looking at the two elves, the spirit frowned. If the darkness had returned, it made sense that they were there.

"I can tell he's a Kaetiel, and he's a Zarthein. And you." She turned to Aiden, saying, "You're an Altira, but…"

"I have no magic," Aiden replied.

Waving at him, she commented, "No, that's not it. You feel like him. Regardless, I can't tell you more than I have. I didn't know what I had to do until I had to do it. No one can tell you what to do. You already know. These men can only get you so far with their power, courage, and determination. The rest of the way, you must find alone."

"Well, that's a lot of nothing," Celiaen muttered. "And I'm a Kaetiel as well."

Eirian chewed her lip. "What did Shianeni do to bind you to this land?"

The question sparked a curious look from the elves and a throaty chuckle from the spirit. "You know more than you let on last time. I told you of things I'd done, don't expect to escape the same outcomes simply because you're her daughter."

"I only learned these things in the last few days. What did she do?"

"I wish I could tell you, but her power was indecipherable to me, despite my knowledge. She took my blood and that of a Kaetiel prince, mixing it with her own. I barely remember what happened. It was hazy and I've been dead for a long time. Whether she gave some of her command of the land and that of…" She cocked her head and frowned, muttering, "Gosh, I don't remember his name. I only crossed his path a handful of times in those turbulent days before he died. But whether Shianeni gave me command or simply allowed me the right to use the land, I don't know."

Dropping her gaze to where Aiden held her hand, Eirian asked, "Why did she bring you and your people here to end the war?"

"Well, for a start, we had already left to save as much of the population of our home as we could. War ravaged everywhere, not just the twin cities."

"But not everywhere had Altira mages fighting the war."

Galameyvin arched a brow. "Why is that significant?"

The ancestor nodded. "Indeed, not everywhere had Altira mages. In desperation to reach this place, I blighted a once beautiful and alive region, condemning it and its people to death. My hope was it would slow down the forces controlled by the darkness. I did that alone. No other magical bloodline could. To be the Altira is to be the heir of death. We serve the god of death himself."

"The most human of human fears, one which elves and daoine don't grasp quite the same way," Eirian murmured.

Not taking her eyes from her hand, Eirian did not need to look at the men to know they were staring at her. There was more to it. She had to remember.

"It comes from the gods themselves. Malfaer is born of life, Kaetiel is born of emotions, while Altira is born of death. Three gods, three bloodlines."

Eirian remembered Vartan mentioning the link between the gods and the bloodlines, but something was wrong. The whispers screamed in her mind that it was incorrect. Three was not the right answer, and the four endless loops of the quaternary knot flashed through her memories.

"What else can you tell me?"

"Shianeni told me this place was significant because the waters came from the beginning. That there is power in these lands because of the power in those waters."

Closing his eyes for a moment, Faolan searched through the memories he no longer trusted. "The beginning of life?"

"Yes, loyal wolf, the beginning of life. I assumed she meant somewhere in the mountains is the sacred place where the gods created life in this world, and the source of these waters flows from there."

Realization dawned on Eirian. "Not all life, just a few lives, which is why she needed you and a Kaetiel. If you can't tell me how to rebind the darkness, can you tell me how the binding works?"

"Not really. I know her actual body is entombed somewhere, somehow. Banished, so only a shadow of her power can touch what is in all of us. When the wards weaken, her power can manifest, growing stronger until she's too strong for them to contain."

"What would happen if they failed?" Celiaen asked, hoping it made more sense to Eirian than it did to him.

Aiden quietly said, "We wouldn't be able to stop her. She's a god. The other gods were the ones who entombed her. Something happened between the gods that resulted in her being locked away and the rest leaving. That's the only thing that makes any sense."

Smiling, the spirit confirmed. "You're a quick one. Clearly, you take after my grandson. He may have done some terrible things to our family, but he was not stupid, and he was a quick thinker."

"He was on the right road, wasn't he? Just heading in the wrong direction." Recalling what Nolan and Vartan had told her, Eirian understood the cost of her ancestor's actions. "And by going in the wrong direction, it led to this. It's happened before because you were in the same position as I am. The only Altira with magic."

"The mad god hunted down those with Altira blood, but I had children before the end."

Covering her mouth, Eirian stared at the two elves while her thoughts connected. The history she had been told only spoke of a daughter.

"They bound her tomb to us and the strength of our magic in the world. The only way they could free her was if we were dead. She is breaking free because magic has nearly died out of the Altira line."

"Plenty of us," Galameyvin said, glancing at Celiaen. "What reason would the gods have to bind her imprisonment to our bloodlines?"

Aiden muttered, "Because they're assholes?"

"He thought she'd be secure forever if there were no Altira mages left. What he should have been doing is making sure Altira mages were everywhere," Eirian said.

Bowing her head, the spirit confirmed, "I knew it, but I was so wrapped up in the war that I couldn't find the right time to explain it to him. My daughter knew, but the war took its toll."

"Are you telling me we need to tell your brother to go out and sow his seeds?" Faolan's mouth twitched, and he added, "He's had plenty of practice."

Letting go of Aiden's hand, Eirian held the wards that had awoken her ancestor and crossed her arms. The cut over her palm had stopped bleeding, and turning over his, Aiden looked at the red line that marked his flesh.

"Well, at least I know what needs doing after the war. Thank you. They weren't the answers I hoped for, but you've given us more help than we realized."

Pointing at Celiaen and Galameyvin, the spirit smiled. "Are you bound to them?"

"Yes."

Smiling darkly, the spirit moved through the pile of stones marking the burial place. It stopped directly in front of Eirian, staring straight into her eyes. The whisper of memories tugged at her, shadows dancing at the edge of her vision.

"Then you already know the cost, but you're not yet willing to pay."

Eirian swallowed, refusing to flinch away from the knowledge she saw in the formless eyes before her. "I'll pay the cost, willingly, when the time comes."

"I'm sure you will. Now, release me."

Letting go of the wards binding the spirit, Eirian closed her eyes and took a deep breath. The men watched the figure vanish, exchanging looks of concern. Taking a step toward her, Celiaen reached out and brushed his fingers over her arm. His action caused Eirian to look at him.

Seeing sorrow in her eyes, Celiaen realized the flecks of lighter brown had faded. He loved those flecks. They always glittered when Eirian was happy. Blinking, she turned away and picked up the knife from where it dropped, swiping the blade against the fabric of her trousers to clean it off before slipping it back into its sheath.

"Eirian," Faolan whispered.

"Take them back to camp, Faolan," she replied, tilting her head back to look at the tor.

Galameyvin argued, "We should talk about what she told us."

"No, not yet. Right now, I need you to leave me alone. When I'm ready, I'll talk."

"I don't think there's much you need to explain, Eirian," Aiden said.

She had shared enough with him previously that Aiden felt he understood most of what the spirit had said. He would tell the other two what he knew when she was not around.

"Besides, I'm a soldier. All you need to do is tell me who to kill to clear your path. After that, the magic is yours."

"No, Aiden, you're not just a soldier." Glancing at him over her shoulder sadly, Eirian murmured, "And I need you to live. Though you may not like my conditions."

Unwilling to leave her, Celiaen did not move, growling, "Ree, you're upset. We don't have to talk, but I'd rather remain with you."

Gathering her magic, Eirian glared at him. The whispers reminded her she needed him and brushed against the bond.

"You'll return to the camp, and I'll speak to you when I'm ready."

Aiden said, "You can't expect us to leave the Queen of Endara unguarded."

"I'm not the Queen of Endara right now. No, right now, I'm just a person who needs some time alone, and I ask you to respect me as a person and give me that. Give me time, and I assure you that tomorrow, we ride north so I can see the mountains before I face the darkness."

Searching her face, Galameyvin saw she knew something. That she understood many things they did not, and he doubted she would ever share those things with them.

"Okay, we can do that for you. Besides, there's nothing any of us could protect you from that you couldn't deal with easily enough by yourself," he stated.

Nodding, Faolan shifted back into his wolf form and leaped over to Eirian, licking the hand she had cut. Turning, he looked back at her before picking his way down the slope, Galameyvin trailing behind him. Huffing, Aiden shook his head and opened his mouth several times to say something. Unable to find an argument he felt worked, he finally shrugged and turned to follow. Left alone with Eirian, Celiaen closed the distance between them and placed his hands on her shoulders, leaning in to press his forehead against hers.

"Please."

Lifting her uncut hand to his face, she cupped his cheek, murmuring, "Let me have some alone time, Celi. Then, when I'm ready, you can come and find me."

Nuzzling her hand, he placed a kiss on her palm. "I'll be waiting."

"I know you will."

Letting go, Eirian stepped back carefully. The others were waiting, and she watched him make his way reluctantly. Every few steps, Celiaen cast a look over his shoulder at her. A slight breeze picked up the loose strands of her hair, bringing them across her face, and he stopped to take in the sight. Sunlight shone on Eirian, but a shadow shrouded her, and he felt the sorrow.

Celiaen wanted to run back, but a hand closed around his wrist, stopping him. Glancing at Aiden, he scowled before turning his gaze back to where Eirian had been standing. Unable to spot her, he realized she had used the distraction to hide. He felt the temptation to reach out through their bond, but he had to respect her desire for solitude.

"Come on, Captain, let's get your hand looked at."

Nodding at Aiden, Celiaen watched the mixture of relief and regret pass over his face.

FOUR

Confidently picking her way over the slope of the tor, Eirian looked at the land. She did not need to watch where she placed her feet among the rocks and loose scree, her magic guiding her steps. Winding its way into the horizon, the waters of the Arianell glittered in the lowering sunlight, and she saw livestock dotted about where farmers had remained on their land, either out of trust that the army would prevail or from stubbornness.

Pushing thoughts of the war and her people from her mind, Eirian continued to move across and downward. Stopping to drink in the beauty surrounding her, she released the grasp on her magic. Glancing around, she located a rock she could sit on and crossed to it, perching carefully. Kicking at a stone, her attention caught on a cluster of white flowers, bright-yellow centers standing out.

Taking a deep breath, Eirian let her gaze drift further and saw that the plant covered the entire slope. It was a carpet of white and yellow spreading further with her magic. Reaching down, she plucked a flower from its stem, the green plant it grew from creeping over and between the rocks. Lifting the bloom to study it, Eirian traced the delicately rounded petals with a fingertip before tucking the stem behind her ear.

She had never seen the flower before and suspected it did not call the southern regions of her kingdom home. It reminded her of Fayleen, and thinking of her in Riane summoned a smile. Pushing off the rock, she resumed her aimless walk, careful not to tread on any of the flowering clumps. She imagined Fayleen's cheery voice babbling on about random things and let the memories fill her mind.

They made Eirian long to cling to her hand as they ran over the land, laughing with the abandon of youth not yet burdened with the harsh reality of their world. A time when being the queen was both the worst and the best thing they could imagine. Chuckling, she rubbed her face and felt the dampness of tears she had not realized she had shed.

"What would you say now, Fay? I don't think you'd make fun of court politics anymore. Instead, you'd probably suggest we run away, build ourselves a hut somewhere far from everything where no one would find us."

Mocking her words, the whispers dragged at the memories. Instead of fighting, Eirian let them come. None of them made sense. Flashes of buildings and gardens, people she thought she knew. Something told her the memories belonged to Shianeni, but how that was possible, she did not know. Nor did she know if it was something she could ask Neriwyn about.

"I wish you were here to give me advice, Fay. I could really use it right now." Eirian sighed. "I could even use your scolding. It's not that I want to do this, but I don't think I have a choice."

Turning her gaze to the west, Eirian took in the sun's position and wondered where the hours of daylight had gone. It was a reminder that midsummer had passed and the days were slowly growing shorter. Soon enough, First Harvest would be on them and they would enter the months of autumn. Feeling the breeze catch her hair, Eirian reached up to undo the cord binding it, dragging the leather over her shoulder as the freed tresses fluttered in the wind.

Wrapping it around her wrist, Eirian brought her thoughts back to the war. She no longer fooled herself into considering anything other than how she would fight the god trying to destroy the world. Thinking about how to ensure farmers had enough to get them through winter or what to do about the increasing reports of deaths and madness spreading throughout would get her nowhere. There was only one thing that would solve all those problems, and that was defeating the enemy.

Her gaze lingered on the water ahead, her feet guiding her toward the stream. Glancing back, Eirian took in the distance she had wandered without noticing and the blanket of white flowers that covered everything. There were splashes of other colors scattered among the white. Most of the blooms were unfamiliar, except for one. The same plant that followed her everywhere. Dandelions blossomed on her trail. As much as Eirian usually loved them, she loathed their presence among the others.

Finally reaching the waters of the Arianell, she stood on the bank and stared into the clear swirling depths. The words of her predecessor regarding the waterways sat uncomfortably in her mind, and kneeling, Eirian reached a hand into the water, letting it drag at her fingers. Closing her eyes, she concentrated and drove her magic to seek anything it could find. When it found nothing out of the ordinary, she sat back on her heels and rubbed her wet hand on her knee.

"This is going to be cold."

Staring at the sky, she breathed in the cooling air and sighed heavily. Barely any clouds marred the western horizon. The setting sun's light turned the blue into soft shades of pink and yellow, lighting up the few clouds in brighter shades. Eirian knew her magic was correct and there was nothing different about the land or water. It left her confused why Shianeni would tell the previous Altira there was.

The only thing Eirian could conclude was that it had been a lie intended to bring the Altira family closer to the other bloodlines. Thinking of the Kaetiel bloodline drew her thoughts to Celiaen, and her heart clenched with anguish. She knew what she had to do, and the prospect of it broke something inside her. Biting her lip, Eirian shoved her emotions down and reminded herself of the lives depending on her doing what was needed.

"Never shy from duty, Ree."

Standing, Eirian unlaced her jerkin, pulling it off to toss to the side, away from the water's edge, before following it with her haubergeon. It was grassier along this stretch of the stream, the soil a gray-brown where the water flow wore away at the edge. Moving on to the bracers, she smiled faintly when her aim was true, and they landed on top of the jerkin. Removing the rest of her clothes, she rubbed her arms and flinched when she felt the blood smear over her skin.

Grumbling, Eirian said, "Nicely done, Ree. Just get blood on everything."

Turning her hand over, she studied the cut, which had bled while she undressed. It was only a small amount of blood and nothing to be concerned about. She barely registered the sting. Picking her path, Eirian carefully waded into the water, sucking in a deep breath at the iciness that made her question her decision. The water was shallow, barely covering her waist when she reached the middle.

With the fading sun to her left, she faced north and stretched her arms out wide over the water, tilting her head back. There was no need to let her magic go. She had not withdrawn it, and closing her eyes, Eirian let life fill her. The beat, the vibrancy of every spark, and the potential it held. All of it commanded her senses, and she ceased to know where it ended and she began.

Louder than usual, the whispers took over her thoughts, and Eirian focused on what they were telling her. She had spent so much time denying them that letting their words take form went against her instincts. They were more than words. Memories of places she had never been. People she had never met. Fragments of conversations with faceless people that the whispers screamed she loved.

"Who are you?" she whispered. "Why do you haunt my dreams?"

Eirian tried to focus on those faceless memories because she suspected some of the answers she needed required remembering them. There was a flash of a familiar smirk, one she knew she had seen for herself. It brought an image to her mind of a lake stretching out in front of her, water reflecting the stars on a moonless night. With it came a feeling of hands tracing over her skin, bringing an exquisite agony that tore at the fabric of her existence.

"*Darling.*"

Groaning, Eirian tried to block the voice from her mind, uncertain if it was a memory or something real. It reminded her of the man in the alley who had witnessed her kill the man hired by Athnaral. The stranger who had made her magic react peculiarly. Thinking of him brought forward more flickers of memory and flashes of agony. Embracing them at the urging of the whispers, Eirian remembered the feeling of gold curls slipping through her fingers and of dark eyes filled with mischief. She knew who they were, three names at the tip of her tongue, but she could not quite remember them.

They were names Eirian knew as well as she knew her own. But there was a wall between her and the ability to speak them. It stopped the memories from completing and prevented her from truly remembering. Frustration made her want to scream. She tried to blame herself for blocking the whispers out for most of her life, but Eirian suspected it was not her fault. The memories were not hers in the first place, and they were things that had never happened to her.

Bringing her focus back to the water, Eirian felt the chill that had settled into her bones. It provided her with a tether to cling to while she regained control over her mind. Which was not a straightforward task. Eirian felt like threads were pulling at her, similar to the bond with Celiaen, but not the same. They were there, present at the edge of her mind, frayed but persistent. Two felt of conflict and death, while the third made Eirian's skin crawl. It was her, the god who had become the darkness.

"*Darling Life.*"

The whisper across her mind dragged the memories back. Finally, Eirian understood what Shianeni had been. Everything was a manipulation. A game to pass an eternity of existence. What they were going through resulted from the gods tormenting each other. Her life was nothing more than a sacrifice, and they bound her to Celiaen to strengthen it. They were both intended to die, but Eirian was determined to ensure it did not happen. Her death she could accept, but not his. Never his.

Forcing herself out of the spiral of thoughts, Eirian opened her eyes and stared at the ripple of water surrounding her. Dashes of silver marred the surface, scattered reflections of the night sky. Her power remained spread out, fueling growth for miles with no effort. It simply existed, doing what they intended it to do. A long time had passed since she had let herself go like that, and the feeling was almost freeing. But the knowledge of where the magic had come from stirred her resentment.

Turning to look at the shore, the sight of Celiaen standing there made her lower her arms. She was stiff, her joints protesting the chill and the time spent holding the same position. The cold had not helped matters, but Eirian was unconcerned by the icy ache that had seeped through her bones. He observed her with concern, emotions flooding over the bond. They were strong enough to wash away the lingering sense of the other threads.

"Aren't you cold?" he asked softly.

"A little, I think." Her eyes flickered to the small fire illuminating him. "I forgot how easily time slips by."

Watching her drift through the water, Celiaen grunted. He had felt her calling through the bond hours earlier and had come. But once he found Eirian, it became clear she was so caught up in her magic that she was unaware of the summons. Celiaen had watched, and she had not moved the entire time. All he had seen was Eirian standing in the water, with her eyes shut and arms spread, naked and glowing.

"And what did you learn?"

Stopping before she was out of the stream, Eirian waved at it. She could not tell him everything, but there was enough that she hoped to satisfy him with the answers she gave.

"That my mother lied. There's nothing different about this land."

"There isn't?"

The ends of her hair were cold and wet against Eirian's back, weighing the tresses down so the wind could not move them. Celiaen did not think he would ever get used to her having long hair. He had experienced a vision of her once, not long after they met, and while she was not yet the same as she had been in it, she was getting close.

"It was always the people that mattered and the potential, always so much potential. I've felt it for as long as I can remember, a soundless beat at the back of my mind that I allowed Riane to dictate constraints to."

Eirian sighed, shaking her head, and he arched a brow. Remaining silent, Celiaen knew she was gathering her thoughts.

"I let them dictate because I thought they were right, that there should be limitations to what magic could do. Instead, I should have been believing what I already knew."

"And what did you already know?"

Running a hand through his hair, Celiaen could not take his eyes off her. He noticed the distant look on Eirian's face, the one that told him she was considering the weight of her choices.

"That magic is life. It is the spark of potential that exists everywhere and in everything. I've held back for so long, Celiaen, because I feared my power and what those around me would think. How could they not fear it? None of them could hear the beat, the echo of a heartbeat that didn't exist yet but which had already ended long ago." Setting foot on dry land, Eirian felt the grass beneath her acutely and said, "That's what I'm fighting for."

"How did you come to that conclusion?"

She cocked her head. "I stopped thinking and started feeling."

Nodding slowly, Celiaen understood her logic. He was a red, and he knew he was not thinking about the actions at the height of his abilities.

"Okay."

"Dance with me, Celi."

Holding her hands out, Eirian took a step toward him. Surprised, Celiaen stepped back. The bond called him, and there was a flicker of magic in her eyes. But there was something else, like dark lines twisting across her skin. He thought it was a trick of the shadows, but a niggling voice at the back of his mind told Celiaen they were a promise.

"You hate dancing, Ree. Besides, there's no music."

"When have we ever needed music?" she asked.

Chuckling, Celiaen remembered saying those exact words to her at her coronation feast. Eirian had told him she would remember what he said, and from the knowing smile tugging at her lips, it was what she had planned.

"Remember that one bonfire night on the beach?"

He arched a brow. "You might need to be more specific. There were many bonfire nights over the years."

Slipping her hand into his, Eirian moved around behind Celiaen and put her other on his shoulder, standing on her toes to whisper, "You know which one. We danced under the stars, by the light of the fire, and that night you didn't leave me to find another."

"And you didn't leave me when Gal called. Instead, you stayed with me on the sand until dawn came. I know you love him, but I don't regret what I did."

"I'm tired of regrets, Celi. I don't want to regret anything anymore. We can't change what has already happened, but what is ahead isn't set in stone. So dance with me under the stars, and we can stop fighting, stop regretting, and we can simply be."

Chuckling, he tilted his face toward hers. "Why, dear heart, it sounds as though you're suggesting more than dancing."

"And if I am?" she asked.

"This isn't the way I had it planned in my mind."

"You're terrible at plans, Celi."

Watching her lips twitch in the corner of his eye, Celiaen pulled her to him and turned to catch her. It was not how he had pictured it, but it seemed fitting. Thoughts going to the two rings secured in a pouch, he knew he would never have a more perfect opportunity to give Eirian hers. Holding her close, he resisted the urge to kiss away the amused smile taunting him.

"I always pictured a nice soft bed where I could take as much time as I desired to show you how much I love you."

Staring at him, Eirian ran her fingers through Celiaen's hair. She loved feeling the silky strands against her skin.

"Plans are fine, but it's time we stopped planning and simply were. Just you and me because we love each other."

"You're not doing this because you feel you have to?" Celiaen asked.

At the back of his mind, a voice told him to refuse the chance. It suggested Eirian was doing this out of obligation. Seeing a flicker of hurt in her eyes, Celiaen flinched, scolding himself for doubting her reasons.

"I'm doing this because I want you. I don't want to die without loving you completely. We're incomplete, Celi, but we don't have to be. They might have intended us to be mates, but they never expected us to love each other. Now it's time to accept it if we want to stand a chance at living."

Wrapping his arms around her waist, Celiaen buried his face in her hair. To him, Eirian smelled like home. He did not know when he had begun to associate the sweet floral scent with belonging, but that was what he thought of every time he smelled flowers. Even when she was far away, and the flowers were just flowers, the smell made him long to be home again, wrapped in her arms.

"We'll live, love, and die together, Ree."

"I hope I'm wrong, and we can avoid the dying part."

"You say the sweetest things, dear heart. How am I supposed to compete with that?" Celiaen chuckled.

Pulling away, she winked cheekily. "You could start by proving all those stories are true."

Watching Eirian saunter away, Celiaen unbuckled his bracers. He wanted to take his time and use it to be confident they were doing this for the right reasons. Besides, while dragging things out, he could memorize every line of her form. Not that he had not done so in the past when seeing her naked. This time, he could be honest about why he was staring at her so intensely.

"Oh, believe me, they don't even come close."

Laughing, Eirian discovered the white flower still tucked behind her ear and pulled it from her hair. Staring at it curiously, she did not watch Celiaen undress. Instead, she twirled it between her fingers until he joined her. The yellow center gave her something to focus on that was not the myriad of thoughts chasing around her mind. Plucking it from her grasp, he flicked the bloom against her nose with a grin.

"They're beautiful flowers, these snow daisies, but I didn't notice them earlier."

Her eyes followed the flower as it fluttered to the ground, free of his grasp. It felt significant, but Eirian was not sure why. Attempting to dismiss the feeling, her mind brushed against the other threads that had made themselves known earlier. They felt slightly different, a mixture of agony and delight coming from two of them, while the third brimmed with resentment. Not wanting to dwell on them, Eirian smiled at Celiaen and crinkled her nose.

"You know me, Celi. I'm good at making things grow."

The whispers laughed at her, and Eirian hoped he would never find out how good she was at making things grow. But it had to be done if she wanted Celiaen to stand a chance of enduring her death. She needed him to live, and she needed Galameyvin and Aiden to survive as well. So long as they all lived, she could die in peace.

Snorting in amusement, Celiaen held out a hand. He sensed the turmoil across the bond, but it was clear Eirian did not want to speak of it. In his other hand, he felt the press of the two rings against his palm as he gripped them tightly. They would be more than a token of his love, and he was thankful for anything that would remind her of what she had.

"That I do, Ree. I also know that I love you. All of you, just as you are."

"I love you too, Celi. So very much."

Lifting his other hand, Celiaen uncurled his fist to reveal the two bands resting on his palm. Gasping, Eirian looked between them and his face, taking in the solemn expression he wore. She suspected he had been carrying them for a while and smiled faintly. Placing her hand on the one without the rings, Eirian felt Celiaen let go of his magic, but there was no anger present. It brought the bond between them to life, and she closed her eyes, drinking in the magic.

"I've been waiting for the right time to give you this," Celiaen told her. "Originally, I was going to give them to you when you fell in my arms while agreeing to marry me."

"And they call me cocky."

Rolling his eyes at her quip, Celiaen lifted her hand to his lips and placed a gentle kiss on her knuckles. He wanted to keep going, dotting more kisses along her arm until he found a spot that would make Eirian squirm.

"You are cocky."

She scoffed. "Not as cocky as you."

Crinkling his nose, Celiaen replied, "Well, I do have a cock. So that does technically make me cockier."

"Celiaen Kaetiel!"

Laughing, he released her hand and picked up one band from his palm. Holding it up, Celiaen squinted while he tried to work out which one it was. Then, putting it back next to the other, he waved at them.

"They're not both for you."

"I gathered from the size difference. You've got bigger fingers than me."

Smirking, Celiaen purred, "And I look forward to showing you what my bigger fingers can do."

"You should be careful about overplaying your abilities, Celi. I'd hate to be disappointed," Eirian replied before plucking the larger ring from his palm. "I take it they're matching like everything else you've ever given me?"

"Of course. We're a pair, after all."

"A pair of idiots."

Grasping the ring intended for Eirian between his fingertips, Celiaen smiled. He reached for her unadorned hand and lifted it so he could slip the cold band onto her finger. The gold caught the light from the fire, a flash in the darkness. Pressing a kiss to it, he heard the sharp intake of her breath before he let go.

"Blade of my blade."

Mimicking the gesture, Eirian slid the second ring onto his finger, and Celiaen clenched his free hand when he felt her lips brush over his skin.

"Song of my song," she murmured.

"Ree," Celiaen whispered.

Turning his hand over, Eirian traced her fingertips over his palm and across the inside of his wrist. Desperation seeped across the bond, the magic pleading with both of them to stop resisting. Meeting his gaze, she licked her lips and smirked when he grabbed her hand to pull her to him.

"Do you know why I decided on rings?"

Drawing her bottom lip through her teeth, Eirian said, "I'm sure you have a good reason."

"We wear rings to show what order we belong to. So I thought it fitting we also wear rings to show that we belong to each other. I am yours, and you are mine. Always and forever."

Reminded of the four endless loops of the quaternary knot again, Eirian did her best not to let Celiaen see the discomfort she felt. She wanted to enjoy their time together, and taking a deep breath, she banished the whispers tugging at the edge of her mind. They would not ruin this chance for a moment of happiness. Frowning, he saw the hesitation flicker across her face.

Burying a hand in his hair, Eirian pulled Celiaen's head down so she could kiss him. He was thankful they were already naked. There was no fabric to stop his fingers from dancing down her spine. There was nothing between the sensitive skin of her sides and the light patterns he traced. She had always been so ticklish, and he knew how to take advantage.

"*Good girl.*"

Groaning against his lips, Eirian tried to block out the whisper that caressed her mind. It was not the voice that had called her darling. She did not want to hear them. All she wanted to know was Celiaen. Everything else did not matter. Even the plan.

"I love you, Celi," she told him. "Always and forever."

FIVE

Picking up the last of the dry wood, Aiden tossed it on the dying fire. It was nearly dawn, and he had not slept. At first, sleep had evaded him out of worry for Eirian, but as the night had crept on, he could not sleep because he felt restless and his skin crawled. His hand had itched where she cut it, and upon unwrapping the bandage, he had discovered it completely healed.

Most of his men slept, and the elves were unconcerned that their prince was off somewhere with the Queen of Endara. Aiden was not sure how long he had sat by the fire staring at the flames, but he had known the moment Eirian and Celiaen returned from wherever they had been. The feel of her magic was unmistakable. He suspected he would always be able to pick her out of a legion of mages. It felt different, but he knew what it meant.

"You couldn't sleep either?"

Aiden glanced up as Galameyvin sat next to him and replied, "I couldn't settle until I knew she was back safely."

Snorting, Galameyvin crossed his legs and propped his elbows on his knees, leaning toward Aiden. "No, it was more than that, wasn't it? You felt it."

"I don't know what you mean."

"Yes, you do, Captain. How is your hand, by the way? Why did you have to be so stubborn about having it healed?"

"You tell me."

Holding his hand out, Aiden revealed his clean palm. Galameyvin grasped it, peering intently at the unmarked skin.

"It healed? How?"

"Again, you tell me. It started itching, and when I removed the bandage to check, it had healed," Aiden explained as he closed his hand into a fist with a sigh.

Letting silence sit between them, Galameyvin stared into the last of the flickering flames. "We knew it would happen."

"Knew what would happen?"

"You know what I'm talking about." Glancing at him sideways, Galameyvin watched the anger appear on Aiden's face. "It's most peculiar that either of us knows. We shouldn't, and yet we do."

Clenching his jaw, Aiden looked up at the sky. "Wouldn't all of you mages notice that her magic feels different now?"

Arching a brow in surprise, he turned to Aiden. "It felt no different to me."

"Then how do you know?"

"I assumed the same as you. I've been too unsettled to sleep, and I just know. My theory was a combination of our having shared blood with her and our love. Magic works in strange ways."

Aiden had to agree with the sentiment. "I don't want to know every time they're…"

He waved over his shoulder at where Eirian's tent was. Snorting, Galameyvin understood.

"Neither do I, but it makes me curious."

"About?"

"Was it because they completed their bond? Or are we bound to her and will always feel it? If that's the case, would we feel it if it were one of us and not him, and would he feel it too?"

Aiden frowned, considering the prospect before saying, "We'll never find out. She was never ours, and we deluded ourselves into thinking we could be with her."

Lifting a finger to his lips, Galameyvin nodded at someone approaching, making Aiden realize he was not as alert as he should have been.

"Good morning, Lord Faolan."

"Good morning, Galameyvin, Aiden. Funny finding the two of you chatting alone." Faolan stood close to the fire and cocked his head, regarding them in amusement. "Or perhaps not."

"Your damn nose?" Knowing he had a way of sniffing things out, Aiden chuckled resentfully. "Have you been lurking around the Queen's tent to get a smell in?"

Laughing, Faolan grinned. "Are you jealous, Captain?"

"Not of your fucking nose."

Shrugging, Faolan sat on the other side of the fire and said, "Tell me, did I confirm it for you, or did you know already?"

"We knew it," Galameyvin answered.

Looking away, Aiden explained, "It made my skin crawl all night.

Do we tell them?"

Sighing heavily, Galameyvin shook his head. "I know Celiaen. He won't miss a chance to lord it over us for his amusement. Particularly you, Aiden."

Faolan smirked knowingly from the other side of the fire. He had smelled the things unsaid between the men.

"Before we change the subject from the delightful antics of our little queen and her mate, I want to share something I expect you to keep to yourselves."

"What is that, wolf?" Aiden asked.

"I knew and loved her mother. So did Vartan. We weren't her mate, but we knew our place, we accepted it, and we took what she gave us. Consider what I'm saying and make of it what you will." Lifting a hand to his mouth, Faolan bit at a nail, grumbling, "Now, do we go along with this plan to ride north? How far north? Are we following this dear little stream? What exactly does she want from this journey?"

"I don't see why not? What difference will it make? I think Eirian knows what she has to do. Something our ancestor said yesterday told her far more than it told us, and I don't think she'll tell." Aiden shifted his position, bending his knees and stretching his arms.

Nodding, Galameyvin agreed. "I had the same thought. Watching Ree during the conversation, I saw her making links. As for the difference? I believe my uncle has more forces coming. Perhaps himself if he feels the southern regions are safe enough. My father is more than capable of holding them. I sincerely doubt Athnaral has more to spare to outnumber us up here."

"No." Aiden shook his head, saying, "I've seen the reports. Unfortunately, the numbers aren't adding up. I've been through Athnaral. I've seen their garrisons. They have reserves somewhere."

"Do you have any idea why she wants to go north?"

"Not the damnedest clue. Eirian enjoys listening to Fox and Mac talk about the Roof. So maybe she just wants to see the mountains. But you know what, she's so sure she's going to die in this war that I don't care if we take months to ride there and back if it means she lives a little longer."

"An endearing sentiment, Captain. Sometimes you say the sweetest things to me." Her voice was soft as Eirian joined them, each man startled by her appearance. "Dawn is breaking. Does anyone have anything I can eat?"

Blinking, Faolan pointed at the apple in her hand. "What's that, then?"

"It's one apple. I'm hungry." She bit the fruit.

"How are you feeling?" Galameyvin asked cautiously, sharing a look with Aiden.

Taking another bite of the apple, Eirian sat halfway between Aiden and Faolan. She did not look at them, staring at the fire.

"Hungry, but I said that already. I've come to some conclusions, but they can wait for the full light of day and when we're all together."

"You know how to defeat the darkness?" Faolan asked outright.

"Maybe I do. Maybe I don't."

Seeing the mischievous gleam in her eye, Aiden shook his head, growling, "It's a serious question, Eirian, and it doesn't deserve a flippant answer."

Regarding him thoughtfully as she finished the apple, Eirian nodded slowly. "You're right, Aiden, it's a serious question, and that was an honest answer. Maybe I know, maybe I don't. We won't know for sure until the time comes. And by your own words, you don't care if it's months before I face her."

"If I knew you'd survive, I'd take you back right now. Do you think I want to risk the lives of so many? I don't want you to die tomorrow. Or at all."

Aiden watched her toss the apple core into the embers of the fire. Getting to her feet, Eirian brushed her hands on her trousers and approached him, resting a hand on his head.

"Don't worry, Aiden, I won't die if I don't have to. Nor will I risk the lives of everyone by not being quite ready. Just trust me."

"I want to, but then I remember you've proven rather happy to trample all over my trust."

Looking at the sky, Eirian took in the deep red hue of the clouds as the sun rose, lifting her hand from Aiden's head to point it out. She knew what it meant, and she felt the early ripples of energy from the storm to come.

"It's a red sky this morning, somewhere shepherds are warning."

Muttering curses, the men looked where she was directing, and Eirian smiled, turning to walk away quietly. Taking in the red dawn, Faolan chuckled and glanced at where she had been, intending to ask if she was sure she wished to continue. Noting her absence, he sighed, ran a hand through his hair, and shrugged at the other men.

"You may as well stamp that fire out. Everyone will be awake soon if they aren't already. Might be a good idea to ride hard northward and hope we find some better shelter than these tents of ours."

"The horses won't enjoy being out in a storm," Aiden said.

Pulling a face, Galameyvin pushed himself up onto his feet. "Don't worry about the horses. Eirian can control them."

"Your cousin made that suggestion ahead of another storm, but she refused because of the numbers," Faolan replied.

"Yeah, our numbers are nothing for Ree. Especially if she can use me. It wouldn't be the first time." He glanced at them briefly. "I'm going to check on Celi and see if I can get any sense out of him."

Left alone with Faolan, Aiden continued to look at the dawn. Despite the rising sun, the day was not getting any brighter, and he felt it reflected his mood.

"Were you her mother's lover?"

Not surprised by the question, Faolan scooped up a handful of dirt and chucked it half-heartedly at the fire. "Yes, I didn't earn my moniker without good cause. Once, I thought Shianeni Malfaer was perfect and could do no wrong. But I know better now. She was perfectly imperfect, a flawed creature like the rest of us."

"I have vague memories of my mother telling Eirian how beautiful and kind the Queen had been while rocking her to sleep. Then, as I grew older, I supposed she must've been a special woman for King Nolan to refuse to wed again and have more children. Is Eirian much like her?"

"Sometimes she is. Captain, you know better than to judge a child by their parent."

Standing, Faolan walked around the fire and offered him a hand. Remembering the beatings his father had given him and the cruelty that Tegan had displayed toward him and Eirian, Aiden nodded, accepting the hand.

"Yes, I do."

"I hope that as my people learn what our late queen did, they don't turn their backs on her daughter because of it."

"You plan to change the reason people call you the loyal wolf?"

Green eyes glittering with amusement, Faolan winked. "I wasn't intending on trying to elbow you and Galameyvin out of your places in line for her bed. But, you're right. I'll be her loyal wolf, and I'll die for her if I must. Not because she is her mother's daughter, but because I believe she could change the world given a chance."

"Won't she be changing the world when she defeats the darkness?"

"Absolutely, but that's not the change I imagine. Now, I'll take care of this fire, but I believe your men are waiting for orders."

Turning, Aiden spotted Merle watching from a distance with his arms crossed over his chest. Nodding when he joined him, Merle fell into step beside him.

"It's a bad day to be traveling. You know what they say."

"Yes, I heard the saying already this morning from Her Majesty."

"She knows it. Surprising."

Aiden arched a brow. "Might I remind you she shared a living space with the daughter of a shepherd? She wasn't an isolated lady of the court."

The last part of his statement made Merle laugh loudly. "No, she wasn't. Nothing should surprise me anymore with her. Do you want to send a rider to confirm we're going north?"

"I told Everett I doubted Eirian would change her mind. He believed it might be for the best if she was away from the nobles for a little while."

"You disagree with him."

Halting, Aiden gave Merle a serious look, replying, "Honestly, I'm torn. The world I thought I understood has gone to shit. We should bide our time to see if we can win this war. Why destabilize the kingdom by forcing her from the throne for something she had no control over when she may well die soon?"

Lips thinning, Merle said, "When you said you wanted to offer me the adventure of a lifetime, I wasn't expecting this."

"I don't recall calling it the adventure of a lifetime, Merle."

"No, but that's how I heard it. I mean, being stationed on the border is not as exciting as being a royal guard. Especially for a farm boy from Caerwel."

Puzzled, Aiden's eyes narrowed. "What are you getting at?"

"She's given us orders, and over the last day, we've all talked about them. You're going to be an earl. Either because she died or because she walked away in triumph to do whatever. We won't be the Queen's Guard, but you'll be Earl of Tamantal and brother to a king." Glancing at the ground, Merle spoke seriously.

Knowing what orders Eirian had given the man, Aiden sighed in frustration. "She's ordered you to protect me and be my guard."

"She might be our queen, but you're our captain. We all owe you something." He scratched his nose. "And who's going to want the men who couldn't keep their queen out of danger serving them as guards except for the man who knew what an impossible woman she could be."

"Impossible woman? That's not a nice thing to say about Fionn," Devin said as he strode over to the two men he respected most. "We fed the horses. Gabe and Fionn have started saddling them while everyone else breaks down the tents. Also, if you were wondering where the Queen is, she's standing out in the open and staring at nothing."

"Anyone watching her?" Aiden asked.

"Fionn and Gabe, but um…"

They looked at him, taking in the perplexed look on his face, and Aiden arched a brow. "What is it, Devin?"

He waved in the direction he had come, muttering, "I know I'm not as, uh… close to her as you are, Captain, but she seems different. I don't know exactly. When she looked at me, I felt like she saw through me and weighed me up. Gabe spoke to her, and when I spoke to him before coming to find you, he was puzzled."

"And we all know he reads her moods better than anyone," Merle chuckled. "Except you, Aiden, but we never see you plying her with food before she figures out she's hungry."

Hearing shouts, Aiden took in the combined efforts of his men and the elves as they took down the small tents. "How do you think the princes will handle the lack of luxury?"

"The only luxury I need is the warmth of your queen beside me," Celiaen commented, coming to stand with them. "You like making derogatory assumptions about me, Captain. If you only knew what sort of beds Ree and I have made for ourselves in the past. Those tents are luxury compared to a cliff face or a hollow at the base of a tree."

"Did Galameyvin speak to you?" he asked, ignoring the uncomfortable looks sent his way by the other two men.

"He did."

"And?"

Blinking at him, Celiaen shrugged. "It's not my place to tell you what Ree knows or doesn't know. I'd hate to get the wrong point across and mislead you."

"You don't know, do you?"

"Not really, no, but my way sounded better. I can tell you she's all about truth, love, and acceptance at the moment, with a good helping of living life with no regrets."

Merle grimaced, muttering, "The sort of things expressed by someone who knows they're going to die."

"Don't say it," Celiaen snarled, pointing at him. "If we believe we can do this without her death, then maybe we can. It's bad enough hearing her talk so casually about sacrificing her life for this war without hearing it from others."

Agreeing with Celiaen, Aiden said, "All we can do is support her, no matter what she thinks the outcome will be. We're the Queen's Guard. We're just not guarding her the way we thought we'd be."

Unable to resist a chance to make a dig, Celiaen commented, "Well, Captain, you certainly weren't doing a good job guarding her last night."

"I didn't need to. You had that all covered," Aiden quipped back, trying not to let the comment get to him.

"I hear someone calling," Devin muttered, inclining his head over his shoulder in a suggestion to Merle that they depart. "We're needed elsewhere, Merle."

Watching his men scurry off in a hurry, Aiden scratched the back of his head and glanced at Celiaen, taking in his amusement. "Feel better now you've made your jokes?"

"Oh, Captain, I'll never stop making jokes to rile you. It's one pleasure I have in life. Besides, I've resisted reminding you I said I'd make sure my sword found your queen."

Smiling coldly, he replied, "But how does it feel to know Gal got there first?"

"Not as bad as you must feel since you never got there at all." Resting a hand on the hilt of a sword, Celiaen watched people bundling equipment together, ready to secure on their horses.

"Don't worry about me. I know the press of Eirian's body against mine."

Spotting Eirian walking among the people packing up, Aiden started forward, but Celiaen grabbed his arm, yanking him back.

"How did you know?"

Aiden held out his healed hand and asked, "How did my hand heal?"

Examining the offered hand, Celiaen said, "So did hers. I noticed it after…"

"Go on."

"Well, after the first time. Ree didn't notice, and I assumed it was something to do with the magic of the bond."

"I don't need to know the details, Prince Celiaen."

"Why do you love her, Aiden?" he asked softly.

"Why do you?"

Exhaling, Celiaen thought back over the years and his countless memories of the woman they spoke of. "Because how could I not? I had a vision once. In it, she was a beautiful, vibrant woman with long hair cascading everywhere as she looked over her shoulder and held her hand out to me to follow her. When it faded, it left me looking at a curious child with a cheeky smile, and I knew I'd always follow her wherever she'd lead me. I've told no one outside our group of that vision, so I'll ask you don't either."

Appreciating what he had been told, Aiden knew he would keep the secret. "The first time I met her again on the road from Riane, she looked at me and smiled. It felt like coming home. Everett expected me to love her like a sister, but on that road, I knew I couldn't, and like you, I knew I'd always follow her. Not out of duty, but because I wanted to."

"Do you think either of us ever had a choice?"

"I suspect not, but if we didn't, then neither did she."

Nodding, Celiaen clapped a hand to his back. "This was a wonderful talk."

"What was a wonderful talk?" Eirian asked as she joined them, smiling faintly.

"We agreed we should travel fast to find some decent shelter," Aiden replied.

Her eyes narrowed suspiciously, and she murmured, "Of course you did. I think we're almost ready to leave. Fox said there should be a grove of trees about half a day's ride away."

"You haven't tried finding it yet?" Celiaen questioned.

"No, but I know it's there," Eirian answered, tapping a finger to the side of her head. "I was just on my way to get those. Thank you, Tobin."

Holding out her swords, he glanced nervously at Aiden. "Yes, ma'am. We thought you might like them. Fox took your bow to Halcyon. Captain, nearly everyone is ready."

Staring out over the remnants of the camp, Aiden scowled while Eirian secured the swords to the baldrics crossing her back.

"A pity we don't have those fancy Telmian tents," he said.

Mouth twisting, Celiaen agreed. "He has a point. They're very comfortable tents."

One of her brows rose as Eirian smirked at Celiaen. "I'm sure you'll make yourself comfortable. A little mud has never bothered you in the past."

"And while you're standing around talking, those clouds are getting closer." Tara approached, hand on the hilt of her sword and eyes darting between each of them. "Celi, Ree, Aiden."

"You look rather cheerful this morning, Tara," Celiaen replied.

"I don't suppose I can talk you out of this insanity, Ree?"

Eirian murmured, "You're welcome to return to Kelsby, Tara."

"You know I go where he does." Tara turned to Aiden, grumbling, "You and I need to knock back more than a few flasks of wine and have a good time complaining about our jobs."

Eirian spread her hands and winked at them before moving toward the horses. Watching Celiaen follow, Tara shook her head, and her short hair flopped over her eyes. Blowing at it half-heartedly, she glanced at Aiden.

"I don't know about you, but I don't get paid enough for this."

Giving her a blank look, Tobin blinked. "You get paid?"

"I like you, boy." Lightly smacking his back, Tara hurried off to make sure her people had collected everything.

"She has a point, though, Captain. We don't get paid enough."

Aiden growled, "How much we're paid is the least of your worries, Tobin. Now make sure all the fires are out."

"I don't think that's going to be a worry once the rain hits."

"Tobin."

"Yes, Captain!"

Saluting, Tobin darted off to follow his orders. Striding in the direction Eirian had gone, Aiden found her with the big brown gelding he knew she loved. Halcyon flicked his ears, nostrils flaring as he stamped an impatient hoof, earning him another scratch. Glancing at the people completing their tasks, he looked at the dark clouds looming on the horizon. Licking his lips, Aiden tasted the rain in the air.

"Don't fret, Cap'n. It's an easy ride," Fox commented as he went past, leading his horse with a rein draped over his shoulder.

Locating his mount, Aiden quickly checked the tack and made sure they had secured everything. People were mounting and throwing wary looks at the sky. Eirian moved among them confidently. She was the only one who did not appear concerned by the weather. He could see they had broken down the tents and that the last few people were joining them. Moving in beside him, Gabe regarded the gaggle with boredom.

"There's some dissension among the masses, Captain."

"I know," he replied.

Dark eyes unreadable, Gabe stared at Aiden. "Just making sure."

Hearing Eirian whistle, Aiden nodded and kicked his horse into motion. "She's determined. The rest of us can come or go."

"Don't worry, I'll talk to her."

"And what do you think you could get out of her I couldn't?"

Almost smiling, Gabe clicked his tongue and said, "We understand each other."

Guiding Halcyon in beside Faolan, Eirian gave him a sideways look. "Faolan, do you think there's more to the world than there seems?"

He frowned, watching the green landscape stretching out before them, broken only by the line of the Arianell. "I don't know because I stopped questioning things. It felt wrong to question. Tharen never stopped, he always had doubts, but I fell into a life of making beautiful trinkets by day and love by night."

"Like a fog?"

"Yes."

"If you'd permit me, while we're away from Neriwyn, I'd like to try undoing what my mother did to you." Eirian did not look, but she knew Faolan was staring in amazement.

"I'm not sure I want to remember," Faolan replied, then looked at the storm clouds in the distance. "But then, the torture of knowing things are locked away in my mind bothers me. I question my entire existence. What is the truth?"

Not answering, Eirian let the horses walk in silence. She understood how he felt, the whisper of memories growing more persistent after she had allowed them in the night before. Quiet chatter surrounded them as the others talked. Bringing their horses in closer to her, the princes exchanged looks with Faolan, and he shrugged, scratching the mane of his horse. Ignoring them, Eirian rested her hands on the pommel of her saddle, reins held loosely. Making his move, Aiden situated himself on the other side of Faolan.

"Don't suppose you lot know any weatherproofing wards? We might need them."

"It's going to get colder," Galameyvin said, crinkling his nose.

Grinning cheekily, Faolan winked at Aiden. "I'm happy to volunteer to keep you all warm. There is much to be said for sleeping in a pile."

"Do you ever stop flirting, wolf?" Eirian asked quietly.

"No."

Growing serious, Galameyvin swept his gaze over the surrounding group. "It's as light as I suspect it will get today. You said—"

"I know what I said," Eirian replied.

Puffing his cheeks out, Faolan shared a look with Aiden. "It's just that we're curious. Our lives depend on this."

"I'm very aware of that. You think I've had a breakthrough about how to defeat her?"

"Are you saying you haven't?" Aiden questioned.

"She fears my blood."

Galameyvin was the first to respond. "Because it can bind her?"

"But how do you bind her again?" Faolan asked what they all wanted to know. "I mean, we don't know if it's wards, or something else."

"For all we know, her physical body could be in a cave somewhere wrapped up in chains reinforced by magic." Snickering at the thought, Celiaen added, "I know it's unlikely, but it's a funny suggestion."

Riding silently behind them, Gabe closed his eyes for a moment before saying, "Could we forget this fight and try to find her body? I know I don't know everything, but I've gathered enough from what you've all said."

"A practical suggestion, Gabe. However, we can't kill a god," Eirian answered.

"Have you tried killing one?"

His question gave them all pause, and she turned to stare at him. "Have you?"

"Would I tell you if I had?" Gabe replied with a dark smile.

"The world is a big place, Gabe, and I wouldn't know where to look. It's not worth the lives lost while I search. So I bind her, and you'll record everything we know, copies made, and held in locations so that those to come will have our knowledge."

Faolan realized where she was going. "Which is why you want to know if you can undo what your mother did to us."

"Yes, I'm sure she had her reasons, but she's not here to give them, and I don't trust Neriwyn." Her gaze flickered to Aiden for a moment, and Eirian wondered how he would react to her next point. "There is something I found concerning out of what we learned yesterday. That the gods tied her bindings to our bloodlines. If she has gotten free because the Altira line has declined in magical strength, then we need to do something."

"What do you suggest?" Celiaen asked.

"It just so happens that the Altira line is rather prosperous. There's a lot of them, with the potential in their veins, and if the Endaran nobility married mages, that'd help. Our ancestor chased magic from his bloodline by ensuring only those without power lived."

While he saw the practicality of her solution, Galameyvin doubted the humans would agree to it. "I don't think you'll be able to convince your nobles to agree to what amounts to a breeding program. They're people, not livestock."

Faolan chuckled. "And yet you trade your young to each other in marriage every day for lands, titles, coin, prestige, or whatever excuse suits your purpose."

"Some would protest, but I wouldn't force anyone. We could send those of an age to marry to Riane to interact with mages of a similar age and perhaps find someone they like."

"Many will protest what they see as a thinning of noble blood," Aiden spoke knowingly.

Rolling her eyes, Eirian said, "There's no such thing as noble blood. Blood is blood. The only difference is if you carry magic. All that sets them apart is that somewhere in the past, they took over an area of land and decided they were in command."

"You have such a glowing view of your nobles." Faolan laughed.

The first distant rumble of thunder reached their ears, and several horses neighed nervously. Halcyon continued walking with his head high and ears flickering, but a muscle twitching in his shoulder told Eirian he was nervous. Stroking his neck gently, she peered into the distance, hoping to spot shelter.

Lightning cast a glow through the clouds above them, brightening the day for a moment before the ominous dark grays of poor weather returned.

Even with the fabric covering her arms, Eirian felt her hair standing on end with the energy of the storm. Closing her eyes, she breathed in deeply and let her magic settle outwards over the land. She searched for anything to provide protection from the weather and located the cluster of trees Fox had mentioned. Returning to herself, Eirian opened her eyes and clicked her tongue.

"If we pick up the pace, we might beat the weather."

"You found shelter then?" Celiaen asked.

"Well, I found the trees. It's better than nothing."

Nudging Halcyon, Eirian encouraged him into a trot. Getting the feeling they would not get anything else out of her, the four men followed suit and pushed their mounts at a quicker pace. The storm continued to rumble, the time between flashes of light growing shorter. She kept her focus on the horses as they trotted along, her magic held at the ready.

Making a judgment call after casting a wary eye at the approaching storm, Celiaen called out to his companions to hurry. Aiden signaled his men to do the same. Sensing hesitation from Eirian, Celiaen leaned over and snatched up Halcyon's reins, giving her a narrow-eyed look.

"Don't. I'm not sure what you're thinking but don't."

He clicked his tongue at the gelding, nudging his horse into a canter and dragging her along with him.

"I wasn't thinking anything!"

Laughing, Celiaen did not let go of the reins. Rolling her eyes, Eirian glanced at the storm before letting her gaze sweep over the land. It glowed with an eerie light that she knew was her magic perceiving the energy of the storm. The beauty of it took her breath away, and she was glad Celiaen was leading Halcyon.

A niggling sense at the back of her mind told her that something else was coming, but she could not decide if she should fear it or not. The whispers mocked her hesitation, the echo of the voices she had heard the night before cutting through the rest. Staring at the scenery as they cantered along the track, Eirian let her focus drift. Someone at the front of the group shouted, directing attention toward the dark splotch against the green where the trees could be located.

"Thank the powers!" Galameyvin muttered.

Eirian sighed, wishing she could have drifted for longer, and gathered the reins, tugging them from Celiaen's grip, earning herself a sharp look. "I think we can risk a race now."

"Weather doesn't wait for anyone!" Kip whooped.

Checking Halcyon's pace, Eirian watched everyone speed up and felt his eagerness to race. Staring north, she tasted the anticipation of what the mountains would bring. Giving the horse his head, she crouched low in the saddle and laughed when he leaped forward. Thunder drowned out the thud of hooves against the earth, but it did not take away the pleasure she felt letting him run like they both loved to do.

SIX

*C*arefully extracting her arm from Celiaen's grasp, Eirian slipped free of the blankets. It was dark inside the tent, the lightning a distant flicker in the sky. He felt her move away and turned his head to peer sleepily as she picked up his coat to drape around herself. Sensing his gaze, she returned to the bedroll they shared and knelt next to it.

"Go back to sleep," she whispered.

Smiling lazily, Celiaen lifted the blanket and replied, "If you're having trouble sleeping..."

"Don't worry about me, Celi. I need to go for a little walk, but I'll be back."

Leaning down, Eirian kissed his forehead and brushed her fingertips across his cheek. Groaning, he caught hold of her arm before she withdrew. Pulling it to his lips, Celiaen trailed kisses along the inside of her wrist. He hoped to convince her to forgo the walk and remain in bed with him.

"Stay," he murmured against her skin.

"I'm too restless."

"I've got a wonderful solution for that."

Eirian knew what he had in mind and chuckled softly. It was tempting to remain, but the prickle along her spine demanded relief. Another wave of storms chased the first, the power calling to her. She wanted to walk away from the camp, free of any watching eyes, and embrace the lightning.

"Stay here, Celi, and when I come back, we can work through that solution."

Smirking against her palm, Celiaen said, "I'll hold you to that."

Her response died in her throat when Eirian felt his teeth graze her skin. Celiaen knew how to make it difficult for her to walk away. The bond pulled, urging her to stay. It was in direct conflict with what the rest of her magic wanted. Closing her eyes, she let him continue, and he took the opportunity presented to him.

"Celi—"

"I thought you were leaving."

The storm was drawing closer. Eirian felt the tingle of the energy accompanying it and clenched her jaw. Yanking her hand from Celiaen's grasp, she ignored his chuckle and stood. He knew she was struggling to go, but it did not surprise him. The lure of the coming storm was stronger. It was no secret among them what it did to her, and he anticipated it.

"Don't miss me too much, Celi," Eirian told him, turning to leave.

"I'll do my best, but don't be surprised if I go looking for another's company."

Glancing back, she suggested, "Aiden's tent is the next one over."

"What an enticing thought. He could keep me warm for you."

Chuckling, Eirian wriggled through the tent door. Her hands held the canvas, and she stuck her head back through to give Celiaen another look.

"That is if Gal hasn't gotten to him first."

Her laughter as she left him alone made Celiaen growl. Unconcerned by the watching eyes of the handful on guard, Eirian closed the coat tightly and picked her way through the camp. The storm was rolling in from the northeast, so she headed in that direction. It was dark, the cloud layer blocking out any light that might have come from the stars. Rubbing the silk between her fingers, she watched the distant flicker of lightning.

Away from Celiaen, the pull of the bond weakened, and the whispers grew stronger. She listened to them, allowing the fragments of memory and voices to fill her mind. The answers were there, and Eirian knew it, but first, she had to make sense of the mess. Nothing was complete, and she hoped something would string together if she was patient enough. It was the only hope she had to cling to.

The rain had left the ground wet beneath her bare feet, but Eirian did not care. With nothing between her and the earth, the connection she felt was substantial enough to reach for the distant energy. If she wanted to draw on it, it was there, and glancing over her shoulder at the figure following, it tempted her. There was little need to go far. All she needed was enough distance that anything she might say would be unheard.

Finding a spot to kneel, Eirian avoided getting Celiaen's coat filthy. Releasing her grasp on the hems, she placed her hands on her thighs and stared at the storm. She felt his approach, but did not turn to look at him when he joined her. Kneeling beside Eirian, Faolan studied the arcing bolts of light that connected the earth to the sky.

"You smell delicious," he joked softly.

Rolling her eyes, Eirian muttered, "Do you ever think about anything else?"

"It's a bit hard to avoid when you reek of him."

"I think the next storm is going to be worse."

Faolan grunted. "Can you do something about it?"

"Don't worry, I'll make sure you don't get hit by lightning."

He had suspected she could do that, and Faolan was glad to have the chance to see it happen. Glancing at Eirian, he admired the warm glow of her skin and the way the coat hung off her shoulders. There was no flicker of power dancing in her eyes, but he expected it would come. Sniffing, he thought he detected something different about her scent, making him frown.

"Are you feeling alright, Eirian?"

Eyes widening, she glanced at him. "I'm feeling a little different. Figured it was just because of the bond."

"Should you play with the storm?" Inclining his head to the horizon, Faolan added, "It might be dangerous."

"Better to play now, while Kelsby is still close. I'm sure it'll be fine, but I need to make sure I can control it."

"That's a good point. So, how's the rage going?"

"Strangely. It's right there. His and mine. I feel like it's easier to reach for, and I'm a little concerned about my temper," Eirian admitted.

Nodding slowly, Faolan understood her worry. He had seen enough bonds in the past to know that it would take some time before either of them was in complete control of their magic again. More so when they were close. The excitement he felt toward the prospect of seeing the two of them in battle together made him swallow back guilt. Sighing, he rubbed his face tiredly.

Her hand left her leg to touch his gently, and Faolan chuckled. Power washed through him, energizing and addictive. It would be so easy to fall into the trap of being around Eirian all the time, letting her magic carry him along. He had observed the way she invigorated people. The elves took it for granted, and he doubted any of them even noticed the exchange. Looking at her face, Faolan knew she would give every drop of herself to them without being asked.

"You know how to end this war, don't you?"

"The darkness needs to kill me."

Breath leaving him in a rush, Faolan felt like someone had kicked him in the stomach. She had not kept it a secret that she thought the war would take her life, but to hear Eirian specify what was needed came as a shock.

"That's it?"

Eirian chuckled. "Herself. Not one of her servants. My blood needs to be on her hands."

Hearing the bitterness in her voice, Faolan covered her hand with his own. The heat of it surprised him, and he glanced at Eirian. With her lack of clothing and the chill of the night, he had expected her to be icy. He was completely naked and regretting it, but she appeared unbothered.

72

"Aren't you cold?"

Thrown by the question, Eirian glanced at her hand. "Not really. I should be, but I'm not."

"The bond?"

"Maybe. Most likely just my magic. It's not the first time I haven't noticed the weather."

Grunting, Faolan squeezed her hand and said, "So we've got to keep you alive long enough to piss off a god. All so she comes to kill you herself?"

"Something like that. I can feel her, Faolan. At the edge of my mind, connected to me somehow. I suppose I can blame my mother for that."

She could not tell him the whole truth, but Eirian knew what handpicked information she gave Faolan was safe. There was no one else she trusted to help her cope. As much as she loved them, the others would let their emotions get in the way. He had seen enough to know what was at stake.

"You said you wanted to try undoing what Shianeni did to my memory. So try now."

"I don't know if that's a good idea," she admitted. "I'm struggling with my mind, and I'm worried what that might do to yours."

Faolan understood where she was coming from, but suspected Eirian wanted to try as much as he needed her to. Noticing a flicker of lightning reflected in her eyes, he pushed on.

"Please. Try while we're away from the well-meaning intentions of the others. You'll have a better chance of listening to your instincts without them."

Still hesitant, Eirian searched the horizon for the next bolt of lightning. The whispers told her where to look and she counted the forks before they appeared.

"I don't want to hurt you, wolf."

"What if I know something that might save your life? Maybe Shianeni kept me close for a reason that she made me forget."

Eirian knew he was right and nodded. It was the same reason she had let the whispers talk to her instead of banishing them. Shifting her position, she provided her protesting legs with some relief. Stretching them out, she ran a hand through her hair and made her decision.

"Let's try this." Scoffing, Eirian asked, "I don't suppose you have any advice before I go blindly looking for magic that isn't yours?"

"I'm the wrong one to ask, perhaps if Saoirse was here. But I'd rather you didn't leave me a drooling mess," he joked.

Sighing, Eirian hoped it was not a possibility. The storm was getting closer, and it would become harder for her to focus. Offering Faolan her hand, she waited for him to lace his fingers through hers. She relaxed her hold over her magic and felt his power rise to meet it when he did. It made the whispers get louder, reminding her of all the times he had seemed familiar.

Closing her eyes, Eirian listened to the voices and followed their urgings.

They told her to look for something familiar, so she heeded the advice. With nothing better to go off, she hoped her mother's magic felt close enough to her own to find it. Sniffing, she thought she smelled rain. The sort of light rain that bordered on being mist. It carried a hint of flowers and the sickly-sweet scent of overripe fruit left in the sun.

"Eirian?" Faolan whispered, watching the flutter of her eyelids.

He felt her in his mind, a soothing presence lingering at the edges. It did not feel like when Saoirse or others used their power. There were no subtle attempts to sway his thought process in a particular direction. Eirian was simply there. Her hand remained entangled with his, the warmth seeping into his limb. In the distance, the storm rolled closer, and the faint rumble of thunder reached Faolan's ears.

Following the scent that Eirian was sure only she could smell, she found the layer of magic entrenched in Faolan's mind. It felt like her own power, but with a few differences, and she was glad the voices were right. Touching the veil sent a jolt down her spine. It gave the sense of a connection, tugging at the threads of her power. She was certain she could undo it, provided enough time to untangle everything.

It was disconcerting to contemplate how much Shianeni had hidden from the daoine. Tugging at the edge of the manipulation worked on Faolan's mind, Eirian let her magic examine its weave. An uncomfortable feeling settled in her stomach at the recognition of the way her mother's power twisted. Aspects of it were similar to the simple tricks she used to sneak out. The wards she used to make people forget they had noticed a door open or seen movement against a wall.

"Do it, or I kill her! I'll kill every single fucking one of them if I have to, darling."

A memory of a knife held above her drove Eirian to gasp. The voice sounding in her mind was one she had heard while standing over the body of a man she had killed. Eyes opening quickly, she pulled her hand from Faolan's grasp and pressed fingers to her forehead while trying to calm the racing of her heart. Instinct screamed that the memory had been hers, but she did not know how it was possible.

"Are you okay? What happened?" Faolan asked in concern.

He wanted to reach for her, but the panicked look on Eirian's face stopped him. Shaking her head, she continued to take slow breaths and block out the whispers of memory crowding in on her. Faolan's nose twitched, detecting the scent of another on the breeze, and he turned to see the guard striding through the darkness toward them. Winking at him, Gabe crouched on the other side of Eirian and held out a hand to her.

"Hungry?"

Lowering her hands, Eirian looked at Gabe and took in the dark forms resting on his palm. Feeling a pang of hunger, she tentatively took one and put it in her mouth, chewing with little thought. Frowning in suspicion, Faolan stared at him and wondered why he had not picked up his scent sooner. It seemed strange that he had appeared as suddenly as he had.

"How do you always know?" Eirian muttered.

"It's my job, ma'am."

Faolan caught a whiff of the food. "Where did you find karkalla up here?"

"I haven't had it in months." She plucked another one of the deep red fruits from Gabe's hand. "I loved going searching for karkalla along the coast. Sometimes Celi and I would steal it from gardens in Riane, but wild ones were more fun."

Smirking, Gabe told Faolan, "If you know where to look, you can find most things."

Consuming the fruit gave Eirian something to focus on that was familiar and comforting. However, the memory of the knife and the voice lingered in her mind, driving the whispers to scream. She wished she could drown out the noise and flinched when a rumble of thunder sounded closer than before. It triggered something in the memory. The echo of deafening thunder and the rattle of glass windows.

"There was a storm," she whispered, ignoring the men.

"What happened?" Faolan prompted. "Did you learn anything?"

"She definitely did something to you. I recognized it because it's similar to my magic."

Grunting, Gabe brushed his empty hand on his leg and said, "Why do I have a bad feeling about what the two of you are up to?"

Eirian replied, "I'm trying to undo something my mother did to the daoine. She made them forget things, including things about the darkness. Faolan and I think he might know something that could help us."

"While it sounds like a good idea, ma'am, I need to tell you that some things shouldn't be meddled with."

"Why would you say that?"

"You don't know why she did it, but maybe it was to protect them? If you could undo it, who might you hurt in the process?"

Furious, Faolan snarled, "Shianeni manipulated our entire people! We have the right to know what happened to us."

"Perhaps." Gabe arched a brow. "And say Her Majesty undoes it? We're in the middle of a war. Hardly seems a good idea to disrupt the Telmian army."

Able to see his point, Eirian nodded slowly. Neither of them knew what they might uncover if she unraveled the fog shrouding Faolan's mind. Lightning flashed closer, thunder following in its wake. There was rain coming, and she tugged at the edges of Celiaen's coat. She would not give up on understanding what Shianeni had done to the daoine, but Gabe was right. It was not worth the risk to the Telmian forces.

"He has a point, Faolan. That's not to say we should stop, but maybe we should keep it between ourselves for now. If I focus on just your mind, there's a chance we'll have a better idea of what was forgotten."

Scowling, Faolan replied, "Fine. First, you figure it out using me, and afterward, we work out how to fix the rest of my people."

Sighing, Gabe muttered, "Pair of idiots."

"Why are we idiots?"

"Because some shit needs to be left alone! I'm not stupid. Queen Shianeni was obviously powerful, and I'll bet there's a good fucking reason for what she's done."

Eyes darting between the two men, Eirian held back, saying nothing. She disagreed with Gabe, but the whispers did not, leaving her torn. Shaking her head, she silently pleaded with them for silence. They taunted, replaying the flash of a knife repeatedly. It felt significant. Even if it was important, she could not afford the distraction it would bring trying to chase it.

"I'm surprised by you, Gabe," Eirian spoke quietly.

Gabe stared at her blankly and answered, "Because I'm telling you, it's a bad idea? My job is to protect you, ma'am. Including from yourself."

"And you think doing this is dangerous?"

"I think it might lead you down a path you'll regret."

"They're my memories," Faolan argued. "And if Eirian can give them back, then I want to know what Shianeni took from me."

"I'm not saying to never try."

Pressing her lips together, Eirian sucked in a deep breath. "Then what are you saying, Gabe?"

"I'm suggesting you leave it be until after the war." Clicking his tongue, Gabe said, "You're worried about keeping Endara stable. It has thrown the Telmians to find out your mother was their queen. Do you really want to add to that instability? What sort of leader are you if you do that to them? They're your allies."

Muttering curses, Faolan did not need to see the look on Eirian's face to know Gabe had gotten through to her. He understood the concern about causing more disruptions, but his anger over Shianeni was consuming. The prospect of Eirian's death did not help. Nothing could convince him there was no other option. Losing one queen was heart-wrenching, and he refused to lose another.

"We can't lose you as well," he informed Eirian.

Her shoulders slumped as Eirian said, "Always the loyal wolf. I'm not going to stop trying to figure this out with you. But Gabe is right. We can't do this to your people."

Watching another flicker of lightning in her eyes, Faolan asked, "But what if?"

"We'll try some more tomorrow. There's no point telling anyone else what we're trying to do when we don't know if I'll be able to unravel it. I don't want to disappoint you, but what if I can't restore your memories?"

Nodding, Faolan stood up and brushed a hand over her head. Green eyes darted to Gabe, lingering on his form in the darkness. Something had always unsettled him about the guard, but now he was sure there was a familiarity to his scent. Lifting his face to smile, he made a show of looking over Faolan's naked body.

"Celiaen is probably waiting for you to come back," Faolan said.

Shaking her head, Eirian dismissed him. "I'm going to stay out a bit longer. There's a storm coming, wolf."

"Something tells me it's already here."

Watching Faolan walk away, Gabe murmured, "He worries about you."

"With good reason, I'm sure," she answered. "You can go."

"And leave my queen alone, unprotected? It wouldn't impress my captain."

Detecting the sarcasm in his tone, Eirian arched a brow and glanced at him. The whispers died down, giving her enough silence inside her head to focus on the rumble of thunder. She wanted to walk out to meet the storm, her power seeking the energy coursing through the earth.

"What do you want, Gabe?"

He chuckled. "What makes you think I want something?"

"Because of all my guards, you're the one who can work out when it's best to get the fuck away from me."

Sparks arced between her fingertips as she connected with the storm. Gabe smiled slowly, delighting in the sheen of magic coating her. The prospect of witnessing Eirian in a storm fascinated him a great deal. He was confident she would not risk hurting him, and it gave him the courage to defy the hint of rage rippling through her power.

"That's true, I do."

"I don't see you getting up to leave," she muttered.

"Because now is not one of those times."

"I disagree."

"Well now, I don't see how you're in a position to disagree, Your Majesty," Gabe informed her. "You're still the queen of Endara, and I'm your guard. I have my orders."

Rolling her eyes, Eirian decided not to argue. Easier to get to her feet and pretend he was not there. Gabe's ability to fade into obscurity meant it was simple to do. Her knees and legs protested the change in position, prompting her to stretch. While she did, he looked away, avoiding the sight of her naked form when the coat shifted.

Glancing at him, Eirian snorted. "You're welcome to look. I really don't care."

"You might not, but they would."

Laughing, she shrugged the coat off and threw it at him. Catching the garment forced Gabe to look, his eyes following the line of her body. She glowed, the magic shifting across her skin, twisting into the radiance that had been growing brighter with each passing day. It was difficult not to admire in the view, and he hoped Aiden did not find out. Crinkling her nose, Eirian spread her fingers, sparks shooting from the ground to her hands.

"Guess you have two choices now, Gabe," Eirian said. "Run back to your tent and pretend you weren't looking at my ass. Or stick around, keep looking, and hope your captain doesn't give you more than a black eye."

Bunching the coat in his hands, Gabe murmured, "A black eye is the least of my worries."

"If I asked you to kill me, Gabe, would you do it?"

He stared at her blankly, refusing to answer.

"What if I told you the darkness was affecting my judgment?"

"Is she?" he inquired, eyes narrowing.

Shrugging, Eirian waved in the camp's direction. "It would be so easy to destroy all of them."

Lightning darted from the sky in the distance behind her, and Gabe sighed. Waiting for the boom of thunder, Eirian looked at the clouds and imagined the stars beyond them.

"If I truly thought for a moment you were being influenced by her, then yes, I'd kill you."

"See, my question wasn't hard to answer."

"Maybe I'm influenced and plan to kill you now," Gabe grumbled.

Smiling, Eirian let sparks of energy dance between her fingers. "I'd like to see you try."

"If things don't go to plan, we'll find out which of us is better."

Eirian turned her back on him and faced the storm with her arms spread. The deafening boom of thunder drowned out her laughter, but Gabe caught the start. It carried a note of desperation which prompted him to consider why she had asked. Feeling the brush of a plant growing beside him, he stood and tossed the coat over his shoulder. Her magic spreading carried the scent of flowers with it. Sweet and intoxicating, like a meadow of wildflowers on a spring day.

"What are you planning?"

Glancing over her shoulder at him, Eirian smiled and took several steps. He did not move to follow, sensing the approach of another. Bowing his head, Gabe watched Aiden come to a halt beside him. Eyes locked on Eirian, Aiden observed the small darting bolts of lightning she was drawing out of the air.

"Faolan told me she was out here," he said. "He thought you might need some help to convince her to return."

"Thank you, sir. Unfortunately, she's not in the mood to listen."

"I heard that!" Eirian called out.

Aiden held out his hand. "Hand it over. I'll take care of this."

"We could try knocking her out," Gabe replied.

"Get some sleep."

Surrendering the coat, Gabe turned and started back to camp. Smiling faintly, he cast a last look at them over his shoulder as he walked away. Draping the silk over his arm, Aiden watched Eirian twist her fingers through the air, the glow of her skin making her every movement clear. Sparks spread from her, and he flinched when one came close to his face.

"Careful, darling. You wouldn't want to damage my pretty face."

"Why, Captain, I believe there are a few sparks between us," she joked.

The absurdity of her comment made him laugh, and Aiden covered his face. Feeling a finger stroke across his wrist, he lowered his hand to gaze at Eirian. Her eyes shone, a reflection of the storm summoned by the power coursing through her. Dropping his gaze to where her finger traced a pattern on his skin, Aiden swallowed nervously. An unfamiliar sensation filled him, like a rush of energy burning his breath away.

"Didn't you like my joke?" Eirian asked softly when the thunder faded.

"I thought it was hilarious."

Arching a brow, she lifted her other hand and held it up in front of him with the palm facing upward. Energy crackled over it.

"Beautiful, isn't it?"

"Very," Aiden said and hoped she would not realize he was not talking about the power.

"You've got nothing to fear from it, Aiden. I wouldn't hurt you intentionally."

He wanted to run his hands over her and chase the flickers of magic. They darted and twisted, leaving glittering trails that faded before the next wave began. Nothing Aiden had ever seen compared to Eirian as she absorbed power from the storm.

"You didn't look like this last time I saw you in a storm."

Eirian smirked. "Last time, I was trying to avoid letting the daoine know about my heritage."

"And this time?"

"What do I have left to hide?"

"More than a few secrets, I imagine."

A shadow of remorse appeared on her face, and Eirian stepped back. Without her touch, the strange sensation Aiden had been feeling vanished. He felt empty without it. Touching her stomach briefly, she shrugged and turned from him. The air crackled with energy, sparks appearing in the space between her moving feet and the ground. Letting her walk away, Aiden clung to the coat that smelled like Celiaen and watched as Eirian strode toward the storm.

Spreading her arms wide, she reached out with her magic. Whispers sang in her ears, telling her to do it. They always did. The whispers had told her she could draw on storms, but Eirian could not admit it. She did not want to see the looks on the faces of her friends if she told them voices in her head had guided her all her life. It would drive them to seek evidence of the darkness on her.

Eirian turned her thoughts to the tiny flicker she had been coaxing along with her magic. It had only been a day, but she needed to encourage it. Aiden had been spot-on with his comment about secrets. Breathing an apology, she closed her eyes and tilted her head back. Palms facing upward, she prepared for what she was about to do.

A wave of rage startled Aiden as he watched a bolt of lightning strike her. Shouting her name, he ran forward, only to be stopped by a wall of power rippling outwards. Eirian stood still, unmoved and unharmed, her hair shifting in response to the magic surrounding her. Thumping a fist against the invisible wall, he called out repeatedly until she faced him.

"What the fuck, Eirian? Are you hurt?"

Clasping her hands together on her stomach, Eirian walked over to him, and the wall vanished. Winking at Aiden, she did not stop moving, making him hurry to match her stride. There was no sign of injury, but lightning danced in her eyes while the sheen of magic coating her skin was brighter than before.

"What are you doing?" he demanded.

"I'm going back to bed."

Unimpressed by the answer, Aiden went to grab her, but Eirian stopped him.

"I don't suggest doing that unless you want to join Celi and me."

"What?"

"He won't say no, trust me," Eirian purred, giving him a sly look. "You'd enjoy it."

Exasperated, Aiden said, "You were just struck by lightning!"

"Well, yes, I was. But only because I made it happen."

"You made the lightning hit you?"

"Yes."

"I don't understand."

Sighing, Eirian replied, "No one does. It's just something I can do. The camp will be safe from the storm. Using the power from the strike, I warded the tents from damage."

"You can do that?" he asked in surprise.

"It's complicated."

"You didn't think that might be useful information previously?"

"Sure. Want to tell me how to break the news that I can make lightning hit me?"

Screwing up his face, Aiden acknowledged her point. "Fair enough. Why didn't you do it earlier?"

"Because that part of the storm wasn't so bad. What's coming now is worse. I just wanted to make sure everyone would be safe."

"And the elves know you can do this?"

"Yep."

The truth angered him, and Aiden glared at the tents that had appeared in the darkness. Lightning lit the sky, forming lines across the clouds to make them appear to be sundered apart. There was a vicious beauty to the storm that he likened to Eirian. It seemed like the perfect description. She was a raging storm trapped within a vessel that could barely contain her. Cracks would appear, letting the lightning escape as her magic, but then things would shift, and the gaps would vanish again.

Halting, Aiden watched her continue walking before Eirian realized he was not with her and stopped. Turning to face him, she cocked her head. Neither spoke while they stared at each other with the storm raging. The first drops of rain began, and he shook his head.

"The invitation wasn't a joke," she informed him.

"I know."

"But you won't."

"No," he murmured, though he wanted to join them.

Nodding, Eirian left him there and continued to the tent where she left Celiaen. The bond called, confirming that he was waiting. Gazing at her glowing figure weaving through the tents, Aiden wondered if any of the others realized what she was. He was not even sure she knew, but it was clear Eirian was a weapon. A weapon forged of flesh and magic intended to battle a god.

SEVEN

*C*raning her neck, Eirian stared at the towering mountains. She had known they were huge, but her mind was struggling to wrap around the true enormity of them. Massive peaks reached far into the sky, a shine of white where the clouds met the snow covering them. It made her appreciate how small she was in comparison and left her reluctant to release her magic. The whispers told her to let go, those memories shrouded in fog screaming out that answers were among the clouds.

She sat on the ground while everyone else set up camp in the trees growing along the mountain slope. They grew as far up as possible, and she looked forward to walking among the twisted trunks. Riding between them, Eirian had marveled at the way the leaves filtered the light through and created a dappled carpet of shadows over the ground. Some were a fascinating blend of colors, bright red bleeding out over silvery-white bark.

A distance away, the Arianell tumbled down the face of the mountains, no longer snow and ice. Its banks showed evidence of frequent animal visitation, well-worn tracks providing easy access to the water. Fox had explained the area was home to moose and deer, hunters often visiting to cull the numbers. The closer they got to the Fingers, the colder the water became, and Eirian noticed Fox and Mac were the only ones willing to spend much time in it.

Sighing, Eirian dug her hands into the rich soil and decided she could spend a lifetime staring at the mountains and never understand all their secrets. Sensing Celiaen approaching, she continued to gaze upward and ignored the protest of her shoulders, neck, and wrists. Carpeting the sky, the clouds appeared as though someone had lined up clumps of cotton so that each was not touching the other.

"You've been sitting here for a long time, Ree," Celiaen said, standing over her with a concerned frown.

"And I could sit here a lot longer and still not find satisfaction," she replied, letting her head drop and shifting her weight to give her shoulders a break.

Brushing his hand over her head, Celiaen peered upward. He did not understand what had her so fascinated, but he wished he did.

"The Fingers are impressive, the Roof even more so, but they're just mountains."

"They're not, though, not to me. I know none of you see the world the same way I do, but surely you can appreciate the magnificence of these mountains."

"You're right. I don't see things the way you do, and the powers know I wish I could. The look of amazement you wore when you first saw them made me envious. It's the same look you wear staring at the ocean, at a simple flower, or a bird. I envy the way you admire everything." Waving at the range, he added, "And I know you haven't let yourself feel them yet."

"I'm scared too."

"Why?"

Sighing, Eirian dragged her bottom lip through her teeth. "Because they're so vast, and I'm worried I might get lost in them. Fox said they're all connected and continue to grow further and further into the sky as they go north."

It was not the whole truth, but she did not know how to explain that they had brought out memories of a vast, glistening lake surrounded by sprawling buildings and gardens. Those memories were creeping more and more into her thoughts. Banishing the whispers and images was increasingly difficult, worsening with each attempt Eirian made to unravel what Shianeni had done to Faolan's mind.

Bending, Celiaen kissed the top of her head, careful not to lose his balance. "I wouldn't let you get lost. As long as our hearts beat in time, I'll always find you and bring you home."

Eirian returned to staring at the looming peak, murmuring, "It's strange not being able to shut you out like I used to."

Nudging her, Celiaen smiled in amusement. "When have you ever been good at shutting me out?"

"I'd argue I'm extremely good at shutting you out," Eirian replied with a laugh and crinkled her nose at his unimpressed expression.

"You know that's not what I meant for a change," he grumbled. "Seriously, Ree, you've never been good at keeping secrets from me. Sometimes I let you like I am now, but if I wanted you to tell me, you would."

Lifting a hand, Celiaen cupped her cheek and stared at her sadly. Guilt flashed through her, and Eirian glanced away to avoid him seeing it.

"I'm not keeping anything from you, Celi."

"Yes, you are. I understand, though, and I know when you're ready, you'll tell me. I trust you, and I always have."

Turning Eirian's face toward his, Celiaen leaned in to kiss her gently. His tenderness added to the heartbreak she constantly felt.

"I'll never tire of saying I love you. I wish I'd told you years ago."

Leaning her forehead against his, Eirian chuckled. "I don't know that the outcome would've changed."

Arching a brow, Celiaen watched the people they were traveling with. He chose not to argue, even though he wanted to. It was not worth wasting what time they had together.

"I think I heard mention of a hunt first thing in the morning. Venison would be nice."

Pursing her lips, Eirian liked the idea. "It's been a while since I could hunt."

"Hunting with you is rarely fun."

"That's because you're a terrible shot!" Pushing Celiaen, she grinned. "You're an embarrassment to reds everywhere. I don't know how you can call yourself one."

"I'm going to let that slide, but don't worry, I'll show you how good my aim is when I take down a deer before you."

"Oh, no, no, that won't happen. It's never happened, and it never will."

Celiaen's eyes narrowed, and he said challengingly, "Want to wager on that?"

Giving up on restraining her laughter, Eirian rose. "And how would you propose we make hunting one deer into a competition?"

"We make sure anyone else who goes knows they're not to take a shot. Then the first deer we sight, we get one arrow each, and the kill shot wins."

"I only need one shot." Smirking with a hand on her hip, Eirian glanced at the camp before shifting slightly to watch the pacing man monitoring them.

Stretching his legs out, Celiaen stated, "No magic."

"Magic or no magic, I've always been the better archer."

"Fine, it's a wager."

Eyes following Aiden back and forth along the outskirts of the line of tents, Eirian tapped a finger to her lips. "You didn't name the terms."

"You always enjoyed bragging rights, but I was thinking about something else."

"Oh no, bragging rights is perfect. I'll win, and someone else gets to remind you I'm the better archer whenever he wants."

His smile faded, and Celiaen stammered, "That's hardly fair."

"If you beat me, the embarrassment will teach me a lesson you won't let me forget."

Picking her way downhill carefully, Eirian listened to the sound of Celiaen scrambling to get up and follow. Taking in the way they picketed the horses among the trees encircled by tents, she noticed their guards had built fires outside the circle. Rubbing her arms, she recalled Mac saying there would be packs of wolves. Fox had mentioned the occasional mountain lynx and snow leopard ventured down from the mountains. The fires would act as a deterrent and help them avoid any encounters with the predators in the area.

Offering her arm to Celiaen, she said, "Cheer up, Celi, at least we didn't set the target as something dangerous. I'd be amused to see you go after a lynx."

Paling at the thought, he muttered, "Why do I have the feeling you're hoping one shows up?"

Batting her eyelids with an innocent smile, Eirian replied, "I'd never wish such a thing. I hear they're extremely dangerous animals."

"Is she talking about lynx?" Aiden caught the tail end of her words as they drew close. "Ever since Fox introduced her to their fur, they've been on her mind."

"Aiden, I have something to tell you I think you'll rather like."

His eyes narrowed suspiciously. "I'm not sure about that."

"The Prince and I have a little wager regarding hunting a deer. We each get a single shot, and the first to bring down a deer wins."

"I see. And what part of this did you think I'd like?"

Celiaen grunted and gave Aiden a frustrated look. "The part where if she wins, you get to remind me as often as you like that she's a better shot."

Pursing his lips, Aiden considered it for a moment before pointing at Celiaen to ask, "And what do you get for winning?"

"I get to remind Ree that I beat her."

Watching Eirian take in the tents scattered through the trees, Aiden saw a hint of wistfulness in her eyes. Glancing at Celiaen, he gave a slight nod, acknowledging the look of concern directed back.

"I believe Fox was discussing tracking down a deer with several of the elves."

Her face lit up, and Eirian said, "I can find a herd easily."

"No magic!" Celiaen declared.

"Not even to locate a herd?" She groaned. "Come on, Celi, that means we have to track them down rather than knowing where they are and getting on with it."

"Good thing you have two skilled hunters serving you. I'm sure Fox and Mac know what they're doing."

Snorting, Aiden waved at the central fire. "Why don't you go talk to them. They were planning over there last I saw."

Nodding in agreement, Eirian dropped Celiaen's arm. The trio was silent, moving through the tents until they joined the small group gathered at the fire. Taking in that it was unlit, she cast a wary glance at the foliage. She noticed they had chosen a spot with minimal coverage. Looking at Eirian in excitement, Fox fluttered his hands in front of him with a grin.

"Fancy a hunt today, ma'am?"

"Celi and I were planning on one, with or without you," she answered.

Rolling his eyes, Aiden said, "They have a matter of pride to settle. I don't think any of you will get a look in."

Fox told them, "I've already done a little scouting around and found signs this area has a resident herd. But, ma'am, I don't suppose you could find them for us?"

"She's not allowed to use her powers, and they have one shot each to take a beast down," Aiden replied. "Hopefully, they both miss, and you can take the kill from under their noses."

"Aiden," Eirian grumbled, crossing her arms.

"Yeah, I've seen her take out a moving target without seeing it. I don't think she knows how to miss." Mac chuckled, giving Fox a knowing look.

Tara planned to join the hunt, and she glanced between Celiaen and Eirian blankly, commenting, "Celi, you're outmatched by her with or without magic. We all know it. You may as well let Ree locate them so we can go kill a deer, and if we work fast enough, there can be a roast over the fire for dinner tonight."

"I don't know about you, but I could do with some fresh venison," Kenna agreed.

Giving in, Celiaen pointed at Eirian. "I suppose you may as well. Just no magic when we go to kill."

Scoffing before closing her eyes, Eirian released her magic and let it chase out through the forest. The whispers tempted her to delve into the mountains, but her fear drove the desire from her mind. Instead, she focused on locating the deer and sifted through the energies of all she encountered. When she found the herd grazing in a glade, she lingered to enjoy it. She felt their natural nervousness, the constant drive to be alert for any danger. Withdrawing, Eirian memorized the way through the forest. Opening her eyes, she blinked, her magic settling around her comfortably. They stared expectantly, waiting for her to speak.

"Found a herd, not far, and no need for horses. A handful of does and fawns."

Curious, Fox asked, "Would you be able to tell which does are without young? Wouldn't want to kill a mother if we can take another."

Shrugging, Eirian started looking around for her tent. "I should be able to, but I haven't tried something so specific before."

Nodding to Aiden, Fox scratched his chin. "By your leave, Cap'n. We'll head out as soon as we're ready to go."

"I need to grab my bow," Eirian muttered. "Just have to find my tent."

Pursing her lips, Tara bit back a chuckle. "It's over there, away from the rest of us a little. Obvious reasons."

Her gaze flickered between Eirian and Celiaen, delighting in the slight blush that reddened Eirian's cheeks.

"I'll come along as well." Aiden shrugged, giving Celiaen a knowing look. "Since my right to annoy the fuck out of you depends on the outcome, princeling."

Not interested in listening to their exchange of insults, Eirian turned to her tent. Filled with purpose, she strode to the small canvas shelter and pulled back the flap covering the entrance. They had propped her bow and quiver against the side next to her bedroll. Hooking her fingers through the straps, she hoisted them and secured the buckles to her belt. Rolling her head, she massaged the back of her neck, feeling a pinch.

Spotting her cloak, Eirian grabbed it before shuffling out of the tent. Draping it around her shoulders as she walked back to the group, she made sure she could draw her swords. Others wore their cloaks, except for Fox and Mac, who seemed at ease with the temperature. Looking around the camp, she took in the busy people going about their tasks.

"Come on, let's go while we have enough light."

Celiaen joined as they were passing the line of fires. "Gal isn't interested. He said to have fun and not to hurt me."

There were a few laughs, and rolling her eyes, Eirian ran fingertips over a low-hanging branch. "Fox, can you tell me about the trees here as we go?"

"The trees? Why?" Fox asked curiously, glancing up and down one of the silvery-white barked trees with its mottling of red.

"She likes to know," Tyrone replied, chuckling.

Pointing at one of the taller trees with blueish-green lance-shaped leaves and a grayish stringy bark, Eirian asked, "What's that one? Does it have any uses?"

"Can't you ask questions after we've found those deer?" Celiaen muttered.

Peering through the trees, he tried using the bond to sense the animals like Eirian, but lacked her instincts to guide him.

"I could, but we're not close, and I don't feel like walking in silence."

Sighing, Fox answered, "It's alpine ash. You'll find them all along the base of the mountains and higher up. My ma extracts oil from the leaves to use on wounds and for treating coughs and other sicknesses."

Cocking her head as they skirted around a fallen tree, the rotting trunk collapsed against another, Eirian said, "That's handy to know."

Mac chuckled. "They're also called woollybutt."

"What an unfortunate moniker."

Glancing at her, Kenna asked, "Can you tell how far off we are?"

Reaching up, Eirian let the leaves of a tree run through her grasp and recalled the layout of the land imprinted on her mind. "Not much further. What about those trees that look like they're bleeding out?"

"Snow gum," Fox responded in amusement. "Good firewood, excellent medicine, much like the ash."

Feeling a prickle on the edge of her senses, Eirian halted suddenly, lifting a hand to stop the others. "Wait…"

Her reaction had those with bows pulling them into their hands with an arrow ready, Aiden and the reds reaching for their swords. Shaking her head, Eirian looked around the forest while frowning. Fox tilted his head to the side, his keen hunter instincts picking up on something, eyes widening before he spun and drew the bow in his hands. Not far behind, Mac loosed an arrow moments after, leading Eirian to realize that what she had sensed was the herd of deer running past them in a panic. Pushing her back against the trunk of a tree, Aiden drew his sword, Celiaen and several others doing the same.

"Fox?" Aiden spoke quietly, giving Eirian a warning look.

"I think we dropped one. The question is why they bolted. What do you sense, ma'am?"

Rolling her eyes, Eirian muttered, "All it took was a few months, and you're relying on me to do half your job."

"You're always boasting you don't need us," Aiden bit back. "So, make yourself useful and do your thing."

Huffing in annoyance, Eirian let her magic go. She first encountered the dying doe lying on the ground. Continuing to where she had initially located the herd, she regretted not doing a broader sweep. A group of humans and dogs were in the glade, the lingering taste of death on the ground telling her they had also taken a deer. There was no hint of the darkness, and pulling back, she lifted a finger to her lips and pulled a knife from her belt.

Pushing to the front of the group, Eirian strode through the trees to the downed animal and stopped by it long enough to drag the weapon across its throat. Murmuring apologies to the dead doe for the suffering they put it through, she wiped the blade off on its coat before signaling to the people following to remain quiet. As she moved, she exchanged the knife for her bow, nestling several arrows in her fingers.

"What is it?" Tara whispered.

Celiaen kept his swords close, replying, "People and dogs. They killed a deer."

"Did you say dogs?" Fox said loudly, halting.

"Yes."

He slipped his arrow back into the quiver on his back and slung the bow over his shoulder. No one asked how Celiaen had known what Eirian picked up. It was not the first time.

"I know who they are, and they're no threat to us so long as you lot don't attack."

Studying him, Aiden's eyes narrowed. "Who are they, Fox?"

"Indari. You call them the lawless people, but that's not what they call themselves. They've always lived throughout the Roof."

Nodding, Mac said, "They're peaceful. They always welcome strangers and offer sanctuary if needed."

Eirian shared a look with Celiaen before lowering her bow. "Well then, Fox, introduce us to these Indari. I'll lead the way."

No one else put their weapons away, and Eirian did not ask them to. Before they went further, Tara sent Link back to the camp to fetch others to retrieve the deer. No one wanted the kill to go to waste. Eirian had to laugh because neither she nor Celiaen had downed the beast for all their bold words. It no longer mattered. She was more interested in meeting the Indari.

Tempted to ask Fox more questions, Eirian took stock of the expressions on the faces of those surrounding her and decided it would be better to keep silent. They were on edge, despite the assurances of Fox and Mac. Fear of the war overrode everything else. Even the trees lost their appeal. Her power was not the only one crowding the forest. Simmering rage from the handful of reds tempted her fury to the surface, but she pushed it down, not wanting to meet new people with it in charge.

Feeling them in the glade ahead, Eirian stopped. "They're not far away."

"Let me do the talking." Fox sounded more confident than she was used to. "If you don't mind, ma'am, Cap'n."

Aiden replied, "Go right ahead, Fox. You seem to know more about this than anyone else except Mac. Just, if you're wrong and they're hostile, I'll make sure you regret it."

Staring at him blankly, Fox lifted a shoulder to half shrug. "If I'm wrong, then fair enough. She didn't say how many, but if it's a typical Indari party, there'll be around eight people and maybe ten of their dogs. The leader will be a woman."

"That's right," Eirian answered in surprise.

Not bothering with more discussions, Fox and Mac elbowed each other for lead position as they picked their way through the low-hanging branches. They were not quiet about it, making Eirian flinch. Fingering the fletching of the arrows hanging at her waist, she shared a look with Celiaen. Knowing how silently they could move, she suspected their noise was intended to alert the strangers.

When they stepped into the glade, sunlight lit the area enough for Eirian to see raised hackles on several of the dogs dotted around the clearing. They bared their teeth, the animals more on guard than the humans they accompanied. Kneeling over the deer, two men and a woman worked while the remaining five stood guard. The guards wore furs, but not the three on the ground, and they had strange contraptions lined up. Their clothes were made from hides, and Eirian wondered if they were fur-lined for warmth.

"By the powers, they're bloody wolves!" Tara hissed.

Flinging his arms out, Mac said, "They're not wolves. Look like them, but they're no more actual wolves than Lord Faolan is."

Taking in the trio working on the deer on the ground, Fox turned to a short woman leaning on a spear, watching them, and said, "May the sun melt the snow and clear your path."

"May the moon guide your feet and show you the way home," she replied, signaling to the others of her group. "I am Liluye of the Two Gum tribe."

"I am Fox, and my family trades with the Fork in Stream tribe," Fox informed her, glancing over his shoulder at Eirian and Aiden.

Liluye cocked her head and looked over at the elves curiously. "It has been many summers since I last saw a full-blooded elf."

"I'm Celiaen, and I've never met an Indari," Celiaen said, bowing in respect.

"We don't find ourselves welcomed among you downlanders, though we welcome downlanders into our families."

Gaze settling on Eirian, Liluye smiled. Returning the stare, she studied the many braids mixed in her dark hair. She had worked feathers and beads through them, giving Liluye a wild look Eirian admired.

"I'm Eirian, and until now, I'd never heard of the Indari. It's an honor to meet you, Liluye."

"You're an Earth Mother." Tilting her spear forward, Liluye pointed it toward the other mages in the group. "They're your protectors. They feel of the earth's power but not like you do."

"Earth Mother?" Eirian asked curiously.

Clearing his throat, Fox explained, "The Indari teach their mages their own way."

"Oh." Amazed, she stared at the Indari, asking, "Do you have many with magic?"

"Enough. The Earth Mothers and Fathers guide and protect us as the Great Mother intended. I've heard from the downlanders among us it has been many generations since you did the same. So perhaps we're better off than you." Smiling, she whistled, and a man stepped forward. "This is Mika. He's my best scout. Mika, tell the downlanders what you saw."

His dark stare swept over them, and he shifted the bow in his grasp. "I was scouting the trail we planned to take home. I saw many men and great wooden things dragged by your horses. More men than I've ever seen before. Long lines stretching as far as I see."

They understood what he was telling them, and Aiden cursed. "Athnaralans. Fuck! I told you they had more men somewhere."

"Hush, Captain, let Mika tell us everything," Eirian scolded him.

"They used the pass. I watched for three days before I was sure it wouldn't be safe for us. I cannot tell you where they were going, but they were slow. The great wooden things hindered them. So did the strange sleds you call wagons, laden with stones."

Crossing his arms, Celiaen stated, "Siege weapons. Thank you, Mika."

Leaning on her spear again, Liluye said, "See, I told you, Mika. Downlanders fight with each other, and it isn't our business."

"We're very grateful for the information. You may have saved many lives." Tara looked worried as she turned to stare through the trees. "I'm sorry, Ree, but I insist we continue at first light. We need to confirm the information and return to Kelsby."

"Liluye, we've also taken a deer, and if there's anything you can use from our kill, you're welcome to it. Would you share our camp tonight? I'd like to learn more about your people if you'd indulge me," Eirian said.

Ignoring the startled expressions on the faces of those accompanying her, Eirian looked at the three people working on the deer.

"It would be an honor if you'd share our campfire tonight." Supporting her, Celiaen smiled reassuringly. "I, for one, would welcome the opportunity to correct assumptions my people have of yours."

"You speak as though you can," Liluye commented, looking puzzled. "We gathered you're not an ordinary hunting party. Too many weapons and the pretty armor. That's why I had Mika tell you what he saw. We don't get involved, but we wouldn't neglect to share information."

Fox sat on the ground, one of their dogs in his lap, receiving scratches to its stomach as he said, "Yeah, she's right, we stick out."

Glaring at him, Aiden shook his head in disapproval, muttering, "And you're doing an excellent job protecting your queen. I presume there are no threats hidden in that dog's coat?"

"Nope, not a single one, Cap'n."

"Queen? That's the ruler of your lands? Like our chieftains." One of the other hunters spoke, sharing a look with Liluye.

"Indeed, I'm the Queen of Endara, and Celiaen." Waving at him, Eirian explained, "He's the future king of the elves. His father is the current king. We've been at war with Athnaral, and while we're at a stalemate, I wished to see the mountains. I'd never seen them before."

Watching Eirian turn her gaze to the towering peaks, Liluye pushed back a fur draped over her shoulder, and the guards glimpsed the knife hidden beneath it.

"I've met a downlander ruler before. He lives further north, and we count him as a friend. He saved the life of a chieftain once, and among the Indari, that counts for something."

Suspecting she knew who it was, Eirian asked, "Is his name Llewellyn?"

"Yes."

"He's my cousin. His mother is my father's younger sister. He's currently in my home to the south, acting in my place while we face our enemy. He just married a wonderful woman. It's why he didn't ride to war with us. I expected him to spend time with his new bride."

Laughing, Liluye pointed her spear at the woman working on the deer. "I'm sorry, Kishi, you should have made your claim sooner."

Throwing a sneer over her shoulder, Kishi made a gesture with a bloody hand, snapping, "Speak for yourself, Liluye."

"I think we'll get on well, Liluye of the Two Gum Tribe. Will you join us tonight?" Grinning, it did not surprise Eirian to hear Llewellyn had bedded either of the women.

Meeting the gazes of each of her people, Liluye nodded. "Yes, we will. Better protection in numbers. You can tell me what it's like further south, and I'll tell you of life among the clouds."

"We'll return to the camp and prepare the rest of our people. Fox can guide you when you're ready," Eirian said as she approached Liluye, holding out a hand in an offer of friendship.

"Thank you. Are you near water? My people will wish to clean." Grasping the offered hand, Liluye stared intently at Eirian.

"We're next to a stream. Will your dogs be safe around horses?" Celiaen asked with a glance at the wolf-like animals.

Snorting, Fox rolled the dog from his lap, only to have another leap into its spot. "They're bloody useless guards. They'll be fine. Horses don't work in the mountains. That's what these idiots are for."

Open-mouthed, Eirian stared at the dogs. "You use the dogs for what?"

"You'll see, they're useful. Part of our families, we look after them, and they help us." Letting go of Eirian's hand, Liluye smiled. "We'll come when done. Thank you."

"I'll be waiting."

Bowing her head, Eirian turned around, but Liluye stopped her.

"We may keep out of downlander happenings, but we've been down from our home for several cycles of the moon now. People talk of your war, and they fear the outcome. People also talk about things I've heard talk of among my people. Tell me, queen, would you warn us if we had something to fear?"

Silent, Eirian looked around the glade at the faces staring at her and pursed her lips. "I would, and you do, but not for much longer. That which we should all fear is mine to fight."

Scratching at the ground with the butt of her spear, Liluye clicked her tongue. "You think you can win?"

"When you face a predator, do you think you can win?"

"I try to, but I always ask the Great Mother for strength. I have not lost yet."

"There's your answer then," Eirian said, and strode over to Celiaen. "We'd best be off."

Aiden scowled at Fox on the ground, surrounded by dogs. "You know what to do."

"Cap'n." Grinning, Fox chuckled. "Don't worry, I got this."

"And that's precisely why I'm concerned," Aiden muttered, shooting a look at Eirian.

As they walked in silence, picking their way through the trees and low scrub, the tension was so thick Eirian felt sure she could cut it with a knife. They directed some of it her way, but the rest was, to her, an understandable feeling. She felt it as well. An infuriation toward Athnaral and the fact they had not considered the turn events had taken. Frustration that overconfidence had led them to dismiss warnings Aeyren had held something back.

"What should we do with this news?" Eirian finally asked, glancing at the more experienced members of the party. "If it's true…"

"I'd like to say everyone has scouts, and they're aware of what's coming. We should go that way and see what we can find out. You can hide us," Tara replied, her tone flat, and the look she shot over her shoulder at Eirian was blank.

Giving Celiaen a sideways glance, Eirian chewed on her lip. "You've fought against siege weapons before, Tara?"

"I have."

Celiaen grunted. "My father has them. I've seen them used against towns a few times. They slow things down, and the fact Aeyren has them in transport suggests he had the plan far before he became outnumbered."

"I've seen the Athnaralans use them. One time I was there, a minor rebellion happened, which was part of the reason they sent me. It was horrific. Not just the destruction of buildings, but the way they brutally treated the people," Aiden said.

He hated the memories of what he had seen in Athnaral, and his grip on his sword tightened to reassure himself of where he was.

"I'll be honest. They could level the battlefield with them. They're not fast, but they are deadly. Unfortunately, we don't have nearly enough yellows to prevent widespread damage to Kelsby. The only thing we have against them is you and your little tricks." Tara sighed. "I know you hate doing it, and I've helped the two of you hide enough bodies. But if that's what it takes to ensure we don't get flattened by flying rocks that may or may not be coated with pitch and on fire… well, I'll drag you into position myself."

"When have you ever known me to shirk from doing what I have to?" Eirian replied.

EIGHT

L istening to the crackling of the fires, Eirian inhaled the smoky eucalypt scent that filled the air and stared at the smoke swirling through the foliage above. The occasional snort and stamp of a hoof reminded them the horses were close. Rowdy chatter came from another part of the camp where Fox, Mac, and others exchanged stories with the Indari. Things around her were subdued, and she wished they were not.

Her gaze flickered to Aiden with his head bowed as he listened to the laughter. Beside her, Celiaen was running a sharpening stone over one of his swords, the repetitive work helping him focus. On the other side of the fire, Liluye worked with a piece of wood. The small knife in her hand continued to move even when she was not looking at her creation. Eirian's mind was constantly churning, listening to snippets of conversation she caught from various directions and the questions directed to Liluye.

They had returned from their hunt to find those left behind busy at work butchering the doe Fox had brought down, the smell of cooking meat making their stomachs rumble. Sharing the news had sent the small camp into a frenzy of preparation. Faolan had remained reserved, not sharing if he had known of their existence with the humans and elves. He had grown quieter over their journey as each attempt to undo what Shianeni did to him failed.

When the Indari materialized out of the forest with Fox, the sight of the dogs pulling sleds had caused more surprise than the mountain people themselves. Liluye and her hunters had been patient as they explained their dogs to the group. By the time they had satisfied the curiosity, everyone was more than happy to sit around fires and eat.

"You live in caves?" Galameyvin questioned in amazement, excitement spreading through his magic.

Liluye nodded. "Yes, systems of caves in the mountains."

"I've heard of people living in caves, hiding out in them. There are some fascinating ones near Riane. I just cannot imagine tribes of people making them their homes for thousands of years. You live in such a hostile part of the world."

"Just because you cannot imagine something doesn't mean it isn't possible. The caves are safe. They provide us with a shelter that won't collapse. During the summer, we gather the things we need to survive while the snow restricts us. We come down and trade with those willing."

"It works, Gal, otherwise they wouldn't have survived for so long." Eirian rolled her eyes, muttering, "Everything has to adapt. Adapt or die. If people can survive in the Red Desert, then why not in the mountains where water is more abundant?"

Hands stilling, Liluye peered across the fire at Eirian. "I've heard stories of that place, but I've never seen it. Have you?"

"No, I haven't. Aiden, you've been into Athnaral. Did you go to the desert border?"

He scowled, replying, "No, I never went that far. I was there to do a job, not take in the countryside. Taking in the countryside is something I leave to you, ma'am."

Tilting his blade to catch the light, Celiaen inspected the edge. "Would you say she takes in the countryside or does it take in her?"

"Hush you!" Smacking his arm, Eirian huffed. "I've been working on it. Haven't you noticed the lack of things growing as often?"

"Yes, you've been showing some restraint and not making the countryside grow every time you sneeze. Well done, Your Majesty," Aiden replied.

Curious, Liluye resumed her carving, asking, "You can make things grow with your magic? There are some Earth Mothers and Fathers who can do that. We value them among our people. You must be powerful indeed."

"I've been told I'm the most powerful, but some days I doubt it." Eirian uncrossed her legs to stretch.

"It is natural to doubt yourself, but the Great Mother wouldn't give you gifts if you couldn't cope with them. Trust that what she intended for you is not too much. She'll test you, but her tests will strengthen you."

"Who is this Great Mother you speak of?"

"Our creator. Aren't you taught of her? The great god who made this world for us, who made us. She's the mother of all life, first among the gods."

Exchanging looks, the mages debated how to respond when Aiden said, "We know of the gods who made our world. We also know how the gods abandoned us to our choices. Though not always to our fates entirely, as my queen can attest."

Liluye frowned, studying the small carving in her hand. "The gods did not abandon us. The Great Mother knew we didn't need her and so went to rest until such a time as she needed to be reborn. It is said the gods sleep in a sacred place awaiting her return."

"Do your stories speak of another?" Eirian asked.

"No, should they?"

Rubbing his chin, Galameyvin reached for a fresh piece of wood to toss on the fire, catching sight of the guards lurking further away. "You know of our war, but our enemy is not the men of Athnaral. It is a god who is manipulating them."

"You'd fight a god?" Eyes wide, she turned her gaze from him to Eirian. "How can you fight a god?"

"That's a good question. Only someone with the right blood can do it. You need—"

"Descended from the First Children?" Liluye held up her hand with the knife in it.

"Yes," Celiaen replied, mouth twisting as he gave Eirian an amused look, sliding his sword into the sheath, satisfied with the job he had done.

"You're descended from one of the First Children?"

Waving at the three men, Eirian said, "Each of us here is. Two, in my case."

Swallowing, Liluye did not blink, awe apparent as she looked at each of them. "By the Mother! To meet descendants of the First Children? It is the greatest honor."

"Llewellyn is as well." Giving her a sly smile, Eirian chuckled. "Now you can claim you've bedded one."

"Perhaps I can make it two."

She looked sideways at Galameyvin, and he choked in surprise. The grin directed his way by Celiaen and the sullen look on Eirian's face left him flustered. Meeting Aiden's contemplative stare across the fire, Galameyvin could see the question on his mind.

"I'm not   We have an early start planned."

"Come now, Gal, no need to play hard to get." Celiaen laughed.

"I'm sorry, Liluye, but—" he apologized, but she cut him off.

"No need. I said it in jest, though I wouldn't turn you down."

Relieved Galameyvin had turned Liluye down, Eirian tucked a loose strand of hair behind her ear and avoided meeting the eyes of the others. Her jealousy had surprised her, and she wondered if Celiaen had experienced it through their bond. She did not need to remind herself that Galameyvin would have felt it. Hearing the yips and howls of the Indari dogs, the urge to release her magic came over her, and Eirian closed her eyes, allowing it to reach out. Assured no threats lurked in the dark, she let herself drift thoughtlessly.

"What is she doing?" Liluye asked.

"She's reading the land. I suppose she is looking for dangers. Your dogs must have made her concerned on top of her failure to search far enough to find you earlier." Aiden waved at Eirian. "Probably the only time we're protecting her."

Celiaen pulled a disgruntled face, muttering, "Nope, even now, she's not defenseless. Her magic will protect her from attack. I know. I've seen it happen."

"No, you thought you'd test it out and attacked her. It didn't go well. She nearly killed him," Galameyvin snickered.

"I wasn't to know she's less in control of her killing side in this situation."

Feeling the delight from Aiden, Galameyvin said, "He was licking his wounds for weeks, but he made her feel so guilty over it, even though it wasn't her fault. I think he was just milking it for her attention."

"You're all very close to her, and your man, Fox, spoke highly of his queen." They looked at Liluye before exchanging looks, and she laughed. "I'm a woman and a hunter. I see things you think you hide. She's lucky to have the three of you warming her furs. If she is as powerful an Earth Mother as you say, it's her right."

Clearing his throat, Aiden shook his head. "You're wrong, only that one does that."

Following his pointing hand, she stared at Celiaen before looking at Galameyvin with a predatory glint in her eyes. "Are you sure you're not interested?"

Maintaining a neutral expression, Galameyvin stared at the dancing flames. There was a challenge in Celiaen's stare while they waited for his response. He suspected Celiaen wanted him to say yes, prove he was not waiting for Eirian or trying to spare her feelings. Flicking a glance at the frozen woman with her focus wherever her magic had taken her, he clenched his jaw and nodded slowly. Leaning back, Galameyvin looked at the night sky and scratched his face.

"It's getting late. Tara won't wait in the morning for those stupid enough to avoid sleeping when they had the chance."

"Getting old, are you, elf?" Hearing the unspoken thought beneath his words, Aiden arched a brow.

Shrugging, he screwed up his face. "Maybe, but I'll still look good long after you're dead, Captain."

"Why is my captain dying this time?" Eirian asked, opening her eyes to blink in confusion.

"He suggested I'm an old man." Stretching his legs, Galameyvin stood. "Because I'm going to bed to get some rest."

The thought made Eirian yawn, and she covered her mouth sheepishly. "Sleep sounds good, but I'll continue talking with Liluye. There's so much I want to hear about her people."

Arching a brow at Liluye, Galameyvin met her stare and watched her smile as he told them, "Well, you can talk. I'm going to bed."

"Have a good sleep, Gal." Smiling, Celiaen waved fingers at him before turning to Eirian. "He has a fair point. We should get some rest."

"If you're tired, Celi, go to bed. I'm fine."

Shaking her head caused the decorated braids to flop over her shoulders, and Liluye slid the knife she had been using back into its pouch. She tossed the piece over the fire to Eirian, who caught it without thinking.

"We rarely get to sleep so protected when we are out of our lands. Forgive me, but I'm tired. We can talk more when light breaks."

Cradling the little carving in her hands, Eirian glanced between Liluye and Galameyvin, understanding dawning on her. The whispers mocked her for not stopping them.

"Of course, enjoy your rest. Thank you, Liluye. You've been more than patient."

"No, thank you, Eirian. Downlanders rarely want to listen." Bowing her head gracefully, Liluye smiled. "Keep it. A small token."

Sighing, Eirian watched them walk away from the fire. Jealousy coursed through her, and she saw the pleased look on Celiaen's face. It made her question what she had missed while she explored the land. Looking down at her hands, she opened them up to expose the carving. The work showed signs of great skill for the time spent on it.

Taking in the wooden wolf, Eirian rubbed her thumbs against it, feeling the roughness against her skin. Liluye had captured the animal in motion, one paw raised as though it was stepping forward. The head hung low with tiny little alert ears. Smiling, she continued to rub it with her thumb and hoped Ona would like it. Thinking of the girl made her stomach clench with anguish, and Eirian looked at Celiaen again.

"You should get some rest, Celi."

He glanced at her. "Let's go to bed. You need rest as much as everyone else."

"He's right, and you know I rarely agree with him," Aiden said, wondering if any of them would get rest that night. "I'm going to get what I can."

He had seen the look on Eirian's face when Galameyvin left with Liluye, and he wished he could find out if her face would look the same if it had been him. Galameyvin's choice pleased Celiaen, and Aiden suspected he had only taken Liluye up on her invitation because of it. Pushing to his feet, he rolled his shoulders and grunted, nodding at them before moving away from the fire to his tent.

"Sleep well, Captain," Celiaen murmured, bowing his head.

"What did you say to Gal?" Eirian asked quietly, her tone cold.

Scratching the tip of one of his ears, Celiaen's mouth puckered. "I don't know what you're talking about."

"Why did he change his mind about Liluye?"

"Beats me. I'm not Gal's keeper, and neither are you," Celiaen growled, his eyes narrowed, glaring at her. "You're upset that he did. I felt your jealousy.

You're my mate, Eirian. I thought you'd accepted it."

She closed her hand around the wolf. "Don't you dare try to make me feel guilty, Celiaen! I love you, and I accept our bond."

"Then why are you so upset over Gal bedding another? It's not like he hasn't done it before."

Unwilling to admit how much it had always stung her to find out about either of them taking other lovers, Eirian groaned in frustration. The noise in her head was deafening, whispers competing to be heard.

"Because as much as I love you, I still love him, and I always will."

It was his turn to feel the sharp bite of jealousy, and Celiaen said, "If he beckoned you to his bed, would you go? Would you feel guilty if you did?"

"I wouldn't betray you, Celi."

"And if I told you to go?"

Her mouth opened, but Eirian could not answer his question. "I'll never be just yours. Or his. I'll never be just mine. I've always known that, and you know it because you're the same. We belong to more than ourselves or each other. Our lives belong to our people."

Closing his eyes, Celiaen sighed. "I never expected not to share you like that. It's your heart I wish was wholly mine. I want to be the only person you love like that."

Filled with sadness, she whispered, "I know."

"I suppose I should be glad you have some idea of how I felt every time I watched you leave with him." It was a bitter thing to say, but Celiaen could not stop the words from leaving his mouth even as he watched the hurt cross her face.

"Go to bed, Celiaen."

Nodding, he understood the dismissal in her voice and knew Eirian would not welcome him to share her bed that night.

"You need to sleep as much as I do."

Unfolding her legs from where she had tucked them, Eirian got up without stumbling and picked up her cloak. "I'll see you in the morning."

Watching her walk away, shaking her cloak out before tossing it around her shoulders, Celiaen cursed quietly. "Stupid, jealous fool."

She did not know where she was going, but Eirian needed freedom from the tents and fires. Away from the tug at the edge of her mind that she knew was Galameyvin. Guards watched her slip through the space between fires, and she flashed a warning look in the direction of the guard who thought to follow her toward the dark line that was the stream. Flinching back, Gram saluted silently and remained outside the fire where he could still see her. He did not fancy the punishment he would receive if something happened and Aiden found out he had not been doing his job.

A slight noise drew his attention, and he looked at Faolan materializing from the shadows of several trees. The silvery-gray coat of his wolf form caught in the light of the fires, giving him an ethereal glow. Trotting with the quiet grace of a predator, he caught up with Eirian. Stroking a hand over his head, she glanced at him.

"Did you want to try again tonight?"

Faolan shook his head and sat, leaning against her leg. Nodding, Eirian watched the water sparkle with a mixture of starlight and firelight. Her magic flickered, tugs of yearning against her consciousness. The whispers died down, giving her a reprieve, but they continued to drag at the edge of her mind. She felt the threads connecting her to Galameyvin, the emotions leaving her nauseated.

Fingers digging into the fur at the back of Faolan's neck, Eirian let go when he whined. In her other hand, the carved wolf felt warm, and she fumbled with the pouch hanging from her belt. Slipping the figure into it, she ensured it was secure before glancing at the camp. Gram was watching, leaning against a tree that was a little closer to a fire than she was comfortable with.

Another tug at her magic made Eirian turn her gaze to the forest on the other side of the stream. It beckoned, shadows dancing between ghostly trunks. Releasing her hold over her power, she closed her eyes to embrace the beat of the land. She needed to run and to be away from this place. The more distance she put between her and the men in their tents, the better.

"Keep up with me if you can, wolf."

It had been months since she had let herself run, and Eirian surrendered to the magic guiding her feet over the earth. Her sudden leap startled Faolan, and he watched her clear the Arianell easily. The way she flowed across the land like water disturbed him. Tossing his head back to howl, he bound after her, ignoring Gram's shouts to stop.

She was a fraction faster than him, Faolan struggling to contain his amazement at how Eirian's feet missed every obstacle that crossed her path. He could have sworn branches moved out of her way. Not even the cloak trailing behind her caught on anything, the wool the most obvious sign of how she flowed.

Eirian's power thrummed everywhere. Faolan felt it beating with his racing heart as he fought to keep up without magic. In the end, the growing gap forced him to release his hold and summon a burst of speed. Finally stopping, she bent over with her hands on her knees and sucked in a deep breath, trying to calm the thudding beat of her heart.

When she could mutter the words, she rasped, "I'm out of shape."

Barely able to control the transformation, Faolan flopped onto the ground beside her, gasping, "You call that out of shape? How?"

"I can't explain it. It's something I've always been able to do. I've never done it in front of anyone, not even Celi or Gal. I just needed to run." It took

Eirian longer than usual to explain, her breathing a pant of exertion.

"I've never..."

Collapsing onto the ground, Eirian watched the puff of her breath in the chilly air. She felt the cold slip of sweat over her skin and laughed, the sound turning into coughs as her lungs continued to battle with her pounding heart.

"You did well to keep up."

He scowled, grumbling, "I had to use my magic."

"There's no shame in that."

"Without magic, I'm faster."

She grinned, chuckling. "That you are."

Silence settled as they stared at the branches above them. Eirian hoped Gram had not gone running for the others. She was unsure how long they had run, and flickering her gaze to Faolan, she wondered if he knew. The niggling sense of Galameyvin had ceased, taking many of the whispers with it. Eirian did not dare reach out to touch the thread, unwilling to test it. Her bond to Celiaen was calm, suggesting he was unaware of her fleeing the camp.

"Why did you need to run?" Faolan finally asked.

Eirian knew she could trust Faolan with the truth. She could trust him not to think badly of her for it.

"Gal took the Indari hunter to his bed."

"Ah."

"Celiaen got upset because I was jealous."

Rolling onto his side, Faolan gave her a concerned look. "He hasn't loved another as you have. He doesn't understand that you can love more than one at a time."

"I used to think that was the way it should be. I mean, most people do," she replied without looking at him. "My mother loved you and Vartan, didn't she? It wasn't just that she desired people other than Neriwyn."

"Each of us filled a need and a hole in her heart the others couldn't fill. I cannot tell you what you should do or what you need from them. All I can tell you is that loving each of them doesn't make you a terrible person. Wanting each of them doesn't make you a terrible person. But being dishonest with yourself and them will cause things to unravel."

A breeze rustled through the leaves above, and in the distance, her ears picked up the sounds of howls.

"Celi asked me if I'd go to Gal's bed if asked. If he told me to go."

"What did you say?"

"I couldn't answer, but I don't think I needed to. I think Celi knew the answer."

Finding the strength to sit up, at last, Faolan shook himself free of debris that had stuck to his skin. "What about Aiden?"

Swallowing anxiously, Eirian brushed against the faint thread that had formed in her power. It was less than the one that let her feel Galameyvin, and she was not sure if it was the lack of magic on Aiden's part.

"He's as entwined with me as Gal is."

"What?"

"I don't know how long it's been there, but I've noticed it. I can feel Aiden and Gal connected to me. The more I tried to unravel what my mother did to you, the more aware I grew. Somehow, I've bound them to me," she said, feeling relief at finally voicing what had been bothering her.

Pursing his lips, Faolan murmured in understanding, "That's how they knew. They knew when you and your mate completed your bond. While the two of you were busy rolling around in the grass, they felt it."

His words were news to her, and she blinked at him. The whispers mocked her for not realizing the depth of the connection. Briefly, her mind darted to the memories haunting her, reminding Eirian of her suspicions.

"They what now? They knew? Not just a logical suspicion, but knew what we were doing? Oh, no wonder they've been so agitated. Well, fuck."

"That's what they'd like to do to you," he quipped with a chuckle. "Both of you."

She rolled her eyes, snorting. "You're still hanging out for gossip on Aiden."

"You know, we have dreams. Nightmares."

The sudden change of subject made her head whip around in surprise.

He continued, "They've gotten... more... since you started trying to undo things. Now I wonder if they're glimpses of what they made us forget."

"What do you see in your dreams?"

"Many strange creatures. Earlier today, I could've sworn I glimpsed a short woman with iridescent wings dancing among the leaves. She had wings like those of a spike tail but shining like jewels. I'd seen them in my dreams so long ago that I don't remember when." There was no sign of jest in his eyes, nothing but deadly seriousness, and Faolan said, "I've seen no one do what you did tonight. It was like you were a part of the forest, a part of the ground. You flowed like water in a stream and the wind through the trunks. The world parted so you could run."

Her blood went cold. Not because Faolan's words shocked her, but because Eirian knew precisely what he spoke of.

"A flicker that makes you think there's something at the edge of your vision. Memories begging to be remembered, but which slip through your fingers when you try."

"You've never asked what your mother's animal form was."

"I've thought about it, but I can't decide how I feel about her."

Faolan continued to stare at her, whispering, "She could be whatever she chose. I thought... we all thought it was because she was the first. The chosen one. But now..."

"Now you wonder, and you're not the only one. Vartan..." Eirian closed her mouth with a shake of her head. "Shianeni Malfaer was a duine. It does us no good to question."

"Was she?" he asked, and she knew the question was for the world around them.

Staggering to her feet, Eirian held out a hand and pushed the protests of her body from her mind. "Come on, we better go back."

"Could you go a little slower this time?"

Flashing a grin, she said, "Sure, I'll go slower so you can keep up, old man."

The challenge in her voice made his eyes narrow, chasing the seriousness away.

"I'll show you old, little queen."

Laughing, Eirian watched Faolan shift into his wolf form and leap in the direction they had come. She let him get ahead before allowing her magic to guide her to the camp. The desperate need to run had gone, and she enjoyed it, taking in the surrounding forest. It allowed her to note what Faolan had pointed out. Her magic guided every step she took, like she danced with the world.

Not wanting to appear at the camp breathless and exhausted, Eirian stopped running when she felt the others nearby. Stopping with her, Faolan's head hung low, his sides heaving as they fought to catch their breath. Searching with her magic, she could sense no one outside of the camp and assumed it meant Gram had not gone running to alert the others.

"They don't seem to miss us."

His tail flicked back and forth, tongue hanging out as he whined in response. Eirian ruffled his fur with a chuckle and started walking toward the distant lights of the fires visible between the trees. When they reached the stream, Faolan cleared it, and she dragged up enough energy to take a running leap. On the other side, Gram waited against his tree, arms crossed and agitation apparent.

"You're lucky I didn't tell the boss man," he grumbled. "But I figured I'd struggle to explain what I saw and decided I'd keep it to myself. Tully agreed with me, and neither of us switched out when it came time to change the watch."

Following his thumb, Eirian looked at the eastern horizon with a low curse. The glow of dawn approaching told her they had taken longer than they realized. Looking back, she wondered how far they had run through the trees, how much distance they had covered. It had tired her, a hint of exhaustion lingering beneath the last of the thrill. Yipping, Faolan trotted off into the camp to find his tent and the clothes within.

"Thank you, Gram. I appreciate it."

"You're welcome."

Picking her way to her tent, Eirian was thankful Celiaen was not there and slipped inside. She had barely sat on her bedroll when she heard voices outside laughing. Closing her eyes, she listened to Galameyvin and Liluye, hearing Tara join them. Doing her best to block them, she stretched out and focused on the discomfort caused by her weapons, the pinch of leather catching her neck. Her body ached, the burn of muscles protesting the strain she had put them through.

"Ree?" Galameyvin's voice sounded from outside her tent. "I know you're in there, Ree, and I know you're alone."

Opening her eyes, she pushed herself to sit up. "Come in, Gal."

He held the flap open and slipped in, eyes adjusting to the change of light. "You haven't rested, have you? Don't bother lying. I can feel your tiredness."

"Fine then, I won't."

"You're always so testy when tired."

Grinding her teeth, Eirian tightened one of her hands into a fist, feeling the dig of her nails against flesh and leather. His presence had brought the whispers back in full force, shadows flickering at the edge of her vision.

"What do you want, Galameyvin? I was trying to grab some rest before we go."

Crossing his arms, he studied her, taking in the way she avoided his gaze. "You're fucking pissed at me."

"Go away."

"You were jealous, so jealous I couldn't believe it was coming from you. It felt more like Celi's jealousy than anything I'd encountered from you. I liked it."

Bristling, Eirian narrowed her eyes. "And what, by the powers, is your point?"

Spreading her hands at the question, she glared at him. They both knew he did not have one, and Galameyvin sighed. Any pleasure he felt over her jealousy faded at the sight of pain in her eyes.

"I'm sorry, Ree. I shouldn't have been so obvious about it when I know what you feel. In the future, I'll be more discrete."

"No."

"No?" Galameyvin asked in surprise.

Standing, Eirian closed the distance between them. Hands at her side, she cocked her head, chin jutting toward him. Galameyvin saw the flecks of dirt on her face where it had stuck to her sweat, confusion rising until the possessiveness became apparent in the way she looked him over. Briefly, he contemplated taking a step back. He imagined the black eye Celiaen would give him. If he were lucky, that would be the worst of it.

Then he felt it. A tug on his magic, a gentle caress that reminded him of her hands running over his skin. Eyes widening, he stared at Eirian, and she gazed back, unflinching.

"How?"

"I don't know. I only realized it was there during this excursion and not just to you."

"Aiden," Galameyvin whispered and searched through his memories to all the times they had shared magic, the times their blood had mixed. "That explains why we've felt it every time you and Celi...."

She flinched, muttering, "Yes, I heard about that."

Chuckling, he grasped why she was telling him. "You felt me with Liluye. Before that, you didn't know how deep the link between us went."

"No, I didn't. I realized it was there when I started trying to free Faolan. Or maybe I've always known but didn't know it. They're not quite the same as the bond to Celi."

Eirian blinked at him, and Galameyvin saw a flicker of something in her eyes that made the light brown spots glow, but it went as quickly as it appeared.

He said, "You have to tell them."

There were voices outside, shouts from Tara directing people to get a move on, and Eirian sighed. "I know. He'll behave like a brat about it, though. We argued after you left. My jealousy hurt him."

"He's always been a brat when it comes to you."

Snorting, she touched his cheek, murmuring, "I don't know how long I have left, but I won't disrupt what little peace I can find."

Turning his face, Galameyvin kissed her palm, the corner of his lips touching the leather of her bracer. "Is that your way of saying you won't tell either of them about it? Am I to suffer from this knowledge as punishment for bedding another woman in front of you?"

"Maybe." Her hands itched to be buried in his golden curls so she could draw him in for a kiss.

Tasting the desire in her magic, Galameyvin chuckled. "You feel you've violated us."

"Yes."

Sometimes her lines of morality made him laugh. "You can kill us all with a flex of your mind, but you're feeling guilty over linking yourself to two men who love you."

"Has anyone woken Ree yet?"

Tara's voice was louder than it needed to be outside the tent, and they knew it was a hint. It was a reminder that Athnaral was not waiting for them. War was continuing, and they needed to catch up. Shaking her head, Eirian turned away and began gathering her things. It was a mundane task that would help her collect her thoughts.

"Ree."

"Just go, Gal. We can't waste time. Tell Tara I'm up."

Nodding, he slipped back out of the tent and gave her a last look. "If we survive this war, he'll expect you to marry him."

"That's Future Eirian's problem."

Left alone, she finished shoving things into her pack before rolling the bedroll. Her tiredness crept up on her again, and Eirian promised herself when they stopped next, she would go to bed. Unfortunately, it did not chase away the swirl of thoughts circling in her mind, each competing for attention. Hearing footsteps and the rustle of the tent opening, she startled and berated herself for drifting off. Merle stood there, sharp eyes looking her over with disapproval.

"You look like shit, ma'am."

"Thanks, Merle, you sure know how to flatter a woman," she replied.

He picked up her pack, reaching for the bedroll tied tightly that she did not remember finishing. "Good thing I'm not trying to flatter you. The Captain is barking orders. So is that pretty elf in charge of your prince. I'm never sure if I'm supposed to call her captain, and I don't hear anyone else calling her a rank."

"Tara doesn't have a rank. They're not called guards, though they function like them. They're companions. If he weren't a mage, they'd be guards."

Snorting, Merle looked at her bow and quivers. "You can bring them."

"You can call me by my name, Merle. I might not be your queen when we get back to Kelsby." There was a sharpness in her tone that made him pause.

"I know you're hoping for it, but even if they took away your title, you'd still be our queen. We're loyal to you and only you. Well, the Captain as well, but you know what I mean." Merle could tell it was not the answer she wanted. "It doesn't feel right to call you by your name. As companion-like we might be, you don't call us friends."

Waiting for him to leave, Eirian whispered, "You're a good friend, Merle, and I wish I was free to call you mine."

He glanced over his shoulder with a grim smile. "After the war, we'll discuss it."

Everything protested as Eirian moved, her fingers catching the straps for her quivers. Her bow remained strung, and she scowled, berating herself for forgetting to unstring it. Leaving the tent, she swept her gaze over the people getting ready to go. Indari pitched in, helping where they could. Liluye surveyed them from a spot beside their dogs, and she tightened her grip on the straps in her hand as she approached.

Smiling warmly, Liluye flicked a hand at the alert animals. "I thought it would be a good idea for someone to remain with them."

"They're beautiful, Liluye," Eirian said. "I wish I could have one."

Giving her a sideways look, Liluye replied, "You have a wolf already. I saw how that... duine... looked at you in his wolf form. The utter devotion to his mistress that I see in the eyes of many of our dogs."

Eirian knew the truth. The devotion was not to her but to the memory of her mother, regardless of the bitterness Faolan felt.

"When the war is over, I'd like to come and visit your mountains."

"You'd be most welcome. We'd enjoy hunting together. The Great Mother would bless us."

"I hope when the war is over, we can build a friendship between our people. We've much we could learn and share with each other. I'll talk to Llewellyn about it. It's time we understood there's an entire society in the mountains, not just those who wish to escape our laws."

"After the war," Liluye murmured.

Nodding, Eirian looked at the people and wondered who would live to see after the war. "We have treaties with our other neighbors. We should have treaties with you. It may take many years before you find welcome among us downlanders, but I want your children to come down from your caves and trade with confidence."

Giving Eirian a look filled with appreciation, Liluye patted the dog's head. "When you come to visit, I'll gift you a pair of our dogs chosen from the best. Then, I'll teach you how to handle them."

"I'd like that."

It was a dream Eirian could cling to.

NINE

"Now that's a fucking sight and a half!" Rylee muttered, sharing a look with Jaren. "How many did they say?"

Gazing at the sea of tents surrounding Kelsby, Tessa said, "At least three legions worth. The Telmian numbers are higher."

Pinching the bridge of her nose, Fayleen shook her head. There was only one thing on her mind, but she could not walk away from her post to go find Eirian. It would have to wait until they observed formalities. Giving her a look, Luke knew what she was planning and chuckled.

"The archmage won't let you anywhere near the greetings," he commented.

"Doesn't matter. Ree's guards will recognize me, so I'll go later. And no, Rylee, I will not help you sneak into her room. Celi would gut you. Best you keep your distance and avoid causing problems between them."

Laughing at Rylee as she sulked, Jaren said, "Poor little Rylee."

Snarling at him, Rylee's hand went to a knife, causing more laughter.

"At least we got here before Paienven." Tessa redirected the conversation. "That should put Baenlin in a good mood."

"Ree's going to be surprised to see you, but I think you'll find she'll be happy you're here to help," Fayleen assured Tessa.

"I'll take your word for it."

"She doesn't dislike you, Tessa. Trust me."

Smiling faintly, Tessa shrugged. "I know."

There was no true rivalry between them, merely the expectation of one. A city that wanted a show of strength from Eirian had foisted it on them. One of them had been a child carrying the weight of too many expectations, the other a girl buckling under the onslaught of her father's vitriol. But they had under-stood each other enough that Eirian had helped Tessa escape. No one else knew the truth of it, just the two of them and Jaren.

"How long before you're called away to play pet?" Rylee joked.

Shifting in her saddle to look for Baenlin, Tessa did not admit it surprised her he had not kept her at his side from the moment they broke camp. The night before, he had made it clear that she was not to get involved with the discussions. It had been easy to agree, wearing her best innocent smile as she did. Tessa had no intention of keeping out of anything, but first, she needed to see Eirian.

"I won't be. He doesn't want me getting involved. Apparently, it's not my place."

Snorting, Fayleen asked, "Then what is your place?"

"A silent cage in the corner."

"It's not too late to turn down the grand mage position," Jaren reminded her. "In fact, it would be a good time to do it while you have Ree's influence."

"That's true! She'd help in whatever way she could," Fayleen agreed, waving at Kelsby.

Dragging her hand over her mouth, Tessa observed the large group of riders heading in their direction. There were no banners and little need for them when it was clear where they had departed from. Magic was thick in the air, but it lacked the comfortably familiar tang of Riane. It was unlike anything they had experienced, and voices murmured throughout the ranks. No one needed to state the obvious. What they were feeling was the magic of thousands of daoine.

Closing her eyes, Tessa embraced the sensation. The magic carried a hint of something intoxicating, making her wish she had fled into Telmia instead of a remote part of northern Ensaycal. She imagined how easy it would have been to forget everything about her past and what waited in Riane. Someone poked her arm, forcing her to open her eyes and glare at Jaren.

"You alright?" he asked in concern.

"Just imagining the outcomes if I'd made some different decisions."

Grunting, he nodded at the group as it came to a halt in front of Baenlin. Shading her eyes, Fayleen stood in her stirrups, gaze sweeping over the lines of riders with worry on her face. Her focus locked on a brown-haired man before she huffed and dropped into her saddle with a thump. Shaking her head, she looked at each of them fearfully.

"Ree's not there. I don't see her. Everett is, but not Ree. Neither is Celi."

Zack scratched his cheek. "What?"

Pressing her fingertips to her lips, Rylee wore a look of concentration as she gazed at the group and muttered, "Fay's right. I can't feel Ree."

"Why wouldn't they be among them? That doesn't make sense. She's the Queen of Endara. All reports have claimed she's at Kelsby, so where else would she be?" Luke argued.

Jaren said, "Maybe they remained in the town where it's safer?"

"That's a fair point."

Scoffing, Fayleen disagreed. "Ree and Celi wouldn't do that. There's no way either of them would miss out on greeting an army of mages from Riane."

Rolling her shoulders, Tessa sat straight in her saddle and gave each of them a determined smile. Unwilling to give her companions a chance to stop her, she pressed her heels to her horse. Distracted, the lines of mages between her and the group in front parted without thinking to let Tessa through. Chasing after her silently, Fayleen and the others were careful not to call out and cause a scene.

"What do you mean the Queen isn't here?" Baenlin demanded as Tessa reached them.

Glancing at the six riders, Everett's gaze found Fayleen, and he smiled. "Lady Fayleen! What an absolute delight to see you."

Sucking in a deep breath, Baenlin tightened his grip over his magic and hissed, "Where is Eirian Altira?"

"North."

Something about the man who answered took Tessa's breath away, and she gazed at him. Dark eyes glittered with amusement from beneath a mess of dark curls, and he winked when he caught her staring. Blushing, she dipped her head, looking away to hide how affected she was by the magic oozing from him. She did not need anyone to tell her he was one of the daoine.

"King Neriwyn is correct. Her Majesty has ridden north with a small company to seek information," Everett said.

Lifting her head, Tessa did not feel guilty for openly staring at Neriwyn. She was not alone in doing so. Most of the mages gazed in shock at the King of Telmia, but his attention had not left Tessa. A small smile tugged at his lips, and she had a distinct feeling he knew something about her.

"Lady Tessa Valkera, future grand mage of Riane. It's an honor," Neriwyn said, ignoring the outraged look on Baenlin's face.

Everett let out a low whistle. "Future grand mage? Seems like everyone's planning to be here for this fight."

Seeing her opportunity, Tessa smiled warmly. "The honor is all mine, Your Majesty."

Waving at the mixture of people beside him, Neriwyn introduced the important ones. "Duke Everett Altira, General Cameron, General Darragh, Lord Vartan, and Duke Marcellus."

"This is all well and good, but would anyone like to explain why the Queen of Endara has ridden north to seek information?" Baenlin demanded in frustration.

"Because it's her information to find," Vartan answered, sharing a look with Neriwyn. "There's no one here who could stop her from doing whatever she wanted."

The dumbfounded look on Baenlin's face had Tessa pressing her lips together to bite back her laughter. Crinkling his nose at her, Neriwyn behaved with the confidence of a man who knew no one could stop him. He extended his hand in Tessa's direction, fingers curling to summon her. She did not resist the urging of his magic, nudging her horse forward.

"No point standing around out here. Come, let's resume this meeting inside the city." Neriwyn instructed, turning his horse. "Ride with me, Grand Mage."

Leaning toward Darragh, Cameron asked quietly, "What do you know about her?"

"Not much. The Valkera are a powerful family in Riane. Her father is Archmage Hugh, but she's considered… different," he answered.

"Different, how?"

"I've heard that her parents call her deranged. They say she makes things unlike anyone else. Personally, I've seen none of her inventions, but I'm not the sort to dismiss someone capable of thinking outside the square. If she's here, Baenlin must think she's got a use."

"All of this is starting to feel like overkill for two Athnaralan legions," Cameron muttered.

Darragh agreed. "It does. But perhaps not so much for a god. Let's hope Queen Eirian gets back soon. Baenlin and Paienven don't get along, and I have a feeling Neriwyn won't help."

"Fucking royalty. Why can't any of them stay on their thrones and keep out of the way?"

Watching Neriwyn lead the group toward Kelsby, Darragh chuckled. "You can't tell me you'd rather your queen wasn't here? Not if she's a weapon like the daoine claim."

"True, she's useful. The rest of them, though? I suppose Neriwyn looks like he'll join the battle, but you can't tell me your king will."

"I'm looking forward to watching her slaughter hundreds with a click of her fingers."

"So it's true then?" Baenlin asked, alerting them to his presence. "Did Eirian stop a battle with a slaughter?"

Scratching his nose, Cameron studied him thoughtfully. "She did. I watched it happen. The battle was a fucking mess, and then the Athnaralans were fleeing back on themselves. What they left behind were withered corpses and flowers and our queen."

"What are you going to do with that information, Archmage?" Darragh questioned, knowing the high council would not take kindly to what Eirian had done.

Even though Cameron was not a mage, Baenlin respected his judgment. However, hearing directly from him that the reports of Eirian's actions were accurate, he was at a loss. He had never heard of a mage being able to do what Cameron described, and it led to his next question.

"Is it true what they're saying about her mother?"

The two generals looked at each other before Darragh said, "Yes. Unless you want to claim Neriwyn is lying. Eirian's mother was Queen Shianeni Malfaer of Telmia."

"And the god part?"

"It appears as though Athnaral has a god driving them. My blues and the daoine have been tracking down people on our side who have been influenced—"

"Influenced?" Baenlin demanded. "What do you mean by that?"

"She's able to twist minds and influence people to do her bidding. It leaves traces, but we can cleanse them."

Cameron added, "We saw her confront Eirian. So none of us has any doubt about what we're up against."

Mulling over the information they provided, Baenlin recalled the reports he had intercepted from the greens. They had kept it from the high council, but he doubted he was the only one who had found out about the increased rate of insanity spreading through the lands. It made him wonder what part the god played in it all.

"Is my nephew with Queen Eirian?"

Smirking, Darragh replied, "My prince is traveling with his future wife. They make a magnificent couple."

"Don't get ahead of yourself, Darragh," Cameron chided. "Eirian's convinced she'll die in this war."

His statement made Baenlin freeze. That a mage as powerful as Eirian Altira could die in a war against a god left him fearful for all those behind him. What hope did they have of surviving if she did not expect to? Swallowing, he shook his head and indicated the retreating backs of the greeting party and those who had followed Tessa. Officers waited to the side for orders from their generals, Soren, and multiple other masters, doing the same.

"We had better catch up. Have your aides coordinate with them." Baenlin waved at the red masters.

"Worried your newest target might find herself swept away by a king?" Darragh mocked. "Is she any more interested in being wooed by you than the last two purples were?"

"Good luck to King Neriwyn if he tries. Tessa Valkera is a defiant brat."

Chuckling, Darragh winked at Cameron and turned his horse to trot after the others. Remaining beside him, Cameron could not resist asking while Baenlin held back.

"What was that about?"

"The archmage fancies himself a kingmaker. Or, in this case, a queenmaker. His pursuit of Grand Mage Mayve is legendary, and reports have it he had his eyes on your queen. He wants to control Riane, and Tessa will be his next target."

"Do you think that's why she's here? If he keeps her close...."

"Nope. He's not stupid enough to risk the future grand mage on a battlefield for the sake of bedding her. Not with Riane's laws. Like I said, she'll be here because she's useful."

When they caught up with the others, Cameron's attention was drawn to where Everett rode with the vaguely familiar blonde woman he had called Fayleen. They were deep in discussion, ignoring everyone else, so he guided his horse to join them.

"Wait, she did what?" Fayleen gasped.

Clearing his throat, Everett nodded at Cameron and said, "General, I don't know if you remember Lady Fayleen. She visited Amath with the archmage earlier this year, and she's a close friend of Queen Eirian. They shared quarters in Riane and grew up together."

The memories clicked, and he nodded, extending a hand to Fayleen. She allowed him to take hers, and Cameron kissed it gently. He observed her small selection of weapons, including the carved quarterstaff strapped to her back. A yellow ring told him Fayleen was no warrior, but he knew the reputation of shield mages, and suspected she had adapted to keep up with Eirian.

"My lady, it is a pleasure to see you again. I'm sorry our queen isn't here to greet you."

Fayleen snorted. "I'm sorry not to be off with her getting into trouble."

"I hope she's not getting into trouble."

"Trust me. If she's with Celi, then they're causing chaos somewhere."

Everett asked, "What about Prince Galameyvin?"

"Gal's with them? There's some hope then. Maybe between him and that delightful captain of hers, they'll manage to keep Ree and Celi under control."

Catching the admiring look Everett gave Fayleen, Cameron commented, "That's if Aiden doesn't kill Prince Celiaen."

"I'm disappointed I missed their meeting," she grumbled.

"It was... tense."

"Cameron was there. Aiden told me all about it later," Everett said.

Sighing, Fayleen waved at Tessa. "Whatever Baenlin might say or do, don't let him make you think she has nothing to contribute."

"I recall Eirian saying something about her to me, but I don't remember exactly. It could have been that she was better suited to the grand mage position."

Studying Tessa laughing at something Neriwyn said, Cameron decided she bore a similarity to Everett. He could not put his finger on it, but it was there, and it bothered him. Rubbing his face, he looked across the sea of tents and wondered where they would put everyone. The numbers were unwieldy as a camp, and it would worsen once Paienven arrived.

Catching his concern, Fayleen said, "Don't worry, General. You have an army of mages."

"That's part of the problem."

"I'm not talking about the reds. They're useful but not nearly as valuable as the rest of us in this situation. We know what we're doing."

"I suspect you'll tell me more than the archmage, so please, go on."

"As soon as possible, the shield mages among the yellows will begin erecting wards around the perimeter of the camp. Then, the stonemasons will set to work on Kelsby, reinforcing absolutely everything they can, starting with the walls. The greens will set up dedicated healing locations and sweep through the forces gathered here to help where they can. Meanwhile, the reds and blues will sit still and look pretty until they're needed. Though the blues will offer their services to those in need of them."

Realizing he had not considered the other mage's orders, it relieved Cameron to have Fayleen lay the plan out simply. The Telmians had been doing much the same as she described, but it would be good to have a more coordinated effort. Everett was giving Fayleen an admiring look again, and Cameron decided it was something he could get behind. If she had half as clever a mind on her as he suspected, she would be a worthy addition to the court.

"Thank you," he told her. "I'll remember to ask you for information if the archmage plays difficult."

Her blue eyes slid in his direction, and Fayleen murmured, "I'm more than happy to make myself useful."

Everett chuckled. "You're hoping to take Eirian up on her offer?"

"Yes. Just don't mention it to anyone. I've said nothing about it out of concern the archmage will attempt to stop me to spite Ree."

The comment intrigued Cameron. "Why would he do that?"

"Because he's still angry that she turned down the grand mage position. That, and they don't like it when they think a mage might slip out of their control. The high council is hardly a forward-thinking group," she explained with a faint smile.

"So, you're a yellow. What do you do?"

"Besides protect your queen in a fight?"

Blinking, Cameron searched for a hint of jest in her eyes and found none. He was aware of Eirian's experience fighting before she returned to Endara, and he wondered how much of it Fayleen had witnessed. Moreso, he was interested in what part she had played and how much blood was on her hands.

"Yes, besides that."

Fayleen shrugged. "I'm a leatherworker. My most recent project has been making new armor for Ree, but I guess I have to wait until she returns to give it to her. Otherwise, I'm just another yellow."

"How do you protect her in a fight?" Everett asked.

"Some yellows are good at fighting. We use offensive wards as effectively as weapons. That's what makes us a shield mage, and some claim we're more dangerous than reds. In a fight, I shield Ree's back and thin out the numbers if she looks like she might be overwhelmed."

"Has she ever been?"

Snorting back her laughter, Fayleen pressed a hand to her chest and gave Everett an amused look. He dropped his head, shaking it as he realized how ridiculous his question had been. If Eirian could kill hundreds without lifting a blade, it was unlikely someone had ever overwhelmed her in a fight. Ahead of them, the open gates of Kelsby beckoned, and Cameron glanced over the two next to him, taking in Fayleen's calculating gaze.

Face blank, Fayleen's sharp eyes danced from wall to wall, giving the buildings a cursory look. Cameron had seen similar expressions before and wished he had time to determine her assessment. Unfortunately, it would not be long before they dragged him into meetings with Baenlin that would likely result in arguments.

"You should join us in the meeting," Everett said. "If anyone has a clue how Eirian might do this, it's you. Everyone else with ideas is with her."

"The archmage won't like that," she replied.

Supporting the idea, Cameron said, "His Grace has a point. It appears you know our queen better than anyone else here."

Lips thinning, Fayleen made it look like she was considering their words when she had already made up her mind. She had meant it when she told them she was happy to be useful. Whatever it took to smooth the way to remain in Endara with Eirian. Soldiers hurried over to take the horses away as they dismounted. Moving quickly, Everett offered a hand to Fayleen the moment her feet touched the ground, and she accepted with a smile.

"You know Eirian would tell you to agree," he muttered.

"Widen your eyes just a little more, Your Grace, and you'll almost mirror Ree when she's pleading with me to go along with one of her plans."

Tossing his head back to laugh, Cameron patted both of them on the back and made his way over to join Darragh. Slinging her arm around Everett's shoulders, Fayleen grinned when Tessa looked in their direction.

"What does she want?"

Fayleen hummed. "Who, Tessa?"

"Yes."

"Lots of things. Including a high council that isn't under the thumb of a certain elf."

Nodding slowly, Everett said, "Celiaen told us Paienven wants to rewrite the borders. Do you think we can count on the future grand mage to side with Endara?"

Keeping her arm around him as they followed the rest of the group into the garrison, Fayleen peered up at the sky before it disappeared. What Everett had told her came as no surprise. She knew enough about Paienven from Celiaen to suspect he had been planning a move for longer than Eirian had been friends with his son.

"Yes, you can. Baenlin as well. If we tell Tessa what you know, she'll take it to him."

"Why can't I just tell the archmage directly?"

"Because Tessa is trying very hard to make an alley out of Baenlin, and if we want a sympathetic high council, we need to help her."

Whistling, Everett grinned at her. "You should marry me."

Giving him a surprised look, Fayleen replied, "Don't make jokes like that. Never know when a girl might think you're serious."

"What if I was?"

"You're the next in line to the Endaran throne. I attended all the extra lessons Ree had, and I know how this works."

"We already know we get on well."

Nose flaring, she whispered, "Ree doesn't know about any of it."

"Which? Your recent visit to Amath? Or any of those times in Riane? Why are you worried about her finding out?"

"I don't... just... no one can know, Everett. Please."

Hurt by her reaction, Everett shrugged the arm off his shoulders and bowed stiffly. "I'd better join Marcellus. It looks like your grand mage wants you."

Closing her eyes, Fayleen sighed heavily before looking at Tessa. She had not intended to hurt Everett, but she could not see a way for anything more than the smattering of moments they shared. He was all but a prince, and she was nothing more than the daughter of a shepherd who grew up as a companion to his cousin. Hurrying to Tessa, Fayleen forced a smile to her face and ignored the looks Zack and Luke directed at her.

"Is everything?" Zack murmured.

Brushing him off, Fayleen spoke to Tessa, "We need to talk after this little meeting."

"Have you been fishing for information?" she replied, arching a brow.

"Well, you were fishing for a king. Figured someone had to collect information."

Jaren choked. "Fay!"

"What?" Fayleen spread her hands. "You know it's true. Besides, Everett and I have met before, so it wasn't hard to pry news from him."

Eyes following Baenlin while he worked through the crowd of nobles and officers, Tessa murmured, "And?"

"Ree and Celi left a couple of weeks ago. Everett said their plan was to go north to see the Fingers."

"I thought they were looking for information?" Rylee asked, screwing up her face. "Are you telling me they've run off and abandoned a war front?"

"That doesn't sound like something Celi and Ree would do," Jaren commented.

Snickering, Fayleen disagreed. "It sounds exactly like something they would do. Gal's with them, so at least Tara and Aiden have someone sensible to help control them."

"Aiden? Who's that?"

"The poor sod stuck trying to protect Ree."

Frowning, Rylee thought back to the day she delivered Eirian to the Endarans and the tall, broad-shouldered warrior accompanying the man Fayleen had been talking to. She vaguely remembered talking to him before leaving, but her focus had been on Eirian.

"Tall, broad?" she asked Fayleen.

"Sounds like Aiden. He's a good man. But, powers know, he's got more patience for Ree than she deserves."

Arching a brow, the comment surprised Tessa. It was not like her to sound so scathing of Eirian. She was not the only one startled. The others shared looks while Fayleen stared at Everett, tracking his movements through the crowd. Something was bothering her, but it was neither the time nor place to try finding out. People were carving some organization out of the mess of people filling the hall, and Tessa did not want to let Baenlin exclude her from the discussions.

"Tessa, I told General Cameron and Everett not to let Baenlin dismiss you. Ree might not be here, but I'll do what I can to help you make allies with the Endarans." Fayleen glanced at Tessa. "You have a chance to prove yourself."

He had said it before, but Jaren reminded Tessa. "Don't waste any opportunity. Make them respect you, my brilliant sister."

"You might be able to take advantage of whatever Ree has done here."

Blinking at Rylee when she spoke, Tessa cocked her head and waited for an explanation.

"Both of you are purples, right? Ree has set an example for the people here. How are they to know you can't do what she can?"

"Huh," Tessa breathed. "You know what, Rylee? Maybe you're not as thick-headed a red as I thought you were."

Making a rude gesture at Tessa, Rylee's planned response died in her throat when she saw Soren pushing his way over to join them. Crowding closer to Tessa, Luke and Zack watched Jaren and Rylee while Fayleen crossed her arms and smiled at him. The slate gray of Fayleen's coat was lighter than the iron gray of Soren's, but the difference in rank did not stop her from keeping herself between him and Tessa.

"Feeling pluckier with your Endaran friends close?" he hissed.

"Not in the slightest. Let's go with my realization that I'm more powerful than you like to think. I'm not afraid of you, Soren."

Growling, Soren stepped closer and held Fayleen's challenging stare. It tempted him to clash with her, but the confident curl of her lips gave him the slightest flicker of doubt. It was a strange feeling.

"Remember who you are."

"Someone capable of going toe to toe with Galameyvin Kaetiel?" Fayleen said sweetly. "Thank you for reminding me, Soren."

Clamping his mouth shut, he breathed out slowly through his nose and looked at Tessa. "You're to return outside and join the others."

"No," Tessa replied, crossing her arms.

"I beg your pardon?"

"You can have it. I'm still not going anywhere."

Soren ground his teeth. "Baenlin has given you orders—"

"That's nice. The King of Telmia invited me to attend this meeting. Would you like to tell him why I dismissed his invitation?"

Backing down at the mention of Neriwyn, Soren muttered curses when Fayleen chuckled. He accepted he could not force Tessa to follow Baenlin's command, but he could do the next best thing. Sweeping his gaze over the circle of people surrounding a table, Soren picked out Baenlin and nodded.

"You make a logical argument. We'd hate to upset King Neriwyn."

Tessa's confidence faltered at his tone, and she said, "I'm pleased you agree."

"Of course, you should tell the archmage before he misunderstands the situation. We wouldn't want him to think you were defying his orders, would you?"

Smirking, Fayleen informed Tessa, "Don't worry, I've got an invitation to participate as well. So let's go tell our dear archmage."

Fayleen fluttered her eyes at Soren's blank expression, holding her arm out. Slipping her hand around her elbow, Tessa forced a smile. Remaining where they were, the other four watched in silence as Soren led the two women over to the table, making a space for them to slip in beside Baenlin.

"What do you think you're doing?" Baenlin whispered in Tessa's ear.

"I'm establishing who's in control," Tessa replied.

Staring across the table at Everett, Fayleen gave a subtle shake of her head and glanced at Tessa to convey her meaning. He inclined his head, unsmiling, as he turned to whisper to Marcellus. It would be difficult to gain access to him in the keep, but Fayleen wanted to apologize. She needed to.

Switching his attention to Fayleen, Baenlin asked, "And what's your excuse?"

"I have friends in high places, Archmage." She chuckled. "Try not to forget."

TEN

Splashing water over her face, Eirian tuned out the exchange between Tara, Celiaen, and Aiden. They stood a distance from the stream they had come across, but did not keep their voices low. The sun beat down from a clear sky, the pale blue hazy when she cast a glance at it to gauge the time. They had ridden hard over the northern countryside for days and not seen a single Athnaralan.

Instead, they had found signs of their passing, the ground so trampled by the sheer numbers that Eirian wondered how long it would take to repair the damage. Great furrows cut into the soil like wounds, and the sight had cast both dread and fury into the group. After finding the route, Tara had insisted they cut at an angle away from it. She did not want to stumble on the tail end accidentally.

Tara doubted any of them would stand a chance at stopping Eirian from trying to wipe the thousands of men from existence. Even more so because the ruins of farms fueled the fury oozing from her. She had ridden in silence for a day after they finished burying the mangled remains of an entire family. None of them had been able to stop her from digging the grave of the mother. Tobin had worn his black eye well after she punched him for trying to take her makeshift shovel.

They knew she was pouring her magic into their horses and into them, ensuring they could ride in pursuit of their enemy. Eirian could not continue to do it for much longer, but she dared not admit it. Not out of fear of looking weak, but because she desperately wanted to confirm their suspicions before they raced back to their forces. Galameyvin had suggested one night that the generals would know about the Athnaralan reinforcements, and they were wasting time. It was the last time he dared argue with Eirian to her face over the matter.

"She's going to kill herself if we continue," Galameyvin said quietly to the group huddled in a circle and cast a wary look at Eirian. "We all see it."

Sitting on the ground, his knees bent up in front of him, Faolan grunted. He had been doing his best to feed energy to Eirian without her noticing, and it was showing.

"What do we do? She won't see reason until she's gotten her hands on some Athnaralans. We may chase them to Kelsby and into a battle," Aiden muttered.

He was long past the point of regretting their decision, and he was not the only one. Tara stared blankly out at the rolling green. She was exhausted. They all were. Not physically, Eirian prevented that, but mentally. What they had seen left no dream undisturbed.

"That last farm was fresh. There's a group moving across the land here," she said.

Celiaen did not need to touch the bond to grasp the deep-seated fury Eirian felt. "I know you're going to argue, Captain. But, you need to trust me, trust us, when I say that once we catch up with them, we need to stay the fuck out of her way."

"What?" Aiden arched a brow.

"You think it's likely to end badly?" Tara asked.

Nodding, Celiaen knew what she was referring to, and Galameyvin let out a low hiss.

"I doubt she'll leave enough to bury."

Reminded they had seen Eirian do things that he and his men had not, Aiden dared ask, "Do I want to know, or is it best I don't?"

"Imagine the worst kind of killing," Tara answered quietly.

"I've seen her drop hundreds in a matter of moments."

Galameyvin shook his head. "Yes, but that was different. They were husks with the life drained. We're talking the sort of slaughter where she turns them into chunks."

"She shreds them to pieces that no longer resemble people. We covered it up last time because if the council knew what she was capable of when her anger and hatred is..." Shuddering, Celiaen rubbed his face.

"We destroyed all evidence of what she and those men she killed had done."

There was no need to ask what they had done to trigger such rage from Eirian. Aiden had seen it on her face each time she had gazed at the mutilated remains of her people.

He said regretfully, "We should never have set out on this path."

Turning to him, Tara agreed. "I'm sorry I pushed it. We should've turned around, returned to Kelsby, and trusted those generals to do their jobs. That's what scouts and spies are for. When we get back, they'll probably laugh because they knew about it before we left."

"There's nothing else we can do bar leaving her to chase them alone. It's not like we aren't heading in the direction we need to go," Faolan spoke.

Deciding to suggest something, Galameyvin wondered if they would take it. "If we declared we were stopping for a day, do you think she'd stay or ride on alone? I mean, if we stopped, we could get some rest, and I could try to lull her to sleep."

Eyes narrowing, Celiaen said, "Do you think she's exhausted enough not to stop you?"

"I don't know. If Ree was human or elf, she'd have collapsed by now. What do you think, Faolan?"

"I know I'd have collapsed by now. By the powers, I suspect even Neriwyn would have. I don't know where she finds the power to continue. Either she's running on pure determination, or she's more powerful than we realized."

Faolan thought back to the night in the forest, how Eirian moved through the trees, and he knew it was the second option. Scoffing, Celiaen shrugged, lifting a hand to a hilt at his waist.

"I've known her for twenty-odd years, and if there's one thing I can say with certainty, it's that she has more determination than sense."

Guilt crossed his mind, and Faolan plastered a sad smile on his face. "Her mother swam in it."

"Anything interesting?"

They turned to look at Eirian, the shadows under her eyes the first noticeable sign of her exhaustion.

Tara smiled, replying, "We're admiring the land."

She regarded them coldly. "I thought we should stop here for the night. There's water and clear sight. The horses could use the rest and a chance to graze. Then in the morning, I'll do a reading. We're chasing blind, and it's time we stopped."

"Good idea." Aiden was quick to agree, casting a quick look at the sun's position to remind himself that it was indeed the middle of the day.

"I'll give the orders to set up camp," Tara said, giving Eirian a hard look before hurrying off.

Nodding absently, Eirian turned and walked away, leaving the four men alone and concerned. Slumping, Celiaen sat on the ground opposite Faolan and sighed. Putting a hand on his shoulder, Galameyvin met Aiden's gaze and gave a slight shake of his head, mouth twisting with worry. Spurred by Tara's orders, the others began setting up a camp, several mounting to search for wood.

"I feel her anguish through the bond. With each dead body, it's felt like her heart is breaking into a thousand pieces, and there is nothing I can do." Celiaen's voice was soft, and he dropped his mask to let the other three see how worried he was.

"She's seen death before," Galameyvin reminded him.

"Not like this, not her people, not innocent people she feels compelled to protect."

Remembering how Eirian had looked at the dead boys in the farmhouse, Aiden knew what had gotten to her. "It's the brutality. I watched her look at dead children once before, dead in their beds by their grandfather's swift hand, and she was not like this."

"Brutality for the sake of brutality." A sneer curled Faolan's mouth, his distaste clear. "There's no honor in it, no need for it. Just a waste of life. She feels the insult to life in ways you cannot understand."

Galameyvin frowned, muttering, "It almost sounds like you're implying she's something different to all of us."

"She is."

"I disagree."

Meeting his gaze, Faolan rose and stepped close enough to Galameyvin that their noses were almost touching. "You do not know everything about her, and you never have."

"I don't think it's a good idea for us to be fighting," Aiden grumbled. "It does none of us any good to fight among ourselves, and it certainly doesn't help her."

Constantly aware of the bond, Celiaen reached out to Eirian. He had propped his head on his hand, fingers digging into his chin, but his hand dropped into his lap, face turning in the direction she had gone. She felt further away than she should.

"Where's Ree? Can any of you see her?"

They turned to look for her while Celiaen leaped to his feet. His first instinct was to look for Halcyon. Tents sat in two circular rows while they staked the horses close by with enough space to graze. Halcyon was not there, and he started cursing, striding toward his horse. Chasing after him, understanding clicking into place, Aiden and Galameyvin echoed his sentiments. Remaining in place, Faolan stripped to shift into his wolf form to follow the scent.

"She's run," Aiden said to Gabe when he hurried over to them.

His response was frank. "What do you want us to do? We can't all go chasing after her."

Glancing at the princes, Aiden said, "Leave Merle in charge. I want you, Fionn, and a few of the others, the ones in the best shape."

"Yes, Captain."

While they tacked their horses, Faolan had circled the camp several times and picked up the scent. Unfortunately, what Celiaen sensed over the bond was not enough to guide them. He gave thanks to the powers for Faolan's nose and Fox's tracking. No one spoke as they chased after the wolf. The closer they got to Eirian, the stronger the feeling of rage thundering across their bond. He tasted her hate and knew she had found her quarry.

"Well, fuck," Tara swore, yanking her horse to a stop. "If we'd pushed on…"

Rippling in the wind, the fields of golden barley stood between them and the collection of farm buildings. The sight of a dozen horses hitched to fencing made most of them curse. Halcyon was grazing without a tether on the other side of the rails, ignoring everything going on around him. In contrast, the other horses tugged at their reins and struggled to escape.

As they approached the buildings, they saw no sign of anyone around the farm, no one guarding the horses or watching to alert the others to those who would stop them. Getting closer also allowed them to understand why the horses were struggling, the echoes of screaming filling the air. It was more than that. It was more than the screams of people dying painfully. The air seethed with Eirian's fury. Her magic was so palatable that they recoiled in horror with the taste of blood on their tongues.

"This is where we don't go in, isn't it?" Aiden whispered, staring at the house.

His face was pale, skin crawling with the feel of her power. Casting a sideways look at Celiaen, Tara rested her hands on the pommel of her saddle. A muscle twitching in her cheek was the only sign of her feelings.

"Do we clean this up the usual way?"

"That's what you're concerned about?" Fionn was incredulous, staring at her with an open mouth. "What exactly are we expecting to see in there?"

Gabe was the only one willing to dismount, and he tossed his reins to Fox. "Death."

"You can't go in there," Celiaen said before Gabe walked toward the open door.

"She won't harm me. I'm the only bloody one here who understands this part of her, and she knows it." Tossing a look over his shoulder at them, Gabe did not smile as he said, "If we're lucky, I can salvage something for questioning."

Watching him slip through the doorway, Galameyvin turned to Aiden. "You didn't even try to stop him. What if she kills him?"

"She won't," he replied. "Gabe's right. She won't harm him. He can speak to this part of her in ways the rest of us can't. I feared they'd bring out the worst parts of each other, but maybe I'm wrong. Maybe he can bring her out of the worst part of herself by understanding her."

"And if you're both wrong?" Tara whispered.

Waving at Galameyvin, Aiden arched an eyebrow pointedly. "Well, isn't that what he's for? Isn't it your job to stop mages like her from going crazy? What about you? You're her fucking mate; can't you do something?"

Celiaen turned his gaze from the house to Aiden. "Not against this. It's like Ree shuts down part of her mind and becomes something else entirely."

The house was dark, but Gabe heard several voices screaming. Flicking his tongue out, he tasted the metallic tang in the air, the smell of blood overpowering his nose. Streaks of it smeared the walls, pools on the floor linked by drag marks. He wondered who had done the dragging and if the person had been alive when it happened.

Ears pricking, Gabe detected the sounds of someone whimpering from the room he was about to pass by. Carefully peering around the edge of the doorway, he located the source of the sound and sighed. Moving cautiously, he approached the naked girl tied to the table. The ruined scraps of clothing littered the floor, soaking up blood. Her left eye had swollen shut, the bruising transforming what he assumed had been a comely face into a mess of purple and red.

It was not the only place that the mottling of colors blended into the blood covering her. Hacked off, her hair was a blood-matted pile under the table. Watching in terror with her uninjured eye, she attempted to fight her bonds when Gabe pulled a knife from his belt. Shaking his head, he went to her feet first and grunted at the mess the ropes had made of her ankles. Deciding not to cut the cord away from her skin, he worked the blade through in another spot, slowly freeing her legs before moving to her arms.

"Don't move quickly," he muttered, taking in the angle her right arm was at. "I can tell they dislocated your shoulder, and I don't know what other injuries you have. Outside are some people who can help."

She stared at him in terror as she croaked, "Why?"

"We're not the enemy. We were just too late to stop this. Do you know if there are others in your family alive?"

Eye darting to the door, the young woman's fear increased. "I don't know."

"You saw her, didn't you?"

He pictured what had been going on. The Athnaralans having their fun with the girl when Eirian slipped in. The fact she knew well enough to leave the girl alive reassured Gabe that he had a chance to get through to her.

"She scared them."

"She's a terrifying woman," Gabe answered, making his way back to the door.

The girl did not move, whimpering, "My sisters."

"If they're alive and I can save them, then I will. Remember, there's help outside if you think you can get there. Otherwise, stay put until we're done cleaning up the men who did this."

He did not glance back, keeping the knife gripped tightly in his hand. Following the screaming, Gabe wondered what he would find. Checking another room, he discovered the first lot of remains. If that was what anyone could call them. Blood covered everything, even the ceiling. It took a moment to make sense of what he was seeing, picking out the chunks that had once been human, dotted about the place.

Not daring to go any further, Gabe attempted to determine how many people had died in the room. Stepping back, he continued on his way and drew closer to the sounds. At least he knew she had not slaughtered everyone yet. Screaming did not bother him. It was something he tuned out. Instead, excitement crept through him, eagerness to see Eirian at her darkest, making him hasten into the room at the back of the house where he heard them suffering.

"Ma'am?" he said, ignoring the blood dripping from the ceiling and the mangled remains of several men. "Eirian."

Eirian stood in the middle of the room, a hand outstretched either side. They pointed at the men pinned to the walls.

"Leave."

"Nah, I don't think I will. I've been asking to play, and here you are, having fun without me. I'm hurt."

She looked at him, and Gabe did not flinch at the smoldering fire he saw in her eyes. "What these men have done."

Looking at the closest man, Gabe admired the desperate agony on his face. "Oh, I saw a sample. They deserve everything you've done and more. Far more. However, we need to ask them some questions."

A third man huddled on the ground, and he lifted his head, reaching out to Gabe to plead, "Please…"

Arching a brow, Gabe walked over and crouched, ignoring the blood. Showing the Athnaralan the knife he held, he smiled slowly.

"Was that please help her kill me slowly?"

"Help us."

"I don't think so," he said in disappointment. "What a silly thing to ask. No, you'll answer some questions my boss has. When he's done, I'm going to ask that poor girl you left strung out like meat what she thinks you deserve. No doubt she'll enjoy your cock and balls on a plate. I'll happily oblige."

Before the cowering mess could croak out another word, Gabe flipped his knife around and drove it through the back of his hand, twisting. Glancing over his shoulder at Eirian, he saw a flicker of the control she typically wielded, trying to claw its way into place. Judging by the state the men were in, it was clear they would not make a run for it if she let her magic drop.

The one on the floor beside him was nursing legs broken in multiple places, and from the markings on his uniform, Gabe knew he was the leader. His rank was probably why he was still alive and mostly in one piece. A little voice at the back of his mind prompted him to be thankful that she could still make judgment calls like that.

"They bashed in the baby's head." Her voice was calm. "A tiny, defenseless baby."

The two men on the wall began screaming again, her magic twisting their bodies in ways he knew would kill them if she took it further.

"Eirian, stop. We need to question them. Be logical about this."

"The one on the floor can answer those questions. You don't need these two as well."

"You know they'll want to verify the information."

The man whimpered. "What is she?"

Looking down at him in amusement, Gabe flashed a rare smile. If he had not been struggling to hold on to a shred of sanity and consciousness, he would have felt fear at it.

"She's our queen. Isn't she beautiful?"

"Please, I'll tell you anything."

He barely got the words out before pain overtook him again. Shaking his head, Gabe yanked the knife free and looked around for something to clean the blood off it with.

"Yes, you will."

Managing hysterical laughter in between sobs of pain, he said, "You take orders from a whore."

Her eyes flashed, and Eirian flexed her powers. The soldier on the floor flew upward to hit the ceiling.

"That whore is going to destroy your armies," she snarled as he hit the ground with a thud. "That whore is going to make your pathetic excuse for a king suffer far, far worse than you can imagine for what he has done."

Moving carefully, Gabe stood and walked over to her, daring to reach out to place a hand on one of her arms, purring, "Alive, darling."

Sneering at his gentle command, she let the two men held against the wall drop. Something about Gabe's voice stirred the whispers that had been silent while she took care of the Athnaralans.

"And when I'm done with your king, I'm going to lock your master back in her cage."

"Other than the girl in the kitchen, are there any others alive?" Staring at her face, Gabe hoped the question would direct Eirian away from torturing the three Athnaralans. "I freed her, but I don't know if she tried to go out to the others."

Eirian's magic remained as she lowered her arms slowly, its presence almost suffocating. "There is another girl. She's in a worse state."

"These men aren't going anywhere. Let's get the girls outside and help them. Just think, these three can lie here in pain and suffering while they wait for the next round."

Blinking, Eirian cocked her head to the side and peered past him at her victims, muttering, "Fine. You take the one you helped, and I'll get the other."

Remaining close, Gabe followed her out of the room without a backward glance. He would have his time with the three men once Eirian was out of the house, and Aiden gave him the nod of approval. There was stickiness on his face where blood had dripped from the ceiling onto his skin. Nothing would erase the image from his mind of the walls painted with blood, and a small part of him was glad Aiden would finally see the darkness that he had always seen in her.

She stared at him coldly before turning to a door he had not looked in. When Eirian pushed it open, his gaze settled on the shape stretched out on a bed in the corner.

"You sure you can handle it? There are plenty of big, burly men outside who can come in and carry her out."

"Just worry about your task," she growled, stomping into the room.

Returning to the first room, Gabe found the girl where he had left her. She had rolled onto her side, and looking her over, he noticed her twisted knee. Grunting, he nodded and watched her fearful expression melt away. Silently scooping her up, he carried her out of the house. He admired her strength, pain evident on her face, and he could tell she was biting down hard on her lip. Occasionally, a whimper escaped her control.

"Close your eye. You'll want to do it before we go outside. I'm gathering you haven't seen daylight for a little while."

"Thank you," she whispered, following his suggestion.

The rest of the group had dismounted, adding their horses to the collection tethered to the fence. They started forward at the sight of Gabe coming out of the house with the injured woman cradled in his arms. Fionn gasped in horror, reminding Gabe he was one of the gentlest among the guard.

Quick to shift from his wolf form, Faolan clicked fingers at Kenna, demanding the long cloak she wore. She did not argue, laying it on the ground where he directed so that Gabe could place his cargo down carefully. Crouching by her head, Galameyvin offered a calming smile, and Gabe watched her fear melt into a dazed look, a sense of euphoria settling on her.

"She's got the other one, but she's in a far worse state. There's still three Athnaralans alive. I stopped her, but I wouldn't dawdle around out here."

Aiden nodded at Tara "Good work, Gabe."

"I'm coming with you. This is what I'm paid for." Pushing himself up, Gabe dusted his hands off, noticing more blood splattered on his clothes.

"Fine."

Appearing in the doorway, Eirian carried the smaller girl, and Celiaen hurried forward to take her. Snarling, she strode past them toward the fields.

"Get out of my way."

Gabe saw how much blood covered her and glanced at the others to take in their reactions. They did not disappoint.

"Captain, I'd recommend we go. If that girl dies, she'll be back to finish what she started and fuck our questions."

Staring at him with hard eyes, Tara asked, "How bad is it?"

"Bad."

Her gaze shifted to Eirian, and she murmured, "At least it's not my first time."

Galameyvin looked up from assisting Faolan and Kelsey. "Get what you need and kill them."

Freezing, none of them moved, all their focus shifting to Eirian. She had laid the girl on the ground between two fields, and Celiaen hovered behind her. The feel of her magic had gotten no less suffocating, but Gabe noted it did not feel the same. They exchanged something, and Celiaen turned on his heels, striding back to the watching group. His face was grim, eyes narrow, and a hand rested on the hilt of one of his swords. Shaking his head, he pushed past.

"She's going to heal her," he explained on his way to the house.

No one moved, and he huffed, turning to watch. Eirian remained kneeling beside the barely breathing girl. It did not look like she was doing anything, but they could not miss the way the crops withered and crumbled as she drew the life from the plants and fed it into the girl. They all heard the scream of terror when she began thrashing, Eirian falling back out of the way of the moving limbs.

"By the powers," Fox said, the sentiment shared by everyone.

"Right, no time to waste." Aiden turned, nodding to Gabe and Tara.

Making their way into the house, Tara and Celiaen were the first through the door, and they waited in the space beyond for Gabe to lead. They barely looked at the blood, but Aiden could not avoid staring. Comprehending it was a shock, Tara put a hand on Aiden's shoulder. She offered him a grim look of understanding with sympathy mixed in.

"I knew she could torture and kill without a second thought, but this?" he murmured, swallowing bile when he stepped over a lump.

Tara replied, "I know. Why do you think we cleaned up the mess and kept our mouths shut? If people knew she could turn like this, they'd have killed her, fuck the political consequences. Though I suppose your nobles would've brought their excuses that she was too dangerous to live."

"Right now, I'd agree."

"You don't mean that," Celiaen growled. "Just because she can do this when pushed far enough doesn't mean she's too dangerous. You saw what we saw at the other farms. You know how much she cares."

"Can you explain how she turns people into lumps of flesh?" Pointing at a clump of something outside the doorway Gabe had halted at, Aiden shook his head. "What about you, Gabe?"

Gabe yawned before saying, "I knew from the first time I met her. I tried to warn you."

Frowning, Tara scoffed. "It doesn't bother you?"

"Why would it? I mean, I can't pull a person to pieces with a touch of magic, but there's an intimacy in using a knife and getting your hands right in there. You warriors are all righteous and polite about killing. You don't appreciate what it's like to hold a beating heart in the palm of your hand while the life drains out of someone." He let her glimpse the monster he kept hidden.

"You're saying that Eirian feels this way?"

"Of course, but she's as much good as she is bad."

Peering into the room at the three Athnaralans, Celiaen sighed. "We can debate and argue over Eirian some other time. We have more pressing matters to attend to."

Not sure what state to expect the men to be in, Aiden took a deep breath and steeled himself before entering. The others did not need the time to adjust. Gabe had seen it and was more interested in having his turn. He knew the middle one was in the better state and pointed, pulling a knife at Tara's nod. Hoisting the man up by his hair, he grinned at the sobs.

"I said you'd answer some questions." It was a small pleasure to slam the hilt of his knife into the hand he had driven the blade into.

"Is that all you've got?" he gasped, a hint of hysterical laughter in his voice.

Grinding it hard against the wound, Gabe replied, "I know after her, we don't scare you, but I'll still enjoy my time."

Crouching, Celiaen said, "How about you answer our questions, and we'll end your suffering."

He lifted his head, spitting blood as best he could at Celiaen. "Elf scum."

"He called Her Majesty a whore. He's not creative."

"Did he now?" The insult did not impress Celiaen, and he let go of his magic to let the Athnaralan feel his rage. "We're rather fond of the woman who did this to you."

"Does she spread her legs for you?"

Gabe flipped his knife around, ignoring the blood that had made the hilt slick, and slipped it between two ribs in a spot he knew would not kill the man in a hurry.

"You answer questions, not ask them."

Looming over them, Tara had her hands on her hips. "How many reinforcements?"

"You swear you'll kill us before she comes back?"

"Of course." Aiden stared at the enemy officer. "You'll die quicker than you deserve."

Coughing again, blood trickled from the corner of his mouth. "Three legions."

They knew the numbers back at the town. Celiaen nodded, glancing over his shoulder.

"How many siege weapons?" Tara prompted.

"Six."

Aiden's mouth twisted, and he asked bitterly, "Are they counted as part of the legions?"

"No."

"They'd have at least a company dedicated to each. Men trained in setting them up, using them, repairing them. We need to hurry." Tara squeezed Celiaen's shoulder. "Let him take care of this. We should check on Ree."

"No more questions?" Gabe purred in delight. "They're mine?"

"He's Athnaralan. I doubt he's smart enough to lie," Aiden said mockingly.

"Fuck you."

Eyes sliding to Celiaen, Aiden replied, "Better men than you have offered. They're all yours, Gabe, have fun."

Panic set in, overriding the pain the man was in, and he began struggling against the grip Gabe had on his hair. "You said quick!"

"I lied."

Leaving Gabe alone with the enemy, the other three walked away without looking back. They were out of the house before the first scream sounded. Outside, they did not receive any looks from the rest, focusing on the two girls. Eirian was sitting on the ground between the dead crops where they had last seen her. She was facing them, watching as the sisters huddled together with Galameyvin.

He held their hands, talking calmly, wrapping his magic around them and through their minds. Fionn and Fox were standing next to each other, keeping a distance between them and Galameyvin. They looked uncomfortable, Aiden recognizing that they were more put off by what he could do than what Eirian had done. Most of the time, he would have agreed. But if manipulating their minds could help the innocent girls cope with what they had been through, then it was worth it.

"He can help them, can't he?"

Glancing at Celiaen, Aiden's mouth twisted in concern. Turning to stare at him, the prince arched a brow. He knew what the other man meant. Behind them, Tara grunted.

"They're taught to do this from early on. Gal would rather use his power to help someone than encourage politics or stop a rampaging red."

It made Aiden stare at Galameyvin with new regard. "Can he make them forget?"

"Yes, but he won't. It's better to avoid that route. There's a risk of the memories returning. He'll dull their feelings, help them distance themselves from what they went through. They'll remember everything, but it won't hurt so badly."

Eirian stood and walked toward them, her magic no longer filling the air. Blood coated her, and Tara puffed her cheeks out at the sight of Eirian's hair matted into clumps with dried blood. She did not seem to care, gazing at them with weary eyes that held more bitterness than they had the day before.

"Anyone else glad we made camp next to a stream?" Tara muttered, slinking backward to leave the two men to speak to Eirian.

She stared at them, and Celiaen felt her drawing energy through the bond to remain upright. "Did you get your answers?"

"Three legions, six siege weapons, and the people required to operate them," Aiden answered.

"We need to return to Kelsby."

Celiaen placed a hand on her shoulder. "You're drained and using me to cling to consciousness. There's no way we're going anywhere except back to camp to clean you up and put you to bed."

"I want to say I'm sorry I lost control," Eirian murmured. "Except I'm not."

"Are you at least sorry for not telling us you knew they were here and for slipping away to take care of them on your own?" Aiden asked.

Her eyes were dull. "Not right now, but ask me again when my mind is not so heavy."

"You saved those girls, and you healed one. What made you attempt it? You've always said healing isn't one of your abilities."

"I don't know. Since I can restore life to plants, I thought, why not use that energy to restore a human? I don't know if my rage over what happened is what allowed me to do it."

Despite the dried blood, Aiden wanted to wrap his arms around Eirian and tell her he understood why she had done what she had. The look on Celiaen's face and the hand on her shoulder stopped him from taking a step closer to her to offer the comfort he suspected she needed. Eirian's eyes flickered between them before settling on Celiaen.

"I should return to camp and clean up."

He agreed. "I'll take you back. Tara knows what to do, and Galameyvin won't go anywhere until he's sure those girls are good to move."

Shaking her head, she looked at Aiden. "Stay here, Celi. The Captain can escort me. That's his job after all."

"Eirian, you're only standing bec—"

"Remain here!" She shrugged off his hand. "Captain, if you will."

"Of course, Majesty. Let me call Fionn and the others. We'll meet at the horses." He waited for her to walk toward Halcyon before turning to Celiaen. "Don't worry, she'll be fine. We'll get her back to camp, cleaned up, and into her bed."

Celiaen grabbed his wrist, eyes filled with worry. "She won't make it back before she passes out. I'd tell you to make her ride with you, but she'd never agree. Just stay close. She doesn't need to hit the ground when she falls out of the saddle."

"You're right. She wouldn't thank us for the indignity or the pain she'd feel tomorrow."

"We don't always get on, Captain, but I trust you to look after her."

They stared at each other before Aiden glanced over his shoulder at the house. "I think I understand our job is less about protecting her than it is about protecting everyone else from her."

"You couldn't be more right," Celiaen said.

ELEVEN

Shadows crept over the tent walls. They spread, finding cracks to slip through as they reached out for others to embrace. Insidious tendrils seeking a hold on those vulnerable minds closest to Eirian. What everyone had witnessed on their cross-country chase had been unsettling, and the events that unfolded at the farm days earlier left them in a worse state. It would have been easy to recover if she had not fallen into silence.

Her silence was deafening. The haunted look in her eyes told everyone she was struggling. Eirian no longer poured energy into driving them across the land. So they set a steady pace, confident the sheer numbers of the Athnaralan forces would slow them. They would make it back to Kelsby first, with or without Eirian's extra help. It was more important to give her time to wrest with her guilt. More important to provide all of them with time to process their feelings.

Moving silently through the camp, he watched the shadows recoil at his presence. Stepping on one of them, the man clicked his tongue in annoyance and ground it beneath the toe of his boot. The tendrils felt nothing, but he knew the woman controlling them would receive the message.

"If you think I'm going to let you torment them, you're wrong," he murmured.

Gathering together, the shadows formed the vague outline of the woman who had faced Eirian outside of Kelsby. She laughed, the sound unheard by anyone other than the man staring at her. The camp slept around them, encouraged by his power to keep their eyes shut. It would have been easier to be invisible to them, but he knew each company member needed as much rest as possible.

"Are you scared I might break your toys?" she asked mockingly. "As though that isn't your plan already, beloved."

"I won't play your games."

"Perhaps you won't, but she will."

His hands clenched into fists at his side, and he snarled, "You can't touch her mind."

"Can't I? Have you seen inside that beautiful darkness? She barely needs a nudge to step over the knife-edge between noble sentiment and destruction."

Eyes sliding in the tent's direction where Eirian slept restlessly in Celiaen's arms, he forced himself to unclench his fists. The god in front of him was not there, and he knew where her body remained imprisoned. It had been his promises that lured her into the trap laid for her. Meeting her gaze, he let the memories of her golden curls slip through his fingers like silk. No matter what they had done to each other and the world, he could no sooner stop loving her than cut off his hand.

She whispered, "Death is the cruelest of us all."

"I never said I wasn't."

"I'm going to enjoy watching your heart shatter like you did to mine."

Shrugging, he told her, "You can end this. Start over and give our creations the chance to be everything they can become."

Her eyes darted to another tent, lips curling in a malicious smile. Urged on by her power, the shadows darted out, twisting around the shelters again. It was an empty taunt, but it was one she knew to be effective. Snarling, the man overlooked the temperature dropping and the sheen of frost spreading across the ground from his position. Beneath the glitter of ice crystals, the grass withered, but all of his focus was on her.

"Careful, beloved, don't let your temper betray you."

Taking a deep breath, he replied, "Go back to your toys. Leave mine alone."

"It's a pity you can't fix that," she said, waving a hand at the ground. "They're going to blame our darling little life. When they see it, they'll assume she lost control in her sleep because one of her nightmares got the better of her. Do you know what torments her when her eyes close?"

"You don't—"

"The whispers of memories that want to break free fill her dreams. She hears them calling. You're going to throw her at me to die, but are you certain that's the right thing to do? What if I don't kill her?"

He knew what he would have to do if things did not go to plan. It was not ideal, but nothing about any part of this war was. Idyllic was a concept that they had torn apart and trampled over the day they took sides against each other.

"If you don't kill her, I will."

Laughing, she closed the distance between them and trailed the shadows of her fingers across his cheek. It lacked the agonizing pain that should have accompanied her touch, but he did not need to feel it, to remember it. Their separation was something none of them could forget. Not him. Not her. Not the ones who were not there with them. The ghost of her lips on his carried a promise of fire and destruction.

"She might not give either of us a chance to kill her. How her fingers itch to drive a blade into her own heart."

Before he could answer, the shadows dissipated into the night and left him standing alone. He felt the tattered remains of chains binding him to the others and hoped it would not be for too much longer. Redemption was within reach, so close he could taste the promise of it. All he needed to do was push the pieces in the right direction and wait for them to do the rest.

Which brought him to the reason he was there. The parting words thrown at him by the shadow of his former lover were not a surprise. He had felt Eirian's desires, her craving to end her own life to prevent a repeat of the farmhouse. It was an unacceptable option, and he had to meddle to prevent things from taking the wrong path. There were too many things that could go terribly if she killed herself before facing her battle.

Brushing aside the flaps of the tent, he crouched down in the small space available. Eirian faced away from her mate, and he saw the traces of tears glittering on her cheeks. Studying her, he wondered who the tears were for. With a glance at Celiaen's arm clinging to her waist, he carefully leaned in and brushed his hand over Eirian's hair. In her restless state, she shifted, eyelids fluttering.

"You need to go for a walk," he whispered in her ear. "He won't wake when you leave."

Her magic reached for him, and he lingered briefly to make sure his instruction had found purchase in Eirian's mind. Moving his hand to Celiaen, he traced a line down his arm and wove power through him. It would keep him sleeping until dawn, providing Eirian with the time to wake up, take her walk, and return to his arms. Satisfied with his task, he vanished from the tent.

Eirian shifted, eyes struggling to stay closed despite the urge she felt to wake. The warmth of Celiaen pressed to her back was comforting, but his hand on her abdomen brought her guilt to the surface. Wriggling free of his hold, she rubbed her face and peered blearily around the tent to chase the echoes of her nightmares from her mind. With consciousness came the whispers and press of memories that grew more relentless with each passing day.

Grabbing Celiaen's coat to wrap around herself, Eirian crept out with a glance to make sure he remained sleeping. It was odd that he had not stirred the moment she moved. He normally did. Dismissing her concern as nothing more than the fact they were all tired, she stood and stretched outside the tent. Tugging the silk over her arms, she clung to the clasps rather than do them up.

There was a chill to the ground that startled Eirian. Feeling the grass crumble beneath her feet as she walked, she glanced down and frowned at the glittering sheen that coated it. The night did not strike her as cold enough for frost, but it was covering the earth, digging its icy fingers into her skin. Shivering, she pulled the coat closer around her, lifting her gaze to the cloudless sky and the blanket of stars sprayed across it.

"I feel your shine, yet you are so far from me."

The whispers laughed, a sound as smooth as the silk adorning her. They told Eirian she knew the names of all the stars, and she wished it was true. No one stopped her from leaving the circle of tents. Lingering influences kept the watchful eyes of those on guard closed against the night. She did not notice the soft snores of Ianto as she walked past him.

She noticed when the unusual frost ended, leaving damp grass beneath her feet. Seed stalks brushed against her bare legs, mixed with the sensation of petals tickling her skin. Eirian wanted to question the change, but the lingering taste of her nightmares led her to suspect the frost had been her doing. It was not something she was aware of having done before, which did not mean it had not happened.

Coming to a halt, Eirian rubbed her arms and gazed at the sky. Her magic curled around her, ready for whatever she might need. It chased the memory of the frost from her feet to welcome the beat of the earth instead. Drawing on the energy, she offered it to the flicker she carried. Mocking her for doing so, the whispers pressed in closer, and she tried not to let the guilt overwhelm her.

"I told you to be careful slipping out."

The voice in the darkness sounded like it had stepped out of the memories that haunted her. Eirian recognized it and the response it received from her magic. She doubted she could ever forget it. Deciding there was little point in trying to coax a different reaction from her power, she accepted the lazy way it rolled over at his approach. Refusing to look in his direction, Eirian hoped if she pretended he was not there, it would be nothing more than her mind playing tricks on her.

"It's not your fault."

Eyes widening, Eirian glanced away and pressed her lips together. There were so many options running through her mind that she did not know which he referred to. The whispers had fallen silent on his arrival, but they returned when she did not answer.

"Are you ignoring me, darling?" He chuckled, and the sound sent shivers down her spine.

"I don't enjoy talking to figments of my imagination," Eirian replied. "Go away, whoever you are. I'm not interested in any of this right now."

He kept a safe distance, not trusting her temper to stay away. When he did not answer quickly, Eirian glanced in his direction. She did not know who he was, but the glow of power surrounding him rivaled the stars. It let her see a hint of the dark lines twisting over his skin, barely visible beneath the pale linen he wore. Catching her look, he arched a brow, a faint smirk curling his lips.

"Your latest offering was delightful, but there really is no need to feel so guilty about it."

"What are you talking about?"

The hitch in her voice did not go unnoticed, so he said, "The farm. I assume that was an offering for me."

"Who are you?" she whispered. "Wait, no, don't answer. I don't want to know."

"I wasn't going to tell you an answer you already know."

Eirian grunted, tugging at the cuffs enveloping her hands. The response of her magic to him and the whispers demanding she close the space between them left her confused. If she did not look at him, if she avoided the gleam of eyes she knew were a vibrant blue, Eirian could almost banish the memories of his hands on her skin. Except it was not her skin, and they added to the confusion.

"What do you want?"

"You don't need to sound so hostile, Eirian Altira."

Her nose twitched, and he saw her fingers flex at the same time. There was a familiar ripple through her magic that betrayed her bloodline. It carried the tang of blood entwined with the promise of death. He knew it was the thread of his power Eirian had inherited and which typically hid beneath her other abilities.

"Careful, darling."

"Considering one of your kind is trying to destroy the world, I don't think you get to tell me to be careful," she said.

"Alright then, go ahead and kill your friends."

She growled, hands dropping to her sides. Unsecured, the coat fell open, and he glimpsed her naked body underneath. The scar was a dark line against the pale glow of her skin. It served as a reminder of the price of her overconfidence. Tilting her head to the side, Eirian stared at him challengingly, and he gazed back blankly.

"If you want to succeed, you need to stop wallowing. You have nothing to be guilty about. Those men got what they deserved."

"Yes, they did. I'm just sorry I didn't get to them sooner."

Frowning at her reply, he asked, "So why do you feel so terrible about it?"

Sighing, Eirian did not know how he knew what she had done, and she did not care. Wrapping her arms around herself, she lifted her eyes to the stars. The illusion of warmth they had provided earlier turned cold, reminding her of the frost.

"It wasn't me, was it?"

"You might need to be more specific."

"The frost. I didn't do that because of one of my nightmares."

He chuckled. "No, that was me. Don't worry, darling, you're not freezing things."

"They won't believe it wasn't me." Her shoulders slumping, Eirian muttered,

"I'll fix it. They'll never know. Better they don't. It's bad enough I've let people know we're fighting a god. The last thing they need to find out is that there's more of you."

"I suppose it wouldn't surprise you to find out you mortals get your bad habits from us?"

"Fuck you."

Dragging his eyes down her body slowly, he purred, "Don't make offers you won't follow through on."

Magic flared around Eirian, rage cutting through the lingering promise of death. It was hot, alive, and thrilling, making him inhale deeply when the scent of flowers became richer. He needed her to focus on that anger, cling to it long enough to see her through to the end. Nothing else mattered except maneuvering Eirian into the position he needed her to be in. The one that resulted in her death.

"No."

"No?"

Eirian snarled, "You don't get to walk up to me and make comments like that."

"You have your mother's fire."

"You don't get to say that either."

Waving at her, he said, "I'd never lie to you about her."

"I don't need to know anything about her. Sometimes, choices tell you everything you need to know about someone. They speak volumes about priorities."

He did not think she realized magic was swirling around her, making her glow brighter. Eirian turned to face him, hands raised. No one needed to tell her the man opposite her was something far more powerful than she was. She was well aware of it, and she did not care.

"All of this is your fault!"

Arching a brow when she jabbed a finger at him, he said, "I was hardly alone in it."

"Well, no one else is here for me to yell at!"

"Believe me, I don't deny my part in what happened. I never have. You're my solution."

"Ah, yes, I'm the carefully bred sacrifice. I do so look forward to dying."

"Not as much as I look forward to watching her kill you," he replied, smirking at her exasperated expression. "Your death is one I've been waiting for a long time."

Raising her hand to hit him, Eirian flinched when his hand shot up to block her. Fingers wrapped around her wrist so tightly she was sure they would leave bruises. Eyes widening, his gaze dropped to her abdomen. Wrenching free, she stumbled back and drew on her magic, surrounding herself with it like a blanket. It could not protect her from a god, but Eirian needed the comfort the illusion gave her.

"Leave me alone."

"I'm afraid I can't do that," he informed her, and his bitter tone made her recoil. "I need to make sure you're not going to do anything else stupid."

Tugging the coat closed, Eirian whispered, "I don't need the god of death holding my hand and walking me to my grave."

"I have a name."

"Do you expect me to care?"

Shrugging, he did not answer. Her words stung, but he could not spare the emotions when there was so much at stake. Running a hand through his hair, he looked at the stars and briefly wished they had never left them. Magic filled the air, a layer of existence that shimmered like stardust to his eyes. A never-ending reminder of where they had come from.

"Darling, you make it too easy."

"So do you."

Scoffing, he asked, "What do I make easy?"

"Hating the gods. We don't need you. Any of you. You should take your problematic member and leave our world alone." The whispers mocked her, but Eirian pressed on. "What have you done for us except cause problems?"

"What have we done for you? You mean, besides create you? Not to mention this world you seem so fond of. Which also has a name, if you're interested."

"Tir."

The word slipped from her tongue before Eirian could stop herself from repeating what the whispers had told her. He frowned, cocking his head to study her curiously.

"Yes, but how?"

"It doesn't matter."

He wanted to argue. It would fuel her anger further and help push the guilt from the forefront of her mind. As much as he had appreciated the blood-soaked walls left behind by her fury, he needed Eirian to stop dwelling on her past actions.

"True, you don't really need to know much when you're just going to die, anyway."

Eirian glanced toward the camp, and he watched the emotions flicker across her face. "If my death is so important to you, why don't you kill me now?"

"You know the reason." He clenched his jaw when she laughed. "You find it funny?"

"Yes, right now I do," Eirian replied. "What if I decided it wasn't my problem? Maybe it's time I was selfish. I could walk away and decide that you worthless deities aren't my problem."

Grinding his teeth, he said, "You won't condemn the millions of lives on

Tir to her."

"You're the god of death. I'd have thought you'd enjoy it."

"Would you? All those innocent lives?"

Walking over to him, Eirian cooed, "Maybe I don't care as much as people think."

"My darling little life, you can't stop caring just to spite your fate."

"Perhaps."

Lifting her hand, she ghosted it down the line of his face and smirked when he flinched away. Both of them knew her taunt was a hollow suggestion, but his reaction confirmed to Eirian that he feared the thought she might follow through. Swallowing, she glanced away and wished she had tears left to shed for herself.

"I suppose I should thank you."

"Why?" he whispered.

Her hand hovered close to his cheek. Its closeness was torment. The lingering promise of a touch that would not come.

"Because now I know there is no hope. They all talk about finding another way, that somehow we'll learn something to defeat the darkness without my death. But there's no other way. If the god of death declares your life is the price, who are you to argue?"

Caught by the breeze, the sickeningly sweet floral scent surrounded him, and he closed his eyes. "Eiri—"

"Don't be mistaken. I've got no intention of running from my death. In fact, I'm really quite okay with it. Maybe I'll finally find that peace I want so badly."

"I can't make any promises," he murmured.

Her fingertips brushed against his cheek in the most fleeting of touches. If agony had not coursed through him, he would have doubted she made contact.

"I'm not asking for any. I'm happy to die, and I suppose saving Tir is as good a reason as any. We can keep that between you and me."

"Who am I going to tell?"

"Who indeed," Eirian stated. "Can you take her memories away? Let me have my last days without the torment of those fragments she somehow passed to me."

Dread coursed through him. Gazing at Eirian in horror, he understood what she was referring to.

"Shianeni's memories are leaking through?"

"Bits and pieces. Most of it doesn't make sense," she lied.

"How much do you know?"

Humming, Eirian shrugged. The tug at one side of her mouth told him what he needed to know. He was confident she did not know everything, but she knew more than he had planned. More than she was supposed to.

"An eternal dance among the stars is naught but a breath between life and death. A glistening blanket of sky coats the waters of a mirror, like the silk draped across skin marred with inky lines of the night," she whispered.

She looked to the sky, eyes dancing from one star to the next, before returning her gaze to the man watching her. The temperature had dropped, the feel of his power oozing from him like the chill of a tomb. Eirian wanted to laugh at the thought and settled for shaking her head.

"When the time comes, I'll make it painless," he murmured.

"I don't need any favors from you."

"Perhaps the favor is not for you but for those who'll witness your passing."

Turning her hands over in front of her, Eirian stared in bafflement while the whispers fought to be heard. She pictured the lines covering him as clearly as if she was touching them in the daylight.

"What are they?"

He was not sure what she was asking about. "You might need to give me more information if you want an answer."

Waving at him, Eirian replied, "The lines on your skin."

"Fracture marks where I separated from the other gods."

"And each of you bore them?"

"Why do you want to know?"

"How did I end up with memories from my mother?"

Hesitating, he was careful with his answer. "Shianeni passed her power to you before she died. I assume it somehow caught fragments of her memories."

Chuckling, Eirian turned her back on him and took several steps. The chill had faded again, chased away by the warmth of her power. She wondered how it was possible.

"We'll haunt each other's dreams," she told him.

Lips parting, he gazed at the back of her head in surprise. It was not the first time someone had thrown those words at him. The last time he had heard them anywhere but in his memories had been the night Eirian was born.

"I'm sorry."

"I don't need your apologies."

"You have them anyway," he said.

Turning, Eirian spread her arms. She wanted to scream and hurl accusations at him. The answer to all her questions stood in front of her, draped in shadows and the promise of death. Whispers across her mind assured her that if she pushed a little more, the truth would come. But regret and guilt hit Eirian, a hand darting to her stomach to draw the coat closed. Some questions were better left unanswered, and she would die soon enough that they would not matter.

"Don't let them make me into a hero after I die."

He snorted. "What makes you think I could do anything about that? I'm the god of death, not accolades."

Rolling her eyes, Eirian grumbled, "No one could mistake you for anything but what you are."

"And what's that?"

"An ass."

"For a mortal woman soon to die, you're awfully willing to throw insults at the god who could make things difficult for you."

"Good thing I'm a dead woman walking."

Laughing, he ran a hand through his hair. Unimpressed by his response, Eirian crossed her arms and glanced at the horizon to assess how far off dawn was.

"It's a pity things are the way they are, darling."

"Why's that?"

"Because I think we'd enjoy arguing with each other far too much."

"No more than I enjoy arguing with anyone else."

The smile he gave her was straight out of the memories, and Eirian had to stop herself from going to him. Her fingers itched to bury themselves in his dark hair while she drank the taste of death from his lips. A whisper promised kissing him would be an agony unlike any other she could ever experience. Yet another swore it would be the most exquisite feeling she would ever know. All the whispers agreed it was worth it.

Eirian reached for her bond to Celiaen, letting the faint sensation of his rage draw her in. He was her tether, even when asleep. Shifting her focus slightly, she felt the threads binding her to Galameyvin and Aiden. They were the cords holding her heart stitched together while the weight of the world became too much. It was they who would get her through to the end. For their chance to live, she would give every last drop.

"You can go now," she said, dismissing the god.

"Really?" he drawled. "Just like that?"

"I don't know why you felt the need to reveal yourself to me, but there's no reason for you to remain. I'm not going to do anything to stop her from killing me when the time comes. So there's nothing to worry about."

Gazing at her, he let the variations of her death play out in his mind until he felt confident she was not lying to him. There was so much he wanted to tell Eirian but could not. Not if they were going to save Tir from the vengeance of his fellow god.

"I'd appreciate it if you didn't mention our conversation to anyone."

Eirian replied bitterly, "Another secret for my collection."

"It's quite the collection."

"I don't think you have the right to comment."

Turning to vanish into the darkness, he said, "Don't forget to fix my little…"

Waiting until she felt the taste of his power fade, Eirian sighed. The whispers howled in disappointment. Releasing her grasp on her magic, she let it slip through the earth, repairing the death he had left behind.

"Goodbye, Gebael," she whispered to the stars.

TWELVE

"If we don't stop, we'll reach Kelsby by nightfall." Tilting his head back, Fox peered at the sun. "Not that it'd matter much, I suppose."

Aiden gave him a cranky look. "No, it wouldn't matter all that much. We're only riding toward thousands of armed and nervous soldiers. Scouts spotting us or not, we're better off arriving in daylight."

"Got to let them see the Queen." Merle agreed.

Eirian ignored the tension and nudged Halcyon into a trot. "If you lot don't stay sitting there talking out of your asses, we might make it there before dark."

It was easy to tell they were drawing closer to Kelsby. Soldiers had stripped the land bare firstly to provide fodder for horses and secondly to prevent the Athnaralans from setting it alight. There would be little they could do against a wildfire burning its way over the fields. Eirian knew it would be a minor feat to restore things to the way they had been before thousands of people descended upon them.

Looking over her shoulder at Faolan, she reminded herself that she needed to ask Neriwyn to do it on her behalf. Sensing her glance, Faolan met her gaze for a moment before returning to his light conversation with the two girls they had rescued from the farm. They rode on the horses left by the Athnaralans, no one willing to leave the beasts behind when they were helpful.

The sisters had taken to watching Eirian intently whenever they had the chance to, and the adoration in their eyes disturbed her. Galameyvin had done his best to soften the trauma of what they had been through. In the circle of his confidants, he had expressed his concern for their feelings toward Eirian. Careful to avoid interacting with them, she remained as aloof as she could manage.

Aiden had joked that it had only taken her saving two girls from a terrible fate to learn how to be distant.

They claimed they had kin in Kelsby, an aunt and uncle, with a tailor's shop. The elder sister, Wynn, insisted their parents had intended for her younger sister Mari to move to the town to learn the trade from them. Despite her reluctance to be near them for their sake, every time she looked at them, it filled Eirian with guilt. It was undeserved guilt. She had not needed her midnight visit with the god of death to know what happened was not her fault.

They were a reminder of the reality of war. More than the dead on the battlefield, more than the exchange of insults and empty promises of negotiation, more than burned crops and destroyed buildings. They were the innocents who paid the price for something they did not ask for. In the dark, with Celiaen's arms around her, Eirian struggled to chase away the memories of the dead and brutalized people she had failed to protect.

With no clouds in the sky, the sun's brilliance was almost oppressive against the vast expanse of blue. Occasionally, the shadow of a bird chased over the land, the repetitive call of the little brown falcon accompanying it. Eirian watched in fascination as they hovered low over the ground. Black wingtips held them in position before the birds would return to a spot where they perched to watch for prey. Catching sight of the pair circling each other before they dipped low to hover, Eirian let out a low whistle to Fox to get his attention.

"What are those birds?"

He screwed up his face, peering as he asked, "What, the kestrels? They're common as muck kestrels up this way. Don't see them further north really. They don't much like forests or the mountains. Grassland hunters."

"Nankeen," Tully said, his eyes squinting as he watched the birds. "That's what we call them. Nankeen kestrels. Don't see them near the coast often, and few nobles keep them. Pity, they're sweet little birds and useful around farms. They like insects and mice. They migrate south for winter but not all the way."

"You know your birds, Tully?" Impressed, Fox gave him an appraising look.

Winking, Tully smiled. "My father is a falconer. Luckily, my sister has shown more aptitude for it than I ever did, so the mews will remain in the family as they have for generations."

At the front of the line, Mac hollered and turned his horse sideways suddenly, forcing everyone to halt their mounts quickly. "Riders ahead!"

Looking where he pointed, they could barely make out the forms in the distance. They were too far away to tell if they were human, elf, or daoine, but the prickle of her skin told Eirian that they had magic. Signaling to the group to continue riding, she nudged Halcyon forward.

"It's a welcoming party. I guess they spotted us," Eirian said and dismissed the concerned looks given to her by Aiden and Merle.

"How can you be sure they're not the enemy?" Aiden asked.

Blowing air through her lips in annoyance, she rolled her eyes, muttering, "Magic, Aiden, always magic. If in doubt, assume magic."

"We can feel the magic," Celiaen explained, keeping his gaze on the riders. "Hopefully, they have some good news for us."

Before long, they could pick out the standards fluttering in the wind above the group of riders, and Eirian was not sure which one surprised her more. The triple sword emblem of the Kaetiel family flapped wildly at one end of the line. At the other, the four colored circles with the purple star in the center linking them hung ominously. It was the symbol of the high council. Speechless, they halted to wait for the riders to reach them. Taking the time to prepare, it did not surprise Eirian when she felt the thundering rage of Baenlin.

"Mother!" Celiaen gasped, eyes on Sannaeh, where she rode next to Baenlin.

"Celiaen, my sweet boy!"

Slipping from her horse, Sannaeh held her arms out to summon him. Knowing better than to refuse his mother, Celiaen dismounted and strode over, letting her pull him into a hug.

"Hello, Mother."

Sweeping her gaze over the lines of mages behind Baenlin, Eirian spotted Fayleen and laughed happily. "Fay!"

"Still disregarding protocol, I see." Baenlin leaned forward in his saddle, arching a brow at Eirian. "I hear you're full of surprises."

Confident in Eirian's ability to protect her from Baenlin's displeasure, Fayleen guided her horse forward. At her side, Tessa followed, and Eirian choked when she realized who it was. Looking closer at the mages, she searched for Jaren's familiar face but could not spot him or Zack.

"Did you think I'd miss helping you fight a war, sister? Don't worry, I brought help!" Fayleen declared, waving at Tessa.

"Tessa?" Eirian said, and Tessa waved her fingers with a grin.

Chuckling at Baenlin, Sannaeh kept an arm around Celiaen. "Ignore my brother. He's cranky because he missed half the fun. And possibly because he's struggling to get over the fact he never considered you might be half duine."

"Does Father know?" Celiaen demanded, stiffening beside her.

"He's delighted," Sannaeh replied, releasing him and clapping her hands. "Come, let's keep moving. There's feasting tonight in Kelsby."

Glancing between them, Eirian looked puzzled. "Why would there be a feast? We're at war, and the Athnaralans have reinforcements on the way with siege weapons."

"I suppose you've forgotten what time of year it is while you gallivanted around your kingdom, doing powers know what. First Harvest," Baenlin replied with a shake of his head.

"Is it truly the last weeks of summer?"

Offering a smile of sympathy, Sannaeh returned to her horse and said,

"Don't listen to him. It's easy to lose track of things when you have greater concerns. Honestly, I doubt there'd be anything if it hadn't been for two kings with a need to strut around crowing."

Holding the reins to the heavyset gray mare his mother was riding, Celiaen took the chance to look over the collection of mages. He was as equally surprised as Eirian at the sight of Tessa. Drawn back on each side in plaits, a purple ribbon secured her brown hair at the back of her head. While the rest of the mages wore shades of gray, Tessa stood out in bright purple that matched the ribbon in her hair. Blue eyes gleamed with amusement when she caught him staring.

Snorting at Celiaen, Baenlin glanced at the target of his stare. "We had to find a new candidate for grand mage when Her Majesty refused the position. It was amusing to see Hugh forced to rescind his harsh words regarding his daughter. She shouldn't be here, but a certain group helped her sneak out of the city."

Tessa heard him, lips curling into a smirk. "Oh, Archmage, I thought you got over that."

"I'm happy to see you, Tessa. I have so much to tell you about." Eirian bit her lip, remembering their parting. "And honestly, you'll make a far better grand mage than me."

Cocking her head, Tessa regarded Eirian thoughtfully, replying, "Thank you. I look forward to hearing all about it. You've always known how to get me excited."

"Let's just say trees used for a network of wards."

Groaning, Celiaen patted the neck of Sannaeh's mount before jogging back to his horse. Remaining at the back of the group with Faolan and the two farm girls, Galameyvin waved.

"Your Majesty, you look well."

"Don't worry, Galameyvin. Your king is not angry with you for taking off with Celiaen instead of remaining with the King of Telmia," Sannaeh informed him with a smile.

Torn between riding with Celiaen or taking the chance to catch up with Fayleen, Eirian looked at her friend for help. Fayleen inclined her head at Sannaeh and Baenlin, nodding before turning to Tessa. Shrugging, Tessa ran a hand over her hair, then moved her horse toward Baenlin. Mages rode in front, the heavily armed reds leading the way. Knowing the mages outmatched them, Eirian's guards sat at the group's back, and Celiaen's companions remained with them.

Sharing a look with Tara, Aiden muttered, "So that's your queen?"

"Let me tell you, Ree's a kitten next to her, no matter what she's capable of."

"What about her? Tessa?"

"Now she's an interesting one. Tessa's father is Archmage Hugh, he's a blue, and her mother, Riona, is a purple master. There's no family in Riane with as much power and influence as hers," Tara informed him. "Except for the one that

Baenlin and Sannaeh come from. She's mixed blood. Tessa is older than you realize."

"How old?"

"A little over forty, she was roommates with Nadinna. Until Ree arrived, she was the most powerful purple in Riane. However, Tessa is special. She tinkers and makes things like no other mage I've ever met. She has an imagination that none of us understands and the magical ability to bring her ideas to existence."

Bringing her horse around to the other side of Celiaen, Eirian kept him and Sannaeh between her and Baenlin. Aware of what she was doing, Celiaen chuckled and glanced at her with a wink.

"I thank you for coming to the defense of my kingdom, Your Majesty, and for bringing further reinforcements," Eirian said politely.

Glancing past Celiaen, Sannaeh was serious as she said, "I fear you won't like what I have to say. I knew the truth of this war years before you were born, but I was forbidden from sharing the information."

"My mother?" Swallowing back a fresh bout of anger and frustration, Eirian tightened her grip on the reins, feeling the dig of the leather against her fingers. "I suppose it shouldn't surprise me. But why?"

"Why would she tell me? Because she knew I'd listen. Paienven isn't good at listening. He'd treat everything she told him with suspicion and disregard her advice. I did my best to hint that things were not all they seemed to Baenlin and others I trusted. When Baenlin informed me you were in Riane, I convinced my husband to order Celiaen to the city to befriend you." There was a flash of dismay that crossed her face, and she admitted, "It took very little convincing. Paienven is an ambitious man."

Celiaen frowned, asking, "Is that why you always cautioned me about my relationships?"

She nodded, making him laugh in disbelief.

"If that's what you're asking, then the answer is yes, I knew the powers fated the two of you to be mates."

"Mates? Are you mated?" Baenlin demanded in shock, and he looked from Sannaeh to Celiaen before resting his hard stare on Eirian.

"Yes."

Returning his stare, Eirian tilted her head to the side, daring him to challenge her. Waving her fingers at Eirian, Sannaeh smiled happily.

"Good, I wasn't sure, especially after you initially refused to marry him."

Baenlin pressed fingers to his forehead and growled, "You recall the high council forbids such bonds, sister."

"I do, and that never stopped Paienven and I. Honestly, brother, sometimes you are so narrow-minded that I question your parentage."

Unsure how to respond to the news, Celiaen turned to Eirian and noted she was gazing at her hands resting on the pommel of her saddle. "When did

Shianeni come to you?"

Pursing her lips, Sannaeh knew he would not like her answer. "Before you were born. Shianeni told me that one day your love would help her daughter save us all."

"Tell me, did you ever seek Shianeni out once she had married my father?" Eirian asked quietly, recalling Nolan's reaction to Celiaen.

"Yes, I visited your mother in Amath. Before that, I'd visit your father and grandparents. Trying desperately to strengthen our friendship and warn them of what was coming. I think I was trying to find a spark of the power that once ran through your family."

"I don't recall you doing that," Celiaen said with a hint of confusion. "When?"

Arching a brow, Sannaeh snorted. "My dear son, I'm the Queen of Ensaycal and a Zarthein. Do you think you knew everything I was doing?"

"Well, no, I suppose I—"

"As it stands, you'll be pleased to hear that with a little sweet-talking, I convinced the high council to send an army of mages to aid in this conflict. I reminded them it was their duty to intervene and that if they failed to do so, why should any of us answer to their laws or pay taxes." Eyes flickering to Baenlin, Sannaeh said, "Besides, Eirian, I got the distinct impression my brother hoped to come to your rescue with his beloved reds."

"I had no such hope."

Sannaeh dismissed him with a wave. "I didn't tell my husband of my intention to rally Riane, so it was a surprise when we met on the road. You'll be pleased to hear the yellows have begun reinforcing the town and preparing other defensive measures."

"All I need is the time to lure the darkness out. Buy me that time, and I'll end the war," Eirian replied.

On the other side of Fayleen, Tessa said grimly, "You know, Eirian, you're not the answer to everything."

"Believe me, Tessa, if you had the right blood, I'd gladly let you fight a god instead of me."

Closing her eyes, Eirian did not respond and listened to the arguments on either side. She felt the magic surrounding them. It was like home to her, and she regretted she would never set eyes on Riane again. Beside her, Celiaen remained silent as well, mulling over the news that Paienven had arrived. Glancing over her shoulder, Eirian noted the gap between them and her guards, the humans looking uncomfortable with the situation. Meeting Aiden's gaze, she gave him a slight nod. His jaw clenched, but he returned the nod.

"Enough!" Eirian snapped. "That's enough. We have bigger things to worry about."

Reaching over, Celiaen squeezed her arm, murmuring, "You want to ask, don't you?"

"Ask what?" Baenlin enquired.

"Am I still the queen?"

Her brows furrowed, and Eirian was unsure what answer she wanted to hear. She knew which one would make her life easier, but a look at Baenlin dragged her agreement with him to the forefront of her mind.

Sannaeh said, "You're still the queen. I believe your nobles trust a queen with magic to lead them against an enemy with magic."

"You can always rely on Endaran nobility to be logical. If you could sell practicality, it would be your greatest trade commodity." Baenlin shook his head.

He did not need to look in Eirian's direction to sense the mixture of relief and disappointment.

"Of course, the most logical and practical solution is to leave things as they are. I suppose it helps that the direct line is unbroken. So, I remain the queen for now. It makes little difference to what I have to do, and it certainly won't change the outcome," Eirian told them.

Finally looking at her, Baenlin did not see what he had expected to see. Instead, a look of resignation confronted him. She looked tired, flickers of grief crossing her features when she thought people were not paying attention.

"We all must play our part and do our duty."

Her eyes shot to him, deep fury fueling a fire in them while her magic flared outwards. The faint scent of flowers deepened, bordering on sickening.

"Do not presume to speak to me about duty! I understand far better than you what my duty is."

Clearing his throat, Celiaen noted the sheen of color creeping across the land. "Ree."

"No, Celi." Holding up a hand, she pointed at Baenlin. "You don't know what the cost of this war will be."

"Are those wildflowers appearing everywhere?" Tessa asked, receiving a scolding look from Fayleen that silenced her next question before the words left her tongue.

"Well then, girl, why don't you tell me what the cost will be?" Baenlin demanded without flinching, his horse striding along calmly beneath him.

Dandelion seeds filled the air, Eirian's power fueling the rapid development of the plant. Vibrant colors covered the ground, the signs of what the soldiers had done vanishing beneath the influx of growth.

"My life. It may cost the life of your nephew as they bound him to me. If I'm not powerful enough on my own, I might have to draw from those around me."

Sannaeh had never seen such a display of power, awe filling her face and those of the other mages accompanying them as more and more flowers covered the land. Horses attempted to snatch mouthfuls of the lush grass they moved through. Accustomed to her displays, the guards did not bat an eyelid at the array of colors spreading as they continued.

Swaying in the breeze, flowers turned cheery faces toward Eirian instead of the sun. Many of the mages swore it appeared the plants were reaching out for the powerful woman in their midst. The sounds of insects came chasing the petals of the flowers, the magic causing an influx of life. Brushing strands of hair away from her face, Fayleen realized that her straw-colored locks were growing again and huffed.

"Every time you get annoyed with the archmage, I end up needing my hair cut," she grouched at Eirian, causing her to stop glaring at Baenlin. "At least here you aren't creating extra work for some poor gardeners."

"Have you always been able to do this?" Tessa asked enviously.

Eirian murmured, "Yes."

"How long have you known about it, Celiaen?" Sannaeh asked.

He shrugged. "Since we met. I helped keep it a secret from the council."

"How long have the two of you been bound?"

"Ten years, give or take," Eirian answered, omitting the fact that they had only completed the bond recently.

"How curious that you made our agreement." Pretending to be unimpressed by her display, Baenlin said, "Did your mate and future wife tell you about our agreement?"

Their dark eyes were almost identical, but the cold look Celiaen directed at Baenlin made him suppress a shudder. "Aye, she did. I wish you luck holding her to it."

"Surely you agree she belongs in Riane, not Endara?"

"No, I don't. Eirian's the daughter of Nolan Altira and Shianeni Malfaer, heir to both Endara and Telmia. Do you believe the position of grand mage means anything to someone with such a destiny as hers?" Celiaen threw his response at Baenlin.

Beside him, Eirian sighed. "That doesn't matter. I have one purpose left."

"But you're the most power—"

Sannaeh cut him off, silencing his argument. "No more, brother. It's the eve of First Harvest. Let's forget the politics, the power plays, and, dare I suggest it, the war as well. Now tell me, Eirian, those two girls don't strike me as noble-women, and I wasn't aware you took any ladies with you on this little jaunt. Who are they?"

The question brought a chill to the air. Memories of mangled corpses and her actions made Eirian shrink slightly into her saddle.

"We rescued them from a band of Athnaralans who were murdering, raping, and pillaging their way across my land. They have kin in Kelsby, so we brought them with us to reunite them with their surviving family."

"They're fortunate you reached them before anything terrible happened," Tessa spoke, a hint of hope in her voice.

Knowing the look in Eirian's eye, Fayleen felt a pang of grief for the two girls behind them. "I hope you made them pay for what they did."

"Do you doubt it, sister?" Eirian said, her voice hoarse.

Nodding to Celiaen, Baenlin asked, "Did you get any useful information?"

"Eirian was kind enough to leave us three alive to question. We found out numbers, but I doubt it's new information."

"You have a habit of saving people, Eirian Altira." Sannaeh gave Eirian a deep look of understanding. "I met your sweet little ward. I've dispatched people to locate her parents. Hopefully, we'll reunite her with them."

"Thank you. Ona is a dear child."

More memories of the dead that Eirian wished would stop haunting her rose to the forefront of her mind. They competed with the whispers of her mother's memories, becoming a deafening noise. No matter how much time they spent apart, Fayleen could always sense how she felt. She wanted to cheer Eirian up by telling her about her gift.

"I have a surprise for you when we get back to Kelsby. Remember how I said I wanted to experiment with your armor?"

Thankful for the distraction, Eirian turned her focus to Fayleen. "I do. I told you not to bother because I was leaving for Amath and would hardly need it."

"Well, I finished it with a little help from Tessa. She had some interesting ideas I think you'll appreciate."

Excited to talk about her project, Fayleen caught sight of the three warriors listening in. Unwilling to put a damper on her excitement, Eirian offered her a smile.

"I look forward to seeing it. Though as you can see, I'm wearing mail."

There was a flicker of disapproval on Fayleen's face as she let her magic brush over Eirian. "I noticed. I know every piece of armor you have, so I knew it wasn't mage crafted. What possessed you to wear mail in the first place?"

"I did." Aiden nudged his horse forward until he was partially between them. "I thought it would be prudent to ensure she was better protected since she's determined not to stay out of the fight."

Tessa glanced at him with a curious smile. "And you are?"

"He's the captain." Fayleen giggled, winking at Aiden.

"That's him? I expected someone older."

Looking from Fayleen to Aiden, Eirian clenched her jaw and muttered, "Aiden is more than proficient at his job. I couldn't ask for a better captain to command my guard."

Snorting, Baenlin leaned back to grin at Aiden. "Have you seen what she is yet?"

Turning to stare at Baenlin, Aiden smirked. "I know better than you what she is. I've seen her power personified, a brilliant, pure light against which no darkness could stand."

"Why, Captain, don't quit your job because you wouldn't make a poet."

Clicking his tongue, Celiaen chuckled. "Careful, uncle, you almost sound jealous."

"Anyway, Aiden gave me the mail. It took a little while to get used to it again, but eventually, the weight stopped bothering me."

Dismissing the exchanges between the men, Eirian twisted strands of Halcyon's mane between her fingertips and watched his ears flick. Nodding, Fayleen beamed with pride.

"You'll not need it once I give you your new armor. I spent countless hours searching through dusty tomes in parts of the libraries that hardly anyone visits looking for inspiration. That's what attracted Tessa to my project. I found her buried in one of the oldest library chambers, and she took an interest in what I was trying to do."

"Indeed!" Tessa agreed. "It helped that I knew you'd be more open-minded than others and willing to try new things. Now tell me about these trees?"

"They're remnants from the mage wars. Trees a thousand or more years old growing in a forest to the south, next to Forrestfield. A network of them linked between two ancient keeps built by mages far more adventurous than we are."

"We went through there," Fayleen said.

"In the little time we had, a few of us tested what we could do. At the very least, each person could connect and use it to sense people within varying proximity of the trees." Thinking about the forest, Eirian frowned, her lips parting to ask a question she was unsure how to word.

Sensing her flurried thoughts, Celiaen said, "You've had an idea."

"It's the concept of the network. I mean, we can link living mages over a distance, power to power, but what if we bound wards into objects and spread those out?"

"To what purpose?" Tessa gasped at the idea, her mind swirling with the possibilities.

"Any purpose that could help us dismantle the siege weapons, but I'm not fussy."

Smiling slowly, Tessa glanced sideways and purred, "I'll show you something I've been working on. I think you'll find it... delightful."

"You've got my attention, Tessa," Eirian replied.

Tessa met Aiden's suspicious stare, and the smile became a grin. "You see, Captain, I'm unarmed, unlike the others, including our sweet Fayleen. I'm no skilled warrior, though I can defend myself with a blade. What I am, however, is creative. I see magical solutions to questions you haven't even asked yet."

His eyes shifted to the cheeky woman who called his queen sister. It sat uncomfortably that he had not perceived her weapons and armor previously. Fayleen's smug look in his direction told Aiden she had not intended for anyone to notice them.

"Were you so armed in Amath when we last met, Fayleen?"

"Indeed, Captain, and if you'd taken me up on my invitation, you might have noticed," Fayleen said, glancing him over suggestively, lips curling.

"Are you trying to seduce my guard?" Eirian scoffed, fighting back her jealousy.

Poking out her tongue at Eirian, Fayleen laughed. "I'm still trying, but I fear the good captain has eyes for nothing other than his duty, and I can appreciate that."

"You said that King Neriwyn and King Paienven were..." Changing the subject, Eirian looked at Sannaeh.

"They're like peacocks flashing their tails at each other," Sannaeh grumbled.

"What festivities do they plan for First Harvest? I'm concerned we're on the edge of a battlefield, and such things would leave us vulnerable to the enemy."

"The Athnaralans are also planning celebrations. It's First Harvest, after all. The King of Telmia convinced my husband to let him make all the arrangements by assuring him he would provide everything, including wine. Which I believe was what sealed it. Paienven has a fondness for Telmian wines."

Choking back a laugh, Celiaen glanced back over his shoulder at Galameyvin. "He's not the only one. They are rather fine wines."

Following his glance, Sannaeh said, "Your cousin developed a taste for more than Telmian wines, I heard."

"So Telmian celebrations, which means food and drink, music, and dancing." Sighing heavily, Eirian scolded herself for forgetting about the yearly festival. "I suppose we should be thankful it's just First Harvest and not the First Planting celebrations."

Holding out a hand to her, Celiaen said cheekily, "Oh, I don't know, dear heart. Perhaps next year, we could plant a few seeds of our own to ensure a bountiful harvest."

"That's hardly a respectful thing to say to a queen in public," Sannaeh lightly scolded him with a smile.

"I've heard Father say far worse to you."

Her brow arched, and she told Eirian, "You have my permission to wallop him whenever he thinks he is free to behave as such. These men believe they're allowed liberties because they have cock, and someone told them they're in charge. You and I, though, we know differently."

Eirian inclined her head. "The Great Mother created the world."

"You've met some Indari? Yes, I rather like their version of things, and perhaps they are not so wrong if our great enemy is indeed a god."

Swallowing the sudden taste of bile that rose at the back of her throat, Eirian wished she could tell everyone the truth. The icy whisper of memories reminded her why she could not, and, struggling against their pull, she looked to the sun.

"What do you think of the Indari?" Eirian asked to distract herself.

Looking out over the flowering land, Sannaeh wondered what Paienven would make of Eirian. If his reaction to Tessa was anything to go off, she did not see it ending well.

"I find them incredible. Their ability to not only survive but thrive in a part of the land that others call uninhabitable is a testimony to our abilities to adapt. I don't know if they've forgotten or if it is a secret kept from downlanders, but I couldn't find out why they settled in the mountains."

"Have you been up there, Mother?" Celiaen asked.

"I have," Baenlin replied, tugging at his coat where it had caught under his leg. "The high council tried to convince them to send their gifted children to Riane. Unfortunately, my endeavors were unsuccessful."

"And rightly so." Eirian ignored his annoyed look. "Why change something that works so well? We've no right to meddle in their affairs. Or to demand they give their children over to a far-off city. Especially when it's filled with self-righteous and ignorant people who've buried themselves in doctrines so deeply, they've forgotten half the knowledge of their ancestors."

"Harsh words from one so young!"

"Long overdue words. My ancestor didn't die imprisoning a mad god so that some self-absorbed council of mages could forget where they came from and who founded their home. If it weren't for her, there would be no Riane."

"Eirian," Aiden murmured cautiously.

"Heed me, Archmage. I'll not die so Riane can continue to pretend it's greater than everyone else." Kicking her heels into Halcyon's side, Eirian let him leap ahead into a canter.

THIRTEEN

It was that funny in between light when the sun dipped below the horizon, but its luminescence had not completely faded. When the first stars became visible, the eyes played tricks with the shadows. People called it a tween time, but no one remembered why. Eirian had always felt an affinity for it. Standing beside Halcyon, staring at the fires with people gathering to celebrate the First Harvest, she questioned if it was another thing her mother had manipulated.

Flitting among the humans and elves, the daoine had dressed to suit the ethereal nature everyone believed of them. Neriwyn had done what he could to encourage everyone to forget that they were an army on the edge of a battle-field. A tossed head and the stamp of a hoof brought Eirian back into focus, and she glanced at her guards. They had split from the others, intending to return to the keep before joining the celebrations.

"Come on, ma'am, let's get you cleaned up so you can play with the other royalty." Aiden chuckled, looking forward to watching Paienven meet her.

"I doubt Brenna and Isabella are waiting in my chamber on the off chance I go there."

He did not respond as they walked through the heavily guarded gates into the town itself. The two girls had huddled together. Their memories made them fearful of the sprawling city of tents housing thousands of soldiers. Remaining close, Faolan whistled softly to Eirian, receiving a nod of agreement. Coaxing them away with the suggestion they find their family, it surprised Faolan when Gabe silently joined them.

Directing half his men to deal with their horses and belongings, Aiden remained close to Eirian. Relatively empty, the keep was well-lit, and people had strung wreaths of flowers across walls and above doorways. Knowing some daoine could grow things, she did not question where they had gotten the blooms. It was strange to be back inside the stone walls. A pang of loss settled into her heart at the thought that they had to return to the formality expected of them.

There was no one waiting in her chamber, though the fire and lanterns were lit, and Eirian shrugged at Aiden. "Told you."

"I'll send someone to get water." Rolling his eyes at her smug attitude, Aiden did a double check of her chamber before waving at what they had laid out on her bed. "They might not be here, but they were expecting you."

She stared at it, nose crinkling in annoyance as she said, "I don't want to wear a dress."

"Darling, it's First Harvest. Put the fucking dress on, wear whatever jewels you have, and go down there and charm the bloody world. Your people need to see you relax for a moment so that they feel alright doing so themselves. A lot are going to die. Give them this."

Shooting her a look over his shoulder, Aiden shook his head before leaving. Huffing, Eirian began unbuckling her weapons. She knew he was right. Laying her swords down next to the heavy chest, she knelt to lift the lid and rummage through. Tucked away among her clothes was the pouch with her mother's diadem, which she pulled out and placed beside her. It felt heavier than she recalled, but she dismissed it and moved on, putting her weapons and belts inside the chest.

Not bothering to grab the slippers to wear, Eirian decided keeping her boots on was a more sensible option. Leaning on the chest to stand, a knock at the door startled her, and she called out for the guard to enter. Lyle slipped into the room with a bucket of water, nodding as he filled the washbowl. He left the rest of the water in the bucket on the ground beside it. Then, giving a quick salute, he hurried out so Eirian could get on.

Stripping out of her clothes, she left them in a pile. When she dipped a washcloth into the bowl, her first thought was an amused one, comparing the temperature to that of the streams they had bathed in while they journeyed. While it was not a bath, the cloth did an adequate job of cleaning away most of the dirt and dried sweat. Satisfied, Eirian turned her attention to the pile of material on the bed.

At first glance, it appeared a deep green, but when she picked it up, the light caught the strands of gold woven in. As it slipped through her fingers, Eirian realized it was layers of almost translucent fabric, quite unlike anything she had encountered before. The base layer was solid, and rubbing it between her fingertips, she decided it was not ordinary silk. Its deep green and gold coloration shimmered, feeling much more delicate than the silk used for her coronation gown.

Carefully slipping it over her head, Eirian discovered that when she got her arms into the sleeves, they were not sleeves at all. Instead, they split at the shoulder, leaving great swaths of fabric cascading down. Spinning, she watched the upper layers flutter and knew the gown was of Telmian craftsmanship. The inner layer of silk fitted her perfectly and rolled over, draping low across her neckline. Glancing down, she was thankful there was no train, the hem of the dress only just touching the ground.

Her eyes caught how the layers of transparent fabric sat, realizing they were like flower petals and laid on top of each other. Returning to the washstand, Eirian picked up the hairbrush to drag it through her hair. Flinching at every knot it encountered, she tidied up the long brown tresses before turning her focus to the pouch on top of the chest. Loosening the ties, she tipped the diadem out and gasped when it came out entangled with a second item. She carefully freed the two objects, letting the diadem drop onto the bed while examining the necklace.

"That looks like it's a match," Aiden commented, leaning against the doorway.

"Faolan has been with us, though, so he didn't add it to the pouch."

Walking over, Aiden plucked the necklace from her hands and indicated for her to turn around. "I doubt he had anything to do with this finding its way to you. He may have crafted it, but the only one who'd have had access to it would be his king."

Feeling the weight of the necklace settle against her, Eirian brushed her hand over it. "It feels like he planned this entire outfit."

"Perhaps he wants you to make an impression. I've seen you in some fine gowns, but nothing that suited you as perfectly. Now, all you need to add is that last piece, and I'd say you're ready."

His hands lingered at the back of her neck when he finished securing the clasp of the necklace. Eirian's breath caught at the feeling of his fingers dancing across her skin. Her reaction did not go unmissed, and Aiden chuckled. The whispers in her mind laughed with him. Choosing to step away, she picked up the pile of metals and stones and began working it into her hair.

"I might not be wearing the crown of Endara, but I feel like this one might be a little more symbolic."

* * *

"Your Majesty." Bowing to Paienven, Celiaen cast a sideways glance at Galameyvin, noting his blank expression. "I'm pleased and surprised by your presence here."

Paienven regarded his eldest son coldly, replying, "And your lack of presence here when I arrived surprised me. I sent you here to secure the north and to secure King Aeyren."

"My apologies, sire, but there was something else you wished of me, and it was that which took me away from this place."

"Ah yes, I've heard many things about our dear Queen Eirian Altira since I arrived."

Watching Paienven signal to those surrounding him, Celiaen met Sannaeh's stare, where she lingered in the shadows, observing in silence.

"The news of her mother's identity was a great shock for all of us. Her Majesty has been struggling with the revelation and feels a great deal of resentment toward the late queen."

Eyes narrowing, Paienven snorted. "Have you bedded her yet?"

"She has agreed to marry me."

"That's not what I asked you, boy."

Stepping forward, Sannaeh placed a hand on his arm. "My love, our son has taken a page from our book."

Celiaen swallowed, knowing what she was telling him to say. "Indeed, sire, we're mates, completely and irreversibly bound."

There was a flicker of shock in the pale blue eyes, and Galameyvin felt them shift to him. Surprise turned into assessment, Paienven keeping his stare on him long enough that Galameyvin glanced away uncomfortably. Once he did, the king returned his gaze to Celiaen.

"Perhaps you haven't been a total disappointment, Celiaen. However, I understand she doesn't expect to survive this war with our enemy."

"If anyone can end it and survive, it's her. You don't know Eirian. She's a survivor."

"She's the daughter of Shianeni Malfaer. I imagine she's many things none of us knows." His memories of the Telmian queen were cloudy, but Paienven remembered enough. "Do you realize she may spark a civil war within Telmia if she survives?"

Contemplating the answer he would give, Celiaen glanced at Galameyvin from the corner of his eye. He had lectured him in depth over the subject.

"Eirian feels that considering her father is human, she's not the rightful queen of Telmia simply because she's a female. She believes her older half-brother has a far greater claim. Being both full duine and the son of Neriwyn."

"That is all well and good, but her considerations won't stop those who believe she belongs on the throne."

"She doesn't want it. She barely wants the Endaran throne, but Eirian knows her duty comes before her desires," Galameyvin spoke quietly, half expecting Paienven to strike him.

There was a flash of fury in Paienven's eyes as he stared at Galameyvin, but it faded to the gleam of affection he usually held for him. "I was furious with you, Galameyvin, but I understand Neriwyn suggested you share your understanding of Telmia with Eirian."

Pursing his lips, Galameyvin hid his surprise. "Indeed, he did. He was aware of our long friendship and felt I might help ease some of her turmoil over the news of her heritage. I suspect that had I not been here, she wouldn't have handled it so well."

"You've always had a way with people."

"Apologies, Your Majesties," a man spoke from the back of the tent. "But I thought I should inform you that Queen Eirian has appeared."

Sannaeh held up a hand to Celiaen, seeing his desire to join Eirian, and said, "Wait a while, Celiaen. Your uncle needs to speak with her regarding council business."

* * *

"**Y**our Majesty," Baenlin said, offering an exaggerated bow accompanied by a challenging smirk in Aiden's direction. "May I say that you look exquisite?"

The dress was unlike any she had worn before, and Eirian accepted the compliment without reservations. She felt the intoxicating energy of thousands of people trying to enjoy themselves, and her mind spun from the effects of it.

"You may. What can I do for you, Archmage Baenlin?"

Offering his arm, Baenlin arched a brow in amusement when she carefully placed her hand on it. Her action let him see the Endaran seal that graced her finger.

"Straight to business then? You don't wish to make any small talk?"

"I doubt twenty years at court would see me improve my small talk."

"You've never been good at subtleties. The warrior runs too strong in you."

Snorting, she shook her head. "Or perhaps I'm respecting you by not wasting your time with pointless chatter? I doubt you appreciate these festivities any more than I do."

Giving her a pointed look, he let his eyes drift down the length of her and took in the way the silk clung as she moved. His response earned him a low growl from Aiden.

"I wouldn't say I dislike them completely. They appear to have some benefits, and I'm sure your captain agrees. Celiaen and Galameyvin certainly will. Rylee is fluttering around somewhere. I'm sure she'll find you soon enough."

"Look all you like, Archmage. That's the only thing you'll ever get to do." Eirian rolled her eyes. "I should know better than to expect you to be above such things."

"I find myself most disappointed that I must release you from our agreement."

She had suspected he would, but did not let it show. "How unfortunate. Of course, it would've been near impossible to hold me to it."

"I know you to be a person of honor. If circumstances freed you to fulfil the agreement, you would have done so," Baenlin said and pointed at her hand. "We raised you to know only duty. That is not something you can change overnight."

"Do you know Celiaen plans to renounce his right to the throne of Ensaycal so that he may return to Riane?"

Watching people surrounding a fire, laughing, and sharing drinks while others began striking up the music, Baenlin sighed. "We've spoken about it over the years. He's a Zarthein. Now it depends on you, doesn't it? Celiaen is powerful, probably powerful enough to withstand the breaking of your bond, but only if he wants to live."

Eirian heard the anger in his voice, coupled with anguish. It did not help her guilt.

"It's no consolation, but I want you to know we didn't do it of our own accord. The gods planned it for us without our consent. I also want you to know I'll do everything to ensure he survives. When I die, remember I fought with every drop of blood in my body, every fragment of power, to keep him alive."

"I forgot how predisposed you were toward noble sentiment. It's almost sickening. However, I understand what you're saying, and I'd expect no less from you, Eirian Altira."

She caught the faint lilt of Saoirse's singing. She would recognize that voice anywhere. It haunted the memories, slipping through cracks in the whispers to remind Eirian of lazy mornings in bed, bathed in sunlight and hair that shone a vibrant red.

"There are things I've learned that I fear won't come out should I die. My mother weaved magic on the land that made everyone forget, and Neriwyn either will not or cannot change that. I don't trust him, so I suspect the former."

He frowned, asking softly, "Whatever do you speak of?"

"The gods gave us but one tongue with which to speak. There are lands beyond ours, lands filled with people. Humans. Elves. Daoine. And others, so many others."

"How do you know this?"

Turning to face Baenlin, Eirian tightened her grip on his arm and gazed at him. "A privilege of my heritage. I'm telling you because I trust you not to take advantage of the information."

Baenlin was stiff, mind whirling with the information she had given him. They reminded him of all the stories he was told as a child. Ones he had dismissed as he had the tales involving the darkness.

"If that's true, why have we never encountered them? Surely we would have?"

Looking to the side, Eirian turned back to him with a sad expression. "Shianeni Malfaer did a lot to this world that we shouldn't forgive her for. Think about it, Archmage. For a thousand or more years we've lingered in this stalemate, bickering over the same tracts of land and the same insults. Where is our progress? We haven't improved. We haven't grown since the end of the mage wars. Quite the opposite, to be honest. We treat those who think like Tessa with scorn instead of embracing them. We fear new things, and refuse to change when we should face it like the dawn of a new day."

"You're saying they trapped us in a pit, and we aren't looking for a way out?"

"Yes, and I don't know how to fix it, but I feel as though telling the right people Shianeni did something to us will allow them to help find a way out. If enough people know the lingering shadow in the corner of their eye is real, they can overcome it."

"She's dead and can't stop her magic from being undone. That's what you're saying. So you want me to return to Riane and force the council to look beyond our borders." The prospect intrigued him, and Baenlin mulled over what they might find elsewhere. "But what if her magic is everywhere and not just here?"

Cocking her head to the side, Eirian searched the night sky. "I want you to whisper in the ears of those with the right minds. Those with the desire to go forth and discover."

Behind them, Aiden coughed. Winking over her shoulder at him, Eirian's lips curled in a knowing smirk she directed at Baenlin.

"After all, Archmage, you watch everyone worth watching, so I trust you know the right people to whisper to."

Returning the smirk, he raised his brows. "Why, Your Majesty, are you suggesting I manipulate things?"

"Of course not. I would never be so bold."

The sound of Fayleen calling diverted their attention. Watching her scamper toward them, with Tessa trailing behind, Eirian squeezed the arm beneath her hand and offered him a thankful look. Inclining his head slightly, Baenlin acknowledged her gratitude for things he had yet to do on her behalf. Tessa was tossing a strange object up and down in her hand, firelight catching it occasionally and reflecting off whatever she had made it from.

Before the two women reached them, he turned back to Eirian. "Survive this war, and abdicate the Endaran throne. You belong in Riane."

"If I survive this war, I need to find out what my mother did to the world and why, so I can undo it," she answered.

It was challenging to keep her eyes from straying in his direction. Eirian knew there was no chance of her surviving the fight, but she refused to waste time arguing. Far better to let everyone around her cling to a shred of hope.

"There's no better place to start than in Riane. If you want to fight back against her actions, then start there."

"Eirian!" Fayleen finally reached them, her eyes going wide at the sight of what she was wearing. "By the powers, you look like a queen."

Scoffing, Tessa gave Fayleen a mocking look. "Really, Fay? Of course she looks like a queen. She is a queen!"

"You know what I mean." Waving at her simple gray tunic and trousers, Fayleen shrugged.

Half bowing to the two women, Eirian greeted them patiently. "Fay, Tessa."

"Your Majesty." Tessa tossed the strange ball into the air, catching it easily before throwing it to Eirian. "Catch."

Startled, Eirian caught it and looked at it. "It's glass?"

"Finely blown glass with wards included as I worked it."

"What's inside?"

Rolling it around in her hand, Eirian felt the magic worked through it. But the strange substance inside baffled her. There was a sly look on Tessa's face when she flicked her hand at it, and the ball rose high above them.

"Watch."

Staring into the sky, the three mages and the Queen's guards waited for something to happen. Magic rippled, followed by a bright flash and a bang that startled them. Instinctively, Fayleen cast a ward, and Baenlin regarded Tessa with a newfound curiosity. People were shouting in fear all over the camp, many rushing to find weapons, thinking they were under attack. Responding swiftly, Aiden ordered his men to spread out and inform others it was not an attack but simply a mage doing mage things.

"Okay, I'll bite. What was that?" Baenlin asked.

"I'm calling it fire powder. It's a mix of substances I discovered by accident. I don't have many of those orbs, but I may have enough to help take care of the siege weapons," Tessa said, keeping her gaze on Eirian.

Taking a deep breath, Eirian watched the chaos of people surrounding them. She appreciated what Tessa had shown her, but not the method in which she had done so.

"Why is it that purples have the greatest flair for the dramatic?"

"You approve then?"

"Of course, but you didn't need to show us like that. People are celebrating."

Shrugging, Tessa grinned. "We should make the most of it. We'll explain it was a demonstration of how the mages intended to deal with the siege weaponry. It wasn't my idea. Jaren thought it'd make an impression, and you know what my brother is like."

"She has a point." Aiden involved himself in the conversation. "It would offer some reassurance to the non-magical masses that you lot have a plan."

Biting her lip, Eirian glanced up to where the explosion had happened. "At what distance can you activate the wards?"

"Probably not as great a distance as you can," Tessa replied challengingly.

"You've given me an idea, but I don't know how to execute it. I'm afraid I'm not as creative as you are, Tessa. Those would damage most weaponry, more so if it's made from timber. However, if you could get pitch onto them," Baenlin said and smiled slowly, sharing a look with Aiden as he caught on.

Feeling their gazes settle on her, Eirian sighed. "Don't look at me like that! I can provide the power, the distraction, and probably the precision, but it's up to Tessa and the rest of you to devise how. Honestly, I don't have all the answers."

Scratching her head, the ideas already forming, Tessa focused on Aiden. He blinked at her, mildly unsettled by the intensity in her eyes.

"How easily accessible is clay? For maximum impact, we'd want many, and probably small, vessels to spread something like pitch. We'd need a decent splash zone."

"Thank you for your demonstration, Tessa, but I've seen enough death in recent days that I'd rather enjoy the celebrations. I'll lend my magic as best I can, in whatever way you require it, but I doubt I'm of any use to you while you devise your plans," Eirian said.

She felt Celiaen approaching through the crowds of people, relief coursing through her at the prospect of being rescued from the conversation.

"Are you sure?" Tessa looked baffled. "I mean, it's just First Harvest. I thought you—"

"I'm sure."

Celiaen materialized out of the crowd and stopped short at the sight of her. Beaming, Eirian walked away from the group to join him. Behind her, Fayleen sighed and gave Aiden a knowing look, seeing the conflict in his eyes. Noticing Sannaeh and Paienven a small distance away, Baenlin glanced between them and the younger duo.

When she reached Celiaen, Eirian placed her hand in his, their matching rings clinking, and allowed him to twirl her around. Laughing, she crinkled her nose before looking him over. He wore the clothes he had worn for her coronation, embroidery catching in the firelight.

"You look rather dashing tonight, Your Highness."

He purred, "I'm afraid my dashing good looks pale before the beauty that is the Queen of Endara."

"You're full of shit."

Her laughter died off when she saw Sannaeh leaning on the arm of a fair-haired man she knew had to be Paienven. Closing his eyes, Celiaen wished his parents had not followed.

"Your Majesty, I'd like to introduce King Paienven of Ensaycal."

Paienven looked at her, trying his best to spot something that would identify Eirian as different from the rest of them. Something that would make her stand out. All he saw was a pretty young woman who looked human, despite the glow of her skin.

"So, you're the wondrous Eirian Altira, the one who is to be our savior. I expected… more."

She did not care for his tone and arched an eyebrow. "And you're the great Paienven Kaetiel, the man who united the elves into one kingdom. Thank you for lending your help to Endara at this time of conflict. My people appreciate everything you've done for them."

"Polite and praising. You took some lessons in manners then."

Beside her, Celiaen held his breath and hoped Eirian would not lose her temper with Paienven. He sensed her disapproval and the anger still simmering after all they had encountered in recent weeks. Her hand was in his, and he squeezed it, receiving a sharp look in return. To the side, Galameyvin took a step closer and let his calming influence wash over the more volatile warriors.

A haughty smile curled the corners of Eirian's mouth before she latched onto Galameyvin's power and twisted it into Paienven. She turned it from the simple calm he had intended into something more inebriating, careful not to let it affect anyone else. A dazed expression appeared on Paienven's face, and it startled Sannaeh, making her tighten her hold.

"What have you done?" she said.

"Gosh, it's a beautiful night." Paienven smiled at his wife dreamily. "You're so beautiful, my sweet. Do you think the stars look brighter?"

Continuing to smile, Eirian replied, "He wanted a demonstration. So, I gave him one."

Baenlin had gone cold behind her, sharing a look with Tessa. "You took over Galameyvin's power and used it."

"I did. Would you have rather I choke the life out of him with mine?" She gave him a look over her shoulder that told Baenlin she knew he would have been happy to see her do it.

"Queen Sannaeh, I'd suggest you make the most of the celebrations. Your husband will be in an exceedingly good mood for most of the night."

Paienven stared at the stars in amazement, rambling, "I think they are. Perhaps I should have a new palace built in the northern region of Ensaycal with an open court where we can do business under the sky."

"You know you could have made your point another way," Sannaeh replied.

"I could have, but he'll remember this with more caution. When he comes to his senses, remind him he forgot his manners first. I have no interest in posturing." Turning a warm smile to Celiaen, she inclined her head to a fire. "Shall we find our friends? I heard Saoirse singing, so I know they aren't far."

Celiaen looked around. "That sounds like a wonderful idea. Gal, are you joining us?"

Not letting his anger over Eirian's use of his power show, Galameyvin nodded. "I enjoy listening to Saoirse sing. What about you, Fay?"

"Have you ever known me to turn down drinking and merry-making?" Fayleen flung her arm around his waist. "Maybe I'll find a nice duine for myself since the good captain insists on turning me down."

Stiffening, Galameyvin shot a glance at Aiden, muttering, "Well, they're the giving sort, so it shouldn't be too hard to find one."

"I'm counting on it, Gal. I don't suppose you have any suggestions for me? I hear you have ample experience." Giggling, she nudged him in encouragement to follow Celiaen and Eirian.

Watching them depart, Tessa turned to Baenlin with a hint of fear. "Have you?"

"No."

"Then it made you as uncomfortable?"

"Yes." Baenlin observed Sannaeh attempting to usher Paienven away, the king distracted by every little thing that caught his eye.

"Good to know." Rocking back on her heels, Tessa sighed. "I suppose I can forgive you for wanting her to lead the council."

He turned to study her, remembering what Tessa had shown him she could do. In combination with her exploding glass orb and the attitude she approached the war with, Baenlin saw advantages.

"I suppose. Eirian is immensely powerful, but I see how you might be a different sort of change. Perhaps you're the sort of change we need."

Taken aback by his statement, Tessa made a slight noise of amusement. "Perhaps working with you won't be as great a chore as I feared. Do you want to follow them?"

"Yes. After all, how often does one get to observe the Telmians in their natural state."

She looked confused. "Their natural state?"

"Aye, all of this." He waved at bonfires, saying, "The music, dancing, wine. I suspect many will flock to Queen Eirian, surrounding her like butterflies to flower."

"Are you coming, Tessa?" Fayleen turned back and hollered to them.

Offering his arm, Baenlin inclined his head as she took it. He had been hard on Tessa from the outset, attempting to establish his control over her position in Riane. Soren had suggested she would be easy to win over if he softened his attitude. Watching her show off her creation, he had seen the eagerness in her stance. Every little thing that could be taken as praise had made Tessa preen.

"I'd be wary the young yellow might attach herself to you in the absence of Eirian."

They strolled together, watching the backs of the four ahead. Observing Tessa from the corner of his eye, Baenlin noticed the faint smile curling her lips. He would discuss it with Soren, gauge his opinion on if the careful feeding of praise would be enough to sway her to his side.

"Fay has more potential than you give her credit for. No one thinks of her as anything more than Eirian's lackey. She might not be the most powerful, but she's far from weak. Besides, Fay has a keen mind and a willingness to learn. Hiding things is something she learned from a master."

"She's not the only one who hasn't been given the credit she's due," he said. "You might be the one who saves Kelsby."

Tessa smiled wistfully, lifting her gaze to the sky. Glancing away to hide his smirk, Baenlin decided gaining control of the high council would not be as tedious a task as he thought.

FOURTEEN

Following the sound of Saoirse's singing, Eirian enjoyed the thrum of music filling the air. The drums in the distance complimented the beat of thousands of hearts, calling to her magic. It surprised her that Neriwyn had not appeared, and lifting her free hand to the jewels draped across her neck, she wondered who of the Telmian court would come to her first. Attracted by her movement, Celiaen studied the elegant necklace she wore.

"Matches the diadem."

"Indeed."

"Where did the dress come from? I've not seen anything like it."

"And you're not likely to see anything like it again." Vartan appeared, saying, "It's been a long time since we could harvest the source of the material."

Eirian pursed her lips, dropping her hand. "And where did this dress come from?"

"Why ask a question you already know the answer to?"

"Knowing and suspecting is not the same. Am I taller than my mother, or was the length of the skirts intended?"

"It's spider silk," Galameyvin murmured.

Vartan smirked, enjoying the group's baffled looks. He had questioned Neriwyn's intentions with the dress, and seeing Eirian in it had taken his breath away. If he had not known better, he would have thought it was Shianeni moving through the crowds. She would face that reaction from most of the daoine, which was precisely why Neriwyn had done it.

"Indeed, it is. And yes, your mother was a little shorter, but she was never one for long trains. She liked the freedom of movement when she danced. Do you dance, little queen?"

There was laughter among her friends and guards, making Eirian scowl. Crossing her arms, she shot a glare at Celiaen and Aiden when they grinned knowingly at each other. Unsure why his question had elicited such a response, it was Vartan's turn to look around in confusion.

"No, I don't dance."

"A pity." He bowed to her, murmuring, "I would've liked to dance with you."

"Spider silk?" Eirian asked curiously.

Chuckling softly, Vartan nodded. He suspected she would not appreciate his explanation, but offered it anyway without saying Shianeni's name.

"Yes, in a far corner of Telmia is a forest where giant spiders live, and they spin webs of the softest, finest, and toughest silk. Once, there was one among us who could walk through that forest unharmed and gain the permission of the spiders for us to harvest the silk."

"Say no more."

Unable to resist asking, Celiaen ignored the look on Eirian's face. "I take it the person was the late queen?"

Coughing, Galameyvin glanced at Fayleen. "Read the mood, Celi."

Agreeing with him, Fayleen bustled forward and broke in between her two friends, declaring, "Come on, Ree, I can smell the wine calling my name!"

Grateful for her intervention, Eirian slung her arm around Fayleen's waist. The whispers returned, breaking through the slight giddiness of her magic caused by the crowd. She hesitated briefly, questioning the wisdom of drinking any alcohol, but decided that with her death coming, she deserved a night of loosened control. And maybe, just maybe, the haze the drinks would cause would drown out the memories.

"I think I could do with some wine tonight. Let's enjoy this celebration. Captain, join us."

"Honestly." Aiden chuckled as he stepped around the princes and Vartan. "When a woman says no more, you listen."

"Don't leave her side," Celiaen said seriously.

Smirking, Aiden winked and replied, "I rarely ever do."

It was one of the biggest bonfires Eirian had seen. She wondered where Neriwyn and his people had located the wood needed for all the fires illuminating the camp. Musicians played lively tunes, and several others accompanied Saoirse. Their voices filled the air in a sweet harmony that made Eirian tilt her head back in appreciation. Glancing at Fayleen, she wondered what it would take to convince her and Celiaen to join the singers.

Dancers surrounded the fire, their movements making it almost impossible to distinguish between human, elf, and daoine. Some Telmian women wore gowns similar to Eirian's. Fabric and jewels glimmered in the light, giving them more of a dream-like appearance than they already possessed. Watching them move, she felt the heavy drumbeat vibrating through her body. Embracing it, Eirian thought she was viewing the world through a haze as her magic continued to latch on to the crowd's energy.

Heady from the influence, she turned back to Fayleen to find her accepting the outstretched hand of an unfamiliar duine. She glanced at Eirian with a smile, eyes silently asking for permission, which Eirian gave with a slight nod. Feeling the brush of a hand against her hip, she ignored Aiden and continued to watch the swirl of the dance. The whispers had fallen silent, but she detected the memories of other dances overlapping the sight playing out in front of her.

"Do you want to join in?" Aiden murmured, paying more attention to her than the dancers.

"Not right now. Perhaps once I'm a little drunk, you can ask me again." Shrugging, she waved at the dancers. "But please, don't feel that you must miss out. Join in if the fancy strikes you."

"I'll dance when you do. I know you enjoy dancing with me."

He flashed a grin at her. It was a familiar grin, filled with the promise of his hands guiding her through the motions. Licking her lips, Eirian let herself remember the feel of his firm grasp gently coaxing her through the steps. It was a distraction that hurt deeply, making her hate herself for the opportunities she had let slip through her fingers.

"Fayleen has a soft spot for you. I don't see why."

"Feeling a touch jealous, are you, darling?" His grin remained as he leaned in closer so he could murmur the question in her ear. "You really shouldn't feel jealous of the one you love as dearly as you claim to love her."

Annoyed, Eirian grumbled, "Fayleen is my sister. I'd do anything to ensure her health and happiness. As I would for you."

Hearing familiar laughter, Aiden bit back the response that lingered at the tip of his tongue and sighed. He had seen the mixture of guilt and lust in her eyes. The urge to chase the regret from Eirian struck. A voice said to sweep her into the dance and make her forget.

"It seems you'd do it for everyone. Hardly makes one feel special."

They stared at each other, and the voice continued to tell Aiden to run with her. Eirian glowed brighter than he had ever seen, magic oozing through the fabric of her dress. He wanted to imagine he could drink it from her lips and claim just a small part of it for himself. Something of the energy that made her a vibrant storm of life.

"Ree, I need to apologize." Celiaen slipped his arm around her, leaning in to kiss her cheek. "I let curiosity override sense and disrespected your desire to drop the matter."

The look on his face made her annoyance soften. Leaning in, Eirian kissed him tenderly, hoping her forgiveness was apparent. His arm at her waist tightened, and briefly, she considered suggesting they leave the celebrations.

"I'm sorry, Celi, you know how the subject of my mother makes me feel."

Lifting the hand that was not around her, he held up a flask, chuckling. "I've got some rosehip wine to help us forget about my blunder. Lord Vartan gave it to me to share with you. He said you'll like it."

"Rosehip wine? That'll be a first for me."

She eyed the flask, intrigued by the prospect of what it might taste like. Removing the stopper, Celiaen sniffed at the contents before lifting it to her lips. Watching them, Aiden wanted to listen to the voice at the back of his mind that would not stop. It told him to surrender and let Celiaen and Eirian pull him into the fog created by their proximity to each other. He wondered what magic and wine would taste like from their lips.

"Smells sweet. Tell me what you think before I risk trying it myself."

Trying not to laugh, Eirian carefully sipped from the mouth of the flask. "You're right. It's sweet. Quite strong, but I think I like it. I'll let you know for sure after I drink some more."

"Well, you didn't hate it, so I'll take the risk." He brought the flask to his mouth and took a swig. "Yes, that is strong and sweet. I can't say it's to my taste."

"All mine then!"

Chuckling, Eirian took it from him so she could drink more. He stared at her, seeing past the cheery mask she wore to the deep anger and resentment that never seemed to fade, and beyond that to the grief. Meeting Aiden's gaze, Celiaen nodded grimly and knew he understood it. They turned to Galameyvin, who was sipping at his flask of wine, which he raised. None of them would stray far from Eirian, silently agreeing that at least one of them had to remain with her at all times.

She ignored the way the three of them stepped closer, her gaze following Fayleen among the dancers. Their proximity did not help the conflicting desires coursing through her. Watching a group of daoine dancing with elves, Eirian wished she could let go of her inhibitions like they were. Unfortunately, no amount of talking or suggesting it was possible would change the hesitation she felt whenever the opportunity arose.

Closing her eyes, Eirian released her grasp on her magic and let the music block out all other sounds. It was never enough to drown out the unheard drumbeat of every heart in the area or the whispers when they wanted to be heard. But it was a drum that added to the music rather than detracted. Delving deeper into her awareness, she felt the burning energy of the fires, the clean, unbiased power.

Magic touched magic, and she knew everyone who possessed it sensed her brushing past them. They felt her pouring energy into them. She drew it from the fire, from the ground, from the air that crackled with the power of thousands of people enjoying themselves. Eirian poured her love, desire, and need to live into each person present. No matter where they were, the scent of flowers blanketed the countryside, rich and heady, as intoxicating as the wine the Telmians passed around.

"By the powers," Tessa whispered and breathed deeply, unable to take her gaze away from Eirian with her eyes closed as she swayed slightly to the music.

Scowling, Galameyvin shook his head. "I don't know how she has it in her. We wouldn't have made it as far, as quickly as we did, if she hadn't been pouring power into keeping us going."

"This isn't channeling." It reminded Baenlin that Eirian was something more than simply a mage, and he admitted, "She truly isn't like the rest of us."

"Not in the slightest. Eirian is power, magic, and life, all combined within one being. She just has to realize and embrace it."

Neriwyn appeared, hands grasped behind his back as he regarded Eirian with an odd expression that none of them could figure out. He glowed as brightly as she did, but the power coming from him lacked the same intoxicating influence of hers. Instead, it carried an echo of bloodlust, the alluring promise of a battle and a hard-won victory.

Tessa cocked her head to the side, appraising him. "You say power and magic as different things."

"Aren't they? You can have one without the other." He arched a brow. "You've had magic all your life, but it's only recently that power has come your way. A power denied to you by those who thought you too different. It's interesting the things that slip through the cracks as time goes by, and you're certainly one of those things."

"What are you on about?"

Offering her a hand, he inclined his head toward the dancing. Tessa glanced at them, envious of their grace. It had been a long time since anyone had invited her to dance beside a fire. Her parents had made sure of that. Few people wanted to be seen embracing the crazy daughter of an archmage.

"Has anyone ever mentioned you have an uncanny similarity to the royal family of Endara? They have a type about them."

The pieces connected, and Tessa asked, "Are you suggesting I have Altira blood?"

"It's entirely possible," Eirian commented, making them aware she was listening. "My ancestors did many despicable things throughout the years to those born among them with magic. I wouldn't be surprised if it turned out there was Altira blood in Riane."

"Indeed. Now, dear Tessa, would you like to dance?" Neriwyn continued to hold his hand. "After all, it's a celebration."

Amused by the conflicted look on her face, Baenlin gave Tessa a nudge. He did not want to watch her with Neriwyn, but his newfound understanding told him that encouraging her would only benefit him more.

"How many can claim the King of Telmia asked them to dance? You'll have a story to make all the other women in Riane envy you."

Chuckling, Neriwyn smiled at Baenlin. "I'm happy to dance with you next, Archmage."

"That is quite alright. I think I'll forgo the dancing."

"I promise I won't bite unless you ask nicely. You're most welcome to ask."

Eirian laughed at the look on Baenlin's face, and it startled her companions. It was the first genuine laugh they had heard from her in a while.

"You have a type, Neriwyn."

"As do you, dear heart." He looked at each of the men surrounding her before winking. "And may I say you're a vision of beauty. You're glowing."

Lips pursed, Eirian glanced slyly at the bonfire before spreading her hands. Magic rippled, flashes of light visible to everyone. Tessa held her breath, gazing in fascination. It was a taste of how she saw the world, and she wanted to hug Eirian in thanks. Because knowing the people surrounding her could see it felt like validation, and Tessa never desired it as desperately as she did then.

"Do you want glowing? I can give you glowing."

Feeling every ember and spark that leaped from the fires, Eirian caught them in her magic and floated them into the air. She held them trapped, frozen in the state they had been. Gasps and shouts of awe interrupted the merrymaking as every person turned their faces to the sky to stare at the tiny balls of light hanging above them. Flexing her fingers, Eirian set them spinning and dancing, doing her best to match their motions to the music. Laughing in nervous disbelief, Tessa shook her head and glanced at Baenlin, taking in his stunned expression.

"How?"

"Show off." Neriwyn grinned. "You have a flair, my sweet little life."

Flicking her hand in his direction, Eirian shrugged as she said, "My contribution to the celebrations, aren't they pretty?"

Baenlin looked at her before looking back at the lights hanging in the air. He felt cold. The initial shock had worn off, and the festivities resumed. People did not care that Eirian had done something no other mage could. The wine's influence and magic chased thoughts of anything but pleasure from them.

"They're beautiful, Majesty," Baenlin told her. "But are they safe?"

Before she could answer, a voice yelled out, "Oi, I have a bone to pick with you, Ree!"

The sadly wistful look on Eirian's face morphed into glee, and she turned to face the four people who were nudging their way through the crowds to join them. Rylee marched up to her, eyes drifting over the dress before she stood on her toes to reach up and kiss Eirian hungrily. There were laughs of disbelief from her guards, Aiden blinking in shock before looking between Celiaen and Galameyvin for a sign that they should peel the two women apart.

Dropping down, Rylee tugged at a swath of silk, purring, "I made you a promise."

"Yes, I believe you did. And it involved gowns," Eirian replied with a chuckle. "But you might need to discuss it with someone first."

Screwing his face up, Aiden thought he recognized her and quietly asked Galameyvin, "Who is that?"

"Rylee."

"She delivered Eirian to us at the border."

Galameyvin snorted. "They were sparring partners."

Nudging Aiden, Merle commented, "You're one of her sparring partners, but she doesn't greet you like that."

Exchanging nods, Celiaen greeted Jaren. "How have you been?"

"Tessa's going to be the grand mage. How do you think I've been?" Jaren answered, holding his hand out.

Watching them clasp hands and hug, Aiden felt a pang of jealousy. Glancing at Galameyvin, he saw a flicker of it cross his face and frowned. It was a reminder of the strange situation they found themselves in. Jaren pulled back from Celiaen, turning to greet Eirian with a hug while Rylee stood to the side and rambled on about the idiocy of purple mages.

"And him?"

"Jaren is Tessa's brother. He was a sparring partner of both Celi and Ree."

Understanding the implication in Galameyvin's answer, Aiden sighed. Catching movement in the corner of his eye, he saw Neriwyn lead Tessa into the dance, leaving Baenlin behind with a curious expression on his face. He did not know what was happening there, but Aiden doubted it would take much thought to work it out. Leaning closer, Galameyvin inclined his head at Eirian and Celiaen with a smirk.

"Do you feel like dancing, Captain?"

Arching a brow, Aiden muttered, "Are you asking me to dance with you, princeling?"

"Why not? We're here to look pretty for them. I'm not as good a dancer as he is, but I'm not half bad."

Extending his hand, Galameyvin winked, and Aiden shook his head in amusement. Aware that Eirian and Celiaen were too busy talking to the four newcomers to pay them any attention, he accepted the offered hand. Surprise appeared on Galameyvin's face before he grinned and pulled Aiden into the fray. Watching them go, Eirian cocked her head. The whispers intensified, encouraging her to follow them. She wanted to, even without the voices filling her thoughts.

"Ree?" Celiaen said.

His grasp on her arm stopped Eirian from walking forward, and her eyes met his. To the side, Rylee and Jaren exchanged looks with Luke and Zack. They had all witnessed her forget their presence when the other two men left. Each of them had known Eirian for years, and the woman standing in front of them was not the same person who had left them behind in Riane. Magic dripped from her glowing skin like drops of water and sunlight.

"Don't you want to join them?" Eirian whispered.

Celiaen shifted his gaze to where Aiden was laughing with Galameyvin. He had not expected them to dance with anyone except Eirian. But he suspected their display was as much for his benefit as hers. He returned his eyes to hers and ignored the flicker of magic surrounding them. The desire she felt was obvious, but there was something else beneath it, something he could barely taste through the bond. It carried notes of regret and longing.

Slipping his fingers through hers, Celiaen raised her hand to his lips. Kissing the ring he had given Eirian, he smiled knowingly and nodded. Relief crossed her face, but she did not move in their direction. She waited for a response, feeling the desire seeping across the bond. Celiaen wanted to join Aiden and Galameyvin as much as she did.

"It's a celebration."

Those words were enough to set her feet moving. Dragging Celiaen with her, Eirian slipped through the people, dancers shifting out of her way like water parting around a rock. Her free hand touched Aiden's arm first before reaching for Galameyvin. Closing his eyes, Celiaen breathed in the scent of flowers, noting it had become something sweeter than usual.

"Ree," Galameyvin groaned when her fingers tugged at his hair. "Are you drunk?"

"Does it matter?" she murmured.

"That depends on if you're going to affect every person here."

Aiden felt the magic tugging at them and thought the question was irrelevant when she had already affected everyone. From the moment they joined the festivities, her magic had been there, twisting and weaving through the crowds. Flowers bloomed where feet did not tread, and above them hung thousands of embers.

"It's a bit late for that," he said.

A hand slid down his back, and Aiden stiffened briefly, meeting Celiaen's mischievous grin. The snarky comment he had planned to say died in his throat when the grin became a silent plea. It was a request that they did not argue for the sake of the smiling woman drifting between them. A reminder that battle waited for the light of day. Smiling faintly, Aiden saw the relief in Celiaen's eyes and the hand on his back slipped lower.

"*Careful, darling.*"

Shaking her head, Eirian tried to banish the whisper of Gebael's voice through her mind. His presence was not the distraction she wanted. Careful not to let her apprehension show, she focused on the three men she danced with. Spotting Celiaen's arm slipped behind Aiden, she grinned and crinkled her nose at them.

"You know, if you drink a little more wine, Aiden, you might find you'd enjoy what Celi could do for you."

"What makes you so sure it wouldn't be the other way around?" Aiden replied.

Leaning against Galameyvin, she chuckled. "Well, why don't you prove me wrong?"

"That sounds like a challenge." Celiaen wriggled his brows at Aiden, purring, "Are you going to let her taunt you like that?"

Swinging Tessa into their midst, Neriwyn quickly exchanged her hand for Eirian's. Pulling her away from the three men, he smiled apologetically.

"Don't worry, I'll return your queen in one piece."

Allowing Neriwyn to draw her into the dancers, Eirian studied his face and listened to the silence in her mind. It was one of those times when the quiet was more deafening than the noise of them fighting to be heard. Fingers dug into her hip, a pain starkly different from the agony that had hit her at his touch.

"You're dangerously close to losing control," he murmured.

Tilting her head back, Eirian said, "Are you frightened, Lord War?"

"What did you call me?"

"Tell me, Neri, what would you do to stop me?"

He spun her away, eyes on the swirl of silk catching in the firelight. The scent of flowers surrounded them, and Neriwyn drew her back, holding Eirian easily. She smirked knowingly, the hint of daring in her eyes encouraging caution.

"Stop you from doing what?"

"There's no need to play games with me. I know. Or did Gebael not fill you in?"

Sighing, Neriwyn asked again, "Stop you from doing what? Turning this celebration into a bloodbath or an orgy?"

"I'd never turn a celebration into a bloodbath!" Eirian huffed. "But an orgy does sound tempting."

"Is that what you want?"

"Does it matter what I want? It's not like I have a choice. I mean, I'd really like to not die soon, but there's nothing I can do to change that."

Looking away, Neriwyn wished he could tell her everything. He wanted to give her the promise of more, the assurance that she would not simply die, but the icy gaze watching them prevented it. Those blue eyes reminded him of what was at stake.

"I'm sorry, Eirian."

"I don't want or need your apologies, Neriwyn. What I want is for you to stay away from me. My days are numbered, and I'd like to enjoy what time I have left with the people I love. That doesn't include you."

Neriwyn swore he saw lightning dance across Eirian's skin as she pulled free of his grasp. Dark hair tumbling over her shoulders, she reminded him of her mother more than he wanted to be. She shimmered with power, raw life energy seeping from her into the ground and surrounding people.

"I'm going to die to keep your mistake imprisoned. Neither you nor Gebael gets to dictate what I do with my last days."

Holding her gaze, Neriwyn said, "Careful, dear heart. You wouldn't want anyone to ask why you're arguing with the king of Telmia when you're supposed to be dancing with him."

"You're no more the king of Telmia than I am the queen of Endara," she replied.

Extending his hand to her, Neriwyn waited for Eirian to take it reluctantly. Drawing her in, he chuckled at the anger simmering in her eyes.

"You are the queen of everything," he whispered in her ear, spotting her companions watching them closely.

"Don't worry, I won't spill your secrets, Lord War."

Releasing her to the waiting hands of Celiaen, Neriwyn bowed. Keeping her head high, Eirian turned on her heel and dismissed him without a word. When she swept her gaze over her friends, she drew from the familiar comfort of their presence. The agony of Neriwyn's touch vanished, but the whispers returned. Determined not to let them take away her pleasure, she let Celiaen wrap his arms around her.

"You're still a terrible dancer," Fayleen joked, an arm slung over Aiden's shoulder.

On the other side of her, Tessa said, "Even I'm a better dancer."

"Mother would've drowned you if you couldn't dance," Jaren muttered.

"Oh, because she hasn't been threatening to do that since I was born?"

Aiden looked between them in amusement. "Are you normally like this?"

"Who's like what?" Everett inquired, joining them.

Eirian watched Fayleen pull away from Aiden suddenly, her eyes on Everett. Glancing at him, she studied the careful way he avoided looking at Fayleen and cocked her head to the side thoughtfully. The silence unsettled Everett, and he greeted Eirian.

"Did you enjoy your escape?"

"It started out well, and then we found some Athnaralans. They've got several legions coming," Aiden said.

"I heard. Our scouts reported them, but you're the ones who got the numbers. It'll soften the blow of your absence." He shrugged, glancing at Fayleen. "I'm glad you're back."

Dipping her head, Eirian replied, "I'm sorry I was away for so long."

"With everyone gathered here, I guess the war is nearly over."

"You're right. It's nearly over."

Exchanging looks, Celiaen, Aiden, and Galameyvin knew what she left unsaid.

FIFTEEN

The great hall no longer resembled a place for gathering and feasting. Instead, they had placed tables together for people to work at. Maps covered the largest cluster, little carved tokens scattered on top of them to show where reports told of Athnaralan troops. They piled smaller tables with documents, and assistants stood ready should anyone require them.

Officers gathered at designated spots, discussing what to do with the companies they commanded. Paienven lorded over everything, the Endaran nobles struggling to make themselves heard. Even the mages bowed to him in Baenlin's absence, though they primarily kept to themselves and their work. When Eirian strode through the open door, her arrival caused everyone to stop what they were doing so they could turn and stare.

"I see you've made yourself quite at home in my town, Your Majesty."

Paienven was the only person who did not turn to look at her. It took all of his control to hide his anger. Her voice brought back the shame of what she had done to him the night before.

"Someone had to assume control of this rabble while you were off carousing."

Bristling at his words, the Endarans looked at Eirian, and she nodded to them. "Someone was in control, but of course, you wouldn't respect that."

"An old man, an untested boy, and the most irreverent man I've ever met. I'd hardly call that control."

Pretending to gasp in horror, Eirian winked at Cameron. He choked back laughter, trying to hide how much he was enjoying her performance.

"Why, General, he's calling you old when you're not half his age! Sire, you certainly know how to make friends."

"Eirian," Everett cautioned her quietly.

Finally, Paienven looked at her, a marker in his hand, which he rolled through his fingers. "And what would a girl like you know about making friends?"

Crossing her arms, Eirian smiled at him. The difference was noticeable to those who had not seen her since before she left Kelsby. Magic dripped from her, rejuvenating energy affecting everyone within proximity.

"Clearly, not as much as you do. All I know is how to kill people without touching them. Great big swaths of men fall with a snap of my fingers. Now, do you require a demonstration, or was last night enough to make you realize I'm not someone you can dismiss or trample over?"

"Yes, you made that quite clear."

"Good. Then I'll remind you again that you're in Endara, and I am the queen here! My people answer to me, and when I leave someone in charge, I expect them to receive the same respect I'm owed. Even more so when the person I leave in charge is my heir." Looking first at Sannaeh, then to Celiaen, Eirian huffed. "Now, considering both your wife and your eldest son are here, I presume that means you left Princess Awena in control of Ensaycal. How would you feel if someone came into your kingdom and completely disrespected your decision?"

Paienven sneered. "Awena would never let that happen."

Clicking her tongue at him, Eirian waved at Everett and Marcellus. "Even when threatened with the cessation of a long-held treaty? I'm aware of what transpired upon your arrival. I will not tolerate you strong-arming my people into doing what you want!"

Shuffling some papers, Vartan looked bored as he said, "Your disrespect for my king notwithstanding, I believe Her Majesty has a point. You did bully His Grace into silence. I said nothing at the time as I felt it was up to him to find his voice."

Clearing his throat, Everett scowled. He had allowed Paienven to push him around on purpose, knowing Eirian would react exactly as she had.

"Ma'am, we don't have a lot of time before Aeyren's reinforcements arrive. I think His Majesty understands you won't tolerate disrespect."

"Indeed, I think we all understand." Despite his desire to do so, Marcellus did not smile. "Shall we get on with it then?"

Moving to her side, Cameron gave Eirian a sideways look and smiled, saying, "I suspect the young duke set the entire situation up."

"As do I. Do you think Everett got what he wanted?" Eirian asked, gaze drifting from one table to the next in contemplation.

"That depends on what he wanted."

Guiding Eirian to the main table, Cameron paused when she shook off his hand to move to the table surrounded by yellow mages. "Ma'am?"

Eirian nodded to the three mages, only recognizing one of them. "Master Leah, how go the fortifications?"

Leah screwed up her face. "Well. This is an old keep, and we keep finding things we need to study."

"When the war is over, I plan for yellows to study the old keeps. I suspect they'll amaze you. I'm sure whatever you do will be of great help."

"Anything is better than nothing, am I right?" The only male in the trio grinned at his fellows and stuck out a hand. "Master Nial. Your reputation precedes you, Majesty. I'm sorry we never got to cross paths in Riane."

Chuckling, Eirian clasped his hand. "With good reason, I'm sure. May I suggest you discuss plans with Tessa? She has a potentially viable solution for the siege weapons."

"Did you see them?" Scratching her head, the final yellow spoke, not lifting her gaze from the drawings and plans laid out in front of her.

"No, I didn't. It wasn't worth the risk to do so."

Making a disappointed noise, she waved vaguely. "Pity, I hear you could've wiped them out."

Leah sighed. "Please excuse Meela. She doesn't leave the catacombs often."

"There's nothing to excuse. If there is anything at all that I can do to be of help, let me know. Your work is invaluable."

Shrugging, Eirian turned to Cameron and allowed him to direct her to the main table, where arguments had erupted.

"We only have one viable option open to us." Darragh was waving at the table, shaking his head. "Waiting until the reinforcements arrive is stupid."

Paienven disagreed. "If we hold off, it gives the yellows more time to build, and we can take care of the Athnaralans in one hit."

Glancing at Vartan, Eirian saw his boredom and said, "Am I to understand you're suggesting we sit here waiting until Aeyren has more forces?"

"Indeed," Marcellus grumbled.

"I have to agree with Darragh. Waiting is stupid."

"We have the superior numbers and power. We should use that and wipe out Athnaral now." Another elf dared support Darragh's plan.

"Lord Vartan, you've been rather silent." Paienven stared at him. "Please, share some of your ancient wisdom with us. I'm sure it's invaluable."

Sighing, he raised his brows and looked at Eirian pointedly before shrugging. The sarcasm in Paienven's voice was not lost on anyone.

"We should have attacked weeks ago, but there was no point doing it without her here to counter the darkness. Well, she's back."

Everett spoke, frustration in his voice. "So, you're saying we should attack now?"

"Yes!" Vartan declared, spreading his hands. "Why, by the powers, would we wait to fight a bigger force when we could be certain of victory against two smaller forces?"

Drumming his fingers against the table, Paienven could tell it was not going his way and turned his attention to Eirian. "While I doubt you know little of battle tactics, surely you'd rather a more decisive victory that will leave an impression on your enemies."

"You're right. I know a little about battle tactics." She twisted his words carefully. "Engaging with two smaller armies is a far easier victory to claim than fighting a single large force. Right now, we can simply overwhelm their men. Once the reinforcements arrive, we will have other things to contend with. The battle is likely to be chaotic and on multiple fronts. If we wait, the victory might not be so definite."

"We have an army of mages."

"I thought you were here to win a war, King Paienven."

Groaning, Celiaen rubbed his face. "Please be reasonable, sire."

"Honestly, you lot could argue until the earth ends, and nothing would happen!" Baenlin declared as he strode through the doors, boots sounding heavy against the floor. "I gave my forces the orders to attack tomorrow at sunrise. Are you joining me?"

Cameron looked for confirmation, and Eirian nodded. "With my queen's agreement, Endara is with you."

"Neriwyn has already given it." Vartan chuckled, flashing his teeth at Paienven. "Ensaycal is welcome to sit this out."

"Shall I give the order then, sire?" Darragh regarded Paienven with narrowed eyes.

Saving him from speaking, Sannaeh agreed. "Yes, we'll support the others. If you insist on doing it this way, then there is no point sitting back and missing out on the fight."

"Well then, it looks like we have a busy day." Marcellus turned to one of his guards to say, "Please find the Duchess and tell her it's time to leave."

Eirian held up a finger to the guard as he passed her. "Her Grace was intending to take Ona and Isabella to watch some training when I left her. They won't have gone far. Ask them to see me before they leave."

The man nodded his thanks, saluting Aiden on his way past. Not missing the opportunity to make a snide comment, Paienven snorted.

"How will you manage without your ladies?"

"The same as I always manage. If you can't dress without the help of your gentlemen, then that's your failing and not mine," she replied, giving him an amused look. "If it's any consolation, your son is more than capable of both dressing and undressing."

Spluttering, Celiaen turned from the table. "I'm not sure how that's relevant, Your Majesty."

"It isn't, and that was her point," Baenlin muttered, frowning at Celiaen.

Laughing, Faolan nodded to her from his place beside Vartan. "Tell me, little queen, why do you cause kings to fall over making fools of themselves?"

"I don't know," Eirian said. "Perhaps you should ask them."

Unimpressed by the exchange, Darragh smacked a hand against the table. "Why don't you all shut up and focus."

Turning to Cameron, she nodded. "I'll withdraw and leave matters of strategy to you, General. Please keep me appraised."

"Is there anywhere you'd like to find yourself in the battle?" Cameron inquired.

"I think I might pass on being with the archers again. It wasn't very satisfying. Put me with the bulk of our infantry. I'll be of more use there."

Shaking his head, Baenlin exchanged a knowing glance with Darragh. "No, I should think it wasn't satisfying at all."

"If it had been, the outcome last time may have been vastly different." Giving a little shake, Eirian directed a smile at everyone around the table. "Pleasant plotting to you all."

Watching her stride out of the hall, Baenlin scowled and crossed his arms. Then, glaring at Paienven first, he gave each of them a frustrated look.

"Dare I ask why the most powerful person here just walked out?"

"She agreed to leave the battle to us while she focused on the one we can't fight," Darragh informed him.

Pressing fingers to his eyes, Vartan sighed. "What he means is she knows where her attention needs to be, and it's not on this fight. We are to provide the stage and the distraction, and she'll provide the closing act."

Understanding the concern, Sannaeh asked, "Does she know what she's doing?"

"Of course." He lied easily, flicking a glance at Faolan. "She can pull off her part."

"Indeed, our little queen has found her strength," Faolan said.

"What you're saying is she doesn't know what she's doing." Sannaeh smiled wryly, eyeing Celiaen. "You can't lie to me, son."

Celiaen drew himself up. "She might not know exactly what she's doing, but Eirian knows what has to be done, and she'll do it. It's our job to make sure she has the chance and the strength to do so."

"So, whatever we do, we need to make sure she doesn't feel a need to do anything extreme again." Marcellus puffed out his cheeks. "I'm assuming we're to prevent her from using any more power than she needs to."

Vartan drummed his fingers on the table. "Unfortunately, we can't keep her from the field because she needs to draw the enemy out. Hopefully, we can end it with one battle."

Meeting Celiaen's gaze, Aiden nodded and turned to chase after Eirian. He had remained, easily forgotten in the crowd of people surrounding the table, to listen to what they had to say after she left. As he went, Aiden noticed word of the battle orders was spreading quickly. When he caught up, he did not question why she was heading toward the corner stairway leading to the roof.

People were already there, but the soldiers and mages moved aside for Eirian. Wedged open, the door had seen more people passing through it in recent days than it had in a hundred years. Scattered around the rooftop, a handful of yellow mages were busy working. Looking them over, Eirian knew there would be more of them in the deepest parts of the town, working their magic through the foundations.

Aiden leaned against the wall beside her and watched the mages working while his men scattered themselves around. "So, tomorrow."

"Do you think I'll ever stop being so antagonizing? I try, but I just can't help myself," she said in annoyance.

"From what little I've seen of him so far, King Paienven is an ass. I suddenly have sympathy for your prince."

Remembering the comments about his father, she gave Aiden an apologetic look. "I'm sorry if he has reminded you of your father."

Dismissing her concern, he shrugged. "Don't worry about it. He's dead. Speaking of dead, I don't suppose I could ask you not to get us killed tomorrow?"

"I'll try my best."

"Eirian…" he started, but stopped with a shake of his head.

The sun shone brightly, and it was early enough in the day that it did not have the harshness it would later. Eirian did not look at him, shading her eyes as she peered into the distance, pretending she could see the army they faced.

"No, go on, Aiden, say what you want to say. I won't judge you for it."

"I don't want tomorrow to happen."

"I know."

He grumbled, turning to stare at her. "It's not my death I dread. It's yours."

"I know that too." Eirian watched from the corner of her eye as she said, "I promise I'll try to avoid dying, but I can't say if it's possible."

"You know we're going to have to get ourselves killed as well if you die? I won't go down as the captain who let his queen die in battle and lived to tell of it." He hoped the comment would make her smile, but it did not receive even a slight twitch.

"Your queen forbids such action. It would serve no good."

"It was a joke, ma'am."

"I forbid you from dying in this war, Aiden." Eirian reached out and clutched his hand. "I mean it. You're going to survive, marry, have children, a family, and you're going to fucking live because that's the whole point. If you don't, then my death will be a waste."

Eyes downcast, Aiden wanted to shout at her but remained silent. He could not answer without betraying his anger over the situation. Taking a deep breath, he lifted his gaze to meet hers, the grief in them a knife to his heart. Aiden wanted to wrap his arms around her and forget the war.

Standing there, they stared at each other and ignored the yellows' uncomfortable but curious glances. The guards did not look at their queen and captain, their focus shifting to the blonde woman standing in the doorway with a chest grasped in her hands. Fayleen tossed her head toward the stairs, and the other yellow mages gathered their things to leave.

Swaggering over, Gram wriggled his brows at Fayleen. "Let me take that for you, fair lady."

"Thank you. Then you can leave." She gave him a cool look and walked toward Eirian. "I've been looking all over for you."

Sighing, Eirian gave Aiden's hand a squeeze. "We can finish this conversation later."

His mouth twisted in frustration, and he looked at Fayleen. "I suppose you want me to leave as well."

"That depends, Captain."

"On what?"

Fayleen clicked her tongue, looking him over. "If you'll show a woman some appreciation for her fine craftsmanship."

"What's in the chest, Fay?" Eirian nodded to the object on the floor between them.

"Take a look. It's my finest work yet."

Perching on the wall while Eirian moved to open the chest, Aiden signaled Gram to join the others in the stairwell. Squatting in front of the chest, she stared in at the piles of leather it contained. Her eyes took in the rich shades of brown, the hints of detailed embossing and contrasting embroidery that were not present on the armor she was already wearing.

She knew what it was. Fayleen had talked about crafting it for a long time, but she had constantly turned her down, believing it was unnecessary. Gripping the sides of the chest tightly, Eirian felt her nails digging into the wood and lifted her gaze to look at Fayleen. She hated the dread creeping down her spine as she realized it was the armor she would die in.

"Well? Aren't you going to take it out and try it on?" Fayleen said impatiently, waving at her work. "Do you know how much time I dedicated to that?"

"Fay." Eirian sighed, letting go of the chest to press her fingertips to her mouth.

"Don't you bloody dare."

Concerned they were going to burst into some sort of crying argument that he would not know how to deal with, Aiden cleared his throat. "Can I ask a question? Why leather? All you mages seem to like your leather."

Deciding to let Fayleen answer the question, Eirian stood and began stripping off her weapons. Coming over to assist, Fayleen shrugged at Aiden.

"It's just the way it's always been."

"That's it? The way it's always been? That hardly seems like a good enough reason to use leather over plate and mail." Her answer baffled Aiden.

"Truthfully, you haven't seen them fully armored for war. You've seen everyday armor." Fayleen blinked at him, blue eyes almost the same color as the sky, and she explained, "Every red is different in what they prefer. Ree has always liked leather. Maybe that was my influence. Working leather was my calling, and I practiced on things for her."

He pointed at Eirian, watching her pull the jerkin over her head. "But you hadn't worn mail before."

"Incorrect," she answered.

"She's worn mail, but Ree didn't believe there was a reason to train in more than leather. Something to do with being the future Queen of Endara and doubting she'd need armor."

Giving Eirian a knowing look, Fayleen turned and bent to lift the first piece of armor out of the chest. It was a beautiful work, and Aiden could not imagine it covered in blood or shielding Eirian from blows. Hopping off the wall, he walked over to join them, reaching out to feel the leather. It was supple and thicker than he had thought, but he sensed the magic worked into it.

Eyes widening, he glanced at Eirian, noticing that she was not paying him any attention. It did not seem all that long ago that he would have thought she appeared smaller without her armor and weapons. But looking at her in her plain gray linen clothes with the sheen of magic coating her, he decided she was a thousand times more intimidating unarmed when he knew what she could do.

Turning back to the armor in Fayleen's hands, he took in the long sleeves and the way the neckline looked higher than the other. It was longer. Where her jerkin had sat on her hips, the new one looked as though it would come down to midway along her thigh. Complex swirls of knots covered every part, silvery thread embroidering the edges of the symbols he knew were wards. On the shoulders hung buckles, and Aiden wondered what they were for.

"What do you think?" Fayleen asked anxiously.

Rubbing her lips with her thumb, Eirian nodded slowly. "I think it's magnificent work, and I'm honored you have created it for me."

Aiden gave Fayleen a broad smile. "I think it's too pretty to wear in a battle, to be honest. Do you need a hand putting it on, ma'am?"

"She's a bloody queen. She needs to stand out." Hearing the admiration in Aiden's voice, Fayleen returned his smile. "Hurry and put it on so I can give you the rest."

Eyes dropping to the chest, Eirian saw there was more. Taking the garment from Fayleen, she did not blink when Aiden put his hands out to hold it while she slid her arms into the sleeves. It was not a tight fit, and she was thankful to find she could move comfortably. Fayleen had listened to enough of her complaints about armor to know what Eirian liked to wear.

There was an eerie similarity to the last battle when Aiden began tightening the laces at the front of the bodice, his eyes staring into hers. His assessment had been correct. The lower part of the tunic flared out from her hips to reach midway down her thighs like a short skirt. Glancing at the chest, he hoped there was something more in there for protection because he was not sure that what she had on was enough.

"It looks as lovely as I thought it would." Fayleen pursed her lips in self-admiration. "I did a good job. Now, Captain, the next item, please."

"You want me to do the honors?" Aiden asked in surprise.

She winked at him. "There are a lot of things I'd like you to do, but for now, dressing my sister in my handiwork is enough."

Rolling his eyes, he left Eirian to continue stretching and picked up the next item from the pile in the chest. It seemed like a belt, but Aiden had not seen one as wide as it was. Holding it out, he realized it was another layer to protect the vulnerable areas of her abdomen. There were two buckles at the front and loops for her regular belt to thread through. Like the rest, symbols adorned it, matching in completely.

Aiden returned to the chest and retrieved a pair of pauldrons, the layered leather heavier than the belt. They were unlike the pauldrons he was used to. Instead, they resembled flower buds, with the tips curling down to form a point. Seeing the straps, he realized the buckles held them in place. Under Fayleen's watchful gaze, he helped Eirian position the shoulder protection and secure it.

"This is incredible!" Eirian pretended she was drawing her bow, admiring how the leather gave to the motion. "What gave you the idea?"

"I saw it in a drawing and thought it would look fearsome on you."

Letting out a low whistle, Aiden moved on to the next item. "New bracers?"

"They needed to match."

Fayleen cast a sad look at the older ones on the ground as Aiden helped Eirian pull the new ones on. They were the same style of bracer but came closer to her elbow, leaving only a small gap. Flexing her hands, Eirian smiled in appreciation.

"Please tell me this is everything. You've done so much for me, Fay."

"There's more, but I'm fine if you don't wish to try the trousers on with the Captain looking. The boots, however."

Aiden saw the look directed at him by Fayleen and bowed stiffly. "I'll join my men. I look forward to seeing the completed outfit."

Waiting for him to pull the door shut, Fayleen sighed. "Is it true?"

"You might need to be more specific."

Sitting on the ground, Eirian pulled her boots off. She wanted to avoid the conversation for as long as she could. Fishing the trousers from the chest, Fayleen flung them at the seated woman in frustration.

"You know exactly what I mean. Are we going into battle tomorrow?"

Catching the garment, Eirian said, "Yes."

Groaning and running a hand through her hair, Fayleen looked devastated by the confirmation. "I had hoped... I don't want..."

Slipping the linen from her legs, Eirian exchanged them for the leather trousers. "You lined them!"

"Why are you so calm? How are you so calm? You said you might die!"

"They're more comfortable than I expected." Eirian admired how the leather gave to her movements while doing some squats and kneeling. "Your technique has come far."

Giving a little squeal of annoyance, Fayleen stamped her foot. "By the powers, you are the most irritating person in existence."

"I'm sorry, Fay, I have nothing to say on the matter." Ducking out of the way when Fayleen flung the boots at her one by one, Eirian asked, "What do you want me to say?"

"I want you to tell me the truth!"

Picking up the shoes, she sat to pull them on. They came to slightly below her knees. The leather curved up at the front to protect and act as padding when she knelt.

"I'm not calm. I'm fucking terrified. You don't know how much is resting on my shoulders in this. None of you do! I know what I have to do, but I don't know exactly how to do it. And I know the price is my life. There are no ifs, buts, or maybes. I will die."

Swallowing, Fayleen nodded in understanding. "I get it—"

"No, you don't! You can't say you get it because you don't. What do you think is going to happen? That there's going to be some glorious battle between a god and me?"

"Well—"

"Because there won't be! There will be blood, and death, and grief, and then I'll have to let her kill me. Kill me so that with my last breath, I can bind her back in her prison." Smacking a hand against the warm stone of the rooftop, Eirian blinked back tears. "So, what am I supposed to say, Fayleen? Because all I can fucking think is that I have to say goodbye to everyone I love and hope that they don't realize I'm saying goodbye."

Dropping to the ground, Fayleen stared at the sky hatefully. "Why do you have to die?"

"Because no one else is what I am. They created me purely for this. Intended as a sacrifice before I was born."

"And there is no other way?"

Shaking her head, Eirian rubbed her face. "No."

"There has to be something. We need to find the time to search." Fayleen was adamant. "And find the time for you to have your child."

"I forgot you could do that."

Giving Eirian a disbelieving look, she snorted. "A likely story. Whose is it?"

"Celi."

"It's not like you not to be careful, Ree. I find it hard to believe you'd make such a mistake when you knew you were going to die."

Eirian let out a shaky breath. "Because I didn't make a mistake."

"Fuck, Ree, you wanted to be pregnant? But why?" The revelation made Fayleen feel sick.

"For the unification of the bloodlines. It won't be my blood and power alone that binds her, but that of my unborn child. I'm not sure how to explain it to you or anyone else."

Grinding her teeth, Fayleen glanced at the shut door. "Why don't you try."

"They created her prison from the three bloodlines. The plan was to bind Celi and I together so our deaths would strengthen it. I'm trying to prevent him from dying with me... and not just him."

A coldness settled over her, and Fayleen shook her head, mouth open in disbelief. She wanted to hate Eirian for what she was doing, but she knew her well enough to know it was not a decision she would make lightly.

"What do you mean, not just him? What have you done, Eirian?"

Standing slowly, the sun's warmth combined with her emotions left Eirian a little faint. The whispers were strangely silent, but the shadows danced at the edge of her vision as a constant reminder.

"I don't know how I've done it, but I bound Aiden and Gal to me."

Taking a moment to stare at Eirian in the armor she had crafted for her, Fayleen smiled in approval. It was a welcome distraction she desperately needed to allow her to collect her thoughts.

"You could never do things by halves, could you?"

"It's hardly intentional." Annoyed, Eirian scowled, muttering, "I'd never do it on purpose."

"Does your captain love you?"

Dragging fingers through the messy locks of her hair, Eirian flinched when they encountered a knot. "Aiden claims he does, and I stick my fingers in my ears."

With a roll of her eyes, Fayleen arched a brow pointedly. "Typical. Sometimes you are the blindest person I know."

"I love him in my way. In another life, we could have had something. Honestly, if this war hadn't come about, I would have eventually married him. Aiden would make an excellent king, and we'd have been happy."

"I see."

Staring at her feet, Eirian gathered her thoughts and considered what she was about to ask before lifting her face to gaze at Fayleen.

"I know I have no right to ask this, and I understand if you say no, but as you love me, sister, I need you to protect Aiden."

Fayleen returned the gaze with equal seriousness. "Why are you asking me to do this?"

"Celi and Gal have each other. I fear for them, but I know they'll be okay in the end. Aiden will need someone, and so will you. Watch over him in the battle, and make sure he gets out alive because I gave him orders to live. Everett is going to need him. When the dust has settled, you have my blessing to do as you please. I'll tell Everett to give you anything you ask for. Lands, a title, a place in court, anything."

"He won't like it."

"I know. Just keep Aiden alive, and remind him why he has to live."

Chuckling, Fayleen shook her head. "I'll do my best. Luckily, I have a soft spot for him."

Pointing at the chest, Eirian smiled sadly. "Why don't you finish up."

Silently, Fayleen pulled the last items from the chest and unrolled them. New belts and baldrics to replace the ones she had made years previously. Helping Eirian put them on, she showed her where they had slots to go through on the armor to hold them in place. Her last gift was a pair of knives, complete with sheathes to wear on her thighs. Practicing drawing them while Fayleen separated the swords and knives from her old belts, Eirian nodded in approval.

"They're beautiful, Fay."

"I know. Look at the hilts."

Letting her focus on the knives, Fayleen secured the swords in their scabbards to the new belt hanging around her waist. Biting her lip, Eirian's chest tightened. Worked into the hilt in chains was the quaternary knot she associated with her mother. It made her look at the symbols worked in among the wards on her new armor, finding it present.

Closing her eyes, Eirian took a deep breath and let it out slowly. Seeing the symbol had stirred the whispers and the memories. The flashes of inky lines on their skin and the never-ending twists. A scream of frustration lingered at the tip of her tongue, but she could not voice it. Sensing her dismay, Fayleen stepped back with a frown.

"What's the matter?"

Knowing she had to explain her reaction, Eirian slipped the knife back into its sheath. "It's such an obscure thing, perhaps on purpose. You weren't to know that it was once used to represent the bloodlines."

Still frowning, Fayleen recalled the book they had first seen the symbol in. "You liked the symbol well enough when I found that old book."

"I suspect I'm predisposed to the symbol. My mother wore it every day."

"What happened to it?"

Eirian shrugged. "No idea. Vartan said Shianeni was wearing it the last time he saw her. Faolan doesn't know, and I don't care enough to ask Neriwyn. I don't trust him, and no one else should either."

Fayleen stroked a thumb across Eirian's cheek. "I can't imagine how you feel about your mother. But, just in case no one has told you, it's okay to feel the way you do. You have a right to your emotions, and no one can dictate your feelings to you."

"You're right," Eirian admitted. "I don't know how I'm holding myself together. I want to scream at the sky. To cry and yell all my thoughts about the gods and my mother to anyone who'll listen. But, worse than that, I want to run away and let the world burn."

"Let's go. We'll disappear and let them deal with it."

Wrapping an arm around her shoulders, Fayleen turned to face the same direction and held a hand up to frame the sky. Eirian remained silent, letting her speak.

"We could find a nice remote village where no one would ever know who we were. Between the two of us, we're useful."

It was a nice thought, and Eirian imagined it, whispering, "I wish we could."

"We talked about it so often when we were younger."

"If only I wasn't who I am."

"Yeah…"

Leaning her head on Fayleen's shoulder, Eirian sighed, "I love you."

"I love you too."

The door to the stairwell opened, and Everett pushed through, arguing with Aiden. Seeing the two women standing together, Aiden stopped and gave them an apologetic look.

"I'm sorry, ma'am, but Everett insisted on speaking to you."

Eirian did not move, staring at Everett sadly. "It's fine, Aiden. What can I do for you, Everett?"

His brown eyes settled on Fayleen, chewing on the inside of his cheek while deciding if it was worth asking her to leave. Seeing her with Eirian reminded him of the hurt he had felt over her request to keep their encounters secret.

"My apologies, Eirian, but I owe you an explanation for the situation with Paienven."

"No need, I'm not a fool. You allowed Paienven to bully you, so when I returned, it allowed me to put him in his place in front of the members of the council and army."

Opening and closing his mouth, Everett glanced at Aiden, who stared back blankly. "Yes, you're right—"

"I know," she said. "Now, I need to make a demand of you. It's my day for it."

"What do you need, Eirian?"

Meeting Aiden's gaze, she almost nodded. She did not need to make the motion for him to understand.

"I need you to get your guards and the members of your household, get on your horses, and leave. Take Brenna, Isabella, and all the others who are also leaving and go back to Amath."

Everett crossed his arms, shaking his head in refusal. "No, I can't do that."

"You're the next king of Endara. I won't have you risking your life on the battlefield."

"And if you die? Would you risk allowing Paienven the opportunity to take over?" Everett countered.

Pulling away from Fayleen, Eirian grimaced. "And what if we both die? Do you want to leave Endara in Llewellyn's hands?"

Not letting his interest in her new armor override his purpose, Everett said, "I can be here and not take part in the fight. Remember which one of us did as planned and left the battle last time. Someone needs to be in charge behind the lines."

"He's right, Ree. Most leaders don't go charging into the fight." Fayleen made her input, turning to stare at the sea of tents and soldiers.

Torn between agreeing with Eirian out of the desire to protect his brother and understanding where Everett was coming from, Aiden sucked a hissing breath in through his teeth, scratching his chin.

"You know how I feel about it. I'd rather neither of you fought."

"I'm not giving you a choice, Eirian. I'm remaining. Someone has to be ready to pick up the pieces." Glancing at Aiden, Everett asked, "I don't suppose you could leave him alive?"

Before Aiden could argue, Fayleen turned and said, "Don't worry about the good captain. He'll be fine."

"Do I want to know what you've done?" Aiden directed the question to Eirian.

"Taken measures to ensure you obey your orders to live." She smiled grimly. "Because I know you'd disobey in a heartbeat."

Chuckling, Everett agreed. "She knows you too well, big brother."

"Shut up, Scrappy."

SIXTEEN

"Why can't I stay with you?"

Hugging Ona tightly, Eirian met Brenna's gaze and silently pleaded for her to take the girl away. Putting a hand on her shoulder, Aiden crouched to smile sadly.

"Come on, chicken. You need to go with Brenna and Isabella. Remember what we've talked about?"

Ona sniffled. "No. I'm staying."

Stroking her head, Eirian whispered, "Be strong for me. Look after Brenna and Isabella."

Nodding to Merle, Aiden moved out of the way so he could pick Ona up and extract her from Eirian's grasp. Kicking and screaming, Ona fought to break free, but he held tight and followed Isabella out. Covering her face, Eirian tried not to cry. She knew she would not see them again, but the false promises she had made to Ona were a fresh heartbreak.

"You don't have to pretend for me, Eirian," Brenna said gently. "I know what's going on. I know this is goodbye."

"Look after Ona. Whatever happens, promise me you'll look after her."

"Like she's my own."

Pressing her lips together, Eirian nodded and staggered to her feet. Putting a hand on her arm to steady her, Aiden frowned when it looked like she was going to collapse back down. Smiling tensely at his concerned expression, Eirian focused on Brenna.

"I'll make sure your husband comes home alive," she said.

Brenna sighed. "Stubborn girl."

"At least whoever Everett marries will be an easier queen to serve than me."

"I might not go gray from stress."

"Boring is good."

Crossing to Eirian, Brenna hugged her and murmured, "Don't die if you can avoid it."

Tears welled in her eyes, and Eirian blinked them away. Familiar lies slipped from her tongue as she promised Brenna she would do everything she could to avoid death. Aiden watched on in silence, his men doing their best not to look at the two women. They knew what Eirian was capable of, and they had heard the fights between her, Aiden, Celiaen, and Galameyvin over how to end the war.

The guard assigned to Brenna cleared his throat, "Your Grace, we need to go."

Releasing Eirian, Brenna stepped back and smoothed her skirts. "Good luck, Your Majesty. I'll see you for your victory celebrations."

"Stay safe, Brenna. It's been an honor."

Watching her leave, Eirian felt Aiden's hand on her back. The layers of linen and leather blocked out the warmth of his skin, but the weight of it gave her some comfort. She did not have long to get her emotions back under control, even though he would have argued otherwise. There was too much to do before they faced Athnaral on the battlefield again.

"I need to see Tessa," she said.

Grabbing her arm, Aiden stopped Eirian from leaving. "You need to rest."

"No, I'm good. Let's go. Death waits for no one."

After the words slipped from her tongue, Eirian flinched. The whispers laughed mockingly, reminding her that Death was waiting for her. It felt like his presence blanketed Kelsby, the chill of the grave eager to welcome her into his embrace. She had not glimpsed Gebael lurking in the shadows, but the whispers assured her he was there. So long as he kept his hands off her loved ones, Eirian did not care what he had planned for her.

Leaving the chambers that she had occupied since arriving in Kelsby, Eirian did not know if she would see them again. If they were lucky, the darkness would meet her in battle on the morrow, and it would all be over. She would be dead, but everyone would be safe again. For however long the prison would last. Eirian hated the fact the prison was not permanent, but she hoped they would find a solution by the time the war came around again.

"It's not too late," Aiden murmured.

"It was too late the day I was born."

Giving her a disgruntled look, he said, "We've talked about it. Each of us is prepared to walk away today if that's what you want."

"Each of us?"

"Yes."

"Each of us who?" she demanded, even though she knew the answer.

"Eiri—"

Holding a hand in his face, Eirian silenced Aiden before he could say anything else. Looking at Gabe, she nodded, and he returned the gesture, his face blank.

"Get some rest, Captain. Or do whatever you want, so long as it's nowhere near me. Better yet, why don't you go find Celiaen and Galameyvin so the three of you can continue to plot how you're going to convince me to abandon the world."

Sighing, Aiden did not bother to argue. Instead, he turned to Gabe and Fionn, meeting each of their gazes to reassure himself that Eirian was safe in their hands. She was still their queen, and they were her guards until the end. Saluting, Aiden let them leave him behind. He would join them later on after he had met with Celiaen and Galameyvin to discuss their plan for the battle.

"Hungry?" Gabe asked, matching Eirian's stride.

"Do I want to know how you find anything for me these days?"

Smirking, he pulled a wrapped bundle from the pouch hanging at his waist. Catching a familiar, fragrant scent, Eirian's eyes widened, and she stared at him in amazement.

"Muntries? How? Someone brought them all the way from Riane?"

"Something like that."

Accepting the bundle, Eirian uncovered the reddish fruits and carefully put one in her mouth. The spicy apple-flavored fruits were one of her favorites as a child. She did not know how Gabe convinced a random mage to surrender such a delightful treat, but she was glad he had. Eirian took her time to enjoy each one on their way through the keep and out into the town.

Stealing one from her hand, Gabe sampled it and murmured, "Crunchy. Like an apple. Wouldn't say they deserve the face you're making."

"How did you know I'd like these?" she asked between fruits.

"I think it's a safe bet you eat anything that resembles a fruit."

Fionn laughed. "You mean, she eats anything."

"That too."

Ignoring Fionn's laughter, Eirian said, "You spoil me, Gabe. Thank you."

Winking at her, Gabe replied, "I've told you before, I need to stay your favorite. I look forward to getting to play with you one day."

She wanted to point out the chance to do so had passed, but decided not to. It was clear Gabe was trying to keep her positive in the only way he could. Giving him a faint smile, Eirian pointed at the sea of tents. Her eyes swept over them, searching out the familiar banners of Riane. There was an easier option, but she did not feel like using her magic to locate Tessa.

The whispers were loud enough in her mind that Eirian questioned her control. She could not deny they had worsened since arriving back in Kelsby. Smoke lingered in the air, thousands of fires sending eddies of gray into the sky.

Above them, clear blue skies did not match the storm of emotions rolling from the camps. Glancing at her fingers, she wondered if she could draw on those feelings and turn them into something tangible.

"The mages are that way," Paxton told her.

"Thank you."

"We thought it would be a good idea to know where everyone was."

Smiling, Eirian ignored the watching eyes tracking her progress. People called out, and she lifted her hand in acknowledgment. If there had been more time, she would have stopped to talk to officers, but she wanted to find Tessa quickly. They needed to discuss the plan to deal with the siege weapons while there was time. Because she knew defeating the darkness was no guarantee the war with Athnaral would end.

"Ree?"

Halting at the sound of her name being called, Eirian turned to look for the source. Spotting Zack jogging in her direction with a bucket, she smiled warmly.

"What are you doing out here?" he asked. "Shouldn't you be in the keep with all the other self-important pricks making decisions?"

"You're spending too much time with Jaren and Rylee." Eirian chuckled, accepting his hug.

"They're sulking. Baenlin ordered them to keep guard over Tessa. I'm supposed to be bringing this to her."

Looking at the bucket, she screwed up her face and exchanged a look with Fionn.

"Is that mud?" Fionn sniggered.

"Clay."

"So mud."

Cocking his head to the side, Zack arched his brow and studied Fionn thoughtfully. Eirian recognized the look on his face, her lips thinning as part of her took insult on Fionn's behalf. Sensing her annoyance, Zack chuckled and shoved the bucket at her.

"You can bring it to our esteemed future grand mage."

"Zack, I'm the Queen of Endara, not an errand girl." Refusing the bucket, Eirian said, "And why wasn't a yellow sent instead?"

Zack shrugged, nodding in the direction they needed to go. "Apparently, it's because I'm less useful. I'm just a blue, and I can't make anything, so errands it is."

"What about Luke?"

"We're taking turns. Just because Rylee and Jaren have to stay doesn't mean we do."

Laughing, she waved at the tents. "You pricks are torturing them!"

"And enjoying it. Fetching mud is worth the sour looks when we swagger off."

It was not long before Eirian spotted Jaren and Rylee arguing outside a large tent. They had tied the doors to each side, allowing as much light in as possible, and she noticed no flames were lit nearby. Tessa was hunched over a bench with streaks of mud on her face while attempting to shape the clay into a ball. Magic hummed in the air, the distinct tang of it reminding Eirian of something she could not remember.

Whistling in admiration, Rylee turned away from Jaren. "Can I peel those layers of leather off you?"

"Is my ass still adorable enough?" Eirian quipped, making a point of turning so Rylee could look.

"Adorable enough to bite."

Groaning, Jaren covered his face, muttering, "I don't know how you two do it."

"There's going to be a battle tomorrow. If I don't make crude comments to the Queen of Endara today, who knows if I'll ever have another chance."

Leaning in close, Fionn whispered to Eirian, "Did you?"

"You bet."

"Am I allowed to imagine?"

Arching a brow at him, she chuckled. "I won't tell your captain."

"Much appreciated."

Listening to their exchange, Gabe grumbled, "She won't tell, but I might."

Scoffing at them, Zack held up his bucket and called, "Tessa, I've got more mud!"

"Clay!" she yelled back. "I hope you haven't got fucking mud."

"I'll mud you!"

"No, you won't! You'll mud my brother."

Pressing his lips together to hold back his laughter, Fionn watched the broad grin on Eirian's face before looking at his fellows. If the interactions they had witnessed between her and Celiaen's companions had not been enough, watching the group of mages speak to each other was. All their expectations of a prim and proper princess never had a chance. They watched Eirian's tense stance give way, a hint of comfort seeping through the magic surrounding her.

"I don't know, Tessa. I think Jaren is too easy to mud!" Eirian said, wriggling her brows.

Noticing Eirian's arrival, Tessa stood straight and stared at her in amusement. "Speak for yourself! One flash of a red band and anyone could mud you."

Turning to Gabe, Kip said, "I don't think they're talking about what's in the bucket."

"You think?" he muttered in response.

Rylee grinned. "Ree, have you been pretending to be a lady around these poor men?"

"There's no pretending I'm a queen," Eirian replied, giving Rylee an annoyed look.

"So, I shouldn't tell them about that time when you were a queen to feast on?"

Knowing the easiest way to stop Rylee from telling stories to her guards was to make it seem like she did not care, Eirian shrugged and started walking toward Tessa. With her pending death, she was not sure it even mattered.

"They've all seen me naked, so have fun. Maybe even tell them about that time I had you in knots in the armory."

Crossing her arms, Tessa asked, "What about?"

"Nope."

"But—"

"Tessa, let's talk about your exploding balls."

Laughing loudly, Jaren waved at them. "Those are words I never thought I'd hear come from anyone's mouth."

Unable to resist, Luke quipped, "Tessa wants to make Baenlin's balls explode."

"You know, for a group of people with so much magic, you're a bunch of crude shits," Fionn said with a grin. "I fucking love it."

Signaling the silent yellows working with Tessa to leave, Eirian waved at the tent doors. Magic rippled, the wards settling into place with barely any effort. Quiet filled the tent, surprising Tessa, and she glanced between the chatting group outside and Eirian.

"Your wards are improving."

"I'm embracing my power a lot more these days."

Eyes darting to her feet, Tessa whispered, "Can they hear anything?"

"No. They can still see, though, so don't do anything silly like kissing me."

"They'll fret not being able to hear us. Most people still think we dislike each other."

Eirian leaned on the table, careful not to rest her arms in any of the piles of half-dry clay. Lips curling into a sly smirk, she did not look at Tessa, keeping her focus on the lump that had been abandoned on her arrival.

"So, Baenlin?"

"I don't have the brute force to back myself up like you do. If I'm going to be grand mage, then I need his support."

"Be careful with him, Tessa. He's not one to do anything for free."

Sneering, Tessa muttered, "Because you don't ask for anything in return for your help?"

"You didn't exactly say no, and it wasn't the first time."

"Would you have helped get me out of the city if I had?"

"Of course. But you offered, and I didn't say no," Eirian purred. "No wasn't a word that left your lips even once. You can't deny you enjoyed paying me for my help."

Looking away, Tessa did not speak. Her cheeks felt like they were on fire, and the knowing gleam in Eirian's eyes did not help. She had forgotten how easily flustered she became around the other woman, and it was not a welcome feeling. Not when she had volatile substances nearby and an audience preventing her from pulling Eirian into a kiss.

"I started at first light this morning," she said, waving at the lumps of clay. "It's not the best stuff, but we're not making plates for the dinner table."

Poking at a lump, Eirian screwed up her face. "What's the problem?"

"We don't have the resources to make them hold shape easily. Apparently, most potters would use a reinforced skin to maintain the desired shape and size."

"Which we don't have the time to do."

"I won't stop working until I've figured this out."

Clicking her tongue, Eirian studied the lumps before raising her eyes to gaze at Tessa. Shifting nervously at the intensity of her stare, Tessa glanced at the group outside. They continued to chat, but she saw several of them keeping a close eye.

"Are you using your hands or your magic?"

"Both."

"Tessa, you can manipulate air and earth. This should be easy for you. Just imagine you're forming the clay around an orb," Eirian said.

The idea had occurred to Tessa, but she had not dared try it. Sensing her hesitation, Eirian sighed, resting her hands on the table to lean closer.

"You're incredible, Tessa. Considering the displays I've been putting on, don't you think it's time you stopped hiding as well? All you need to do is form the inner layer of the container, and someone else can add extra coatings of clay to make sure the pitch doesn't escape."

"It would use a lot of power to do."

"I'll sit quietly in the corner as your own personal well."

"Don't you have better things to do?" Tessa asked.

Shrugging, Eirian muttered, "Not really. I'm just sitting pretty until it's time to fight."

"Do you really think you might die in this?"

"No."

Breathing a sigh of relief, Tessa said, "Thank the powers."

"Don't thank them. There's no thinking I might because I know I will. Tessa, there's no after this war for me."

"Surely there's—"

"Please do me the honor of being the only person who doesn't pretend there's hope. Tessa, please. Everyone else refuses to accept it, and I'm playing along for their sakes. You and I, though, we know things they don't. We see the world differently."

Reaching across the table, Tessa covered Eirian's hand with hers and murmured, "If that's what you need."

"I need you to be a brilliant grand mage. When this is over, support my cousin Everett. Make mages leave Riane and go into Endara. Fay wants to stay, and I think she'll be an excellent official representative for the high council in Amath."

"There will be resistance."

Eirian nodded, agreeing with her. "Yes, lots of it. Especially from Paienven. Celi plans to abdicate his place as Crown Prince, and Gal will follow him. So use them as much as you have to. The prospect of power will sway the council, and Endara is going through a crisis of belief. You need to take advantage of my sacrifice."

"Until Mayve dies, my ability to do anything is limited."

"Which is why you need Baenlin. I told him something that I'm now going to tell you."

Cocking her head to the side, Tessa frowned and waited.

"We're not the only people in the world. My mother manipulated things to make everyone forget the rest of the world. Tessa, Shianeni was—"

"Don't be stupid, darling."

The words died on her tongue when Gebael's voice caressed through her mind. She knew he was lurking somewhere close, watching over her. Telling someone the truth about Shianeni was not worth the risk of what he might do to them in retaliation. Gazing out at the sunny day beyond the tent walls, Eirian tried to drown out the whispers. Concerned, Tessa squeezed her hand, drawing her attention back.

"What, Ree?"

"She was an awful person who lied and manipulated to get what she wanted. You can't trust Neriwyn either."

Blushing, Tessa cleared her throat, muttering, "Why not?"

"Because he helped her." Eyes narrowing, Eirian suspected why Tessa's face had gone red. "You know he's the father of my half-brother?"

"No, I did not. But I didn't sleep with him, I promise."

Eirian had enough memories darting around her mind to know better than to ask if the flirtation had been worth it. Instead, she hoped Tessa had gained some confidence from knowing a man as powerful as Neriwyn had shown an interest in her. Knowing what Neriwyn was, she had to wonder if he had done so on purpose.

"When you've wrested some control over the council, look beyond the Red Desert. Until then, there is an awful lot of forgotten knowledge sitting beneath the streets of Riane. But I don't need to remind you of that."

"A world beyond our borders?" Tessa murmured. "What an amazing idea."

"Do you understand why I can't avoid my fate?" Eirian asked.

"You've always been one for saving people. So much nobler than I am."

"I'd have thought you'd be happy to see me dead. Then you'd be undoubtedly the most powerful purple mage."

Laughing bitterly, Tessa replied, "Do you even count as a purple mage?"

Noticing the looks being sent their way, Eirian brought the conversation back to the clay vessels intended for pitch. They needed to focus on the crucial matters while they could.

"My suggestion is to decide how big you need them and focus on coating a ball of air. No one else can do what you do, Tessa. So use that brilliant mind of yours to figure this out."

Releasing Eirian's hand, Tessa wriggled her fingers, and the air moved around them, tiny eddies driven by magic. She understood where Eirian's suggestion was coming from. However, the focus and power needed to maintain a solid ball while coating it with wet clay would be draining. It would tax her, but she could not think of anything else that would work.

"What if…" Tapping a finger to her chin, Tessa hummed. "What if I could start the drying process while coating the air?"

"What would that do?"

"If I could harden the initial coating, I wouldn't need to hold the inner ball of air for as long. Then I could give it over to a yellow to finish. I'd only have to do the first part, and it would give us a chance to make more."

Trying to picture what Tessa was suggesting, Eirian gave up and shrugged. "If you think it might work, try it. Like I told you, I'm happy to sit in the corner and provide you with the power to do what needs to be done."

"You need to rest and conserve what you have for your fight," Tessa said. "Regardless of how you act, you're not an inexhaustible well of energy."

"Are you sure about that?"

"Positively."

Eirian sighed. "I'm not even sure how I'm going to lure the darkness out to fight me. She knows killing me herself will reimprison her, so she'll avoid confronting me directly."

"You're a purple, Ree, and we're nothing if not tricksters. What if she doesn't kill you?"

Reminded of what Tessa could do, Eirian felt the stirring of a plan but did her best not to think of it. It was not something she could risk, not yet, not unless she could not think of another way. Unbothered by her silence, Tessa played with eddies of air, twisting the tiny elements that composed each part. They were something she saw clearly with her magic, but no one other than Eirian had ever understood what she was talking about.

"Water."

"What?" Eirian asked in confusion.

"Ice. A paper-thin sheet of ice would harden the clay on contact."

Shrugging, Eirian did not answer and backed away from the table. It was something she had seen before, the way Tessa forgot everything else existed. Her focus was on nothing except her work. Dropping the wards she had raised to keep their conversation private, Eirian returned to the outside, flinching as her eyes adjusted to the light.

"Everything okay?" Jaren inquired, a touch of concern on his face.

"Tessa had an idea. Make sure she eats and drinks."

Gabe looked curious, his eyes switching from Eirian to Tessa. She was peering into a bowl, and he saw what looked like swirls of water dancing across the surface. He knew better than to ask, leaving it to the mages to understand what they were doing with their magic.

Flinching, Rylee asked, "How much time does she need?"

"All the time that we can get her. If it looks like she'll drop from exhaustion, send for me. Otherwise, make her stop and eat, go for a walk, and do anything else that will stave off the slump. Find every damn yellow you can to help."

"There's got to be an easier way to deal with siege weapons..."

"Sure, I could set them and the Athnaralan army on fire," Eirian replied, her expression and tone suggesting it was not a joke.

Even though killing came naturally to the pair of reds, the prospect of what Eirian suggested was not one they liked. Exchanging looks, they attempted to reconcile the woman standing in front of them with the one they had known for twenty years. Sighing at them, Eirian turned to her guards and nodded. The men regrouped, breaking away from conversations to leave.

"Good luck tomorrow," she told Rylee and Jaren.

"It's only a little battle. The Athnaralans won't know what hit them," Rylee replied.

Eirian and her guards stared at the two reds, and she said, "Look after each other on the field. Neither of you is allowed to die. The Queen of Endara forbids it."

Clearing his throat, Gabe commented, "We should go, ma'am."

Giving each of them a hug and a kiss, Eirian focused on Luke and Zack. The two blues watched on in amusement. She expected Luke to comment about sentimental warriors, but he remained silent.

"Make sure they don't do anything stupid."

Luke snorted. "We said the same thing to your guards."

"Rylee and Jaren might be a pair of idiots, but they lack the reckless flair you possess," Zack added.

"Fuckers," she grumbled.

"Yeah, yeah, you love us."

Spotting Galameyvin waiting in the distance, Luke said, "Someone is waiting for you. Better not keep him too long, or he might punish you."

"Yeah, but she likes that!" Rylee laughed. "Her ass is pretty covered in handprints."

Groaning, Eirian made a rude gesture. "Alright, fine. I hope you all die tomorrow."

Walking away from their laughter, she met Galameyvin's concerned gaze and forced a smile. It was a wasted effort, and he saw through the mask before Eirian reached him. Pulling her into a hug, he buried his face in her hair and breathed deeply, inhaling the floral scent. She let him, her fingers digging into his back as she clung tightly to the silk of his coat.

"Celi said you got into a bit of a pissing match with Paienven this morning."

She mumbled into his chest, "Don't want to talk about it. I'm hungry. Can we find food?"

"What was so funny?"

Fionn grinned, replying, "They suggested you might punish the Queen for keeping you waiting and that she'd enjoy it."

Chuckling, Galameyvin kissed the top of her head, blue eyes gleaming with mischief. "Very true, she does."

"Oh, for the love of!" Eirian huffed.

"She gets cranky when she's hungry," Wade said, receiving laughs from the others.

Rolling his eyes, Gabe told Galameyvin, "I gave her some muntries earlier to tide her over."

"How did you find muntries up here?" Galameyvin asked in surprise.

"I have my ways." A faint smile appeared on his face. "But she hasn't had much else for a while."

Glaring at them, Eirian grumbled, "If you're all so concerned, stop talking and fetch me food. Go on, fetch, boys, fetch."

SEVENTEEN

ayleen's observation that he had not seen mages fully armored lingered at the front of Aiden's mind as he waited beside Eirian, watching from his mount. Dawn had barely broken, early sunlight making the sea of plate gleam. More weapons than he could make sense of adorned each red mage. Next to the mages, everyone else looked like they had barely started dressing.

The magical members of Paienven's army had joined their comrades from Riane, leaving the ordinary soldiers as a separate force. It had come as no surprise to Eirian when she was told the mages intended to lead the fight. She knew they would cut through the Athnaralans like a scythe through wheat.

"Don't you feel underdressed?" Fionn asked and waved at the mages.

"And nowhere near armed enough. Why so many weapons?" Merle muttered.

Sitting beside Eirian, Fayleen snorted. "Have you seen the Telmian troops? Not a single bit of plate. They don't need to gleam and shine."

"Really?"

She cast a look at the months of her hard work that Eirian wore and said, "Makes me wonder if something guided my hand when I made that."

Aiden knew precisely what she meant. He had seen Vartan, and the Telmian commander wore armor similar to Eirian's.

"Not the most surprising thing any of us have heard in recent times," he said.

Tugging at Halcyon's reins, Eirian shook her head. "Come on, let's join our people. Baenlin is going to give the command any moment, and I don't think any of you want to be close when it happens."

"How can you tell?" Fascinated, Fox peered at the mages.

"I can feel it," she replied, nudging the horse to turn. "Besides, it's light enough that the enemy will know we're coming."

Almost on cue, horns blared in the distance, telling them the Athnaralans had discovered what was going on. As Eirian and her guards rode, they heard the answering horns signaling the archers to release. It was a harsh sound, but it was the wash of magic that made their breath catch. Eirian had known it was coming and wrapped her magic around them to soften the desire to fight, but it called to her. Warded against the pull, Fayleen glanced at her before turning concerned eyes to Aiden.

"It's going to get stronger," Fayleen muttered. "That's why they ordered anyone not fighting to withdraw past the line of blues and yellows."

Aiden flicked a glance at the quarterstaff strapped to her back. "I expected it to be more overwhelming."

"She's protecting you."

It was clear Eirian was concentrating as she said, "Let's hope they're enough."

"They know what they're doing. We train for this."

Cheek twitching, Aiden understood Eirian's concern. "They don't train for the daoine."

Spotting Celiaen waiting for them with Tara and the other reds of his party, Eirian decided she hated the sight of him fully armored. "I expected you to be with Baenlin."

While he did not need to question how she had known Celiaen was under the armor, Aiden knew there was no mistaking the eyes staring at them from beneath the helm.

"Did you think I wouldn't be by your side for this?" Celiaen cocked his head to the side, not looking at anyone except Eirian. "Magnificent work, Fay."

Beaming with pride, she replied, "Thanks, it's high praise coming from you, Celi."

His eyes strayed to the unfamiliar knives strapped to Eirian's thighs. It surprised him to see the symbols decorating them.

"Who crafted those?"

"Keigh."

"How did you convince him to make them?"

Surprised, Celiaen stared at her. The pleased smile hinted at a superiority that said Fayleen would not share her secret.

"I would've pushed my luck and asked for a matching pair for you, but I know you have your preferred smith."

Flinching, Eirian pressed her lips together, murmuring, "They've begun."

"Father sent his cavalry to harass their camp from the left flank. He hopes to capture Aeyren. Neriwyn sent some of his people along," Celiaen said and turned his face in the fight's direction.

Being at the back of the line frustrated Eirian and the reds, but they did their best to keep their magic in check. With the sheer number of soldiers involved on both sides, the noise of the battle was persistent and accompanied by what resembled the constant buzzing of bees. Aiden and his men did not need to ask to know it was magic in use. Their watchful eyes rarely strayed from Eirian in expectation of her losing control and diving into the fight.

They knew she was waiting and watching, biding her time for some hint of her enemy to make an appearance. It gave her enough focus to maintain control, but Eirian had warned them the pull of the fight might become too much in the end. What she had not told them about was the unending whispers barraging her mind or the shadows dancing at the edge of her vision. Overnight, they had gone from barely manageable to entirely not.

Aiden knew talking would help Eirian and Celiaen to keep their focus. "If Aeyren is our prisoner, Athnaral must concede."

Eirian tilted her head back, staring at the clouds. The white fluffy shapes seemed too clean for what they were overlooking. Mocking her ceaselessly, the shadows told her how easy it would be to change that. She knew soon enough the smoke of funeral pyres would discolor the sky.

"I don't think it matters. She'd only drive Athnaral on until there was nothing left, and then she'd turn us on each other."

"Do you think so?" Merle asked.

"She'll burn the world around her and dance in the ashes that remain."

Randolph was the first to express his impatience. "Then how do we end this quicker?"

"We can't." Eirian shook her head, ignoring the looks given by those closest to her. "There is nothing I can do but wait. If I try to go to her, she'll run. She needs to believe she's winning before she'll face me."

"Well then, how do we make her believe she's winning?" Kane was the next to speak.

Squinting one eye at Aiden, Celiaen waited for him to tell his men to stop asking questions. When he remained quiet, Celiaen looked at the guard.

"Do you think it's an appropriate time to be questioning your queen?"

Shifting in the saddle, Gabe gave Celiaen one of his cold, calculating stares that made most people look away nervously. "There's no better time to be questioning her than when she told us we have free rein to do so."

"Why would you do that?" Celiaen demanded.

Lifting the hood of her cloak over her head, Eirian pulled it as far forward as she could, hoping it would hide the strain she felt. Her grip on her reins helped hide the trembles.

"There is no making her believe she's winning. Something will happen during the battle to turn things in her favor. We just have to hope that it's not something I can't come back from."

Fox waved in the town's direction, making a noise that resembled choking. "That's jolly fantastic."

"What is?" Merle prompted.

They turned to look in the direction he waved and took in the sight of several Telmians riding toward them. At the front and center of the line was Faolan, his expression solemn. Eirian did not look at them, fearful he would see through her guise. Without a word, they slipped among the guards like it was their place, Faolan maneuvering in next to Aiden with a shared look.

"Didn't think you lot would join us." Tobin wriggled his brows.

Slaine snorted at him, her armor doing nothing to make her seem less tiny. "She's our little queen. King Neriwyn gave us a choice to be with her or our kin."

"And you choose her?"

"Always," Ilar declared with a smile at Eirian's back. "We've seen enough to know we aren't wrong to place our faith in her. She is our little queen."

Scowling, Eirian threw a glare at Faolan and said, "You've placed yourselves between the rest of them and me as a sacrifice."

"That is secondary to our need to protect you," Faolan replied.

"I don't need you opting to die for me."

He turned his sad green eyes to Celiaen before shifting them to Fayleen and Aiden. "Or them, and yet here we are, willing to do so. And before you try to say anything about your mother, it's not her I'm placing my faith in. It's you."

Offering his hand, Aiden nodded. "She's stubborn."

"She's our stubborn, though." Clasping the hand, Faolan found a faint smile.

"I'm right here!" Eirian huffed in annoyance and twisted a lock of Halcyon's mane in her hand. "You're so frustrating."

Fayleen grinned. "Don't lie, Ree, you love it, and you love us."

"With so many people having faith in you, Eirian, it's time you had faith in yourself. Let yourself feel it, feel the faith and the hope, and use it. Believe in us as we believe in you," Faolan said and met Eirian's gaze, feeling the weight of her grief.

Horns blasted through the air, and they turned toward the battle. They could see nothing from their place at the back of the lines, but they knew what the call meant. Eyes narrowing, Faolan kept his focus on Eirian, wondering if he was the only one among them who understood that she felt every death.

The horns signaled the Athnaralans had roused themselves to face the attacking mages. It meant the Ensaycalan cavalry would sweep across the flank, accompanied by members of the Telmian army. Archers were withdrawing to avoid killing their people, their orders to return to the town walls and prevent any press of the enemy toward it.

"Eirian."

Faolan whispered her name, watching the clenching of her jaw. He did not need to wonder if she had chewed the insides of her cheek to the point of blood.

"Your people are about to join the fray. Are you?"

"They expect it," she answered hoarsely.

"Are you ready?"

Celiaen said, "You don't have to do this. No one will think less of you if you wait and conserve your energy to fight the darkness."

Releasing her grip on Halcyon's mane, Eirian bowed her head before pushing her hood back. Her friends and guards stared at her, seeing signs of the strain she was under.

"You don't get it. I have to. She needs to see me weakened. So I apologize now, while I can, for anything my influence may drive you to do." Her eyes swept over her guards, wondering if she would see them again. "And I thank you all. I know I've said it already, but I don't think I can ever say it enough."

"You sound like you think we're going to die on you." Mac chuckled. "Don't you worry, we're coming back with you."

"I've warded them the best I can against your influence. They stand some chance of keeping control of themselves," Fayleen told Eirian.

Aiden shrugged, saying, "You know I'd rather you were anywhere else, but here is where you must be. Lead your people, Majesty, inspire them as only you seem to do."

"And do it magnificently." Fionn grinned.

"We always have your back," Merle said, receiving nods of agreement.

She looked like she wanted to either strangle them or hug them. "You're a bunch of bloody fools, but I suppose I can't expect any less."

Grim, Celiaen waved in an invitation for her to lead the way. "Fools for a fool. Let's go show my father why he should fear you."

"You say that like he's the enemy," Merle muttered.

"I've been contemplating that exact thought a lot recently."

"That's not reassuring in the slightest."

Shaking her head, Eirian nudged Halcyon. "The longer we sit here, the more we miss."

Making room for Celiaen to ride between them, Fayleen reached over and knocked on his helm. "Metalhead. It's an improvement."

Pretending to be insulted, he flexed a hand at her, the plate catching in the sunlight, demanding, "What, I'm not pretty enough for you?"

"I have my eye on something a little less aged," she quipped, grinning.

"Captain, do you mind?" Faolan ignored the banter, pointing at the space between him and Eirian.

Cocking his head to the side, Aiden studied Faolan's face, replying, "Of course."

There was little need to go faster than a walk. Eirian did not look at Faolan, despite feeling him watching her. Instead, she closed her eyes to block out the view of people marching on the orders of their commanders. She hoped if she thought hard enough, the image in her mind of the cliffs of Riane overlooking the ocean would be what she saw when she opened her eyes again.

For a moment, Eirian imagined she smelled the salt, the prickle in her nose as she inhaled, and the taste on her tongue. And for that moment, the shadows and whispers faded from thought, allowing silence to fill her mind. Swallowing back her reluctance, Eirian blinked against the light that made her flinch when she opened her eyes to look at Faolan.

"I know you want to say something, wolf."

His green eyes had settled on the knife closest to him. None of the quaternary knots worked among the wards, and symbols on Eirian's new armor had escaped his notice, and Faolan needed to know. Waving at her, he frowned.

"Where did?"

"Fayleen. It's no longer surprising, but we found it together many years ago in a book without understanding what it meant. It drew me then, and she always said she'd use it when she made me new armor. Which, as you can see, she did."

"And the knife?"

"A pair, because one can never have too many knives," Eirian said without smiling.

"It's rather disconcerting and eerily familiar. Perhaps none of us is free from influence even when we think we should be."

Faolan did not need to say anything else for Eirian to understand his implication. She saw the line of horses belonging to her nobles, her mouth twisting when she located Everett among them.

"Powers know, everything is a game to them. Every step along the way, they're there making sure we follow the path they chose for us."

Eirian hoped Gebael was choking on all the death resulting from the battle wherever he was. Beside her, Celiaen and Fayleen shared a look at her bitter tone before Faolan sighed.

"I would say to make the unexpected move, but would it be unexpected?"

"I don't think there is an unexpected move, simply a list of consequences for every choice. I could choose to turn my back and ride away from all of this, but then what?" Shaking her head, Eirian directed her mount away from the nobles, ignoring the calls of her name. "They don't need to lead me down their path because they knew I'd never turn my back on everyone."

"I feel how much this is straining you."

Eyes flickering down to her gloved hands, Eirian fought back against the trembles. "It's nothing I can't handle. Poor Celi is feeling it far more than me."

She tasted his rage through the bond, barely held back from the tipping point. Shrugging, Celiaen could not disagree with her.

"I have more years of discipline than you, dear heart. I'll be fine. Besides, we'll join the fight soon."

Her expression softened, a hint of a smile reaching her eyes. "That we will."

"They won't know what hit them." Holding out a hand, Celiaen waited for Eirian to entwine her leather-covered fingers through his. "You and I have this under control. Together, there isn't a fight we can't win."

They had come to the ridge that swept down across the plain where they had fought the first battle. No longer the grassy space it had been, soldiers covered it in their push toward the Athnaralans. It was just high enough for Eirian to get her first look at thousands of people marching into battle, and the sight made her stomach clench. They were close enough to hear the screams and the ringing clangs of weapons clashing. Magic was so heavy in the air that the guards questioned their ability to breathe, the feeling like a blanket suffocating them.

Waiting ahead, slightly separated from the Endaran forces, was a familiar company of soldiers. Aiden had gone behind Eirian's back the day before, organizing for Todd and his people to be waiting. He knew they were staunch loyalists and trusted them to maintain a shield of bodies around Eirian until every one of them had fallen. Todd had been more than happy to oblige, assuring Aiden that no one would know they had set it up.

Suspicious brown eyes settled on him, and Aiden forced a surprised look onto his face, hoping it would be enough to assuage her. Unwilling to speak, Eirian nodded at Todd, and he saluted, the lines of soldiers behind him following suit. They were close enough to the fight that it was time to dismount and leave the horses behind. They were not cavalry, and there was little point in risking untrained horses in an infantry fight.

Slipping from the saddle, Eirian scratched Halcyon in his favorite spot and rested her head against his neck, breathing in his smell. Removing her cloak, she tossed it over the saddle, aware of the hindrance it would be in battle. Signaling to the younger members of his troop, Todd had them take the horses away. Watching her faithful mount led in the opposite direction, Eirian clenched her jaw in determination.

Keeping close, Celiaen checked his swords and observed from the corner of his eyes as others did the same. Fayleen chuckled as she slipped the quarterstaff from its binds and leaned on it like it was a walking stick. It was their first chance to see it clearly. The other mages in the group picked out the wards engraved into the smooth wood, helping them realize it was more than a stick that hurt when hit with it.

The movement of so many people had torn the ground. Todd led the way, the soldiers under his command engulfing Eirian and her company, surrounding them like a barrier against the rest of the world. She hated it, hated the knowledge that none of them stood a chance of controlling themselves once she and Celiaen let go of their fragile self-control. There was no more banter, no inquisitive conversation. They had nothing left to say. Each person knew they might not come back from the battle that raged before them.

With every step they took, they felt the pull of the bloodlust of the mages already fighting. The whispers of Eirian's power escaping her hold told of slicing blades and blood spilling, of killing anything in its path. Parting before their queen, the Endaran forces cheered, and it was a harsh contrast to the sounds of battle around them. It held a note of hope, expecting Eirian to lead them to victory. Only a few lines of soldiers remained between them and the fight, each ready to give way the moment she made her move.

Finding her voice, Eirian looked at those closest to her. The woman who she counted as a sister. The captain who adored her above all others. The lord who gave her his loyalty, despite the love he had held for her mother. And finally, at the man whose heart shared a beat with hers. Only Galameyvin was missing, and she felt his absence badly.

"I'll see you on the other side."

Drawing his swords, Celiaen held the hilts up, and hands pressed together in front of him. He stared at Eirian in expectation.

"Blade of my blade."

"Celi."

"Ree."

Sighing, she pulled her swords free and held them the same way he did. Celiaen and Eirian rested their foreheads against each other, their fists touching.

"Song of my song," Eirian said.

Placing a hand on Aiden's shoulder, Faolan wondered if he could see the power that swirled around the pair as he said, "All we have to do is let them dance and watch their backs."

Tara shared a look with the other red mages. They knew what was coming. It was a display of power they had witnessed before, though not on the same scale they were facing.

"Here we go," she warned.

Expecting the two warriors to release their control, Fayleen spun her staff around and planted the butt firmly on the ground, her power spreading out over the guards. Aiden thought it looked like she had cast a shimmering net of dewdrops over them, but a blink cleared the vision from his eyes. Her ward caught the wash of bloodlust, preventing Aiden and his men from feeling it in full strength and allowing them to follow Eirian into battle.

There was no desperation to Eirian's magic like last time, and Aiden suspected it was because she was confident they would win the fight. With no need for her to sweep in and save the day, she moved through her people like a predator stalking its prey. A great dark beast that had caught the scent of blood. Beside her, Celiaen was something gleaming, the light to her shadow. Her power energized those already engaged in combat, lending precision to their aim and strength to their blows.

Faced with their enemy falling back to let the duo through, the Athnaralans surged forward. Their initial confusion became fear when Eirian's magic hit. They saw their deaths coming, panic spiking as the blades sliced through their flesh. Diving into the battle, the group of royal guards was clear-headed. Staying close to Aiden, Fayleen fought hard, a sword gripped tightly in one hand while her staff swung in the other. Letting himself admire her fighting, he winked when she slit the throat of a soldier.

Rallying the Endarans, Todd screamed, "For Endara! For your queen!"

Like a roar, the surrounding army repeated the words. Those already in the battle barely registered what was being screamed, but the ones behind heard and answered. Further back, the Endaran nobles understood their queen had joined the fight, and Everett whispered prayers to the powers to protect her. He hoped the darkness heard the voice of the Endarans and knew her destruction was forthcoming.

Elsewhere, General Darragh stood with Paienven and Sannaeh, wishing he could be a part of it. He envied those witnessing what he suspected was a fight unlike any he had previously seen. It had been a long time since he had seen someone command loyalty as easily as Eirian did, and a glance at Paienven left him doubting his own. No army had ever roared their allegiance to the sky for the Ensaycalan king, and the knowledge of that left a sour look on Paienven's face.

Further away, the words brought a tear to Neriwyn's eyes. Closing them, he let images of the fight come, let them flow through his mind and stir regrets for everything that happened and which was yet to come.

Blood, sweat, and death filled his nostrils as his head swung around, trying to spot Eirian among the fighters. Aiden thought he spotted the silver gleam of Celiaen's armor before a pike came at him. He raised his sword to block, but Fayleen appeared between him and the blow. Her staff was on her back, and in its place, she gripped her swords tightly. The sight of a woman facing him stunned the Athnaralan. Taking advantage of it, Aiden drove his sword into the man's gut, twisting it as he yanked back.

"Where's Eirian?" he asked.

"Don't know. That way somewhere." Fayleen swiped her arm across her face, wiping sweat away and waving in a general direction. "I'm following my orders."

His eyes narrowed, and he growled, "She told you to watch my back."

"Got to keep you alive, Captain. Ree doesn't need me to watch her back, but she needs you to not die."

Clicking her tongue, Fayleen looked down at the dying man at her feet. Watching her casually thrust her blade into his throat without flinching, Aiden realized he had severely underestimated her.

"We better find her."

"After you."

"Ladies first," he said and waved his free hand in the direction she had gestured.

Giving him a cheeky grin, Fayleen purred, "Oh, gorgeous, I'm no lady."

Admiring her dive into the fight, he agreed. "Damn right you're not."

Eirian had not stopped moving, magic driving her further and further into the fight. A short distance away, Celiaen was a lethal blur among the Athnaralans. She did not take stock of who was still close by, the ferocious growling coming from Faolan as he fought enough to remind her she was not alone. With each drop of blood that hit the ground, she felt the earth beneath her feet hunger for more.

The darkest aspect of her power constantly whispered in her mind, reminding her how easy it would be to reach out and shatter the opposing army. It grew harder to drown out the urge, the knowledge that the number of mages offered a well of power deep enough that she could do it. They would lose a few of their own in the process. Holding tightly to the thought that it was unnecessary and far too steep a price to pay for victory, Eirian channeled her desire into swift, deliberate strikes.

Rippling through the Athnaralans came an echo of madness, driving them to fight back harder. Feeling the shadows chase through them, the desperation and fear that filled them, Eirian experienced nothing but sorrow. The shadows called to the ones dancing at the edge of her mind, increasing the internal struggle she was dealing with. Yet it did not stop her strikes, the twin blades slicing through flesh and armor as though they were merely cotton.

Men fell one after another, and Eirian barely spared a thought for them before she moved to the next. Blood coated her armor, splashes of it marring her pale face with vibrant red. More and more of the enemy threw themselves at the Endaran queen, pushed by the darkness, who twisted her claws deep in their minds. Eirian felt every moment, felt the mocking laughter and glee that came as a response to her grief over each death. She knew with each desperate swing of their swords, the men were striving to injure her at the very least.

Her armor absorbed the few that escaped her parries, but she felt their impact. Ripping her blade free of a corpse, Eirian hissed through her teeth while rolling her right shoulder. The joint ached from a blow that had landed square across her arm, and the pain was enough to let her overcome her bloodlust completely.

"Fuck."

Faolan stepped up to her, parrying a blow while asking, "Are you hale?"

Her fingers tingled slightly, but she refused to let it stop her. "Yeah, I will be. Just keep them off me."

"I'll do my best, little queen." He smelled the lie, despite the carnage surrounding them. "But they're a little demanding right now."

Eirian watched Faolan swing his sword, gripping both of hers with her injured hand so she could press her good fingertips into the side of her neck. "She's driving them, forcing them into madness."

Grunting, he glanced back at her. "I know."

Returning her sword to her hand, Eirian did her best to hide the wince of pain shooting through her arm. It was a struggle to swing the blade, but gritting her teeth, she pushed through. There was an upside to the pain. It kept her magic from driving her into the fight. Without that urge, she could carefully pick her battles, letting her allies take the brunt. But there was also a downside. The shadows taunted at the edge of awareness, taking advantage of her clarity to scream louder.

She sensed Celiaen's concern through the bond, his mind aware enough to realize that she was not fighting as hard as she had been. Reassuring him, Eirian let him return his focus to the task at hand, the Athnaralans eager to strike him down. They were ordinary soldiers, and she doubted they knew who either of them was, their desire stemming from the mad god.

Feeling her magic whisper to her of danger, Eirian spun to block an attack with her injured arm, the impact more than she could handle. Letting the sword drop, she cradled her arm to her chest and dispatched her opponent with her second blade. Slipping the weapon into a scabbard, she scooped up the one she had dropped and turned to look for Faolan and Aiden.

Sensing her pain, Celiaen began fighting his way back, worry driving every blow. Hearing Eirian shouting his name, Faolan knew she needed to withdraw from the battle. He had suspected she was more hurt than she had cared to admit, but the fight had pulled him a little further from her than he had planned. When he reached her, he found her battling, her right arm held tightly against her chest as she did her best not to let anyone land another blow. He quickly killed her opponent and nodded, eyes sweeping over the line.

"Sheath that sword, let's get you out of here," Faolan growled, pointing his weapon toward safety.

Nodding, she swallowed and did as told. "I'm sorry, I should have withdrawn earlier."

Pressing a hand to Eirian's back, he urged her to move. "Just focus on dodging and warding."

"What about the others?"

"They'll find their way out. Your prince is coming. Now move."

Staggering when he pushed again, Eirian glimpsed Merle fighting nearby. Calling his name, she watched him look at her.

"Find who you can, Merle! Withdraw!"

He saluted quickly, registering the words. Eyes widening, Merle spotted the Athnaralan heading for her with his sword raised and shouted a warning.

Eirian realized too late, moving to draw a weapon for defense. It felt like time slowed as Faolan shoved her clear and intercepted the incoming sword. Bile rose in her throat, nausea threatening, while Eirian watched the blade driving through him.

Lunging forward with her sword in hand, she responded by thrusting it into the Athnaralan's exposed throat, shielded from the worst of the spray by the man between them. Dropping the blade, she cradled Faolan, guiding him to the ground among the dead and dying.

"No. No. No." She could barely speak, his green eyes finding hers. "No, Faolan, it's fine. It's going to be fine. I can fix this."

He coughed, a hand covering his bleeding abdomen. "I'm sorry."

Reaching for her magic, Eirian tried to remember what she had done in her rage to heal the girl from the farm. "You're not allowed to abandon me, wolf."

Wards rippled over them, Fayleen's quarterstaff appearing in the corner of Eirian's vision. She did not care. The sounds of Faolan's rattled breathing drowned out the battle. Voices were speaking, and hands tugged at her armor to get her to move, but she could not. Sitting in the blood-soaked dirt with his head resting in her lap, she could not move.

Eyelids drifted down over the green eyes Eirian knew had seen more than any of them understood. With her hands cupping his cheeks, she bent over his face to press her lips to his. Tears of rage welled in her eyes, the liquid distorting her vision. Her magic had gone still, reminding those around her of the calm at the center of a storm.

"Thank you, my loyal wolf," she murmured, not sure if he heard her. "I love you."

"Shian—" Faolan rasped before his breathing stopped.

The moment his heartbeat ended, the storm broke.

EIGHTEEN

High in the sky, an eagle screamed. Saoirse had kept out of range of the archers, but she felt the death of her twin. She did not need her fellow daoine to reach out with their minds to say what had happened. Caught on a wind current, she wanted to plummet to the ground, but something prevented her from closing her wings. Instead, Saoirse remained watching what would unfold, her eyes following everything.

Grief and rage filled Eirian, her nails digging into the flesh that she clung to. The physical pain from her shoulder vanished in the wake of the heartache coursing through her. Her mind struggled to come to terms with Faolan dying in her arms. He had been the vibrant man who teased and challenged her. The one who understood her feelings about her mother. He had become her friend and confidant, someone she could count on. Her loyal wolf.

Eirian felt his blood on her, and she did not think she could ever wash it away. His death was on her hands. He would be alive if she had done the right thing after being injured and left the fight. If she had kept out of it in the first place, biding her time for the darkness to confront her, he would be alive.

Her hatred chased the tails of anguish, magic pounding against the walls of her mind in demand for vengeance. Memories chased through her mind, and not all of them were hers. Most were Shianeni's. Images of Faolan's cheeky smile and joyful leaping in his wolf form became memories of him bent over a workbench while crafting another trinket. Faolan had been a link to a side of herself that she barely understood, and now he was dead because of her.

Staggering to her feet, Eirian continued to ignore the desperate pleadings of her friends. Magic roared to life around them, making those closest to her stagger with its intensity. Understanding quickly dawned on Fayleen. She grabbed Aiden, ignoring his startled protests as she pulled him to her and held her quarterstaff high, surrounding them in shielding wards. Eirian's magic swarmed, angry and hateful, darting through the Endaran forces.

She sent it seeking anything that bore the taint of her enemy. The power ripped the life from those it touched. There was no gentle crumpling of corpses, no blooming flowers creeping over them as they fell. Instead, it was violent, and she felt no remorse as screams filled the air. Those watching thought it resembled lightning darting through the Athnaralan troops. But shadows dripped from Eirian, swirling at her feet like a tempest.

Thrown into chaos by her actions, the allied forces fell back in shock. Eirian did not draw power from anyone else; instead, she used the energy of the lives she took. She stood facing the Athnaralan camp with her head held high and fists clenched at her side. Magic surrounded her, flickers mirroring the bolts burning through the soldiers. Every part of her body language screamed for the darkness to challenge her. Demanded it. The shadows twisting at her feet hungered for destruction.

Knowing that if they let her continue, the repercussions would be severe, Celiaen muttered a pre-emptive apology before slamming the hilt of a sword into her head. Dropping like a rock, the rush of Eirian's magic faltered. Catching her in his arms, he cast a look at the dead man and nodded to Aiden. Shielded by Fayleen, he understood and sheathed his sword, signaling to Merle to help him. Together, they picked up Faolan, following Celiaen.

Stunned soldiers let them through. The battle stalled while everyone worked out what was going on. Telmians and guards filtered through to accompany the unconscious queen. Bringing up the rear of the procession, Fayleen had gathered the fallen weapons of Faolan and Eirian, the blood-stained blades cradled carefully in her hands as she walked. As they got further from the front line, the battle resumed, lacking the same intensity as it had.

The Athnaralans fought reluctantly, the twisted figures of their dead comrades scattered over the ground to remind them they battled an opponent with significant power. Satisfied with the blow struck to Eirian, the darkness stopped driving them as forcefully. Her whispers changed, slithering into the minds of the Ensaycalans and the Endarans, urging them to fear.

"Keep walking." Ilar fell into step beside Aiden. "He knows what has happened. They're coming."

"I'm sorry." It was the truth, and Aiden could admit it while adjusting his grip on the dead man.

Blinking at him, Ilar nodded. "I know. He's not the only one to have fallen so far today, and he won't be the last."

"He was a good man," Fionn said, striding along on the other side of the body, ready to lend a hand if Aiden needed help.

Slightly ahead, Celiaen kept Eirian cradled close, commenting, "We're going to need some potent sedatives before she comes around."

"What for?" Fox asked.

Glancing down at the woman in his arms, Celiaen's mouth thinned. "You couldn't feel what I felt through our bond when he died. Trust me, she's going to need sedating. A little headache is the least of it."

Slaine exchanged a look with another Telmian. "Don't worry, Tharen will have something for her."

Recalling what she had been like after the last battle, Aiden suspected she would be so much worse. He was thankful Celiaen and Galameyvin were there to help this time. Together, the three of them could take care of her.

"She knew."

"What?" Arching a brow, Ilar gave him a confused look.

"She knew something would happen. Something that would allow the darkness to believe she has the upper hand," Merle answered.

Nodding, Fionn agreed. "She told us before the battle. Just didn't know what it would be, or at least, that's what she said."

Waving at their unconscious queen, Gabe looked even more serious than usual, and Aiden thought he saw grief in his eyes when he asked, "You don't think?"

"We couldn't tell you." Another of the daoine answered, his mouth set in a grim line.

"Kearney is right. Only the little queen and our king can answer that question. So we're left to wait and hope," Slaine said, and reached over to brush a hand against Eirian's leg.

They were clear of the soldiers, the absence of people surrounding them more noticeable than it had been earlier. A glance at the sun told Aiden it had reached its zenith. He barely noticed the heat, too many other concerns dominating his thoughts. Continuing to walk, the approach of riders soon greeted them. Daoine and mages moved toward them, Neriwyn at the front of the group.

Barely looking at Eirian, Neriwyn slid from his horse and hurried to Faolan. Chasing at his heels, Vartan was quick to move to the other side, and the two humans allowed the Telmians to take the body. Holding the dead man, Neriwyn tilted his head back and howled, the sound echoed by the other daoine. Tharen came to stand beside Celiaen, his silvery eyes looking down at Eirian.

"She's hurt."

"Her body or her heart?" Celiaen snapped, gripping Eirian tighter.

Grief was on Tharen's face as he lifted his gaze to the piercing eyes that challenged him. "I cannot be certain without examining her closer, but I think her shoulder is fractured. I can heal the physical, and I can keep her calm. The rest is up to the three of you."

Without blinking, Celiaen continued to stare at him. "I felt her heartbreak when he died. I felt the strength of her hatred, of her anger… her despair."

"And it wasn't just toward the Athnaralans, was it?" Tharen did not need an answer to know the truth. "She blames herself for the death of a friend. And at a glance, I can see her guards are fewer. Their deaths will weigh all the heavier on her."

Joining Celiaen, Aiden brushed a hand over Eirian's cheek. "Will it be like last time?"

"Worse, I imagine." There was no hesitation in Tharen's answer.

Fayleen cocked a finger to Merle and showed him Eirian's sword. Letting him take it, she walked over and knelt to offer Faolan's to Neriwyn. He blinked at her, taking in the blood splatter and the messy hair that had escaped the binding holding it back. Blood had matted clumps of it, lending to the solemn air that surrounded her.

He lifted the blade from her grasp and laid it on Faolan's body, crossing the man's hands over the hilt. Watching her rise to her feet and hold out a hand to Neriwyn left Aiden intrigued. There was a regalness to her he had not noticed before, a comforting air that surrounded her. Fayleen helped Neriwyn to his feet, offering him a grief-filled smile and a bow of her head.

"He saved her." Her voice was barely more than a whisper, but they still heard it.

Neriwyn replied, "I know."

"None of us will forget. None of us will stop being grateful to Faolan. We'll always mourn him."

"He gave his life for the person who mattered most to him, and Faolan wouldn't have had it any other way." Turning to look at Eirian, Neriwyn's gaze was hard as he instructed. "Make sure she can fight. Don't let his death be in vain."

Gabe stared at Neriwyn, speaking when no one else answered. "Don't worry, we will."

Neriwyn's gaze softened when he looked at Gabe, but the expression went as quickly as it appeared, and he said, "I know you will."

"We need to get her into the keep. Where are the horses?" Tara demanded.

Brushing aside his worry for Eirian, Aiden took command of his men, ordering them to locate where Todd had sent their mounts. Aware of the battle continuing behind them, he weighed up their options. Deciding it was better to walk while they waited, he turned to Celiaen and prepared for the argument to come.

"Give her to me," he instructed. "You're covered in heavier armor than I am."

Gripping Eirian tighter, Celiaen snarled, "I can carry her!"

"Now isn't the time to fight with me, princeling."

Most of the daoine had left them, focusing on removing Faolan's body from the battlefield. Aiden dismissed their presence, turning to Tara for support. Her helm was tucked under her arm, hair spiked up with sweat, but she regarded him with understanding.

"I'm not dragging your ass back if you collapse trying to carry her in this heat," Tara said.

Looking between them, Celiaen wanted to fight. Despite his concern for Eirian, the battle still called to him, bloodlust entwined in his magic. He feared surrendering her to another would take away the thing allowing him to remain focused. Inhaling deeply, he tasted flowers mixed in with blood and sweat, then nodded. Carefully taking Eirian into his grasp, Aiden shifted until he found a comfortable balance.

Ripping his helm off, Celiaen wiped a hand over his forehead and turned to look at the battlefield. He had seen the magic pouring off Eirian, and he had to acknowledge it was not a scene he cared to witness a second time. The screams of her victims would linger in his memory until he died. Placing a hand on his arm, Fayleen smiled grimly.

"Come on, Celi. We can't stay here. Not unless you want to rejoin the battle."

Unwilling to risk the reaction leaving with Eirian might garner, Aiden grunted. "Come or go, princeling? Make up your mind."

"This is ridiculous!" Tharen snapped. "Captain, take your queen back to the garrison. Your horses shouldn't be far off, but I don't advise waiting here."

Peeling away from the group escorting Faolan's body, Vartan joined them. There were blood spots on his armor, telling them he had been in the midst of the battle at one point. Shaking his head, he placed a hand on Celiaen's back and shoved him forward, ignoring the protests his action received.

"Don't fucking try, boy," he growled. "I've dealt with Neriwyn for millennia. You've got nothing on him. I will throw you over my shoulder if I must."

Smirking, Aiden nodded to his men, and they kept close. The blow Celiaen had struck Eirian continued to keep her unconscious, but Tharen stayed next to him just in case. None of them wanted to deal with Eirian if she came to while the battle raged on. Despite her state, flickers of magic oozed from her, dripping like shadows. It bothered Tharen to see flowers breaking through the trampled earth, a sign she was still affecting things when she should not have been.

"That troubled look on your face bothers me," Tara said, keeping her voice low in the hope no one would listen.

"What happened to her?"

"Celiaen knocked her out."

Mouth twisting, Tharen inclined his head at a brightly colored flower as they passed it. Shifting her helm from one arm to the other, Tara's eyes flickered to take the bloom in before returning to Celiaen's back.

"Can't say I've seen her summon lightning without a storm."

He had not witnessed what Eirian did and gasped, "What?"

Tara explained, "Faolan died, then she went crazy. I've seen Ree do a lot of things, but not that."

"Grief and rage manifest in different ways. She's powerful enough to turn them into magic."

"Sure, I'd believe it. If I wasn't one of the ones responsible for raising Ree, and I couldn't see the changes she's gone through in the last couple of months as clear as the fucking sun."

Sighing, Tharen shrugged. "I'm sorry. I don't have any answers for you. King Neriwyn might, maybe Vartan, but I'm afraid I have nothing to offer."

"I'm not sure I expected you to. Ree is never what anyone expects," Tara said. "It's always been that way, and I predict it'll be that way until she dies."

"The real question is if your prince ruined her chance to face the darkness."

Meeting his fearful gaze, Tara did not answer. She had considered the prospect straight after witnessing Celiaen knock Eirian out. It terrified her to voice it, and she refused to believe the chance to defeat the mad god had slipped past. Sidling up to her, Kenna still wore her helm and waved a hand at Celiaen.

"We should return to our tents and get cleaned up."

"I agree. One arm each?"

Kenna snorted. "Better giving him the same treatment he gave Ree."

"We need Gal," Tara admitted. "He's got the best chance of getting through."

"To which one?"

"Both. Either. I don't know. It's a fucking mess, Ken."

"What about Queen Sannaeh? He always listens to his mother." Kenna suggested, ignoring the amused look Tharen gave her.

Shaking her head, Tara said, "No, we need her to stay with Paienven. I know that fucker, and he's going to take one look at what Ree has done before demanding her head."

"What?" Fionn demanded from behind them.

"He already hated her. Now he's going to be shitting himself that he can't control her."

"Un-fucking-believable. Merle!"

Merle dropped back to join them and asked, "What's wrong?"

"We need to make sure Her Majesty is under constant guard. Tara said Paienven might try to have her killed."

He gazed at Tara. "Is he wrong?"

"No."

"Alright. We'll reach out to Todd and get him to bolster our numbers. I don't know if we've lost any of us, but I'd rather we have extras on duty. Let's not bother the Captain with this information until we're safely in the keep. Probably safe to say we shouldn't tell the Prince either. Don't need him committing patricide and regicide right now."

"While Paienven deserves it, we need Celi alive," Tara muttered.

Holding a hand in her direction, Merle said, "I don't want to know. Right now, I'm more concerned about keeping my queen safe. Fionn, I need you to whisper in ears. Make sure everyone knows no one is to get near her unless we know them."

"The boss man will catch on," he replied.

"Not much we can do about that. He'll understand."

Spotting soldiers bringing their horses toward them, the group moved quickly to sort themselves out. Hauling himself into his saddle, Celiaen nodded to Aiden expectantly, but he refused to surrender Eirian.

Before Celiaen could protest, Aiden said, "You're not coming with us. We've got enough to deal with. Go get cleaned up, then join us."

Vartan approached to offer his arms and waited for Aiden to give him Eirian. Gazing at her, he studied the blood splatter on her face. The blow Celiaen had delivered to her head had broken skin, blood seeping into her hair and leaving it matted. Once Aiden settled in the saddle, Vartan carefully lifted her up for him to hold.

"Don't let her out of your sight," Celiaen growled. "If anything happens to her—"

"I wouldn't say another word if I were you."

Recoiling at Aiden's harsh tone, Celiaen stared at him. Whistling for the rest of their group, Tara nodded at the guards and grabbed Celiaen's reins on her way past. Forcing him to go with her, she did not look back. Listening to horns blaring in the distance, Tharen turned to Vartan. He saw the worry in his eyes.

"Are you coming with us?"

"I have my orders. Neriwyn wants us to take precautions."

Taking in the way his men kept close around him, Aiden looked from Merle to the two daoine. "What's going on?"

Fionn replied, "There are concerns about her safety. We shouldn't stay here."

He wanted to demand more information, but nodding, Aiden touched his heels to his horse. The daoine mounted, and their magic formed a shield around the group. Fayleen kept her power close, eyes darting back and forth. Riding beside Aiden, her gaze stopped on Eirian occasionally to take in the sheen coating her.

"You're making me nervous," Aiden informed her.

"Sorry."

Grunting, he said nothing else. Fayleen clenched her jaw, trying to keep a better grip over her emotions. She could not voice her worries and avoided looking at Aiden's arm wrapped around Eirian's stomach. Shooting a look over her shoulder at Tharen, she knew she needed to speak to him in private before he examined Eirian. If he told anyone about Eirian's condition, the result would be disastrous.

"I'm going to speak to Tharen about what he needs from us to help her," Fayleen muttered.

She slowed her horse and fell back through the group until she was beside Tharen. He frowned, glancing at where Aiden rode with Eirian in front of him. Leaning toward him, Fayleen waited for him to do the same.

"There's something you need to know about Ree," she whispered.

"Is there?"

"No one can know." Raising her brows, Fayleen gave him a look.

Tharen chuckled. "I'm not a mind reader."

"No, you're a healer. You know things about your patients. Things they might not want anyone else to know."

He knew precisely what was bothering Fayleen, but the faces she pulled to convey her point were amusing. Pressing his lips together, Tharen let it chase away his sorrow and enjoyed a moment to torment her.

"As far as I can tell, my patient has a fracture and a concussion. A few cuts as well."

The strangled noise Fayleen made as a response drew attention from the guards.

"Don't worry, her secret is safe with me," Tharen assured her. "Though I'm concerned by its existence."

"Ree is determined to win."

"I see."

Faolan had admitted what Eirian had revealed to him about the fight, and Tharen sighed heavily. He wanted to be mortified by her actions, but he understood her desire to do anything to protect others. Especially the people she loved most. Nodding at Fayleen, he felt the relief pouring off her. However, it carried an undercurrent of anguish, telling Tharen that she was not happy about what was going on.

Glancing to where the sprawling sea of tents obscured the land, Fayleen said, "I need to check on Tessa. Find Rylee and the others. Clean up. Can you let the Captain know I'll find them as soon as I'm able to?"

"Of course."

Saying nothing more, Fayleen pressed her heels to her mount and hurried off. The guards parted, letting her leave, several calling out to ask what was wrong. Guiding his horse forward, Tharen joined Aiden, ignoring his concerned expression, and focused on Eirian instead. His magic told him her condition remained the same. Exhaustion had continued to do the work of Celiaen's blow, keeping her unconscious.

"Any signs of her coming around?"

Aiden shook his head. "None. Going to say that's a good thing right now."

"I'd have to agree with you."

"I'm not looking forward to force-feeding her your concoctions again."

Snorting, Tharen was not sure they would have a choice. It made him thankful for the additional help Celiaen and Galameyvin would provide. The connection between them and Eirian would offer benefits that had been lacking after the last battle. No one needed to say anything to remind them she would be worse.

"What she did out there—" Aiden spoke, but a whimper from Eirian cut him off.

Holding her tighter, he contemplated pushing them to go faster. Gazing at the approaching walls of Kelsby, Aiden decided the risk outweighed the benefit when she did not stir any further. Magic continued to seep from her, leaving a trail of flowers behind them.

"She wasn't like this last time."

Tharen agreed. "Can't say I've encountered anyone shedding magic like this while unconscious."

Looking at him, Aiden asked, "Should we be worried?"

"Maybe. We've got people coming. Hopefully, between us, we can prevent her from affecting the garrison. At the moment, it just seems to be the flowers and a general sense of her power, but that could change."

"Why did Fayleen leave?"

"She said something about cleaning up and finding Tessa, then asked me to tell you she'd join you as soon as she could." Tharen knew she had gone to deal with her emotions where they would not betray her, but he did not say that. "She's covered in blood, like the rest of you. It was good thinking of her."

Chuckling bitterly, Aiden did not need to be told twice to know they were all a mess, muttering, "We'll have to stagger it."

"Lucky for you, I'm clean. We'll get Eirian out of her armor and into bed, and then while I heal her, you can sort yourself out."

"Doubt we'll have some friendly local women to help this time."

"Why, Captain, are you angling to see your queen naked again?" he asked in amusement.

Kissing the top of her head, Aiden retorted, "Might be my last chance to do so."

The walls rose in front of them, offering the illusion of safety while the battle continued in the distance. Aiden was glad of the stone surrounding them. It blocked out what was happening, and he could pretend there was not a war unfolding on the other side. Soldiers and mages were everywhere, but enough people recognized who they were to keep a path clear. Endarans shouted out, demanding to know if their queen was safe.

"Tell anyone who asks that the Queen is fine," Aiden commanded his men. "Just say she's exhausted like last time. They'll accept that."

Merle replied, "We'll do that. I sent Devin to find Todd. Thought we could use the reinforcements protecting her."

"Good thinking. He's loyal, and so are the members of his company. We'll keep them lining the halls closest to us."

Slipping from his horse, Vartan waited for Aiden to pass Eirian down. "I have trusted warriors coming. We won't let anything happen to our queen."

The words left Aiden's mouth before he could stop them. "She's not your queen."

"You really want to argue that right now?"

Magic surrounded Vartan, and something about it tugged at what was trailing from Eirian. Gazing at the pair of them, Aiden watched as the sheen coating Eirian's skin crept across the man holding her. Sharing a look with Tharen, he dismounted and took a tentative step toward them.

"You're right. Now's not the time to argue anything." Holding his arms out, Aiden added, "You're the better warrior."

Returning Eirian to Aiden's protective grasp, Vartan agreed. "Yes, I am. I was protecting her mother long before Endara existed."

Huffing at them, Tharen pushed past and headed for the keep. "Yes, yes, you're both big, scary warriors. Now shut up and bring her along so I can heal her. We need Eirian in one piece so she can fight the darkness."

NINETEEN

It would have been a lie to say Eirian's actions had not trampled the battle plan into the ground. Baenlin knew this, but he could not help feeling wonder at the sight that stretched out before him. Athnaral had eventually retreated after Eirian had thrown her tantrum, leaving the dead and dying behind on the field. Mages were making their way through the bodies that littered the ground, helping who they could. They put those beyond help out of their misery. People from the other armies were among them. Their mercy was less friendly, and they killed any Athnaralan they found.

There was no question who had died because of Eirian's magic. It had left agony etched into every part of the corpses. Baenlin had been told of her last mass killing, and he struggled to believe the accounts. These had not been merciful deaths; their bodies had not crumbled into the earth to feed the land. Instead, it looked like she had intended for them to suffer painfully.

"It's rather terrifying," Sannaeh said as she approached him.

He glanced at her, taking in the grim expression while her gaze swept over the bodies. There was a calculating gleam in Sannaeh's eyes that Baenlin recognized.

"Paienven is beside himself. I fear if Eirian survives her battle, he'll try to kill her."

Baenlin nodded, admitting, "I can understand why. Have you spoken to Celiaen?"

"I have."

"And?"

Arching a brow at his impatient tone, Sannaeh flicked a hand at the nearest twisted body. "The Telmian, Lord Faolan, died protecting her. That set her off."

"That's it? A man died doing his duty in battle, and she loses the plot. By the powers…"

"He wasn't just a man. Lord Faolan was her friend and a teacher of sorts. The one they call the loyal wolf."

Sannaeh understood the significance of such a death on someone as young as Eirian. Crossing his arms, Baenlin spotted Tessa walking through the dead.

"She places too much emotion in her relationships with others."

"Perhaps you don't place enough, brother." She sighed. "Need I remind you of what you've done in the past?"

Tessa was pale when she joined them and said, "I'd like to assure you that, as far as I'm aware, I'm not capable of this. Though I am capable of much more than you know."

"You held your stomach then," Baenlin replied.

He felt a moment of guilt, knowing that she had lost her brother in the fight. Cocking her head, Tessa stared at him.

"Do you think so little of me, Baenlin Zarthein?"

Looking at her, Baenlin decided she was out of place on a battlefield. No armor or weapons were visible, and Tessa wore a curious black vest. It made him wonder if she ever wore gray anymore. Her coppery-brown hair was high on her head while loose strands framed her face, and she had tied one of her signature ribbons in a bow to hold it together.

Piercing blue eyes held a hint of cunning and challenge, a gleam of amusement that mirrored the slight curl of her lips. There was pain and grief, and he respected her desire to hold herself together. She was not a warrior, but Baenlin doubted his magical ability to best her anywhere else. Bloodlust lingered at the back of his mind, the high from battle not faded, and with a shift of her feet, Tessa smirked when his eyes dropped to the curve of her hips.

"I thought it best to inform you, Your Majesty, that we've placed heavy protection around the Queen of Endara. You will, of course, understand that we've only selected humans out of concern that any elves may suffer from divided loyalty."

Sannaeh did not need more reasons to like Tessa than she had already found, but a glance at Baenlin made it difficult not to laugh. His eyes widened slightly, betraying his surprise. She appreciated the challenge Tessa presented for Baenlin and wished she could continue to watch it unfold.

"Of course, I understand completely. I intended to suggest it to the archmage, but it would seem you've beaten me to it."

"You were?" Baenlin asked.

"I was. I did just tell you I fear my husband might try to kill Eirian."

"King Neriwyn has done the same. I'm sure you can appreciate that the Telmians wouldn't take well to any attempts to kill the daughter of their late queen." Tessa spoke without flinching, her voice dripping with sweetness.

Chuckling, Sannaeh bowed her head with a faint smile. "I shall remind my king of that."

"See that you do."

Walking away, Sannaeh paused but did not look back to ask, "She is well, isn't she?"

"She suffered an injury in battle, but the Telmians have their best healer tending to her. Celiaen and Galameyvin are with her. They'd be nowhere else."

"My son is completely devoted to those he cares about. I'd expect nothing less." Her dark eyes flickered to Baenlin, and Sannaeh muttered, "Much like his uncle used to be."

Without waiting for him to respond, Sannaeh started back to where Paienven would be waiting. Satisfied she had done what she needed to, Tessa dusted her hands on her clothes and inclined her head to Baenlin. Lost in his thoughts, he barely noticed her walk away until a huff drew his attention.

"Where are you going?"

She glared at her boot. The heel had sunk into the mud created by blood and, she suspected, other fluids. Tessa noticed the soldiers had trampled flowers into the ground. It seemed out of place, but she suspected Eirian was responsible for the blooms.

"I'm going back to work. We might have technically won today, but more are coming, and I have a task to complete. Those siege weapons won't blow themselves up."

"You are a surprising and peculiar woman, Tessa Valkera. I don't believe I've ever heard anyone speak a threat to my sister without being laughed at."

He watched her head whip around, eyes narrowing at him. Soren kept reminding him to praise Tessa if he wanted to coax her to his side. What worried him the most was how she would handle Jaren's death.

"Mayve let Ensaycal dictate to her, but I can assure you, Archmage, I won't be a puppet." Her wicked smirk reappeared. "You spent so many years dismissing me without bothering to learn what I'm capable of. I'll enjoy challenging your misconceptions."

Letting Tessa walk off, her hips swaying as she pretended she was walking through a field, Baenlin chuckled, knowing it was for his benefit. "So, it would seem. I'll endeavor not to make that mistake anymore. By the way, Tessa, I'm sorry about Jaren."

She paused, hands clenching at her sides. Feeling a shift in the air, Baenlin glanced around in confusion. The sudden sensation of an icy breeze surprised him.

"Thank you, Baenlin," Tessa replied.

"He was your brother. You can grieve his death, and no one will begrudge you for doing so," Baenlin said. "I was proud of Jaren, and you should be as well. He was a credit to your family and our order."

"It's war, Archmage, and Jaren knew what he was signing up for. Now, I really must get on with my task. I will not disappoint my brother's memory or let his death be in vain."

Feeling the breeze die down, Baenlin questioned his sanity. Deciding it was nothing more than the lingering effects of the battle, he brushed aside his concerns and noticed Tessa had turned slightly to face him.

"I have some Telmian wine. Should you wish to raise a toast to his memory, you know where to find me."

Arching a brow, Tessa turned back in the direction she had been going. "I'll take it into consideration."

Her explanation to him had only been half true. While Tessa knew she needed to complete her task, she also knew that without Eirian's help, the plan would not work. The walk back to the town took longer than she expected, the afternoon sun continuing to shine on the dead without care. Tessa twisted the purple band on her finger, a reminder that her fellow mages would never view her the same way after what Eirian had done.

It would not matter that Eirian was special. All they would see was that she was a purple who had kept the extent of her power secret. If one purple had done it, who was to say that others were not doing the same. Which Tessa knew was true. They all had gifts they hid from the others, and she was no exception. Her momentary lapse of control over her power when Baenlin brought up Jaren had reminded her of that.

Riane treated purples differently. Their raw power never fit into a mold. Her ability to think outside the rigid expectations had made Tessa an outcast, and she knew the first challenge of her future rule faced her. Fayleen and Jaren had done their best to prop her up, but now she needed to establish command for herself. She refused to let down Jaren's faith.

The keep was calm despite the layers of soldiers surrounding it. Tessa passed through the guards with a flash of her hand displaying her purple ring. Endaran soldiers assumed she was like Eirian, and the appreciative looks gave her a thrill. She just hoped they did not overestimate her. Inside, mages were among the Endarans, their eyes following the future grand mage as she strode past. In her mind, Tessa kept telling herself to hold her head high and show no weakness.

Outside Eirian's chambers, the hallway was thick with people. Telmians, battle-ready and willing to kill anyone who looked like they were a danger to the Queen, were the ones who regarded her with the most suspicion. The first chamber was less crowded, and a handful of Eirian's guards were mixed in with the daoine, but the space was tight.

Fox moved to stop her before she reached the next door. "You can't go in there."

Without missing a step, Tessa said, "I think you'll find I can."

He recalled her display and bowed. "Yeah, good luck."

There were only a handful of people inside the chamber with Eirian, none of whom surprised Tessa. But, from their reactions, she knew her presence was a shock. Radiating power, Neriwyn was leaning against the fireplace with his back to her, casting a cold and grieving look over his shoulder. Sitting on the floor beside the bed, Fayleen smiled grimly while Celiaen perched on the edge, glaring at her.

It surprised Tessa to see Galameyvin curled around Eirian, a hand stroking her hair. The surprise faded when she felt the calming prickle of his power. The pale daoine she had only glimpsed once before was standing next to the window, head bowed in conversation with Aiden, neither of them sparing her a second glance.

"How is she?" Tessa asked.

"Who sent you?" Celiaen replied, a touch of accusation in his voice.

Touching a hand to his leg, Fayleen shook her head, murmuring, "Celi, be calm. She remains much the same as when I spoke to you, Tessa. Tharen has finished healing her shoulder. Unfortunately, Ree had multiple fractures, and we're waiting for her to wake."

"Thank you, Fay. To answer your question, Celiaen, no one sent me. I'm concerned for her well-being." Looking to Neriwyn, she sighed. "I'm concerned for all of you."

"How touching," Celiaen sneered.

Feeling a change in Eirian's breathing, Galameyvin hushed them. "Ree?"

"Gal." Her answer was flat.

Moving to the bed, Tharen looked at her. "How do you feel?"

"Like I hit my head on a rock."

A flash of guilt passed over Celiaen's face, and Tessa arched a brow. Fayleen had told her what happened on the battlefield and the actions taken to stop Eirian.

"I'm sorry, Ree, I didn't know how else to stop you."

"He clobbered you over the head with a hilt," Galameyvin explained.

Eirian groaned. "That explains the headache. Why did you need to stop me?"

Every pair of eyes stared at her in horror, but she did not notice. Eirian covered her face, trying to reduce the headache from pounding against her skull and competing with the noise of the whispers. Rubbing his forehead, Tharen looked to Neriwyn, and Tessa suspected they were having a silent conversation. She found their ability uncanny.

Crossing to the closed chest, she sat on it, leaning forward to observe in silence. No one spoke, the tension in the room thick enough to cut with a knife. But the silence lasted too long, and Eirian pulled the hand away from her eyes, struggling to sit while Galameyvin pushed her back down.

"Stop it, Gal!" Eirian growled, batting away his hands. "What happened? Obviously, something happened."

"You snapped and killed a load of people unpleasantly." Tessa offered an answer while everyone else seemed to struggle with one.

The explanation did not mollify Eirian, her head pounding with each push she made to remember what had happened. It was a struggle to wade through the press of Shianeni's memories, fragments slipping past the wall of whispers.

"They hurt me, it was my shoulder, and we were retreating."

"You had several fractures to the joint. Thank your friend for her excellent work because it could have been worse," Tharen commented.

Brow furrowed, Eirian looked around the room slowly before her gaze settled on Neriwyn on the opposite side of the room. The sight of him stirred her magic, and she struggled to hold it in check.

"Where is Faolan?"

"Ree—" Celiaen spoke, but she held up a hand, silencing him.

"Where is he, Neri?"

Neriwyn gave Aiden and Celiaen sharp looks and ignored the shortening of his name. He suspected Eirian did not realize she had done it, but could not discount that her intention was to threaten him.

"You know where he is."

There was a flicker of panic in her eyes, the lighter specks of golden brown standing out. Magic twisted around her, setting them all on edge. No one had worked out why Eirian continued to exude her power while unconscious.

"No! No, you're lying," she argued, shaking her head. "It's not... he isn't... it didn't happen. It was one of my nightmares. All of this is one of my nightmares."

"It's not. You aren't dreaming. Faolan is dead."

"No!"

Her refusal to believe him incensed Neriwyn, and he snarled, pointing a hand at the door. "You were there! He died protecting you. Do I have to take you to see his corpse?"

"I can bring him back." Eirian sounded certain.

"No, you can't. You're not the god of death. There is nothing you can do now."

Concerned by her mind's direction, Tharen held up a hand. "Neriwyn is right. Maybe you could make his heart beat again, but it wouldn't be Faolan. We are not plants. You can't give and take life from us."

Filing away the idea for later contemplation, Tessa spoke gently, "Eirian, you can't blame yourself. Everyone is aware of what might happen in battle. Not a single person went out today who wasn't aware of the risk they were taking."

"Don't you dare speak to me about risks, Tessa Valkera! I didn't see you putting your ass out on the battlefield."

At Eirian's hissed words, the others let go of the fears they were holding. It was the fire in her eyes, a spark that let them know she was still there. Mouth twitching, Tessa inclined her head slightly. The words had hurt deeply, but she reminded herself that she was not a warrior.

"Indeed, you're right. I didn't put my ass out on the battlefield. However, I was working on a solution to the siege weapon issue. Because that's what I do. You can run off and play soldier, but some of us have to do the less glorious activities."

"Do you think now is the time?" Celiaen demanded, furious at Tessa's approach.

"Oh, absolutely," Tessa replied, eyes remaining on Eirian. "Look, I'm not here to make you feel better about yourself, to smooth over the loss of your friend, or dillydally about your feelings. Instead, I'm here to remind you there's still a war raging outside this room. A war that stands to take more than just your friend."

Fayleen shifted uncomfortably, murmuring, "Tessa."

Lifting a hand, Neriwyn agreed. "She has a point, and Faolan would be the first to remind us of it."

"Take the rest of the day to grieve. Tomorrow is a new day and a new battle I need you to be ready for. Save your breakdowns for when it's over."

Tessa knew her words would not endear her to the others, but she also knew someone had to take a hard stance. They were for her sake as much as Eirian's. She could not let her grief over Jaren take hold. Not yet. Not until it was all over.

Drawing in a deep breath, Eirian exhaled again slowly. "You're right."

"Of course I am, but you've always known that."

"Modesty isn't your strong point," Aiden grumbled, unsure if she impressed him.

"Call it what you will," Tessa replied, tossing a dismissive look in his direction. "We need to stick to our plan, Eirian. We need to keep focus and not dwell on what we've lost or what loss is yet to come."

Galameyvin understood where Tessa was coming from, but he wanted Eirian to grieve. "She just lost a great friend, Tessa."

Regarding him coldly, Tessa shook her head. "And I lost my brother! But you don't see me falling apart because it would dishonor his sacrifice!"

"Jaren is dead?" Celiaen was ashen at the news.

"Yes, he is! As are many others. We might be mages, but we're not indestructible."

"Where is she?"

They froze at the enraged voice coming from the next chamber.

Tharen looked at Neriwyn, worry etched into every line on his face. "Sire? I thought Saoirse was being dealt with?"

Neriwyn hesitated. "Healwen assured me she was dealing with it."

"Perhaps you should do something," Aiden grumbled, moving to stand next to Tessa, the two of them positioned between the door and the bed.

Pushing Galameyvin aside, Eirian scrambled out of bed. "No, it's okay. I can handle her. She blames him as much as she blames me. I want all of you to leave and let her in."

"That's not a good idea," Galameyvin replied.

"I wasn't asking." Her voice was icy.

Slipping from the bed, careful not to catch Celiaen or Fayleen with his boots, Galameyvin regarded Eirian with eyes narrowed. "You should let Neriwyn deal with her."

The door slammed open, and Saoirse stood there glaring at them. Her green eyes shifted between Neriwyn and Eirian, magic churning erratically.

"I don't know which one of you I should kill first."

"Get out!" Eirian snarled, her gaze locked on Saoirse, who took several steps forward.

Giving her a worried look, Tharen shook his head. "Don't strain your shoulder."

Offering Fayleen a hand, Aiden flicked his eyes at Eirian, and she understood his silent question. Pursing her lips, Fayleen gave a shrug and grabbed hold of his hand, letting him help her up. They reluctantly followed Tessa out of the room, the two Telmians close behind. The princes stood side by side, torn between her order and their desire to protect Eirian.

Sensing their hesitation, Eirian flexed her magic and gave them a shove. Carefully stepping around Saoirse, they joined the others outside before the door swung shut behind them. Sighing, Neriwyn shook his head and turned to leave, Tharen trailing after him. Guards and daoine watched on in confusion. No one was sure what was going on.

"Where are you going?" Celiaen demanded.

Arching a brow, Neriwyn replied, "I have work to do and people to comfort. Unfortunately, Faolan was not the only one of my people to die."

"What about her?" Fayleen asked, waving at the door.

"I assure you, Eirian can deal with it."

Neriwyn tossed his answer over his shoulder on his way past the guards. Tharen trailed behind him, leaving the chamber with an apologetic look.

Grimacing, Tessa looked around the room with a touch of envy. "I had best get back to my efforts as well."

Reminded of Jaren's death, Galameyvin moved away from Celiaen toward her. She watched him with wide eyes, hoping he would not attempt to coax her into talking.

"Tessa, do you need? Jaren was—"

"No!" She quickly cut him off before he touched her. "Thank you, though.

Ask me again when this is over and I have the luxury of grieving. Right now, I have a point to make."

"A point to make?" Aiden inquired.

A slight snort and the curl of her lips was the only flicker of emotion that Tessa let through her grasp. "Absolutely. I'm attempting to establish my dominance. I will be the grand mage. My brother lectured me not to waste an opportunity, and I will not let him down."

Watching her stride out of the room, Galameyvin gave Celiaen a worried look. "Well, she's as much a mess as Ree."

"Emotion and Tessa aren't two things I'd put together in the same breath," he replied, turning around to look at the shut door.

Crossing her arms, Fayleen huffed. "You're such a prick, Celi! Jaren was your friend. He was Ree's friend. My friend."

"Fay—"

"Fuck off, Celi. Tessa and Ree aren't rivals, they never were, and you're not being some kind of defender by acting like an asshole to Tessa."

Galameyvin knew more than Celiaen and said, "Fay's right."

"I suggest the two of you make some more appearances among your people. Reassure the King of Ensaycal that everything is under control and cross paths with the archmages to do the same. I'll remain here."

Surprised by Fayleen's attitude, Celiaen balked. "I'm her mate. I should remain here."

"Captain, do Everett and the other duke have enough respect for His Highness to listen to him?" Fayleen ignored Celiaen and his blustering.

Aiden sniffed, screwing up his nose while staring at Celiaen in amusement. "Yeah... Everett will listen to him."

"You don't sound very convinced there, Cap'n." Chuckling, Fox scratched his shoulder, watching the frustration appear on Aiden's face.

"They'll listen to him because of his closeness to her, but until they speak to Eirian directly, nothing will reassure them," Aiden answered, his shoulders slumping. "Honestly, every time she gets involved in a battle, all those carefully calculated plans are moot."

Unable to disagree, Galameyvin placed a hand on Celiaen's shoulder and nodded at the exit. "Fayleen made an excellent suggestion. Your father won't listen to Tara's placating words. Besides, you don't want your mother to come looking for you."

Reminded of Sannaeh, Celiaen grimaced. "Fair point."

"Are you scared of your mother?" Aiden mocked him.

Pointing at Fayleen, Celiaen said, "You send for me. One of Eirian's guards specifically, no one else. Anything."

Her mouth twisted, and she rolled her eyes. "Don't worry, Celi, I have this under control. Now go away. Maybe check in on Zack."

Once the two elves and the handful of companions accompanying them had departed, Aiden looked at Fayleen seriously.

"It wasn't long ago you came to Amath, and yet you seem a different person to the jovial woman I met then."

"I learn fast, Captain." Fayleen brushed a loose strand of hair away from her face. "And I learned even though Ree was far away, they still viewed me as a means to manipulate her. Tessa helped me. She encouraged me to be firm and to find my light to stand in."

"Free of Eirian's shadow."

"I also realized that for a long time, I let myself believe I was less powerful than I am. Because standing in Eirian's shadow was easier than fighting for recognition."

Thinking about the constant surprises Eirian threw at them, Aiden snorted. "I suppose it's hard to reach for the sun when they view you as little more than a weed."

"That's the thing about weeds, though." Her mouth curled in a victorious smile. "We're persistent, survivors. Ree was always encouraging. I was the one who held myself back, resigned to be the follower of someone greater, but not now."

"You saved my life today with that little stick of yours."

Remembering the ripple of her shields protecting him, Aiden bowed his head in thanks. She had kept him and many of his men safe while proving she could hold her own.

Winking at him, Fayleen's smile turned cheeky. "You can thank me later."

TWENTY

Words spewed from Saoirse, accusations mixed in with anger, grief, and hate. Patient, Eirian let them flow while she went from screaming in her face to the low hiss of deeply felt emotion. Each word echoed what Eirian already thought. She believed Faolan was dead because of her, and the blame belonged nowhere else. Nothing anyone could say would shake that feeling or change her mind.

She wanted to blame her mother or the twisted god they were fighting, even Neriwyn and Gebael. But deep down, Eirian knew it had not been their choices that led to Faolan's death. Just hers. Her hesitation. Her desire to fight on. Her stubbornness. It did not matter that other gods were floating around and watching on. They had not directly led Faolan to his death.

Eirian bowed her head, eyes on the floor, when she sensed Saoirse was running out of energy and said, "You're right."

Stumbling over her words, Saoirse fell silent and stared at Eirian, lips parted. "What?"

"You're right to blame and hate me. I do. Faolan would be alive if it wasn't for me." Clenching her eyes shut, Eirian shook her head vehemently. "And there is nothing I can do to bring him back. How many others died today because of my stupidity?"

Deflated, Saoirse let her shoulders drop and pressed the heel of her palm against her forehead, rubbing it hard enough to hurt. Crying had made her eyes red, but her cheeks were dry.

"He was the other half of me, my twin. I've never been without Faolan, and I don't know how to be without him."

"If I could take away your pain, Saoirse, I would do so without hesitation."

"You amaze me, little queen."

The words were bitter, and Eirian hated the moniker the daoine used for her. She was no queen. No one deserved the suffering she led them into. Cajoling her, the whispers dug phantom fingers into her mind, telling Eirian how easy it would be to save everyone from the destruction she would bring them.

"I expected you to argue and spout some excuse that he decided to follow you. I didn't expect you to agree it's your fault."

Letting Saoirse see the pain she felt, Eirian sighed. "That's true as well. He chose, but he wouldn't have if it wasn't for me."

"I want to hate you."

"I know, and you're allowed to."

Crying with frustration and grief, Saoirse curled her hands into fists at her side. She did not know if anything would take away her pain.

"He loved you, but not like he loved Shianeni. More like the wishful love of someone who saw what had never been his but loved what he missed out on like it was his own. He loved you because you're you."

Eirian considered telling Saoirse that he had spent his last breath on her mother's name, but she decided not to. She knew her brother better than anyone; she had probably already assumed where his mind had gone in those last moments.

"I won't let his death be in vain."

"I know you won't, but on the way to victory, you'll drag so many down with you. So many of them will wear a smile on their faces because they believe dying for you is the right thing to do. They're probably right."

"These deaths are a waste when there is only one death that will serve any purpose."

Saoirse blinked slowly, her gaze shifting downward before returning to meet the brown eyes staring at her. Recalling what had happened on the battlefield, she did not know how Eirian would react to her admission.

"I watched what you did from the skies as I felt his death. I saw your rage tear apart the lives of hundreds. I enjoyed watching your power shred through them as though it were my talons. I imagined it was my talons."

"I lost control."

It was no excuse, but Eirian offered it as an explanation. She could not explain to anyone how the whispers had taken over. There was no way she could tell them about the well of power she had found within herself when she let the whispers have control.

"Did you? You didn't kill a single Endaran. Or elf. Or daoine. Just Athnaralans. It was almost as though you needed a catalyst to fuel you because last time you pulled power from us, but this time it was all you." Her gaze went hard as Saoirse searched for some sign that she was wrong. "I'm right, aren't I?"

Glancing away, Eirian shrugged. "Only partially. I didn't plan on the death of a friend, and I didn't plan on what happened today. But, you're correct, I didn't need any extra power to do what I did, and I could go out there and do it again right now."

"You're growing."

"I'm learning," she said. "I was always this powerful, but I didn't grasp it. Some knew, but it did not suit their plans to let anyone else find out. Instead, they lurked in the open, pretending to be something they're not while pulling strings to manipulate us into doing what they want."

A spike of fear coursed through her, and Saoirse felt it chase some of her grief away. A gut feeling told her the subject Eirian spoke of was a dangerous one they should avoid.

"Faolan wouldn't want you to repeat your actions."

"That I can agree with."

"Why did it have to be him?" It felt wrong to ask, but Saoirse did it anyway. "Why couldn't it have been one of your guards? Or Ilar, or Slaine, or anyone else... why him?"

So many variations of what had happened on the battlefield had already run through Eirian's mind. Only a handful of people dying could have inspired a reaction similar to what happened. Most of them would have been worse. She would have torn the earth apart in response to the death of one of those closest to her.

"I would've done the same for Faolan. But it's no consolation to any of us who cared for him. He died doing good. He saved me."

"Saved you today so you can die tomorrow?"

"Yes."

Sighing heavily, Saoirse turned to the door, her anger dulled and leaving only grief. A hollow feeling grasped at her heart, a reminder that part of it was missing.

"I know it seems to be what must be done, but that doesn't make it feel right."

"Faolan meant a lot more to me than you realize, Saoirse. You can give me all the looks you wish and remind me I have three wonderful men who love me, but Faolan? Faolan knew me. He was a link to my mother I didn't resent. Don't presume I don't understand the depth of your grief. Just hope that the depth of mine doesn't lead to our defeat."

The look Saoirse gave her was unreadable, and she said, "When the time comes, I'll guide your path through the fight. But your death will never make up for his."

Nodding, Eirian agreed. "No, it won't. It will, however, save countless others who don't deserve to die."

Shaking her head, Saoirse seemed to age. "This will be the last time we speak.

If you survive this war, by the powers, I never wish to set eyes on you again."

"If I survive this war, I promise you won't have to. But I'll spend every breath trying to restore what my mother took from you."

"I'm not sure you should. Some things are better forgotten."

Saoirse opened the door and left as abruptly as she arrived, leaving Eirian alone with her thoughts. Doing her best to ignore the whispers, she closed her eyes and pictured Jaren's laughing face. She had avoided thinking about him until she was alone. His death hurt as much as Faolan's, and she wondered how many of her guards had survived. How many of Celiaen's companions had died. Who else she had grown up with had died fighting a war that should never have happened.

She wanted to scream and cry, to give a voice to her grief, but the shadows dancing along the walls stopped her. The whispers and memories prevented her. Eirian had to hold herself together for as long as she could. It was too soon to give her emotions freedom because it would let the darkness in once she did. So until the time came, she had to be strong.

Concerned, Fayleen and Aiden slipped into the room and took in the way she stood with her shoulders slumped and eyes downcast. Sensing their presence, Eirian lifted her gaze to look at them standing next to each other with equally worried expressions. Her vision was blinded, and she swore she was watching a smiling Aiden twirl a laughing Fayleen, the two of them surrounded by a crop bathed in sunlight and blue skies. Blinking, the sight disappeared again and left Eirian looking at them in bafflement. They sensed her confusion and shared looks.

"Eirian, are you okay?" Fayleen asked tentatively.

Blinking again, she shook her head to clear the vision from her mind. "I am. You need not worry about me."

"I disagree," Aiden said gruffly, and moved away from Fayleen, giving her a funny look. "There's no need to lie to us. We understand if you are feeling…"

"Overwhelmed by feelings," Fayleen finished for him.

It made Eirian smile, a bittersweet smile that understood what she had seen. She drew comfort from the knowledge they had a chance to be happy one day.

"I'm not lying to you. Seeing— I'm fine. You don't need to worry."

Confused by her words, Fayleen pursed her lips. "I'm not sure about that. You're not making sense."

"I don't need to make sense." Answering her concern with amusement, Eirian flicked a glance at Aiden. "I'm glad you found something you can agree on."

"I know what you asked her to do." There was a touch of scathing to his voice.

The amusement remained, and Eirian was glad for it. Thankful for the ability to feel something outside of grief and anger. It would help her get through the time she had left.

"And what was that? What did I ask Fayleen to do?"

His brow arched, and he grumbled, "To protect me."

"She's a yellow, and that's her job. Fayleen has always been a superb shield mage, and I knew you would remain close to me, so it made sense."

"I don't need a mage to protect me."

Sucking her breath in through her teeth, Fayleen cleared her throat. "Just to make it clear to you, Captain, I would have protected you even without her asking me to. If you want to fight with anyone over it, then fight with me."

Aiden glared at her. "Don't bullshit me to cover for her meddling."

"I told you, Aiden, I need you to live. This means I'll meddle as much as needed to make sure that happens. I care for you; I care for you both so very much."

"Ree, we know you do," Fayleen said.

The grief reached past the layer of amusement, and Eirian looked between them. "I've lost friends today, and I don't want to lose any more. You don't need to tell me you lost men today, Aiden. I feel their absences. Their deaths are more for me to carry."

"They knew what they were signing up for," he answered sadly.

Pursing her lips, she disagreed. "No, they didn't. None of you did. Powers, not even I knew what I was signing up for. I refuse to carry the weight of your death, Aiden."

He wanted to kiss Eirian and wipe away the tears gathering in the corner of her eyes. Despite her efforts to appear in control, Aiden saw the signs of her struggle. She was fragile, and it would not take much for her to break.

"The weight of my death wouldn't be on you. We knew from the beginning there was always the chance we would die protecting you. It's our duty, and it would be my honor."

"No." Lifting a hand to her lips, Eirian closed her eyes before dropping the hand to her chest, holding it over her heart. "No, I refuse it, and I release you from your duty. I release all of you."

"And I refuse your release."

Uncomfortable, Fayleen shifted toward the door, murmuring, "I should leave the two of you to argue about this alone."

Reaching for Fayleen, Eirian said, "No, Fayleen, I need you to remain. As the two of you love me, I need you to promise me you'll look after each other."

"What?" Aiden grunted.

"Ree..." Fayleen frowned, giving Aiden a worried look.

"I mean it. Fay, you're my sister and my closest friend. We would do anything for each other, and Aiden will need someone to ensure he does as he's told. Someone to make sure he lives." Eirian dropped the hand away from her heart. "And someone needs to stop you from sinking into a frenzy of studying and crafting."

"I already promised you I'd make sure he lives." Fayleen reminded Eirian of their rooftop conversation.

"Don't I get a say in this?" Uncertain, Aiden ran a finger over the hilt of his sword, staring down at it intently.

Scowling, Eirian huffed. "Neither of you is listening! I want you to promise me you'll be there for each other. Do me that honor. Don't just survive. I want you to thrive. Fay, be his friend, guide him, protect him as you have done for me. And Aiden, protect her, be her friend, serve her as you have done for me."

"It almost sounds like you are suggesting I marry her," he muttered.

Her mouth twitched, a wistful smile appearing. What Eirian had seen lingered at the forefront of her mind, untouched by the whispers.

"Somehow, I don't think that would end so badly. There's no way you could do better than her, Aiden."

Chuckling, Fayleen rolled her eyes and shook her head. "You can't order us to marry."

"Why not? I'm still the queen here. Aiden is a legitimate noble, and I have some say over his future bride." Crossing her arms, she gave them a humorous look.

Aiden did not like the suggestion and said, "Well, for a start, I don't want to marry her."

One eyebrow shot up, and Eirian winked at him. "And yet you were the one who jumped to the conclusion. All I was asking was for you to be there for each other. I just want you to be friends and support each other for as long as you need it. But hey, if you think you could find your way to marrying her? You could not do better."

"I disagree."

The words were softly spoken, and they knew he was referring to her. Eirian's lips thinned. A desire to yell at him threatened the calm she clung to. She wanted to tell Aiden there was no one worse than her for anyone, but she could not.

"Fay is one of the best people I know. If you found happiness in each other, I'd rest easy. All I'm asking, and hoping for, is that you find solace together."

Solemn, Fayleen saw what Eirian was trying to say. "You don't want us to be alone in our grief. Celi and Gal will have each other, as they have always had each other. But, you know they won't have room for me in their anguish, and they won't make room for him."

"Yes," Eirian replied. "More than that, Aiden will need to be there for Everett. If the two of you are supporting each other, you'll better be able to support him. Grieving alone does things to your mind. I won't have either of you fall to melancholy. Endara will need you."

Glancing away, Fayleen hoped Eirian would not notice the look of shame that crossed her face at the mention of Everett.

Angered by her implication, Aiden took a step and snarled, "What do you know of grieving alone?"

Eirian let his anger wash over her. It helped her cling to control. She was aware magic was slipping past her walls, and there was nothing she could do to stop it.

"Aiden."

"No!" Raising a hand, he pointed at her angrily. "Don't you dare!"

"You know me well, Aiden. You've held me when I have let it show. You know I've been grieving for a while. I understand that you're angry with me, but it's not truly me you're angry with. Remember that. Remember the tears of grief you have wiped from my cheeks. I can no more change my fate than I can bring Faolan back." Letting a touch of her bitterness show, Eirian turned her gaze to Fayleen. "You'll hurt for a long time, and I'd change it if I could. You know I would."

Nodding in agreement, Fayleen glanced down briefly at Eirian's stomach. "I know. You will do whatever you must do to protect the ones you love. We should count ourselves fortunate to be among them."

"Do I have your word?"

"Always, sister, I've told you that before. I'll be persistent. Perhaps that will help me come to terms with a life without you in it. Besides, what is there for me in Riane? Endara will give me the purpose I need."

Crossing to Eirian, Fayleen slung an arm around her shoulder and crooked her fingers at Aiden. He glowered at them, refusing the summons.

"I don't need you meddling in my life. I need you not to die!"

"Oh, shut up, Captain, and come here!" Fayleen snapped.

"Fair warning, he sulks worse than a child." Eirian chuckled, earning another glare.

Stomping over to them, he grumbled, "If you think for a moment..."

Wrapping their arms around Aiden, the two women pulled him in for a hug. Closing her eyes while they stood in silence, Eirian let her magic surround them. She pulled carefully at the thread she felt connecting her to Aiden. Tugged at it and Fayleen's power, hoping neither of them noticed her weaving the threads together. Her heart clenched in shame that she was doing such a thing without asking, but she could not risk her death killing Aiden.

Without knowing how the faint bond between them worked, Eirian knew she could only hope to share the impact of it breaking. There was power enough in Celiaen and Galameyvin to protect them, but Aiden had none of his own. He had no way to shield himself and no knowledge that the link was there. If it all went right, they would never know what she had done. Not that it would matter once she died. They could not yell at a dead woman.

Finding a shred of hope in the vision she had seen of them, Eirian carefully pulled back and smiled. Her eyes settled on where Fayleen had slung an arm around Aiden's waist and knew deep down that they would be fine. It gave her more strength than they would ever know.

"Thank you," Eirian whispered.

"What for?" Letting her arms drop, Fayleen stared intently at her.

Half shrugging, Eirian spread her hands wide. "Everything, absolutely everything."

Aiden felt like she was saying goodbye. "Eirian."

"Aiden."

"You've given up, haven't you? Given up on surviving this fight."

Backing away, Fayleen knew it was time to leave. She knew how Eirian had to end the war. There was nothing she could say or do that would change a thing.

Sighing, Eirian turned her back on Aiden and said, "I've known for a long time how this was going to end. You can't say I've kept it a secret from you."

"I thought you were going to try, but you're not. You're just going to die." He could not understand why she was unwilling to fight against her death.

"I accept my fate, Aiden. I don't expect you to, but I need you to keep out of the way when the time comes. You can't stop this, so don't try."

His voice was desperate, the words bordering on a plea. "I love you."

Pinching the bridge of her nose, Eirian glanced over her shoulder at him. It was almost too much, and Aiden knew he was threatening the small amount of control she was clinging to.

"I know. I love you too, and that's why you need to live. Because I love you and in a different life, I would have chosen you, and we would have been happy."

"This is the goodbye you're giving me." The words turned his tongue to stone.

"It is all I can offer, Aiden, though I wish I could give you more. My love, my thanks, my apologies, and my understanding. I give those things to you, and I ask that you accept them."

Reaching out, Aiden grabbed her uninjured arm and pulled Eirian around to face him. He felt her magic swirl around them, the tremble of her hands betraying her.

"Say it again!" he demanded. "I want to hear you say it again."

"What?"

"Those words."

He did not need to say them; she knew which ones he meant. Touching his face, Eirian smiled. If it was what he needed to hear, she would repeat it until the end. She would tell each of them how much she loved them, even with her last breath. He was a tether in the storm, just like Celiaen and Galameyvin. They would unwillingly escort her to her death, and she would go.

"I love you, Aiden, and I would have chosen you."

"Damn you."

Pulling her to him, Aiden wrapped his arms around Eirian and kissed her. Burying her hands in his hair, she let the feel of his lips banish the whispers. She did not understand why they went, but they allowed her a reprieve. Keeping his grasp firm, Aiden shifted toward the bed, taking Eirian with him. He expected her to hesitate and make an argument about Celiaen, but she did not. Instead, she continued to kiss him, a hand leaving his hair to run down his back until it found the hem of his shirt.

Legs catching the side of the bed, Aiden had to chuckle at the look of surprise on Eirian's face when he stumbled out of her embrace. Sprawled out in front of her, he propped himself up on his elbows and waited to see what she would do. Magic swirled over her skin, adding to the glow that never faded. Her surprise was replaced with a smirk that was a little too pleased for Aiden's comfort.

"What's that joke your men make?"

Kneeling on the bed, Eirian straddled him, and Aiden felt her fingers stroke his cheek before digging into his chin to tilt his face up. Gazing at her, he smirked, knowing what joke she was referring to.

"I believe it involves me having you right where I want you," he replied.

"Are you trying to take advantage of your queen?" Eirian purred, lips brushing across his as a taunt.

Carefully shifting his weight onto one arm, Aiden brought a hand up to dance his fingers along her side. It had the desired effect, Eirian squirming away to avoid being tickled. Taking advantage of the distraction, he rolled her over and pinned her beneath him. Meeting her eyes, Aiden thought he should feel guilty for what they were doing. They had both lost friends on the battlefield, and their emotions had undergone immense strain. But the touch of her hands chased away any remorse he might have felt.

"Oh, definitely," Aiden murmured, lowering his lips to hers. "Full advantage."

Quietly shutting the door, Gabe leaned against it and stared at the people lingering in the chamber. Marcellus glared at him, waiting to find out what was going on, but received nothing more than a shrug.

"I want to see the Queen!" he snapped.

"She's in bed. Someone must have given her a sedative."

The other guards exchanged looks, none of them willing to question Gabe.

"I thought you said she was talking to your captain."

Gabe shrugged again. "She was earlier, but I stepped out before. Didn't realize he had left. He's probably gone to get some rest."

Marcellus looked around the room, taking in the mixture of expressions on the faces of the guards and daoine. He did not believe Gabe, but unless he tried barging into the room, there was no way to prove it. Shaking his head, he turned to leave.

"Send someone to get me when she wakes up."

"Yes, sir. Will do."

When the door shut, eyes turned back to Gabe expectantly. He did not look bothered by the scrutiny, opting to remain against the door. His task was to prevent anyone from disturbing the two in the chamber beyond.

"Why did you lie to the Duke?" Fox asked quietly.

"What makes you think I did?" he said with a chuckle. "The Queen is in bed. She'll probably be asleep at some point."

Eyes widening, Fox grinned. "About bloody time."

TWENTY-ONE

No one had bothered her in hours. Outside the tent, mages hurried about, focused on dealing with the aftermath of the battle. Greens tended to the injured and fought to save who they could. Yellows repaired wards, weapons, and armor. Blues helped those in need of their services. Others assisted the Endarans and Ensaycalans with the dead and the dying.

Tessa did not want to think about what they were doing with the bodies of the slain. It hurt too much. She could still smell the lingering scent of oil and wax from the night before, when Jaren had sat on the edge of her bed to sharpen his swords. The memory of his jokes taunted her, forcing Tessa to step back from the table where she was trying to work. Clay splattered onto the surface, her concentration broken.

Gripping the edge, she leaned on outstretched arms and let her head hang. Sucking in shaky breaths, Tessa fought back her tears. There was too much left to do before they went back into battle. She knew that. People depended on her to create a solution to the siege weapons. Something that would circumvent the senseless deaths more traditional methods would cause.

They were all senseless, and nothing would convince Tessa otherwise. But that did not change the fact they had no choice other than to fight. To do otherwise would be akin to lying down to die. Eirian was the only person allowed to surrender to death without resistance. Tessa knew it was up to her to make sure they kept as many people alive as possible to honor that sacrifice. She would honor Jaren's sacrifice.

"It's not fair," she whispered. "You promised you'd come back."

Her fingertips dug into the timber, blunt nails catching and sending pain through her hands. Magic twisted around the tent, Tessa feeling the shift of the ground beneath her feet. She felt like marching out onto the battlefield and tearing the earth apart in her pain. Even though she had told Baenlin that she could not kill like Eirian, Tessa knew she was more than capable of making the ground swallow the enemy.

"I can't do this!"

Hearing the clatter of things hitting the ground, Tessa lifted her head and looked at her table. Panic coursed through her, fueled by fear she had damaged some of the precious clay balls that had taken so many hours to make. Finding several broken, Tessa sunk to the ground, wrapping her arms around her legs. Staring at the fractured clay, she knew her mother was right.

She was useless and could do nothing right. People would die because she failed to control her magic. It was insane to think she could help anyone. Jaren was dead because of her selfish need to show off her differences. He would have remained in Riane, safe and alive, if she had not asked him to help her sneak away with the army. When she returned to the city, their parents would know it was her fault their son was dead.

Tessa stopped fighting the tears and let them come, burying her face in her arms. It was too hard to hold them back. She had tried to hold herself together to get on with her task, but she was not strong enough. Jaren had been her strength. He had protected her from the world as best he could. Without him, Tessa could not see a point in going on. No one would miss her. They might care about losing the power she had, but not her.

Hands stroked her head, fingers tugging at the ribbon struggling to contain her hair. She did not lift her head to look at the person, a gentle power coaxing her to close her eyes. Tessa thought it felt familiar, a reminder of choices not taken and the stillness of time when she watched the particles dance under the influence of her magic. But the person remained silent, offering only the comfort of a warm embrace and their presence. Leaning against their chest, Tessa inhaled the clean, woody scent and the image of sunbathed trees filled her mind.

"Thank you," she whispered.

She felt fingers running through her hair, drawing the wild strands out. They did not respond, and the press of their magic was intoxicating. At the back of her mind, a voice told Tessa that accepting comfort from a stranger was not the best idea when they were on the edge of a battlefield. It was hard to care what danger she might have been in when her power wanted to soak in what it could get from the arms wrapped around her.

"Can I stay like this?"

Hearing a faint chuckle, Tessa thought about lifting her head and opening her eyes. As quick as the thought whispered through her mind, it was replaced with the desire to curl in closer. The presence soothed her, chasing away the edge of her grief and anxiety. Breathing in deeply, she sighed at the feeling of lips on the top of her head. It was the most relaxed she had felt in months, and she wanted to sleep.

"Tessa, are you in there?"

Startled, she realized the person had left. Lifting her head, Tessa looked around, pushing her hair away from her face. Nothing seemed out of place, but the lingering scent assured her she had not imagined the other person. Before she could stand, Neriwyn entered the tent. He gazed down at her in concern.

"Are you hurt?"

Running a hand through her wild mane, Tessa looked for her ribbon with a frown. She remembered the person untying it, but it was nowhere to be found. Unfortunately, it was not the first time one had gone missing, and she found it inconvenient every time it happened.

"Can you see my ribbon?" she muttered.

Amusement crossed Neriwyn's face as he walked to the bed and picked up a long black ribbon. It sat, curled in a spiral, on the pillow. Squinting at it when he held it up, Tessa shrugged. She had not seen it before, but she never knew where the ribbons in her collection came from half the time. They appeared as frequently as they disappeared, and she could never find it in herself to ask questions.

"Thank you."

Delivering it, Neriwyn waited while Tessa bundled her hair back and wrapped the silk around it. He offered a hand to help her stagger to her feet when she finished. Steadying her, Neriwyn took in the tear-stained cheeks and red-rimmed eyes that betrayed why Tessa had been on the floor when he entered.

"I'm sorry."

Offering him a weak smile, Tessa said, "It's fine. I'm fine. Everything is fine. What can I do for you, Your Majesty?"

He did not believe her, and she read the disbelief on his face.

"Honestly, it's fine. I needed a moment, and now I'm ready to get back to work."

"Your brother was a great warrior."

"I don't need to hear those things. No one knew who Jaren was better than Zack or me. Telling us he was a great warrior, or a wonderful friend, or anything like that won't help how fucking awful we feel."

Neriwyn sighed patiently. "I didn't intend it to. I was merely expressing my respect for him. Believe me, I know those words don't help. Not until you're ready for them to help."

He reached for her hands and turned them over to gaze at her palms. There were scars there, faded lines that blended in with the creases in her skin. Marks earned from mistakes made while trying to craft something from nothing. Brushing the tip of his thumbs over the lines, Neriwyn smiled grimly.

"There are those who claim these lines spin the story of our lives. They would tell you that following the lines on your hand will lead you to the other half of your heart."

"What a load of nonsense," Tessa said, meeting his gaze.

"Maybe. Though, don't they remind you of ribbons across your skin?"

"Not in the slightest."

Chuckling, he shrugged and released her hands. Neriwyn reminded Tessa of what had happened, nodding at the broken clay balls. He was so much more powerful than she was, and she wanted to ask him how he maintained control even when it felt like there was a weight on his chest. A weight that would crush every bone beneath it, cutting off the ability to breathe again.

"Tessa, look at me," Neriwyn commanded, placing a hand on her cheek. "Deep breaths, one after another. Listen to me, you can do this."

Shaking her head, Tessa pressed a hand to her chest and tried to follow his instructions. It felt like she could not breathe, the weight of everything stopping her lungs from expanding. Tessa had experienced it before, but there was no Jaren to talk her through it. Knowing that made it worse, and her knees buckled, but Neriwyn caught her before she collapsed.

"How long have you suffered panic attacks?"

Half carrying her to the bed, Neriwyn sat Tessa down. While running a hand over her back, he let his power surround them and felt some of the tension release from her shoulders. Gently encasing her wrist with his other hand, he located Tessa's heartbeat. It beat quickly, a racing thud against the press of his thumb, but the longer he sat with her, the slower it became. Finally, her breathing evened out, slow, steady intakes rather than the rapid gasps that had come on with the attack.

"You're exhausted, Tessa."

"I'll be fine. There's too much to do, and I need—"

"You need to rest," he growled. "Your brother died, and the emotional strain is going to break you if you keep trying to push."

Tessa did not want to admit he was right. "There will be time to rest after the war. But, if I don't do everything I can to help, Jaren died for nothing. He's the only person who has always had faith in me."

Sighing, Neriwyn said, "You're all so stubborn. It's a good thing I came here to help."

"You did?"

"I did." She arched a brow expectantly, and he chuckled. "You want me to tell you?"

"No time like the present."

"You just had a panic attack," he replied. "Your body is exhausted, and your mind is… well, it's also exhausted."

Dismissing his concern, Tessa clung to the thought of her work to keep from spiraling into another attack. It helped. She knew it helped. That was how she kept from having more of them. Locking herself away in her workroom, where no one was bothered by her strangeness, was the most effective method of avoidance she had found.

"If I have to, I will send for Tharen to sedate you."

"No, thank you, and if that's the help you're offering, I'll pass."

Releasing her wrist, Neriwyn retrieved a pouch from his belt and offered it to her. Plucking it from his hand, Tessa jiggled it and frowned when she heard nothing from it. Glancing at him, she carefully untied the cord holding it closed and peered in at the strange mass it contained.

"Are those seeds?"

"Yes, and I suggest being very careful with them. The plant they are from is known to eat buildings. It's called kudzu, and it's an invasive, consuming vine."

Screwing up her face, Tessa tied the pouch shut. "How are these supposed to help me?"

"Eirian can make them grow to full potential in a matter of moments. She could engulf anything with one seed, let alone that many." Snorting, Neriwyn added, "Attaching them to your solution would provide her with a backup plan."

"If she could do that with those seeds, then why bother with my plan?"

"Because I meant what I said about them. Kudzu is highly invasive and doesn't belong in this land. We can't scatter them across the earth and hope some end up where we need them. Besides, if Eirian pushes their cycle far enough, they'll become a flammable material entwined in the weapons."

Rubbing her chin, Tessa considered the plan, eyes darting to the chest containing the glass orbs. They were counting on the combination of fire and pitch to be enough, but neither of those needed Eirian's power. It would not be hard to incorporate the seeds into the clay vessels. They could be embedded into the last layer, and they would lose nothing by doing so. All Tessa needed to do was work out a way to attach them to the glass balls as an extra.

"Before you get caught up, you need to eat," Neriwyn said, watching her eyes darting between the objects of her focus.

Waving him away, Tessa staggered to her feet and moved stiffly over to the table. Poking a bowl of wet clay, she rubbed it between her fingertips and considered her options. The most logical solution was to coat the glass balls with a layer of clay and use it to hold the seeds. But she needed to determine if it would affect the wards worked into them. It did not matter how logical it was if it prevented the balls from exploding.

Neriwyn watched her work in silence. Her lips moved, the voiceless mutterings a reflection of the thoughts racing through her mind. It grieved him to acknowledge how poorly her abilities had been received over the years. His focus shifted to the black ribbon restraining Tessa's hair, lips twisting in amusement. While she did not seem bothered by its appearance, Neriwyn knew precisely where it had come from.

"What made you decide to tie your hair with ribbons?" he asked, trying to sound disinterested.

"Pardon?"

There was a smear of clay on her cheek as Tessa blinked at him. Chuckling, Neriwyn stood and walked over to the table. She had placed the pouch of seeds in a spot away from the bowls of water and clay.

"The ribbon in your hair."

"Oh!" Tessa shrugged, telling him, "Don't know. One day I found a ribbon, tied my hair back with it, and that was that."

"Sometimes, the smallest oddities have more significance than we realize."

"Tessa?" Rylee said, walking into the tent without waiting for a response. "Oh! Your Majesty."

"I'm leaving someone outside to help you if needed. Merrin will summon me the moment you ask." Reaching out, Neriwyn touched Tessa's shoulder. "Eat, rest. You need to. If you don't, I won't hesitate to have Tharen force something down your throat. Believe me, you don't want him to do that."

Humming a vague agreement, Tessa wiped her hands on a cloth and reached for the pouch of seeds. Uncertain what to do, Rylee looked between Neriwyn and Tessa, taking in the concerned expression he wore. Turning to her, he moved away from the table and stopped when he was close enough to murmur.

"Keep a close eye on Tessa. She's fragile."

"Her brother died. What else would you expect her to be?" Rylee grumbled.

"I'm not sure if you're her friend or not, but someone needs to be with her at all times. Preferably someone with a knowledge of panic attacks."

Understanding dawned, and Rylee stared at Tessa in concern. "Okay. I'll talk to my blue and get someone. I mean, ideally, Zack could help her, but he's a mess over Jaren."

"Thank you," Neriwyn said before leaving.

Studying Tessa as she worked, Rylee replayed her promise to Jaren over in her mind. They had hoped to go into battle together, but orders from Baenlin had separated them. Jaren had demanded she promise to watch out for Tessa if anything happened to him. She did not know how she was going to do it. They could barely stand each other at the best of times, and Rylee expected Tessa to resent her for being alive instead of him.

"Hey, Tessa?"

"What?" she snapped. "Can't you see I'm working? Don't you have something to do?"

Biting back the annoyance she felt at Tessa's response, Rylee said, "Yes, it's called helping you. So, what can I do?"

Pausing to look at her, Tessa hesitated before replying, "I dropped some of the clay balls earlier. Could you clean them up?"

"I can do that."

Eyes darting to the shattered remains, Tessa did not tell Rylee that they reminded her of her failings every time she spotted them. The thought of having to clean them up made her heart race again. Keeping her focus on the new vessel she was crafting, Tessa was thankful for Rylee's grumbling presence.

"Did you see what happened this morning?" Tessa asked quietly, scooping a handful of clay to smother the ball of air and water she had formed with her magic.

Glancing at Tessa, Rylee said carefully, "Baenlin sent me with Paienven's cavalry. We were attempting to flank the Athnaralans when it happened."

"Apparently, it was like lightning striking through them."

"Have you seen Ree?"

"Briefly. I checked in on Eirian when she regained consciousness."

There was a bucket for Tessa's scraps, and using it to collect the pile of broken clay pieces, Rylee mulled over what she was going to say. "I'm sorry I wasn't watching his back."

"It's not your fault. You can't defy Baenlin's orders. Besides, if anyone is to blame for Jaren's death, it's me. He wasn't going to come because he didn't want to leave me."

Rylee was aware of that, but it did not change how she felt. He had been her friend and sparring partner. A rival in the square, but not outside it. Crouching on the ground, a hand on the bucket, she observed Tessa lather clay onto the orb suspended in the air. She looked close to unraveling, sweat beading on her brow. It was obvious she had been crying, red-rimmed eyes not leaving her work.

"Luke's with Zack."

"Good. He needs a friend with him."

"Is it true Ree did all that because someone close to her died?"

Sniffing, Tessa nodded. She wanted to pretend Eirian had reacted to Jaren's death and not some duine who had only known her a short time. Whistling, Rylee did not know what to do with the information.

"I know it wasn't the boys. If it had been, Paienven wouldn't have withdrawn from the field when the Athnaralans did."

"It was one of her Telmian friends. The red-haired lord... Faolan? I met him briefly."

No longer adding clay to the ball, Tessa concentrated her magic on lowering the temperature of the air. She had worked out that the quickest way to harden the shell was to significantly drop the temperature inside until it froze. That allowed it to hold a shape until the rest of the clay dried.

"So, how are the pitch balls coming?" Rylee inquired.

Glancing at her crouching on the ground, Tessa kept up the flow of magic. "How do you think?"

"Tessa, what you're doing? No one else could do it. You're trying to save lives by negating the need to march soldiers to capture multiple siege weapons. We'd take them in the end, but by the time we did, how many would be dead?"

"I'm aware of that."

Rylee leaped up, careful not to knock into anything. Waving a hand around wildly, she ignored the annoyed look on Tessa's face and the sudden heaviness in the air.

"We don't always get on, but we don't have to for me to respect what you're trying to do."

"What's your point?"

"I don't know if I have one," Rylee admitted. "But if you need someone to have your back, I'll be there."

"Excuse me?"

Turning to look at the man standing in the doorway to the tent, Rylee frowned. Power oozed off him, sunlight catching his brown curls, adding to the signature daoine glowing skin. In his hands was a plate covered with a transparent cloth. Tessa's focus had returned to the ball in her hand, a finger lightly testing the hardness of the clay.

"I was told to bring Lady Tessa this plate of food," he explained, keeping his gaze on Tessa. "My orders were strict. I'm to make sure she eats."

Squinting at him, Rylee asked, "Orders from who?"

"King Neriwyn."

Approaching the table, the duine smirked when Tessa lowered the clay ball and placed it down on the surface beside the plate he delivered. Her nostrils flared, catching a whiff of the food and a hint of something familiar. He removed the cover, revealing thick slices of bread balanced on top of a bowl. Next to it was a selection of sliced fruits and other things she did not recognize. Lifting her gaze from the food to the man, Tessa met his dark gaze and sighed.

"I recommend starting with the stew." He waved at the bowl. "The bread is fresh. You could dip it in "

"Do I know you?"

"No, we've never met."

Grunting, Tessa returned her focus to the clay. Crossing his arms, the duine arched a brow, and Rylee watched in amusement. She could tell Tessa had no intention of eating the food, and the man would not let her get away with avoiding it. The question was which one of them was more stubborn.

"Tell me, Lady Tessa, you've met my king."

Her eyes slid in his direction, and Tessa muttered, "Yes, I've met him."

Nodding slowly, he looked pointedly at the food. Following his gaze, Tessa rolled her eyes.

"He was very specific about what was to happen here. Either you agree to eat, or I summon him back, and he'll force you."

Cackling, Rylee said, "I'd like to see that."

Ignoring her, the duine reached for the bread, removing it from where it balanced on the bowl. A spoon helped keep it out of the stew, and he stirred the contents slowly. Watching the spoon's motion, Tessa frowned when he lifted it, showing her a lump of something orange.

"So, why don't we make a compromise?"

"What makes you think I'm the compromising sort?" Tessa said.

Picking up the bowl, he leaned against the table next to her with his back to Rylee. Cradling it in one hand, he scooped up more stew and held the spoon out to Tessa patiently.

"I know your work here is essential. If you don't eat, you'll collapse from exhaustion, and you won't be able to finish your task. Your self-neglect will attract the ire of a certain archmage, compromising your attempts to work with him."

Grinding her teeth, Tessa's eyes flickered between his dark stare and the spoon of food. He did not budge, holding it in front of her face, waiting for her to open her mouth. She caught a whiff of a familiar woody scent mixed with the tantalizing smell of food, making her stomach clench with need. What he said was correct. If she did not eat, she would collapse. Tessa could not work indefinitely without fueling her body, no matter how much power she had at her disposal.

"Fine. I work, you feed."

Opening her mouth and letting him feed her, Tessa tried not to notice the delighted gleam in his eyes. Concentrating on forming another ball of air, she heard Rylee's startled gasp when she drew drops of water from the bowl into the swirl between her hands.

"Open," he prompted.

She followed the gentle command, barely paying attention to the food in her mouth. Backing away to sit on the bed, Rylee watched the two of them in rapt fascination. It was strangely intimate, but she did not want to leave Tessa alone with the strange duine. He continued to feed her, careful not to cross her line of sight. Tessa worked, fingers dancing as she held the ball of water and air firm enough to coat with clay.

"Are you cooling the water once you're finished with the basic shape?"

"Yes."

Humming, he carefully broke a slice of bread into the stew, letting it soak up the liquid before capturing it on the spoon. Bringing it to her mouth, he waited for Tessa to take it. Her eyes darted to him briefly.

"Do you have a better idea?"

"The clay mixture you're working with is already quite wet. If you use that moisture instead of adding extra, you'll save yourself the energy needed to cool the water."

Rylee watched Tessa's brows furrow as she considered his suggestion.

Clearly, she had not thought of it, and she stopped adding to her creation. The ball was not fully formed, providing an opening for her to carefully extract the water from the air. Eyes wide, it amazed Rylee to watch the water drawn out, drops hanging above the table like rain frozen in place.

"Alright then. I'll try it," Tessa said before accepting a spoonful of food.

Smirking, he prepared the next. "I knew you would. The balls don't need to be completely dry for the plan to work. Just dry enough to hold shape for the pitch."

"You didn't know I'd take the suggestion."

"Oh, love, I knew."

Tessa added more clay to the spinning ball of air. "How could you know?"

"I know everything."

"No one knows everything. Except maybe the gods, but even then, I'm doubtful."

Chuckling, he shifted off the table and moved to stand beside her, bringing the spoon to Tessa's lips. She opened without prompting, eyes never leaving her work. A whiff of the same woody scent tickled her nose.

"Maybe I am a god."

"Does your king know you have such delusions of grandeur?"

Leaning over her shoulder, he studied the slowly forming clay ball, murmuring, "He knows. Careful, love, it's wobbling."

Forcing herself to focus, Tessa held her breath when she felt a rush of energy. It coursed through her, warm and renewing. Another spoonful of stew pressed to her lips, and she ate it without thinking. Part of her was thankful for his attention and the compromise no one had ever suggested before. Jaren and Fayleen had always made her stop working to have food rather than work with her.

Still sitting on the edge of the bed, Rylee had not taken her eyes off them. She watched Tessa accept each spoonful while continuing to add more clay until a fully formed ball hung in the air. It was fascinating. The way he watched Tessa suggested to Rylee that something deeper was going on. Not that she seemed aware of much other than her task. Finally, the duine man set the spoon down, stepping away, but she did not notice.

Looking at Rylee, he winked. "Make sure she eats some of the fruit."

"What, not going to let her suck the juices from your fingers?" Rylee quipped.

"Not this time." Giving Tessa an amused look, he said, "She's going to last two more balls. Make her rest. You can negotiate her down to nightfall."

"She's standing right there."

"Yes, but she's not listening."

"You're awfully confident about that."

Shrugging, he headed for the door. "Of course I'm confident. I know she's not paying us any attention right now."

Resuming her task of watching Tessa, it did not take Rylee long to admit the man had been right. She was oblivious to everything, and her focus did not leave the clay ball. Hoping it was going to be worth it, she settled back to observe in silence. If Tessa pulled off the task ahead of her and saves lives with her idea, she would gladly kneel for the future grand mage. And not just out of respect for the memory of a dead friend.

TWENTY-TWO

They had left her alone, giving in to her requests for solitude. She imagined it was predictable that she sought the silence of the rooftop, but Eirian did not care what they thought. Laying on the cold stone with her arms crossed under her head, she stared at the cloudless night sky. Despite the lack of clouds, she viewed the stars as though a mist shrouded them, dulling their shine.

Squeezing her eyes shut, Eirian felt the damp of tears and sighed heavily. She had done nothing but lay there, staring at the sky and letting the tears slowly escape her control. There had been no heavy outpouring of grief, no audible sobs for the guards hovering on the other side of the door to hear. There were just the quiet tears tracking down her face and leaving sticky traces on her skin.

Opening her eyes, the stars were clear again, but it would not last long before more tears filled her vision. With each drop, she thought of the dead she had known and those she had only encountered in passing. Her heart broke over losing friends, people she had loved and would never see again.

Her mind lingered on the blunt stories John used to tell of life growing up in Amath, his jaded approach to life, and his love of the city he came from. Paxton's laugh and cheeky grin, the way he would back up his squad commander no matter what, even when Aiden was furious with them. The quiet observing Kane was one of the youngest guards who had served her and one of the least experienced but he had enjoyed learning.

She would miss the way Fisk could rile Aiden with a well-worded quip and their long conversations about archery. While Fox had overshadowed Mac's skills as a tracker and hunter, he had proven himself more than equal. He had been a mountain man born and raised who had been as enduring as his home region. Every time her eyes closed, Eirian would picture them and contend with the guilt that they had died protecting her in a battle she should never have joined.

More than anything, she was trying to avoid thinking of Faolan and Jaren. Or about the desperate way Aiden had kissed her as he took her to bed. The whispers still purred in delight over it, and Eirian did not understand why. She wanted to forget she had used Celiaen to create a life that would never see the light of day. Or the disappointment she had felt over the bond because she slept with Aiden. Guilt ate at her, even as the whispers reminded Eirian of the feel of his body pressed to hers.

She wanted to banish the horror she felt about the extent of her ruthlessness. It had always been there, lurking on the edges of her personality, encouraged to be there for when she would need it. Leaders needed to be ruthless. Eirian had heard that more times than she could recall. Endured lectures from well-meaning teachers who believed the princess with a kind heart would never be as hard as her male counterparts.

Eirian had not bothered to find out how many of them were helping to fight, but she wondered what they thought now. The cold calculation she had seen in Tessa's gaze when she had awoken had not come as a surprise. She knew the other woman had never underestimated her. They simply had not known how much of her power the gods had hidden.

She knew now. Eirian understood her greatest limitation had been herself and her desire to be less than she was. There was no more locking it away, no shielding that would banish it to the depths. Though while she knew, she doubted anyone else had grasped it. No one except the god she needed to defeat and the two gods pulling her strings. The shadows had always haunted her, even when she did not know it.

It was the niggling feeling Eirian felt, the tug at the deepest edges of her mind, the flicker in the corner of her eye, of something that was there but not quite seen. Memories of a life that demanded remembrance. The gods were the whispers toying with her mind, directing her actions, driving her to surrender her life for them. They would take everything from her, and she could not stop them.

Staring at the stars through the tears, Eirian wondered how many other people realized something lingered beneath the surface of what they perceived. Knowing what she did, she could sense it clearly. A coating of magic covered the world like a shroud. The temptation was strong, a compulsion to reach out with her power and pull it back to reveal what it hid. Eirian resisted her curiosity. But, despite her resistance, the memories whispered and tugged, persistent enough that she expected the temptation to become stronger.

Even with the constant buzz of magic surrounding the area, Eirian could easily pick out those closest to her. Try as she might to tune them out, the feeling of Galameyvin's approach was impossible to ignore, an echo of his calm finding its way over the link between them. It was easy to surmise they had sent him to assess her. She could not blame them for being worried. Her reactions had not been what they expected.

There had been no outbursts, no struggle to come to terms with what she had done. All there had been was the initial confusion when Eirian's memory had been vague about what happened. Her denial had faded, giving way to acceptance. A reserved distance from her emotions, born of necessity. She needed to bottle her grief, to hold it in reserve for when it would serve her best.

While none of them had said anything, Eirian knew Fayleen and Aiden had mentioned her attempt to say goodbye. They were probably fearful that she would slip away into the night to end the war alone. It was tempting, but she knew the mad god would not come out to face her yet. She also suspected the other two gods would prevent her from stepping off their path.

The door barely made a sound as Galameyvin slipped through it, the prickle of magic suggesting he was doing his best not to disturb her. She felt his eyes on her, the creep of his magic barely touching the surface of her power. Neither of them spoke, Eirian from the lack of desire to hear her voice and Galameyvin because he could not find the words to address her.

He had not seen her since she woke, but the light cast by the night sky was more than ample to tell she was unarmed. The gray of her clothes was pale against the glow of her skin. A light that had grown with each day. It was like she absorbed all the moonlight that touched her, reflecting it out to the world. There was something else to it he could not figure out. She did not glow like the daoine, and he did not know how to explain it.

Filling his lungs with the chilly night air, he closed the distance between them and sat near Eirian, murmuring, "Hey."

Tears glistened on her cheeks like drops of light, and Galameyvin wondered if they would resemble liquid silver on his finger if he caught them.

"I knew they'd send someone in the end, and of course, it would be you."

"And we knew you knew. Can you blame us for being worried?"

"No, given the circumstances, I can't blame you. No amount of reassuring from me will make you worry any less."

Opening her eyes, Eirian unfolded her arms from beneath her head and stretched them out. The sting of her joints protesting preceded the tingling numbness she felt in her hands. Without her arms cushioning her head, she felt the unevenness of the stone paving of the roof pressing against the back of her skull. Grunting in annoyance, she rolled over and pushed herself up. There was an ache that would fade, a stiffness to her back that was not entirely from laying on the cold rooftop. For all of Tharen's healing, the shoulder injured during the fight had some lingering tenderness.

Galameyvin knew how to read her. "Tharen said to take it easy. He might have healed the worst of it, but your body and magic still need to do the rest."

"I have been taking it easy." Eirian rolled her eyes, grumbling, "None of you have let me do anything but take it easy. Just convincing anyone to let me be alone was difficult enough."

"We're worried."

"Didn't we just cover that?"

Taking a deep breath, he felt a flash of annoyance. Galameyvin knew what had happened earlier between her and Aiden. It was the source of some of her guilt, and he had seen Celiaen storming around in a rage. He wanted to say something about it, except concerns over her stability stopped him.

"Come, Ree, I know you can be more irritating. You're hardly giving it effort."

Sighing heavily, she did not smile at his attempt to rile her. "Please don't, Gal."

"Have you noticed you're positively glowing?"

"My eyes work, thank you, Gal. I also know it has grown with my power."

Scowling over the fact that his second attempt had also fallen short of expectations, Galameyvin asked, "Are you implying it's directly related to your power?"

"That I am."

"Well…" Cocking his head, he shrugged. "That makes sense, I guess. I can't say it occurred to me. I thought it was the daoine blood."

Mirroring his move, Eirian blinked. She watched him shift nervously,

"If it was a duine thing, then why didn't I glow my entire life? I assume it was because I lived in denial of my power, barely letting myself scratch the surface of it." Her gaze lifted toward the stars, and she whispered, "If they had raised me among my mother's people…"

"You would be a vastly different Eirian to the one I know. Or perhaps not. Perhaps you wouldn't be so dissimilar."

"The assumption that the core of my nature would have remained the same."

Galameyvin screwed up his nose, lifting a hand to scratch at the delicately pointed tip of his left ear. This was a discussion he was familiar with as a blue mage.

"You're the daughter of Shianeni. They would have raised you to be a queen. You know your place in life is to give all you can to your people and your land. We're all servants of duty, and you're the first—"

"I'm pregnant."

Words failed him, and sitting there, staring at her in shock, Galameyvin realized he did not know how to respond. Eirian was matter of fact, her voice carrying hints of boredom. Yet, for all the weight her words carried, she could have been telling him she intended to raise taxes. He realized why Fayleen had been so defensive and repeatedly told them they did not know what Eirian was going through. It was not only her life she intended to sacrifice.

Stretching her arms out, Eirian rolled her head and felt a pinch in her back.

"I don't believe I've ever rendered you speechless, Galameyvin."

"Is it— It's Celi's, isn't it?" He shook his head, scolding himself. "Of course it is. You haven't been with anyone else until today. We'd have known."

Her brows raised questioningly. "I thought I'd been doing a better job of shielding you and Aiden from our link. Why didn't you tell me it wasn't working?"

"How could you be so reckless? You know how to prevent this from happening, and you bloody well should have been when you knew what was coming. I'm so disappointed in you right now, Eirian."

It was not the first time she had disappointed him, but the sheer strength of what Galameyvin felt threatened to unravel the calm he carefully maintained. Eirian saw the cracks appearing in his power.

"It is what it is, Galameyvin."

There was no need to ask it as a question, so he stated, "Fay knows, but no one else."

"I had no intention of telling anyone. Fayleen has her little gifts, she knew." Shrugging, Eirian brushed the hair from her face and frowned. "And like her, you'll tell no one."

"You can't ask that of me. I won't lie to him!"

Her eyes narrowed, a gleam of frustration apparent. "You're failing to grasp the reality of the situation for all your ability to read people and events. Has it occurred to you that I planned this? This was my plan from the moment I found out the blood of the three lines was used to bind a god. What do you think will happen if Celi knows I carry his child? That I intend for both myself and his child to die?"

Just as frustrated as she was, Galameyvin screwed up his face, snarling, "It's not fair to keep it from him! We could buy more time to find—"

"There is no other solution! Don't you understand? My death alone is not enough to keep her locked away forever. This might do it, or at least for a long time. Enough time for you and the others to discover something that will prevent it from happening again."

"It's one thing to choose death for yourself, but—"

Holding up a hand to silence him, Eirian sighed heavily. "It exists purely for this purpose, just as I do. At least I'm saving it from having to find out. I'm no different from livestock bred for consumption. Our deaths will serve the survival of everyone else."

"Your life is not worth less than those you would save," he said.

"No, it's worth more. It's worth the lives of everyone alive and those yet to be born. Don't you get it yet? If I don't do this, the world will fucking burn. She'll descend everything into war, chaos, and death. Pointless death. Rivers will run red with blood from everyone turning on each other. We will lose the sky under a haze of smoke from the fires of her victory." Eirian saw him prepare to argue, and she continued, "How will you feel when you drive a sword through Celi?

Or Fay? How about when you watch your father turn on your mother and siblings? Will you still think, 'I'm so glad I stopped Eirian from dying to prevent this'?"

Shutting his mouth, he mulled over her words. Logic screamed that Eirian was right. Her survival was not worth the consequences, but his love wanted to let it all burn.

"I understand, I do. We can hear what you're saying to us."

"Then why are we having this conversation?"

"Because we're all selfish! Would you willingly let any of us walk to our death if the situation were reversed?"

Deciding to circle back to her earlier question, she lifted her gaze back to the stars. "Why didn't you tell me my efforts aren't working?"

Choosing to indulge her question, Galameyvin smiled. "Why would I? I take comfort in sensing you when I turn my mind to it. To know you're there, alive. I know it won't last, so I'll appreciate it while I can."

"Have you told Aiden about it?" Eirian asked softly.

"Do you think me a fool? He's already willing to die for you. I'm hardly likely to give him another reason to do so. Or did he not remind you of that while his hands were all over you?"

Snorting, she could not help but agree. Avoiding the slightly jealous tone of his question, Eirian refused to speak about what she had done with Aiden.

"I did something earlier. Like most things I have done recently, you won't approve."

"But you're not asking for my approval." He gave her a knowing look.

"No, I'm not seeking your approval. It's easier to ask for forgiveness than permission."

"Then what is it?"

Taking several deep breaths before she told him, Eirian noticed the faint glow forming to the east. Sunrise was approaching. She had not realized the time.

"I manipulated the bond between Aiden and I. Included Fayleen in it, hoping to protect him from any backlash caused by my death. You and Celi are both so powerful. You stand more of a chance than he does with no power."

Galameyvin clicked his tongue. "I see. You're right, I disapprove, but if your fears come true, I suppose I'll understand your motives. Where did your morals go? It was not so long ago that you would've found your path abhorrent and condemned anyone for doing such a thing. The link between you, Aiden, and I might be unintentional, but you've brought your best friend into it intentionally and without her consent."

"I'm trying to protect Aiden."

"You know they'd sentence you to death for this."

Her cheek twitched while she ground her teeth. "Fay agreed to do everything she could to protect Aiden for me. To make sure he lived."

"But you didn't ask her if she agreed to that specifically." Cocking his head to the side, he glanced at the closed door. "But then, I suppose, you'd have to reveal you're bound to three men."

"Fay knows. Did you think I wouldn't tell her? I tell her just about everything."

The mocking tone she took made Galameyvin peer at her. "You do? Just what exactly do you tell her?"

Smiling sweetly, Eirian drew comfort from the memories of nights spent curled up in bed talking with Fayleen. "By everything, I mean everything."

Feeling deeply uncomfortable with the thought, he shifted. "Everything?"

"Everything."

"Even…"

"You bet," she said with a grin.

"Oh." Exhaling slowly, Galameyvin found her grin unnerving. "How did we get so far from the topic at hand?"

Eirian chuckled. "Which topic at hand? You might need to be a little more specific."

"Eirian," he grumbled.

"You're the one who went there. Besides, you can't tell me you and Celi don't talk about everything. I mean, I can understand that some things, mostly involving me, might be a little awkward, but Fay and I had no such boundaries to worry about."

"So, what, you'd tell her every time and giggle over it like a pair of girls?"

Her brows raised. "We were girls. Just because you're old."

"I'm not old." Crossing his arms, he huffed at her before letting himself smile a little. "But you're right. Men are hardly any better. Perhaps we're a little cruder."

Scoffing, Eirian thought of the whispered conversations she had taken part in and had overheard. "Yeah… no. We're all as bad as each other. Just because we're women doesn't mean we're any less crude."

"My pride wants to know how we compare," he half-joked, knowing she would not tell.

Mouth twitching, she said, "All I ask is that you keep your silence until after I'm gone."

Hating the thought, Galameyvin grunted. "As much as it pains me to agree…"

It did pain him. Galameyvin desperately wanted to go to Celiaen and tell him everything she had revealed. He needed to tell Fayleen what Eirian had done to her and Aiden. Nodding, she lifted her shoulder and let it drop. It ached at the movement, but she welcomed it.

"I'm sorry I've put you in this position. I'm sorry we're even at the point where I must. There's so much I'm sorry for, and I need you to be the one to tell them that. I need you to tell them how much I loved them, that everything I did was to protect them and ensure their survival." Eirian sighed. "Just be sure you think about it seriously before you tell Celi that I was pregnant when I died."

"Is it your intention to make heartfelt speeches and beg something from all of us?"

"Perhaps. I beg you all to live, to carry on. I want you to find someone, marry, maybe have a child. I want you to be happy. I need to know my death will mean something to you beyond the fact I saved everyone else. I want you to make sure Celi does the same. I need you to protect him from Paienven and his ambitions, Baenlin, and even himself. Help him find happiness without me in his life."

The glow of light continued to creep higher on the horizon as the sun rose. Protecting Celiaen was something Galameyvin would always do, but he knew she needed to hear him reassure her of it. For her, not just because it was what he had always done.

"You know I will. Don't you ever doubt that I'll be there for Celi because, by the powers, I will be. Always. After you're dead, I'll be the one dragging him away from here and pushing him to live. That's if he survives you."

"Thank you for reminding me my death might take him down as well. Because I don't feel enough guilt."

"Forgive me, I shouldn't have made that dig. Sometimes I wish I could have foreseen what chaos you would wreck upon us. I'd have fought harder to keep Celi away from you."

The guilt on her face did not make him feel as bad as he thought it should. Instead, it told Galameyvin she wished the same. Pulling her knees up to her chest, Eirian leaned forward to watch the colors on display across the sky, chasing the stars away.

"I don't know what I'd have done over the years without you. What if it was the three of you, your love and friendship, that made me what I am now? We'll never know if I could have done this without you."

"That's a fair point." Getting to his feet, Galameyvin stretched before holding out a hand to her. "Dance with me."

Surprised, Eirian accepted and allowed him to help her stand. "You know I don't dance."

Waiting while she shook the stiffness from her body, Galameyvin said, "It's not about dancing. I want to hold you and forget everything else. To remember when I watched the morning light chase the shadows from your face. Times when my biggest worry was what I'd do when you realized how much you and Celi loved each other."

Stepping into the circle of his arms, Eirian smiled sadly. There was a familiar comfort in how Galameyvin embraced her, foreheads touching. His arm around her waist held her tightly, and she moved her head, letting it rest on his shoulder while she pressed her nose to the side of his neck. Even so far from his beloved libraries, he smelled like parchment, and Eirian giggled.

Feeling the twitch of her lips before she kissed his neck, Galameyvin held her tighter and buried his face in her hair. It would be hard to let go, but he would cling to the moment for as long as he could. She smelled like flowers. She always smelled like flowers, even when filthy and covered in dirt, blood, and sweat. It occurred to him he had never plucked a flower grown by her magic to see if they smelled like her.

Pulling her face away, Eirian cupped his cheek and kissed him, whispering, "I love you. I loved you first, and I'll never stop loving you."

"Eirian," he murmured sadly.

Burying her other hand in his hair, she kissed him again. She wished they had the time to sink into each other's embrace.

"Remember this. Whatever happens next, remember this. Don't remember me in pain, don't remember my fear, and don't remember your own. Instead, remember the feeling of my lips, the press of my body against yours, my hands in your hair. Remember the sound of my laugh and the way you made me smile."

When she pulled away from him, Galameyvin regretted losing her warmth and wanted nothing more than to grab her back. He would have given anything to lower Eirian to the floor and remind her how those things felt.

"Ree—"

"I better go. A messenger is looking for me, and the poor woman doesn't need to face the gauntlet of my guards."

Glancing at the sky, Eirian felt her tears threatening to return and took a deep breath to gather herself. Magic twisted around her, shifting the shadows at her feet like living things. Whispering taunts, the memories continued to barrage her mind with fragments of someone else's life.

"Don't dwell in the past, Gal, remember it, but don't dwell in it. Honor me by making new happy memories."

Letting her walk away, Galameyvin turned to face the sun and moved to the edge of the rooftop. "You don't realize, Eirian."

TWENTY-THREE

A t the sound and movement of the door opening, the handful of royal guards jolted to attention. It surprised them to see Eirian instead of Galameyvin, and she offered a worn smile. She did not bother to hide how drained she felt because she needed everyone to see it, and her emotions warring within. The darkness lurked in so many, watching them, watching her, and she wanted to make the god think she had the upper hand.

It was easy. Eirian suspected it would have been harder to pretend she was fine than it was to show the world the truth. Gabe was in command, the shadows cast by the torches dancing over his face. His expression was grim, and eyes dark as he regarded her blankly. The whispers stilled, and she thought she saw black lines at the base of his throat, a strange swirl she remembered tracing with her fingers. Those memories slipped away as quickly as they came, and Eirian shook her head, dismissing it as a trick of the shadows.

"There's a messenger on her way up," she explained, slipping through them.

Nodding to another, Gabe sent him on ahead. "Have you left the elf standing?"

"Yes."

"I didn't think it was a good idea to disturb you, but they insisted."

The explanation sounded sincere, and Eirian glanced back at him. She could always count on Gabe to look out for her.

"It's fine, Gabe. Thank you. You've been through a lot, but I know I can count on you."

For a moment, his mouth twitched, and she thought he might give her one of his rare smiles. "No one can offer me as much fun as you."

Giving him a wide-eyed look, Eirian grimaced. "I'm not entirely sure I've lived up to your expectation of fun."

"True," Gabe grunted in agreement. "I expected us to have more years together."

"I'm sorry to let you down."

"What about the rest of us?" Wade said jokingly.

They knew Eirian was closer to Aiden and his chosen. Looking at the back of his head, Eirian wondered what Wade would have wanted from her, given a chance. She assumed it was what most of them wanted. A good ruler, a fair one, someone who would ensure their families and communities remained safe and provided for. A ruler that they could feel pride in serving. Wade sensed her stare, half-turning as he picked his way down the stairs to meet her gaze.

"The rest of you aren't as picky as Gabe," she jested, smiling faintly. "His tastes are that much more particular."

Next to Wade at the front, Kip did not glance back as he said, "You know, I can't say I have ever seen you with anyone, Gabe, just your knives."

It was a wintry smile with the promise of death that Gabe offered them. Eirian thought the shadows crept closer, the whispers petering off when she looked at him curiously.

"Don't fret, ma'am. Seeing your handiwork with those Athnaralans was enough. It was a thing of beauty, a memory that I will always treasure."

"Mate, you are so fucking odd," Lyle commented, reminding Eirian he was not as used to Gabe as the other members of the squad.

Jack snorted. "Yeah, he ain't the boss man, but I know which one of them I wouldn't want to piss off."

Sighing softly, Eirian glanced back at Lyle. "I'm sorry we've broken your squad up and spread you among the others."

"Nah, think nothing of it, ma'am." He shrugged, eyes downcast. "It'll be right. When we get back to Amath and the Captain selects new men for the guard, we'll return to his squad."

"They were your friends."

Blowing air through his lips, Lyle shrugged again. "They were. Do we need to remind you? Because I'm sure we can if that's what you need to hear."

"That's not what I need to hear, but thank you anyway, Lyle."

Her ears picked up the sound of hurried footfall coming up the stairs, and the two guards at the front placed hands on the hilts of their knives.

"It's the messenger sent for me," Eirian said.

Wade scoffed. "We'll be the judges of that."

"Besides, you're not armed," Kip added.

"I don't need any weapons," she reminded them.

"Oh!" They startled the older woman as she rounded the curve of the stairs and stopped short. "They sent me to find the Queen."

"Sent by who?" Crossing his arms, Wade glared at her.

Hissing at the two leading guards, Eirian placed a hand on their shoulders and peered past them to the messenger. Magic seeped from her through their armor, sending warmth down their spines. It replenished their energy without trying. She had struggled to contain her power completely since Faolan's death.

"Hush, boys. I'm here. What do you need?"

Scrambling to bow and salute, the messenger stumbled on her step, and Kip shot forward to catch her. She gave him a thankful look, receiving a wink in return.

"I'm sorry, it's been a long, busy night. You're wanted, ma'am. In the hall. They're all there already."

"They're making preparations quickly. Please, lead the way," Eirian stated with a nod and a wry smile.

"Actually, ma'am, if you don't mind." Looking embarrassed, the messenger glanced at her feet. "I haven't stopped all night, and I'm starved."

Eirian did not mind. She appreciated hunger and the need to stop for a moment to rest. Signaling the guards to keep going, she paused next to the woman and placed a hand on her arm.

"It's fine. We know the way. Eat and get some rest. You'll need it."

Feeling the prickle of magic, the messenger stared at her in awe. The rush of energy made her feel ready for anything. It was such a small thing for her to do, but Eirian knew it meant a lot to the other woman.

"Thank you, Your Majesty, for everything."

Grunting, Gabe encouraged Eirian to move along. "You heard your queen."

Waiting until they were closer to the ground level of the keep, Jack asked, "You think they're going to try attacking again today?"

"What, keep harassing Athnaral until they're out of numbers or the reinforcements arrive?" Lyle said, looking skeptical. "Nah, I doubt it. They'd have to trample over the dead to get there, and no one wants to do that."

"Yeah, that's true." Kip agreed.

Listening to them talk, Eirian drew strength from Gabe's silence. He was the simplest of them for all of his complexities, and she found a shred of peace in his dark nature. His calm was a beacon in the turmoil of emotions that swirled everywhere she turned. Even the blue mages felt the effects, but not Gabe. Not the quiet killer with a twisted morality, the assassin tasked with carrying out despicable deaths on her behalf.

He remained unfazed by the deaths of his comrades. The drama of the battlefield and the politics washed over him like raindrops on a leaf. It made Eirian wonder how he processed it, whether Gabe would slip away some time when he was free and find someone who violated his rules. Someone to kill to vent his feelings.

"Why do you keep looking at me like that?" He acknowledged her continuous sideways glances, dark eyes remaining watchful.

People stared as they passed through shadowy hallways. Whispers followed in their wake, and Eirian decided she did not wish to know what was being said. She did not want to find out if it was condemnation or praise for what she had done on the battlefield. Gabe cleared his throat, reminding her he had asked a question, and she gave him a flustered look.

"Sorry, I was in my thoughts." It was half an apology.

His mouth twisted, and a sense of familiarity struck her again, the whispers drawing back. Eirian sighed, thankful for any moment of peace she got.

"You are what you are, Majesty, and there is nothing you can do to change it. All you can do is own it."

"Is that your favorite piece of advice?"

He had said it to her before, a simple encouragement toward self-acceptance that she long disregarded. The twist of his lips flattened into the straight line they usually held.

"It's my only piece of advice. Own who you are, own your actions, own your mistakes and your triumphs."

The doors into the great hall never shut anymore. Tired officers trudged in and out, mages mixed in the throng. Eirian felt their exhaustion, the promise of rest waiting for them at the other end of their tasks. She relaxed her hold over her magic slightly, letting energy wash over all of them. It barely touched the edge of her power, but it scratched an itch, taking away some of the pressure in her head.

Many did a double-take when they noticed Eirian. The handful of guards a stark contrast to the wall of men and weapons usually surrounding her. She suspected her appearance in simple gray without armor or weapons was equally surprising. Joining the chaos within the hall, Eirian lingered at the back of the gathered people. It afforded her the chance to listen and observe, catching snippets of shouted arguments and muttered gripes.

People slowly grew aware of Eirian's presence, their attention turning as energy seeped into them. With each person who turned her way, more realized she was there, and awareness spread. The arguments came to a halt when the decision-makers learned she was at the back of the crowd. Through the bond, she sensed Celiaen in the hall, a mixture of emotions rolling back at her.

Sneering, Paienven signaled for people to part so that he could see Eirian. "We've been waiting for you."

"I've been here, listening," she replied, carefully slipping through the gap and avoiding the gazes of those she passed.

General Cameron waved for her to stand beside him. "Another impressive display yesterday, Your Majesty."

Tucking her hair back behind her ears, Eirian glanced around the table at people staring at her. She wanted to feel remorse for her actions in battle, but the ache of grief overpowered her emotions. What guilt she felt was not for her victims, but for everyone and everything else.

"My apologies for disrupting your carefully laid plans."

On the opposite side of the table, Baenlin's face was unreadable. He had taken in her lack of armor and weapons, the way her hair tumbled around her face in disarray, and the red rim of her eyes that told of time spent grieving. There was pain in her eyes and fury that ran deep, her magic weighing so heavily around her he thought he might choke on it. A glance at his fellow mages told him they felt it as well, felt the whisper of her power calling.

Baenlin had always known Eirian was dangerous. But knowing was not the same thing as understanding. Now he understood she was the most perilous person any of them had ever encountered. Paienven had realized it as well. Surrounded by people, she did not seem cowed by their stares. Baenlin decided she looked like a caged predator that knew it had to bide time for an open door so that it could fight for survival.

"Athnaral has requested, and we have agreed, that there be no fighting today," Marcellus informed her.

Her eyes flickered to Everett, where he stood silently beside Marcellus and said, "How gracious. I assume it's to deal with the dead."

"Indeed, ma'am," Darragh answered without looking at her, his eyes remaining locked on Paienven. "The dead are their excuse, but they'll make the most of the time to recoup. Their reinforcements are due."

"How due?" she asked, frustrated that no one had informed her sooner.

Sensing her frustration, Baenlin scowled. "Any time. Tessa is aware and is working hard on her solution with as many mages as she can."

"We should disregard any truce and finish them!" Paienven argued.

Chuckling, Eirian inclined her head to Cameron and murmured, "Wasn't he the one arguing to wait for the reinforcements to arrive so we could take them out in one fight?"

There was no attempt made to hide his smirk. "Yes, he was."

"We still have the upper hand. It doesn't hurt us to show courtesy and respect the truce. It is only for a day. Let people rest, tend to the dead and the wounded. It will give the mages time to finish their preparations to deal with the siege weapons," Gallagher said.

He surprised her by speaking against Paienven. There was a bandage wrapped around his arm, faint blood staining suggesting he had taken a blow to it. People stared at him in shock, and he waved as he continued.

"We didn't lose as many as we could have. We still have greater numbers."

Vartan regarded Eirian thoughtfully. "Tell us, little queen, what do you feel is the right thing to do? Do we attack today and take advantage of disarray, or do we honor a day of peace to take care of our dead?"

The question felt heavy, and Eirian did not look at the man who had asked it as she answered, "When the battle is over, there will be survivors. Show them we are people of honor. That we respect a truce, and they can trust us to keep our word."

Bowing her head in agreement, Sannaeh arched a brow at Paienven when he went to argue. "Queen Eirian is correct. Let's remember that we'll have a defeated enemy in the end and that they are people. No doubt King Aeyren has people urging him to turn and flee with his forces while they have a chance."

"Unlikely," Eirian said sadly. "Though I wish it were the case."

"Any adviser worth their title would urge retreat in their situation," Kendall scoffed.

"They're here!" Shouts rang through the hall, diverting attention from the conversation toward the breathless soldiers at the doors. "They've come."

"What are you on about?" Darragh barked.

Baenlin did not need to hear the answer to know, his voice low as he said, "The Athnaralan reinforcements have arrived with their weapons."

She desperately wanted to see them, but Eirian remained in her place. "Well then, that changes everything."

Paienven glared at each of those he felt responsible for thwarting his attempts to direct the war. "We should attack them now while they are unprepared. If we don't, they'll have time to ready their weapons to use against us."

"It pains me to say, but His Majesty has a point." Eirian felt how her words surprised the hall. "We face a tough decision."

"You're the Queen of Endara. Decide, and we'll do as you command," Cameron stated.

A hand touched the small of her back, and Eirian knew Celiaen had worked his way around to her. She had not paid him attention, her focus on the matter of the truce.

"Ree, whatever you decide," he murmured in her ear.

"No, not me. Everett will decide." She shook her head, waving at Everett.

Startled, he held his hands up, protesting. "I cannot make this choice."

"You'll be the king soon, and if this is a decision for queens and kings to make? Well then, make it, King Everett."

Marcellus placed a hand on his shoulder. "She has a point, my boy."

Looking around at the waiting faces, Everett clenched his jaw and nodded. "We respect the day to tend the dead! Archmage, is there anything your people can do about them?"

"There is. If there are no objections, we'll burn the bodies. It's cleaner, less chance of diseases spreading through the armies." Baenlin clipped his words, gaze seeking Eirian again thoughtfully. "Of course, I imagine you could do it on your own."

Eirian blinked, murmuring, "Let's say I did and leave it at that."

"You want to burn the bodies?" One of the Endaran officers asked, his voice betraying his horror at the thought.

"This is neither the time nor place for that debate. Unless you wish to remove the bodies and pile them up, devoting powers know how many people to digging holes for mass graves." Sannaeh knew the Endarans buried their people.

His hand remained pressed firmly against her back, Celiaen watching his father intently. "Tomorrow then? Tomorrow we end this."

"Are we certain this is the path we wish to take?" Vartan asked.

Feeling the eyes on her, Eirian scowled and said, "You can't involve me in making these decisions. They need to rest on the shoulders of those who'll be here when the fight is over."

"You're the most powerful mage among us. You can kill so many, so easily." Paienven sounded disgusted, and the eyes shifted to him.

"The truth remains that we're drawing closer to the actual fight. She did not come to me on the field yesterday, and we can only hope she'll appear during the next battle. After all, with these reinforcements and the weapons, it promises to be a far more fervent fight."

His eyes narrowed, swapping from her to Celiaen at her back. "You remain convinced you'll die in this fight."

Feeling Celiaen's nails dig into her back, Eirian rolled her shoulders before shrugging. He was warning her not to engage Paienven in an argument. It was an unnecessary caution when she had no intention of giving energy to fights that held no meaning.

"Don't worry, Your Majesty, my blood won't be on your hands."

"We know whose hands it will be on, don't we, darling."

Stiffening, Eirian resisted the urge to cover her ears. It would be pointless to try blocking out the caress of Gebael's voice through her mind, and it would only lead to questions. Sneering, Paienven turned his back on her to speak to Darragh. People waited to see if either of them would react, but Eirian forced herself to smile. Clearing his throat, Cameron leaned in to speak to her.

"What are your plans, ma'am?"

"I'm going to find my captain and convince him to let me see the siege weapons." Eirian ignored the flood of anger over their bond. "If I've got a better idea of what I'm helping Tessa with…"

Nodding, Cameron said, "That's a good idea. If Aiden digs his heels in, tell him I ordered it. He might be captain of the royal guard, but I'm still his general."

Laughing at the image her mind created, Eirian nodded. Giving Everett a reassuring look, she quietly slipped from the table. People let her go, Celiaen keeping close as they wove through the crowd. Rage simmered in his magic, a reminder he was unhappy. His hand did not leave her back, the press of it encouraging Eirian to move. Gabe and the other guards formed a wall around them, keeping any courageous people from approaching.

"Celi—"

"Shut up," he snapped.

Gaze downcast, Eirian let him direct them down a dimly lit corridor with no one in it. She did not have the energy to argue. Shadows danced over the walls, the light cast by torches as twisted as the whispers in her mind. Looking at the two of them, Gabe signaled for his men to remain at the entrance. They did not worry about Eirian's safety, but protecting her privacy was part of their job.

Shoving Eirian against the wall, Celiaen growled, "How dare you!"

"I'm sorry for hurting you."

"I felt everything."

She sighed, closing her eyes as she rested her head against the wall. The anger he felt was understandable. Eirian remembered how it felt when Galameyvin had gone to bed with the Indari woman, and she imagined it had been worse for Celiaen. Guilt flooded through her, the unexhausted well of tears overflowing again. Hearing him curse, Eirian did not move when Celiaen buried his face in her neck.

"If you had asked, I would have said yes," he told her, and his breath was warm on her skin. "I love you so much."

"It wasn't planned."

"You used it to say goodbye."

Flinching at the accusation in his voice, Eirian did not ask how he knew. She had known Aiden and Fayleen would tell others of her decision not to fight her fate. His hands tugged at her clothes, seeking the skin beneath. Burying a hand in his hair, she grasped the silk of his coat, moaning when his teeth grazed over her neck. Fingers stroked her sides, following familiar paths that danced between sensitive and ticklish.

"I can smell him on you. Powers, I wanted to join you."

"Celi—"

"I'm not willing to say goodbye."

He lifted his lips to taste the tears on her cheeks. An agonizing gesture that had Eirian wondering if guilt flavored them. She could not speak. Her voice was lost beneath the whispers and the feel of Celiaen's hands on her skin.

"I refuse to let you give up, Ree. You're not allowed to die."

"There's nothing you can do to change it, Celi," she whispered.

Using his body to press her against the wall, he growled, "I'll find something. Anything. Whatever it takes to keep you alive."

"Please don't make this harder for both of us."

"*His hopefulness is endearing.*"

"I'm not the one making this hard! You're the one walking around like a shadow of herself, telling everyone she's going to die."

"If I say it often enough, some of you will believe it! I'm only trying to prepare you for what will happen," Eirian said, her voice becoming a whimper when his fingers dug into a sore spot on her side.

Eyes narrowing, Celiaen gazed at her. Her skin glowed, the sheen of magic unaffected by the grief he felt over the bond. He wanted to scream and shake her until some of the fire returned. The woman in his arms was not his Eirian. She was the shadow he had described her as, an echo of someone powerful and vibrant. Seeing tears glistening on her cheeks again, Celiaen wanted to cry with her, but he could not. One of them had to be strong.

"You break my heart," he told her.

"Better a broken heart than a broken body."

Gebael's voice snaked through her mind again, a momentary distraction. She welcomed it and the cold traces it left. The whispers were silent for him, but the emptiness was a gaping wound. Eirian shook her head, preparing for what she needed to do.

"Oh, darling, you want to be so noble, but I know what you are."

"Go away," she whispered.

Recoiling, Celiaen left her clinging to the wall for support. Hurt was written across his face, and Eirian realized she had said the words aloud. She had intended them for the voice in her head, not him. Laughing, the whispers mocked her for the mistake, but she could not feel any guiltier than she already did.

"Is that what you want?"

Eirian shook her head. "No. I don't want you to go away."

"Then why?" Celiaen asked.

"Because I need you to. Just for now. You should be in the war council, and I need to do things today. But tonight? You can hold me in your arms. It'll be just you and me, as it's always been."

"If you die, I'll die with you. We'll be buried side by side."

It was a promise, and Eirian knew it. She would do whatever she had to do to make sure it became a broken one. Before she said anything to argue with him, Celiaen's lips were on hers. His hands pulled her against him again, the warmth of his body a comfort Eirian did not think she deserved.

"Foolish boy does not know your bones will never rest beneath the earth."

Gathering the determination to push Celiaen away, Eirian looked at her guards and noticed Gabe watching them. Embarrassed they were behaving the way they were in view of anyone who might turn down the hallway, she rubbed her face to hide her feelings. Tugging at his coat, Celiaen sighed heavily.

"I spoke to Rylee earlier. A few of them are going to raise toasts to Jaren tonight."

"I'll be there."

"You need to see Tessa," he said, his voice low. "Rylee said she's close to losing it. Something about panic attacks, Neriwyn threatening her, and fights over resting. Honestly, sounds like something you'd do."

Pressing her lips together, Eirian went through her plans for the day. It would be helpful to include Tessa on her trip to see the siege weapons. They had to work together to make the plan work, and if they both knew what they were dealing with, things would go better.

"I'll ask her to come to see the Athnaralans. It will help both of us to visualize what we need to destroy."

Opening his mouth, Celiaen went to say something, but decided against it and turned away. Reaching out, Eirian grabbed his hand, stopping him before he walked away. She kissed him tenderly, a hand cupping his cheek. Frowning, he did not stop her when she stepped back, putting space between them. He watched a mask slip over her face, but it did not hide what he felt over the bond.

"Good luck in council," she said. "Try to avoid killing your father."

The comment made him smile, and Celiaen replied, "No promises."

"I love you."

"I know, dear heart, and I'll always love you too."

Watching Celiaen walk away, Eirian met Gabe's stare and sighed. Once he was out of sight, she slumped against the wall and ran her hands through her hair, tugging at the long strands. The pain was not enough to distract her from the guilt or silence the whispers. Magic swirled around her, slipping through the fragile hold she had over it.

"Eirian," Gabe spoke, placing a hand on her shoulder. "Deep breath."

"I'm fine, Gabe."

He arched a brow, looking around at the moss coating the stone. "If you were fine, would that be happening?"

Looking at where he was pointing, Eirian muttered, "Beats flowers for a change."

"Hardly the point. We need to find the Captain and make your plans. Arguing with him will improve your mood. Or you could just let him repeat what he did yesterday."

Blinking, Eirian stared at him, a blush turning her cheeks red. Winking, Gabe nodded at his men, signaling for her to move.

"Does everyone know?"

"Define everyone."

"Never mind."

Chuckling, Gabe said, "Don't worry, no one will say anything. The Captain would gut us if we did."

Embarrassment filled Eirian, chasing away some of her guilt and sorrow. Avoiding the gazes of her guards, she clung to the emotion like it would save her. At the back of her mind, a voice screamed above the whispers that it was pointless, and she ignored it. She would take what she could get, anything that would help keep her from stepping over the knife's edge she balanced on. All she needed was one more day.

TWENTY-FOUR

"Well," Tessa muttered, chewing on her lip. "I suppose it's a good thing they're made from wood. It works in our favor."

Watching the Athnaralan legions cautiously, Eirian kept a firm hand on Halcyon's reins. "What is wood can burn."

The smell of smoke and burning flesh filled the air. Mages and soldiers had spent most of the morning preparing the pyres, the day slipping away as they carried out the unpleasant tasks. Eirian had observed as the first was lit before meeting with Tessa to make plans. She intended to return to bid farewell to Faolan, Jaren, and her guards.

"Trebuchets," Aiden grunted, looking around warily in expectation of an attack.

Glancing at him, Tessa nodded. "I've read about them. Paienven uses trebuchets."

Aiden grunted again and let his gaze linger on one of the massive wooden contraptions. "There's a big difference between reading about them and seeing them in action. Will your special powder work?"

"I hope so. I can hardly test it beforehand. What do you think, Eirian?"

They looked at her, waiting for a reply, but she did not move.

Tessa spoke again, "Eirian?"

Her eyes were unfocused, mind chasing after her magic as she explored the weapons. There was no life in them, but Eirian could taste the destructive potential they held. It whispered about them and the great boulders the Athnaralans had transported to use. The stone told of being ripped from the earth, struck with iron picks to make them a desirable size. She pictured the dry valley in the desert where they originated.

Trained men constructed the weapons, assembling the pieces they had divided for transport. Leather and metal reinforced the joints, the heavy central beams cut from single towering trees. Trees that had reached for the sky in competition with the mountains they grew on. Off to the side, wagons of rocks waited for loading into the large boxes attached to one end of the central beam.

"The timber is fresh. Felled after spring melted the snow from the base of the Fingers. That's why they came the way they did. They reinforced parts with metal and leather, but nothing will hold fast once we get a good fire burning. All we need to do is damage the central beam to render them useless." Slowly returning her focus to her companions, the lighter flecks of Eirian's eyes gleamed. "Equally so if I destroy the men trained to use them."

Knowing better than to imagine limitations to what Eirian could do, Tessa squinted. "Could you save us all some time and effort and destroy them now?"

Tilting her head to the side, Eirian shrugged. The whispers wanted her to do something. It would be almost too easy to reach out and pluck the life from the army, taking it for herself. Fingers twitching, she considered giving in to the demands in her head, then reminded herself that killing for the sake of killing was abhorrent.

"I could, but it would likely cause them to launch an attack on us. We agreed to a day of peace. We will not be the ones who go back on our word."

"You're going to be the boss mage. So you should understand how these things work. From what I gather, mage politics are worse than the rest." Aiden chuckled.

"I don't need schooling in politics by a guard and a queen who won't see a year on her throne," Tessa grumbled, frustration breaking through.

Corners of her mouth curling, Eirian smirked. "Except they raised me to be a queen. While I learned politics, your father denounced you, and others labeled you peculiar. All because you approach magic differently to them."

Unimpressed by the reminder, Tessa lifted her hands to the back of her head to unravel the black ribbon binding her hair. It was difficult to hide how badly she was struggling, but anything that allowed her to cling to a sense of control helped. Shaking the brown tresses free, Tessa stared at Eirian before raising a brow and returning the smirk.

"Riane wanted a queen for a grand mage. Well, they're getting a grand mage who'll be the queen they need. I'm not a puppet, and they're in for a rude awakening."

"Good." Nudging Halcyon, Eirian turned him toward Kelsby. "The world is big, Tessa, and Riane needs someone capable of looking beyond the city. You can drag them into the future. Kicking and screaming if needed."

Grinning at Tessa and shrugging, Aiden pursued Eirian. "I almost feel sorry for your council."

Laughing, Eirian beat Tessa to a response. "You've not met them. They deserve everything coming."

"I've met Baenlin," he replied.

Thinking about Baenlin, Tessa said, "He may be the exception. I'm undecided."

Tossing a glance over her shoulder, Eirian shook her hand where she could see it. "He has his faults. He's ambitious, seeking to further his power and influence. If you tell me he's already attempted to worm his way into your bed, I wouldn't be shocked."

"Perhaps my reputation puts him off. Or my father, although he is training his replacement as an archmage."

Tessa said nothing of his offer to share a drink, dismissing it as battlefield niceties. Or of her attempts to hint to Baenlin that she would welcome him in her bed. Someone else had pushed him from her thoughts, and she pictured the brown-haired duine who kept visiting.

Aiden screwed up his face, trying to make sense of the complexity of the situation. "Isn't your father human?"

"Yes. Hugh's on his last legs, but he still has the power to turn a man into a nonsensical mess. I wouldn't want to fight him. He's a sly and vindictive bastard. But I won't be sorry when he dies," she said with a look like she had eaten something foul.

"I thought power decided positions on the council?" Merle asked, curious but not entirely sure he wanted to know the answer.

Sharing a look, the two mages pursed their lips, and Eirian arched her brows to give Tessa leave to answer.

"Mostly. We base the grand mage on power. The rest... well, there's more of them, and sometimes it's harder to pick who's more powerful. There's also a higher chance that a person might not desire a position on the council and all it entails. So, there are political maneuverings, alliances with people already on the council and fellow masters. We also have our version of noble families, and they get involved more than anyone cares to admit."

"Sometimes the candidate is so obvious that no one is going to argue. Like Baenlin. Stories have it that when the man he replaced failed, he stormed into the council during a meeting and told them in no uncertain terms he would be the next red archmage," Eirian said.

Patting Halcyon, Eirian picked at a small clump of knotted hairs in his mane. The conversation was an excellent distraction, providing an external noise to compete with the whispers.

"I used to dream of doing the same when Mayve failed, and then you came into my life," Tessa grumbled. "It was going to be my moment of decisive glory, and I hoped it would happen while my father was alive just so I could watch his face."

"Sorry, it's not like I asked for this."

Looking between them, Merle sighed. "And I'm sorry I mentioned anything."

"I'd like to see what you have crafted so far, Tessa. We should work out if Her Majesty can move so many at once." Latching onto the opportunity to change the subject, Aiden attempted not to let his curiosity show. "She often misleads us about what she can do."

Eirian shot him an angry look. "It's not misleading. Misleading would be to tell you I couldn't do something when I could."

"Here we go again," Fox said, screwing up his face, and his fellows agreed.

Mouth twitching, Tessa regarded him and tuned out the hissed words being exchanged between Eirian and Aiden. "They argue like this a lot?"

"All the time. We're used to it, but some days it's just annoying. So annoying that you want to lock them in a room and throw the key in a river."

Snickers arose from several men, and Merle growled a quiet warning.

"Somehow, I doubt that would solve anything." Giving Eirian a disapproving look, Tessa scowled. "Eirian, do you think you can spare me your focus rather than fighting with your captain?"

Clamping her mouth shut mid-argument with Aiden, Eirian snorted. Remaining quiet for a short time, her eyes took in the city of tents that remained sprawled out over the land.

"Tell me again that your plan is going to work, Tessa. Tell me these creations of yours will disable those weapons before they can kill my people."

Growing serious, Tessa took a moment to consider what was being asked. "I can't, and you know that. All we can do is try our best to pull it off. Don't worry. You're not the only one with a few tricks up her sleeves. Believe it or not, I care about these people as well."

"I never implied that you didn't," Eirian replied shortly.

"Then what was the point of your requests?"

Mouth twisting, she admitted, "Because I'm trying to convince myself that walking out there right now and killing every Athnaralan that opposes us isn't an option."

Her guards exchanged nervous looks, and Aiden choked, but Tessa halted her horse, turning her torso to face Eirian. "Could you do it?"

"I have the power."

"That's not my question."

Letting go of the reins, Eirian crossed her arms and stared at Halcyon's neck. The gelding shifted beneath her, pawing at the dirt impatiently. He wanted to keep moving. All the horses were sensitive to the undercurrent of tension and the magic oozing off Eirian. She could not stop it, no matter how hard she fought to keep it controlled. Flowers bloomed at their feet, covering the damaged earth.

Continuing to move, soldiers hurried about their duties, some packing down the sheets of canvas that had been their homes. Everyone knew the following sunrise could see their last day alive. Many were spending time with their friends, alcohol flowing freely. Her ears could pick up the distant lit of music from somewhere within the camps, the notes telling of mourning.

She knew many sought the companionship of anyone willing, and her heart clenched with a glance at Aiden. Eyes hard, he regarded her with the stony mask he had shown her countless times before when he was trying to distance himself. They had not mentioned what happened between them, and Eirian was unsure if that was a good thing.

"Yes, unfortunately, I could." She shifted her gaze to Tessa. "But I wouldn't be the same woman afterward."

Swallowing, Tessa hesitated. The answer was not the expected one. She allowed her magic to let her see a flicker of the power that Eirian wielded. It was something she rarely did because it always left her with more questions.

"Hold on to that thought because none of us can say you won't need to."

Merle cleared his throat, uncomfortable with the conversation. "Not all of those men are bad. Not all of them want to be here fighting us. They deserve a chance to live."

"Merle," Aiden cautioned as Tessa's calculating blue eyes darted to him.

"You're a country boy. You probably have a large family, lots of siblings. Some of them may already have children of their own."

"As would those men you're condoning the death of!" Merle snapped, glaring at her.

Pinching her nose, Tessa smiled faintly. "I'm not condoning anything, but if you wish to believe that I am, then do so. This is a war. However, consider what will happen if we don't stop them. At least our armies don't wish to invade Athnaral. Do you think those men you are defending would spare the same thought for your family as you do for theirs?"

He saw her point, but the prospect of Eirian taking so many lives with her power sat uneasily. "I'm just saying, there has to be another way."

"And I'm just saying that she needs to do it if there is no other way."

They stared at each other, and Merle could see in her eyes that if she had the power Eirian did, she would not hesitate. Yet, beneath her conviction, he saw the same grief he had seen in the gazes of countless others. The overwhelming grief threatening to tip her beyond her ability to cope.

"This is all hypothetical, Merle. I'm sure it won't come to that. Tessa is right. If I have to do it, then I can't hesitate. Regardless of—"

"Eirian!"

She stopped speaking at the sound of her name being called, and they shifted their focus to the group approaching them. Eyes narrowing, Aiden looked Everett over.

"What are you doing out here?"

"I was looking for our wonderful queen." Everett chuckled, arching a brow at Aiden.

"And you found me. I was planning to see you later." Eirian smiled warmly, thankful for his arrival and the opportunity it provided to escape the conversation they had been having.

Looking into the distance, Everett grew troubled. "Were you spying on the Athnaralans?"

"We wanted to see what we were up against," she answered with a shrug and rolled her eyes toward Aiden. "You can imagine that he was not keen on the idea."

"No, I don't suppose he was." Silence fell uncomfortably between them, Everett flicking looks between Aiden and Tessa.

Sensing his reluctance, Eirian explained, "Tessa and I were about to test out her plan. Would you like to join us?"

It was enough to redirect his attention, and he said, "I'd appreciate it if you tell me about your plan. Lord Baenlin has told us much of the battle ahead depends on you and your contraptions."

Tessa arched her brows. "Well, that makes me feel all kinds of special. I know my contraptions will work. If I hadn't faith in my creativity, I wouldn't have made my suggestion. Likewise, if I didn't have faith in Eirian's ability."

"I think we're all putting a lot of faith in Eirian," he replied.

"Don't worry, she'll deliver."

There was more confidence in Tessa's tone than Eirian had expected to hear. Pursing her lips, she stared at the pommel of her saddle, watching the magic shifting over her hands. The horses walked steadily, Tessa slightly in the lead to guide the group toward the tent city where she had her workspace set up.

"The good captain directed me to someone who sourced a suitable material to work with for the containers."

"Glad I could help." Aiden sounded bored, but Eirian knew him well enough to know his curiosity was eating at him.

They dismounted at the edge of the camp, and several soldiers stepped up to take the horses. It was easier to leave them on the outskirts than lead them through the maze of canvas. Tents were packed close together, keeping everyone as near to the town as possible for ease of defense. With the elves being the most recent arrivals, they should have been on the furthest edge. Instead, the commanders had decided it was better to have the mages around the outskirts to build and maintain defensive wards.

Following closely behind Tessa, Eirian felt the stares. There was some hostility among those watching her, making the whispers hiss in anger. It was a strange shift from the awe she felt from her people. Eirian understood why they felt hostile toward her. Twenty-odd years she had walked among them. They had assumed her bound by the same rules. They had believed the half-truths she had told to cover up what she could do.

Mouth twisting, Tessa glared at one group of older mages huddled together as they stared at Eirian. It was enough to send them scurrying off in search of another spot to talk.

"Ignore them, Eirian, don't let their fear bother you."

"I don't blame them. I've lied and deceived for most of my life." Eirian brushed off the concerned look Everett gave her. "They have every right to their anger and fear."

"It's not lying and deceiving if you were unaware of your heritage," Everett said.

Smiling faintly, she shrugged. "That's true. It is lying and deceiving if you know you can do many more things than you let on."

"You know you're not the only one." There was a sly gleam in Tessa's eye as she said, "Sometimes we're unaware of what we can do until the time comes. Were you born knowing you could do all that you can, or have you learned it along the way? It's do or die, and I imagine a lot of mages will discover that."

"Are you saying you're not frightened by what Her Majesty can do? That you're not angry over the fact that she can?" Merle asked.

Chuckling, Tessa scratched the back of her neck before pointing to a large tent set slightly apart from the others. It appeared people had been reluctant to set up close to the strange woman that would be their grand mage. Eirian had been in it previously, but it was the first time Everett had seen what Tessa could do.

"Does her power frighten me? Yes. It frightens me that a mortal can have the power she does and not go mad. Angry? Not in the slightest. I used to be angry that she was so powerful. Even jealous that they would consider her before me. Now, I'm thankful she's as stubborn and self-sacrificing as she is because someone needs to be, and I'd rather it not be me."

Shaking her head, Eirian waved at the tents. "Coming from someone who knows what it's like to face distrust from her fellows? Tell me their reluctance doesn't bother you?"

A strange look flickered over her face before Tessa offered Eirian a lopsided smile. "Those that are worthy of being our equals will never let their fear of our differences overcome them. They will simply accept them as part of who we are. If we are all the same, the world will never change."

"Late for that sentiment, the world already needs a great deal of change." Everett snorted. "And where will we get with that attitude, cousin?"

Her brown eyes widened at the challenging tone he put forth. "I'm sure you won't disappoint me, Everett. What do you think, Aiden?"

"Why are you dragging me into this?" Grumbling, Aiden scowled. "Why don't you and Tessa focus on what you're supposed to be doing. Isn't that why we're here?"

Agreeing, Gunter huffed. "I'm uncomfortable with this. We have both the queen and the heir out in the open together."

"And the enemy is right there."

Sharing a look, Everett and Eirian grinned at their fussing captains. Stony glares met their grins, neither man interested in encouraging them to linger. A glance at the sun made Tessa hurry, her hands pulling open the entrance to usher them into the large tent. Most of the guards remained outside to keep watch. They were aware they would not fit, and several of them were less keen to set foot in the domain of the strange mage.

Eyes adjusting to the dim light, Eirian could not help but chuckle at Everett's response to the sight. Makeshift workbenches occupied most of the space, a bed tucked into a corner that barely looked slept in. Eyes settling on the twin swords in their scabbards, belts wrapped around them, Eirian could not help remembering Jaren.

Turning to Tessa, she opened her mouth to speak but shut it again when Tessa said, "Say nothing, Eirian. There will be time for that later."

"He was a good man, Tessa. That's all." Eirian rubbed a hand over her forehead. "Show us what you've got so far."

Leaning in to murmur his question to Aiden, Everett kept his eyes on the confusing mess that covered the benches. "Did she lose someone in the battle?"

Nodding, Aiden watched as Tessa stretched up and opened some flaps on the top of her tent, allowing light to flood in.

"My brother, Jaren," Tessa replied without looking at them, moving over to the clearest of the benches. "Now, I demonstrated my glass balls the other night. They work perfectly. The issue we face is ensuring the trebuchets will catch on fire. Someone suggested coating them with pitch, which is a brilliant suggestion. But, unfortunately, I didn't have any containers of pitch."

Gunter moved to pick up a small clay ball, arching a brow when he felt the weight of it. "I'm not so well informed. What exactly is your plan?"

Her eyes narrowed, and she said, "Be careful with that. It's full of pitch. If you notice, I don't have any lit flames."

"Right." He put the ball down, scrambling to stop it when it rolled awkwardly across the table. "Sorry."

"The plan is that your queen will use her magic to fling the clay containers and then my glass ones at the trebuchets."

Keeping her hands behind her back, Eirian examined the clay balls on the bench. "I haven't attempted moving multiple objects like this over distances."

Holding up a finger, Tessa smiled. "Ah, now, have a feel of them."

Arching a brow, Eirian let her magic sweep over the table. There was a prickle of awareness when it picked up the seeds embedded into the clay. Her eyes widened as she registered their long term destructive potential.

"Who gave you that idea?"

"Neriwyn. He said it might help you when he gave the seeds to me. I believe he suggested that if ignition didn't happen, you could use the seeds to tear the machines apart."

"You've been very careful with the seeds, right? They don't grow into a friendly plant."

"He called it kudzu, and yes, I was warned."

Picking up a clay ball with no stopper, Merle nodded to Eirian. "Catch."

Magic flared, stopping the object before it reached her, and Eirian twisted her hand around, causing it to twirl in the air. "Would you say the keep walls are about the distance away we're talking about?"

"I'd say attempting to fly a small object through the air at a highly nervous garrison could lead to a battle," Aiden commented.

Conceding the point, she flattened her hand out, and the ball stilled its movements. "Fair enough. I didn't think of that. So how did you make these, Tessa?"

"More importantly, how many have you made?" Everett asked seriously.

Reaching out, Tessa plucked the ball from the air and cradled it carefully in her hands. She stared at it while considering her answer.

"I have had as many capable yellows as I can get helping. So far, we have twenty balls filled and ready to go. We've been keeping them in separate locations, stored carefully and as dry as we can manage. These balls aren't set, but they didn't need to be. I wanted them easily broken, plus we needed to make them in a hurry. We've barely had enough time to do this, but we will continue to make and fill what we can before the battle begins."

"Twenty." Doing the calculations in her mind, Eirian understood the unspoken message Tessa was giving her. "Whatever you have will be enough. We'll make this work."

Aiden was blunt. "With the size of them and the amount of pitch you can put in there, that will be nowhere near enough to stop them."

Quickly lifting a hand, Eirian silenced Tessa's retort. "It will be enough because my aim is always true. I already have a sense for the weak spots, and I know exactly where to break them to cause the most significant damage."

"She's right. It doesn't need to be enough to burn the entire trebuchet. Just needs to be enough to cause damage to the right places." Rubbing his chin, Everett looked thoughtful and said, "I'd rather not destroy them. We may need them."

A chill ran down her spine, and Eirian said, "Excuse me? We may need them?"

The guards coughed, sharing looks before staring at the dirt floor. Sighing, Tessa shook her head and placed the ball on the table next to several more waiting. An awkward silence filled the tent, Eirian's icy stare making Everett shift warily in his spot. He looked at the two captains, hoping to find some sort of solidarity directed his way. Neither Aiden nor Gunter offered him solace, their expressions blank.

A commotion outside broke the tension, guards reaching for their weapons. Huffing at them, Tessa shook her head again and walked over to the open doorway. Clicking her tongue at the guards outside to silence their arguments, she beckoned a man in.

"Is it done?"

He did not look at the people behind her, holding the tall rod out. "Just like you asked and exactly the wards you gave me. If it doesn't work like the one Fayleen designed, that's your fucking fault and not mine."

"Functional and pretty, just how I like it." Tessa ran a hand down the staff with a smile. "Thank you, Shaun."

"Anything for my grand mage," Shaun said and bowed, giving her a wink before taking a glance at the watching group.

Eirian nodded at him. "Master Shaun, always a pleasure."

"I thought I sensed you nearby, little troublemaker. Can't resist causing a stir wherever you fucking go, can you?" Cocking his head, Shaun regarded her in amusement.

Taking in the cut of Shaun's white hair and how it did nothing to hide the points of his ears, Aiden inclined his head. "Thank you for your fine work on Fayleen's staff. It may have helped her save my life yesterday."

Nodding, Shaun smiled faintly. "Fayleen's a good one. These were her idea, but I understood what she was trying to achieve when she came to me. I'm glad she succeeded."

"Have you been assisting with Tessa's plan for the trebuchets?" Everett asked.

"Nah. Wood is my thing." Shrugging, he glanced at the workbench and the clay balls it held. "She's got better yellows than me for that. I best be back to it. I have reds demanding shit from me. Damn frustrating fuckers think they're all that because they're bloody warriors."

Choking in shock, Everett did not appreciate Eirian's mocking laugh and the hard slap to his back. "I can honestly say I've never heard an elf talk like you."

Shaun bared his teeth, his smile threatening and amused. "What, you think we're all pompous little pricks like that royal fucker Paienven? Don't even get me started on some of the others."

"Thanks, Shaun, but please stop tormenting the poor duke. Isn't it enough that Eirian is his cousin?" Tessa grinned, taking pleasure in the way Eirian's eyebrows shot up.

"Yeah, true. At least you're not a complete fool, Eirian. Better not have broken another one of my bows, though. I ain't got the fucking time to make you a new one before the Athnaralans try to fuck us all up." He started toward the square of daylight, but stopped to turn and stare at Eirian sadly. "Try not to die. I don't hate you."

Aiden grinned once he left. "I like him."

"You'd be one of the few who does." Tessa chuckled.

Licking her lips, Eirian sucked her bottom lip between her teeth and chewed on it. "Look, Tessa, I'm confident I can get these balls where they need to go. Of course, without testing it, we can't know for sure, but let's be honest, I have backup plans."

"Why does it feel you have a request for me?"

Tessa knew Eirian wanted her to do something else on top of the plans already made between them. They had talked and plotted in private, deciding how to approach the darkness so she might not see Eirian coming.

"I need you to ensure that our people aren't between me and those weapons."

The staff in her hands felt heavy, and Tessa nodded solemnly. "Don't worry, I'll make sure Baenlin does as he's told. If he understands, he'll make sure Darragh follows through, even if that pompous prick of a king disagrees."

"Cameron will also do as asked." Eirian knew he would heed the request without asking for an explanation.

"Guess it's a good thing I have this then." Wriggling the staff back and forth, Tessa smiled faintly. "I hope I don't have to use it. Now, off you go. I suspect your dear cousin here didn't come looking for you for no particular reason."

Eirian knew he had not. Her thumb rubbed the band of the royal seal on her hand. "Of course, we'll leave you to your work. We're using precious time you could spend on those. I'll find you before the battle. Don't forget the plan."

"Are you going to stay in the keep? I may need to find you first."

"No, I'm remaining out here."

Not looking at her guards, Eirian started moving across the short distance to the entrance, with Everett barely a step behind. Smirking, Tessa winked at Aiden before he followed.

"I'll find you in Celiaen's tent. Enjoy what time you have, Eirian."

Outside, the air was thick with the smell from the pyres. The wind had changed direction, sweeping the smoke back over the camp and driving those who could escape it into the tents. It would not be long before it permeated their sanctuaries. Everett sniffed the air, screwing his face up while biting back the urge to bend over and retch.

Sparing him some sympathy, Aiden placed a hand on his shoulder and squeezed in reassurance. It looked like Everett would shake him off, the thought crossing his face before he smiled and nodded. Seemingly the least bothered, Eirian swept her gaze around the mage camp.

"Come on, walk with me. You can tell me why you needed to find me, and I'll tell you why I was going to look for you."

His eyes dropped to where her fingers twisted the royal seal. "Eirian."

"Everett."

"Is there somewhere we can talk without an audience? I don't feel like arguing with you in public."

Sighing, Eirian waved at the outer line of the camp and said, "We can go find an open spot and have a casual stroll as though we're not in the middle of a war."

Pained by the idea, Gunter shook his head. "Are you trying to kill us?"

"Gunter, you'll serve Everett well as captain of the King's Guard. I'm sure he is far more cooperative for you than I have ever been for Aiden."

Offering Everett her arm, Eirian felt a calmness settle that ignored the whispers. She knew what it was and welcomed it. It was the calm of acceptance, of relief. Endara would be safe. She would see to that. It would have a fine king to replace her, a man who would make them proud. Everett was the king her people deserved, and he would have the chance to build something amazing out of the fires of war.

"Everett, this is going to be a strange request, but I need you to hear me out."

He stiffened without faltering in his stride, muttering, "Okay."

Watching him from the corner of her eye, she smiled and said, "You need to encourage young, unwed nobles to go to Riane to meet people. Invite mages to come to live in Amath and other cities and towns. There need to be more mages with Altira blood to avoid this from happening again. It will strengthen the bindings on the mad god."

"While I understand what you're suggesting, the nobles…" Everett stopped, shaking his head. "Why did they teach us to fear mages so much when the common folk don't? If there's one thing I've learned recently, it's that people appreciate what mages can do for them."

"Because a man witnessed what his bloodline could do and thought the best way to avoid it happening again was to drive magic out. Unfortunately, it was the wrong solution." Sighing, Eirian lifted her gaze to the sky sadly. "And unfortunately, my mother did nothing. Though I suppose it was because she had seen how it would all play out."

Noticing the way Eirian held her free hand to her stomach, Everett said, "You might still survive this. I have faith that you will."

She carefully slipped the seal from her finger and pressed it into his grasp. He closed his hand around the gold ring, feeling the weight of its meaning.

"Even if I do, this is your kingdom now. You need to understand that what I'm going to do will either kill me or destroy me."

"You say that like they're different things."

Just enough steps behind the duo to give them a sense of privacy as they walked, Aiden ground his teeth and shared a look with his fellow captain. Gunter looked as uncomfortable with the situation as he felt, and a quick glance over his shoulder at the guards behind them told him they would have preferred to be elsewhere. Eirian kept walking, taking her time to respond. Resting her hand on his, she tried to smile, but the expression was more like a grimace.

"They are different things. If I survive, I won't be your Eirian. My battle with the enemy won't be one of swords, and if she gets the chance, she'll rip my mind to pieces."

He halted their progress and turned to look at her, keeping his voice low. "I wasn't sure if I should tell you, but it doesn't feel right not to. Your father—"

"Is dead."

"How did you guess?"

Scoffing, she arched her brows. "Well, what else were you going to say?"

"You're not as upset by the news as I worried you might be." Everett was unsure if her lack of obvious grief should relieve or disappoint him.

"I said my goodbyes to my father months ago and grieved his loss. He is no longer suffering, and I'm thankful for that mercy. Aren't you?"

Tilting her head to the side, Eirian blinked at him thoughtfully. Letting his shoulders slump, Everett knew she was right.

"He was a good man, Eirian, and a wonderful king. If he could have been, he would have been a good father. He was proud of you, and he'd be even more proud of you now."

"He was proud of you as well, Everett. I know you'll be a fine king, an excellent king, and he will smile on in pride from wherever it is we go after we die."

Looking at his fist and feeling the ring within it, Everett blinked furiously. "I'd rather not be the king. Being the king means you're dead. You can do so much good."

Eirian wrapped him in a hug. "You have the potential to do something I cannot. You can unite Endara and Athnaral when the dust settles. So, I need you to let me do what I was born to do and give me your blessings and forgiveness. I'm at peace with what must happen, and I don't fear my death. I fear the rest of you dying. Stay out of the fight, and let those of us better suited to dying to do the dirty work."

"Eirian…" Pressing his face to her shoulder, Everett hugged her tighter. "I forgive you, and you have my blessings to save our people."

"Thank you. You don't know how much that means to me. You're going to be a fantastic king, Everett. I know it, and everyone else knows it. Nolan knew it." Stroking the back of his head, she caught sight of the look on Aiden's face.

He felt her power. It simmered like a cloud around her, and Everett wondered if he was breathing it in or if he imagined it. A floral scent surrounded them, sickly sweet enough to override the smell coming from the pyres. He had felt rejuvenated from the moment their paths had crossed, and he knew it was Eirian's magic.

"It would mean more to me if you lived. I want to see you happy, truly happy."

Closing her eyes, Eirian tried to sense something of the future from Everett as she had with Aiden and Fayleen. She was disappointed when she picked up nothing, but she pushed the feeling aside to return her focus to him.

"I'll be truly happy knowing you're alive and safe. That's all I want."

"For just one moment, Eirian, could you be selfish? You don't have to echo yourself to convince everyone listening that what's going on is fine. You're allowed to fight back! Don't be the cow we blindly lead to slaughter," Everett said, pulling away.

"I don't have a choice, Everett. Who else can save all your asses from the terrible god that wants to destroy the world?"

Slipping the seal into a pouch, Everett lifted his hands to her shoulders and held her tight. "Look, I know nothing we say will change your course of action. However, I want you to think about what I'm about to say."

Blinking, Eirian waited for him to continue. Her gaze flickered to the guards, who were pretending not to pay attention, except for Aiden. His hard stare rested on them, and he gave the slightest nod of acknowledgment. If there was anyone she could count on to make sure Everett would remain true to himself, it was Aiden.

"You're not arguing, so I may as well get it out. We're all responsible for our decisions right until the end. The decisions of others might influence your path, but the choice remains yours. It's always yours, and it always has been. So don't blindly give in. Just because your information tells you it requires your death doesn't mean you have to die."

Eirian took a deep breath, hesitating in expectation of Gebael's voice across her mind. When no mocking comment drowned out the whispers, she shook her head and repeated words she had told herself repeatedly.

"My blood is what will bind her back in her prison."

He let go of her shoulders and stepped back. "I love you, Eirian. I wish we could have had more time together to be a family."

"I know, Everett, I do too. You were the best brother you could be to me."

There was a wistful gleam in his eyes. "Let's imagine it was one of those things where a little goes further. We might have hated each other if we were always around."

Meeting Aiden's gaze, she agreed. "You're right. A little does sometimes go a lot further. Live for me, Everett, live and be happy."

TWENTY-FIVE

"You don't need to do this, Eirian," Aiden said, keeping a tight grasp on her arm.

Magic and smoke swirled around them, the smell of burning flesh so strong it overrode the floral scent accompanying Eirian. She sensed the daoine among the crowd of people making their way to say goodbye. Their eyes found her, a mixture of resentment and sorrow betraying their feelings about the situation. Making no attempt to shake off Aiden's hold, Eirian kept walking.

"Yes, I do."

He growled, "You got to say goodbye to him."

The memories of Faolan's head in her lap and his blood on her hands filled Eirian's head. It made the whispers scream, flashes of Shianeni's past with him slipping through the fractured wall that kept them separated from her mind. Flinching at the assault, her stride faltered, and Aiden took advantage of the opportunity to grab her other arm.

"This won't make you feel any better."

"I need this, Aiden," she whispered. "First Faolan, and then I'll find Jaren."

Pulling her against his chest, Aiden ignored the looks sent their way and buried his face in her hair. She remained unarmed, wearing only the simple gray clothes she had put on the day before. Clothes he had watched her dress in while he laid in her bed. Eirian's arms wrapped around him, holding tight while he refused to let go. It was all Aiden could do to avoid throwing her over his shoulder and carrying her back to the keep. He wanted to lock her in a chamber until the war was over. Anything to delay her death.

"Please."

Eirian sighed, dropping her arms away from him so she could withdraw. His quiet plea brought her guilt to the surface, and the whispers laughed. Lifting her gaze to watch the smoke surrounding them, she was sure she saw shadows twisting the eddies into shapes from the memories. The haze was enough to make most people cough, few able to avoid the irritation to their lungs.

"Come on, they won't wait for me before setting the fire."

She forced herself to walk again. Taking Aiden's place beside her, Merle did not ask why he remained unmoving. None of the guards did, but Fionn stayed with him. By the time they reached the pyre for the fallen daoine, Aiden had caught up. The crowd was not static. Most came to say a few words and left when done. It was a battlefield funeral, and they observed no ceremonies for the dead.

"How are they… you know… how are they burning everyone?" Merle whispered, eyes on the closest line of bodies.

There was no wood in sight. Only row after row of the dead, with naked mages standing at each end. Looking at Eirian, the guards waited for her to explain. They had their suspicions but did not want to assume in case there was something else going on.

"It's a cleansing."

Fionn eyed the nearest naked mage thoughtfully. "Like what you did at that farm?"

"Exactly the same. Well, not quite. They're sharing the task to make it easier. Each group will do one cleanse and then retire to their tents depending on the severity of their sensitivity."

"Which means they won't need to be drugged to get over it?" Fox quipped.

A faint smile graced her lips, and Eirian stared over the lines of dead daoine at the living. They fluttered along, stopping to say farewell to friends and family, sharing hugs with others as they went. She knew where Faolan's body was located, though her feet did not want to move in that direction. One of her guards coughed, the sound reminding Eirian she was not alone. It prompted her to sigh, reluctantly turning to trudge through the crowd.

"Don't worry, darling, your body won't be joining the pyres."

Inhaling sharply, Eirian swept her gaze through the people surrounding her, looking for the lurking figure of the god of death. She wanted to be surprised he was near, but the chill in the air had warned her. Beside her, Aiden touched her arm in concern, brows furrowed with his unspoken question. Shaking her head, Eirian kept moving, eyes darting from one person to the next.

Flowers had grown around the corpses because of her inability to keep her magic under control. Taking advantage of them, many people plucked brightly colored blooms as they appeared, bundling them together on bodies. Watching them do it, Eirian decided not to begrudge her effect on the ground. Instead, she flexed her power, encouraging more to grow.

"Our little life among the dead." Gebael laughed.

Eirian wanted to snarl in response. They would meet any attempts to explain what she was experiencing with fear. Those around her would assume the mad god had affected her, and she could not risk what they might do. Grinding her teeth, she struggled to ignore the chuckle caressing her mind, causing the memories to claw at the wall.

When she spotted Faolan's body, Eirian sighed in relief. Moving out of her way, the daoine bidding him farewell stared silently as she dropped to her knees at his head. He had been cleaned up, redressed in his armor with his sword clutched to his chest, but she knew something was missing. Fumbling with the pouch hanging from her belt, she withdrew the twisted clump of jewels and metal.

"Eirian." Aiden crouched beside her, eyes on the objects in her hand as he said, "You can't. They belonged to your mother."

Baring her teeth at him, she carefully shook the two items apart until the necklace hung from her hand. Draping it across Faolan's chest, Eirian plucked the diadem from the dandelion it had landed on. It dangled from her fingers, Aiden's hand gripping her wrist to stop her from placing it in the red hair that gleamed in the afternoon sunlight.

"Why?"

"He made them for her. No one else should ever wear them."

Tears welled in her eyes, and Eirian blinked to banish them. Glancing away, Aiden released her wrist, letting her proceed. Nestling the diadem in Faolan's hair, she smiled sadly and dragged her fingers through the familiar locks. A touch of her magic ensured no one would take the jewelry away. She wished she could bring him back. Not just him, but all the dead who had died because of the gods.

"I promise I'll find you."

Leaning down, she kissed his forehead before resting her own against it. A hand against his cold cheek, Eirian closed her eyes and let go of the fragile hold she had over her magic. The whispers mocked, dragging claws across her mind.

"Wait for me, my wolf," she whispered into his hair. "I'm coming for you. I'll find you on the other side, and we'll run. You, me, Jaren. We'll be a pack forever."

Sharing a fearful look with Merle, Aiden went to touch Eirian but stopped when he felt a shift in the magic. He was not the only one who noticed it. Daoine and mages alike turned to stare at her. Through the eddies of smoke from other pyres, they could see the carpet of wildflowers her power had grown.

"Darling, don't make promises you can't keep."

Lifting her face from Faolan, Eirian found Gebael standing a short distance away. No one else seemed aware of him, and at his feet, wildflowers withered. The defiance in her stare brought a smile to his lips, and he crossed his arms, chuckling.

"Now, now, don't look at me like that."

Following her gaze, Aiden wondered what Eirian was glaring at. When he noticed the spreading patch of dead flowers, he looked back at her in confusion. Anger began weaving through her magic, the simmer of bloodlust breaking through. He should have been relieved to feel something other than sorrow coming from Eirian, but concern over the cause overrode everything else.

Gebael winked, and Eirian barely stopped herself from leaping to her feet. She wanted to hit him, to find out if she could spill his blood like anyone else's. A hand restrained her, fingers digging into her still-aching shoulder. Snarling, she turned, batting Aiden away. He let her rise, waiting until she was steady on her feet before following. Signaling his men to keep a tight circle, he watched her closely.

"Eirian, what's wrong?"

"Nothing!"

Remaining where he was, Gebael grinned coldly. She imagined wrapping her hands around his throat, taking delight in choking the life out of him. Not buying her response, Aiden huffed, scratching the side of his face while he considered how to handle Eirian. A voice told him knocking her out was not an option, no matter how much he wanted to do it.

"I think the mages want to start their thing," Merle said, hoping it was enough to distract Eirian from what was bothering her.

Fionn screwed up his face, making a show of peering at the naked man waiting at the end of the line. "Yeah, they look impatient."

"As much as I'd like your hands on my throat, you can't fight me, darling."

Her eyes narrowed. Trying again, Aiden placed a hand on her wrist, tugging Eirian's arm to convince her to follow him.

"Go with your captain before you do something stupid."

"Eirian, please don't fight me on this. We need to go. You want to say goodbye to your other friend as well, and the longer we're here, the less chance you'll have," Aiden said, trying to coax her away.

Looking at Aiden, Eirian focused on the concern in his eyes, the worried twist of his mouth, and bowed her head. Refusing to glance at where Gebael stood, smoke swirling around him and the patch of dead growth, she allowed herself to be led away. Feeling the tremble of her hand, Aiden considered asking again what was wrong, but the look on Eirian's face kept him silent.

The guards were unsure which way was the right one, but she nodded toward the next grouping of bodies. It was clear the mages had separated the dead by allegiance, allowing people an easy way to work out where to go so they could say goodbye. None of them envied the task set to the mages, but watching Endaran soldiers carrying a body carefully, they realized everyone was assisting where they could.

"Ree?"

She turned to face Rylee, eyes going straight to Zack beside her. "I'm sorry, Zack."

Dipping his head, Zack rubbed the side of his neck. "I'm glad you're here, Ree. Jaren would be pissed if you weren't."

"He loved you more than anything."

"No, he didn't. He loved her more than anything. We wouldn't be standing here with his corpse if he didn't."

Flinching at the anger in his voice, Eirian glanced at Rylee and Luke, noting their concern. She was thankful Tessa had refused to attend because she suspected Zack might pose a risk to the other woman if he saw her. What he said was an undeniable truth. They all knew how much Jaren had loved Tessa. He had always been a devoted brother, determined to protect his sister no matter what.

"Blame me instead," Eirian told him. "If I had ended this war sooner, he'd be alive. Most of these people would be."

"You didn't start this war, Ree. But Jaren came because Tessa wanted to prove herself."

Putting a hand on his shoulder, Luke sighed. "We've said our part to Jaren. They want to get on with it, so you better hurry."

Nodding, Eirian swept her gaze over the line of bodies until she located the familiar brown-haired warrior. Leaving her guards with her friends, she crossed to Jaren and knelt at his head. He looked strange, dressed in his armor but without his swords. Glancing at Zack, Eirian wondered how many arguments would happen over Tessa's decision to claim the weapons.

"I'm sorry I couldn't protect you out there, Jaren."

Brushing a hand over his hair, she leaned down to kiss his forehead, lingering there like she had with Faolan. Magic rippled around them, drawing the attention of the watching mages. Countless eyes stared at her bowed over the body of her friend. Eirian did not care who watched. She did not listen to the startled comments as fresh flowers overtook the ones already present.

"You and Faolan would have gotten along so well," she murmured, resting her cheek against his forehead. "And tomorrow, when I join you on the other side, we'll find him. Then the three of us can run and fight forever. I promise you, I will find you. Just wait for me, Jaren."

"By the powers…" Rylee breathed.

They watched the shimmer of light radiating from Eirian, the glow of magic cutting through the layer of smoke.

"If we're lucky, Celi won't be coming with me, but I can't promise anything. You'd like it if he did, I bet. He needs to live, Jaren, so I'm going to do whatever I can to make sure he does. You can yell at me tomorrow when I find you. I'll even let you kick my ass for a change."

Tears dripped onto Jaren's face, ignored by Eirian as she continued to stroke her fingers through his hair. Loud enough to drown out anything else going on around her, the whispers made suggestions for what she could do. Life crept through the earth, easy picking for someone so innately connected to it. The shadows told her it was her power to use. They urged her to take it all and bring back the ones she had lost.

"Come on, gorgeous," Rylee said, pulling her away from Jaren. "Don't know what the fuck you're doing, but it's not good."

On the other side, Aiden agreed. "If you don't stop, I'll take a page out of your princeling's book. Do you fancy another headache?"

Eirian wanted to struggle against their hold, but she realized the whispers were urging her to do it. Allowing Aiden and Rylee to guide her from Jaren's body, she forced herself to focus on taking deep breaths. It was safer than counting the heartbeats like she usually would. Every time she heard the echo of a heart, the whispers reminded Eirian how easy it was to stop it.

"I knew this was a bad idea," Aiden muttered to Rylee.

Slinging an arm around Eirian's waist, she grunted and nodded to Luke. He remained with Zack while the guards formed a tight barrier. Fearful of her power, the watching mages backed away, keeping clear of the group. She caught sight of the withered wildflowers from the corner of her eye. As people moved through them, they collapsed in piles of dust, with life completely drained from them.

"Shit," she muttered.

"Yeah."

Glancing at Aiden, Eirian saw his worry. Her eyes shifted to Rylee, taking in the flustered look on her face and the way her free hand crept toward the hilt of a knife.

"I'm sorry, I didn't mean to do that."

Aiden replied, "I know. You're upset. It's understandable if you slip a little."

There was more to it, but Eirian could not tell him that. She was surprised Gebael had not slid into her thoughts again to make taunting comments. From what little she had learned from the memories slipping through the cracks, it was the sort of thing he would delight in. Her losing control and slaughtering everyone would be a feast for him.

"Don't invite me in if you can't handle me, darling."

Clenching her eyes shut, Eirian bit down on her lip. She bit hard, hoping the pain would overcome the press of voices in her head. Nails digging into her side, Rylee muttered something and halted, forcing Aiden to do the same or lose his hold on Eirian. Standing on her toes, she grasped Eirian's shoulder and pulled her down. There were coughs from the guards as they watched them kiss, Aiden letting go in surprise.

"I'm not putting up with your shit, princess," Rylee growled.

Laughing softly, Eirian said, "I'm not a princess."

They felt the wards rise to prepare for the mages beginning the next round of cleanses. Resting her hands on Eirian's hips, Rylee sighed heavily.

"You're a fucking mess, Ree."

"I'm a dead woman walking, Rylee. Doesn't that mean I'm allowed to be a fucking mess? We all knew I'd lose the plot one day."

Rolling her eyes, she huffed. "Well, I'd rather you didn't kill me in the process. Or anyone else we don't hate."

"Do you have a habit of kissing our queen in public?" Fionn asked with a broad grin.

"Are you going to try stopping me?"

He shook his head, earning comments from his fellows, and Merle pinched the bridge of his nose in frustration. Waving at the two women, Fionn spluttered excuses, but Eirian ignored him.

"You're going to have to find someone else to kiss, Rylee," Eirian said jokingly.

"Don't worry, I replaced you the moment I got back to Riane. Like I was going to wait around for you to summon me to your castle." Rylee winked at the guards. "There are plenty of women in Riane who are happy for me to worship them."

Unable to resist joking, Fionn asked, "Are you as good with your tongue as you are with a sword?"

"Maybe I'm better. You'll never know."

Covering his face, Aiden muttered, "Remind me again why I put up with you?"

The lighthearted banter was a balm to Eirian, something to break through the guilt and sorrow. Watching Rylee's face light up with the anticipation of a verbal sparring match with Fionn and other guards, she did not move when Aiden slipped a hand under her tunic. It was warm against her back, the roughness of his fingers sending shivers along her spine with each gentle stroke. A reminder that he had discovered how easily the right touch unraveled her.

"Why don't we return to your chamber?" he whispered in her ear. "I know you want to join your mage friends for drinks in memory of the fallen, but I think you need to forget."

She was tempted to agree when a wave of frustration reached her over the bond. He did not direct it at her, but Eirian felt guilty that Celiaen was dealing with the commanders of three armies without her support. Brushing her mind against the link to him, she wondered how much he had experienced while she struggled to control herself.

"I can't, Aiden. Tonight…"

Her voice faltered. Aiden did not need her to explain anything. He knew where she planned to be. They had argued over it earlier, and Eirian's attempts to dismiss him and his men had been met with refusal. But no matter what she said, there was nothing she could do to convince them to walk away from her.

Hoping the conversation distracted his men enough to miss it, Aiden kissed her temple, murmuring, "Could we negotiate?"

Breath hitching, Eirian imagined what Celiaen might demand in a negotiation with Aiden. Seeing her cheeks flush, he chuckled and slowly withdrew his hand. Clearing her throat, she crossed her arms and glared at Rylee.

"Gal is probably waiting for us. With wine," Eirian said. "Telmian wine. Lots of it."

Giving Eirian a suggestive leer, Rylee replied, "I should tell you boys about what she's like when she's had too much to drink."

Devin looked uncomfortable. "She's our queen. I don't think that's appropriate."

Laughing loudly, Rylee stalked off, waving over her shoulder to summon them. Shaking his head, Merle shoved Fionn to follow, muttering as they went. Waiting for Eirian to move, the others stared at Aiden expectantly, but he shrugged.

"Let's not argue over the 'queen, not queen' matter tonight," he told them.

Agreeing, Eirian said, "It hardly matters anyway. You're a bunch of stubborn fuckers, and I'll be dead tomorrow. It won't be an issue after that."

"None of us appreciate your comments about dying," Kip replied.

"True. It makes us feel like we've failed our duty," Tyler added.

Eirian sighed. "That's not true. You haven't failed anything, least of all me."

Sharing looks with his fellows, Kyson said, "We're supposed to protect you. So if you die, and the rest of us don't, that says we failed."

Studying each of them, Eirian nodded slowly. She hated lying to them more than she already had, but it was one of those lies where she hoped it would help. The last thing she wanted for her guards was a lifetime of guilt.

"I'll try my best to avoid dying when I fight the mad god behind all of this."

"You don't need to mock us," Fox muttered.

"That wasn't my intention. I'm sorry if it came across that way."

Nudging her, Aiden pointed at the group waiting. "You said something about wine."

She snorted. "I don't know that Gal has enough wine for everyone."

Appearing out of the lingering swirl of smoke, Gabe asked, "Where were you? I've been looking for you."

"The pyres," Aiden replied.

There was an apple in Gabe's hand, and he held it out to Eirian. "Thought you might need this."

"Thank you." Eirian accepted the apple but did not take a bite. "You should leave, Gabe. This battle isn't where you belong."

His mouth twisted, the barest hint of a smile appearing. The whispers laughed in Eirian's head, dragging claws across the crumbling wall holding back Shianeni's memories. Grip tightening around the apple, she glanced away, taking deep breaths to regain focus.

"Ma'am, I'm still a soldier. I'll be there until the end."

"Are you fucking coming or what?" Rylee shouted.

Beside her, Fionn quipped, "Have you had to say that to her a lot?"

"Wouldn't you like to know?"

"Actually, yes, that's why I asked."

Spluttering, Merle scolded, "You can't ask those questions!"

"Why not?"

Looping an arm through Eirian's when she joined them, Rylee pointed at Fionn with a thumb and said, "Can you break it to him?"

Arching a brow, Eirian studied the apple in her hand. "Break what?"

"The fact he's never going to get near me."

Biting into the apple, Eirian did not answer. Instead, she listened to her guards joking with each other, their banter lacking some of their usual joviality. She doubted anyone could find any genuine joy from anything when they knew what the following day would bring. Tension simmered across the sea of tents, as thick as the layer of smoke. Rolling her eyes skywards, Eirian wished the wind would change again.

"Any idea where Gal might be?"

Rylee's question broke her chain of thoughts, and Eirian frowned. She reached for the thread binding Galameyvin to her, using it to gain a general idea of his location. Part of her hoped he was with Celiaen in the keep, but the other part felt relief to find him in the sea of tents.

"The Telmian camp."

"You sure?"

"Yes."

Grunting, Rylee shrugged. "Lead the way."

Negotiating their way through the sea of tents was not an effortless task. Many had packed down their temporary dwellings to prepare for the coming battle, opting to clear away anything that might get in the way. No one was sure how it would unfold or when the order to attack might come. They knew Athnaral could strike before dawn, turning their trebuchets against the town.

The Telmian camp was closer to Kelsby, the opulent tents standing out among the simpler canvas choices the Endarans used. Daoine hurried about, but they did not miss the group walking the paths between tents. Somewhere, musicians had struck up a tune, the lilting music carrying a sorrowful note. Grief sat like a blanket, diminishing the carefree nature of the long-lived people.

Stopping at Galameyvin's tent, Eirian detected a brush of rage. It tasted of battle and death, a fury unmatched by the other warriors present at Kelsby. Turning her head, she stared at Neriwyn, where he stood watching them. Sunlight caught his dark hair, making it gleam like a raven's feathers. She had not seen him since he left her bedside the day before, but with the end close and her lingering anger from Gebael's taunts, Eirian wanted to scream at him.

"I was wondering when you'd get here," Galameyvin said, coming out with several flasks in his hands.

"Eirian's been having trouble with her magic," Aiden explained while Galameyvin shoved flasks at his men.

Looking at the carpet of dandelions, Galameyvin snorted. "I can see that."

"How much wine have you got?" Rylee questioned, sticking her head into the tent with a whistle. "Powers, Gal, this is fancier than my room in the tower."

Neriwyn inclined his head, stepping back before Eirian gave in to her desire. She watched him turn and vanish between tents, the taste of his rage going with him. Returning her focus to Galameyvin, she forced a smile when he reappeared with more wine.

"You're not giving up all of your stash?"

He nodded. "What's the point of keeping it? Can't drink it if I'm dead. It deserves to be drunk and enjoyed with friends and loved ones."

"You're not joining us in battle tomorrow," Aiden said with concern.

"Do you really think I'd miss it?" Galameyvin snapped, meeting his gaze. "I can hold my own better than you, Aiden."

"I know you can, Gal."

Eyes flicking over the silent guards, Galameyvin broke into a grin and winked at Aiden. Rylee's brows rose, and she looked from one to the other while Eirian bit back a chuckle. She suspected she knew what Galameyvin planned to say.

"Besides, Captain, if you can't protect her ass, you can always protect mine."

Smirking, Aiden replied, "Shouldn't it be the other way around? Since you can hold your own better than me."

TWENTY-SIX

Watching Celiaen's chest slowly rise and fall, Eirian propped herself up and sighed. He had spent so much of his day helping and attending strategic meetings that his exhaustion had shown the moment she laid eyes on him. The vulnerability that had broken through his carefully held demeanor confirmed his struggle. Celiaen only let it show once they were alone after drinking toasts to the fallen with their friends.

His desperation had shown in every kiss, and the shadow of his fear chased every touch. Eirian had not dared acknowledge the tears dripping onto her skin. It was only once Celiaen drifted into a troubled sleep that she had let herself cry silently, a hand stroking his hair. Sleep was elusive, her mind busy struggling with the whispers. She decided she was thankful for it. The way Celiaen tossed and turned left her doubtful he would wake feeling rested.

Brushing his hair off his face, Eirian sighed again. She did not know how far off dawn was, but she felt an agitation she could not explain. Carefully leaning over, she kissed Celiaen's forehead softly before rolling away. He was sleeping soundly for the moment, and she was reluctant to disturb him. Moving confidently in the dark, she located the clothes she had set out. Slipping them on, Eirian made her way to the closed door of the tent and loosened the tie to go out.

It was lighter outside, fires flickering in their designated spots and one in close enough proximity that she could pick up the sound of wood cracking. Letting the flap shut, Eirian took a step and tilted her head back to stare upward. Despite the quiet of the camp, she could not draw peace from it. The whispers barely gave her space to breathe, clawing away any chance of quiet thought.

There was a slight chill in the air, telling her it was closer to dawn than midnight. Staring at the familiar night sky, Eirian thought the stars were duller. The whispers claimed she knew the name of every star. Shifting her stare to the eastern horizon, she did not detect the first signs of the sun rising, but she let her gaze settle there for lack of a desire to look elsewhere. Faint traces of the smell from the pyres lingered in the air, a bitterness that made her nose twitch.

A rustle pulled Eirian's attention off the sky, a figure moving out of the shadows. Her eyes narrowed, recognizing Aiden instantly. It was hard to feel surprised by his presence, but Eirian was disappointed that he was not getting some rest while he could. Standing beside her, he watched the sky. Keeping her eyes on him, Eirian pushed her hair back.

"You should sleep, old man."

Aiden's cheek twitched. "So should you. You need all your energy for your battle."

Scoffing, she shook her head. "I have this sweet little ability to pull energy from my magic, and the last I checked, you had no such trick up your sleeve. Therefore, you're in more need of rest than I am."

"I swore to guard you until the end."

"As you wish."

He whipped around to stare at her. "What, no arguments? No smart remarks? You're accepting it just like that?"

"Aiden, I don't want to spend my last hours fighting with those closest to me. I'll save my pent-up argumentative energy for the one who deserves it." Brushing her hands over her tunic, she smiled wistfully. "I'm not your queen anymore. Anything you do is purely voluntary."

"You'll always be my queen."

Aiden crossed his arms, tilting his chin forward, and earned a chuckle from her. For a moment, Eirian regretted not putting her belt on when she dressed, her fingers tugging at the ties holding her trousers up.

"I don't recommend saying that to the woman Everett marries. She might not take it very well."

Face falling, Aiden dropped his arms and shifted in annoyance, grumbling, "You know that isn't what I meant."

"And I still don't recommend telling your future queen she's not your queen. They might see it as treason."

"You are so frustrating."

Pursing her lips, Eirian winked, cooing, "You love it. You're going to miss it. Your life will be boring without me."

Conflicting emotions made him hesitate, half turning toward her. "Fuck, Eirian, no one has ever driven me to distraction the way you do."

"It was never intentional."

The words felt like a lie. Her brow furrowed when the whispers reminded

Eirian of what she had done to him and Fayleen. It was not a reminder she wanted to deal with under the blanket of stars. Pinching the bridge of her nose, she sighed.

"Aiden."

"What?" he prompted.

Starting again, she closed her eyes. "Aiden, there are things I've done that are unforgivable. To you and others. Don't pretend I was a good person after I'm gone."

Rolling his eyes, Aiden snorted. "That's horseshit. You're a good person doing your best to achieve good things, even when the choices presented are terrible. If you were a bad person, you wouldn't be prepared to sacrifice yourself to ensure everyone else lives."

"You don't understand, but maybe one day you will. I've done things without consent… taken choices away from people I care for."

"And others have taken choices from you without your consent."

He waved over his shoulder at the tent behind them where he knew Celiaen lay. Turning her head, she glanced back and hoped he continued to sleep.

"You're right, but that doesn't excuse what I did with full knowledge."

Inclining his head, Aiden wondered if a kiss would shut her up. He wanted to pull her to him so he could taste the sweetness of her lips for what might be the last time.

"Why bother bringing it up when you don't plan to tell me what you did?"

"I don't appreciate the sarcasm, Captain."

"Pretty sure I'm not a captain anymore, darling. I mean, you had me legitimized and abdicated your throne. If you're not the Queen of Endara, then I'm not the captain of your guard." The sarcasm remained, his intention to mock her.

Clenching her fists in frustration, she grumbled, "Of course, only fair that you remind me of a point I've made previously. It also means that you, and everyone else, no longer have any say over what I do or where I go. I'm a free person."

The whispers mocked her, shadows dancing at the edge of her vision.

"I suppose so."

"But I'll never be free," Eirian whispered, her shoulders slumping in defeat. "It's all I ever wanted. Fay and I used to pretend it was possible, and we'd make plans for the future."

Closing the space between them, Aiden cupped her face gently and smiled sadly. "Hold on to those dreams."

Eirian searched his face for something she could not name, whispering, "Don't lose your hope. Keep it safe for me."

"Always."

Leaning in, he kissed her, but a sudden whistling sound caused them to pull away in confusion. They felt the thump of impact moments before screams and shouts filled the air. Horns blared, their sound masking the whistling of the next stone flying into the camp. People responded as quickly as they could manage, following orders.

Cursing, Aiden shoved her into the tent and shouted for the other guards to gather. Stumbling, Eirian found Celiaen sitting up and rubbing his face. It took her longer than she expected to adjust to the dark inside, memory taking her to where her armor and weapons were. Moving on instinct, Celiaen scrambled for his gear as well.

"What's going on?" he asked, struggling with his clothes.

Bursting in, Aiden carried a lit torch while another guard held the door to the tent open with a torch in his hands. "Athnaral is attacking."

"We expected that. Are they marching on us yet?"

Grateful for the light they provided, Celiaen worked as quickly as possible to dress. Shoving the torch into a sconce, Aiden stomped over to Eirian to help her with her armor.

"I don't know. They're hitting us with those fucking trebuchets. Tyler, help the Prince with his armor. We can't waste any time. It's not safe to stay in the tents."

"Tessa!" Eirian scrambled. "Fuck. We need to move! We have to stop them. Powers, I hope they haven't hit her supplies."

Clamping hands on her arms, Aiden growled, "Be still, or you're just going to make this take longer. You're losing focus."

Snorting, Celiaen calmly accepted Tyler's help and wondered where his companions were. It did not surprise him that Eirian was an unfocused bundle of energy.

"Did you see Tara out there? What about Gal?"

"I saw Tara. She's organizing your guards. I sent Merle to help her. Haven't seen Gal. Or Fayleen." He arched a brow at Eirian, silencing the question before the words left her mouth.

The ground trembled, the sound of an impact close enough to make them jump. Wanting to get out of the tent even quicker, Aiden shouted for two more guards to join them. Anxious, Eirian forced herself to take deep breaths while Aiden and Fox worked in union to secure her armor. She sensed Celiaen slipping into his power, the simmering rage lurking beneath the surface.

Knowing she could not afford to become distracted, Eirian shoved her battle lust down as best she could. It was a tentative hold, made worse by the barrage of whispers dragging at her mind. The shields she placed would only last so long, but they did not need to. They just needed to give her time to deal with the trebuchets.

"Right, stick close together and don't stop moving." Aiden finished securing Eirian's swords, giving her a sideways look as he asked, "Can you guide us to

Tessa?"

She nodded, letting her power seek outwards.

"Good. Then let's go." Grabbing her arm, he pushed her to the open door, stopping only to extinguish the torch.

"Aiden, don't leave her side, or I'll kill you. We'll be right behind you," Celiaen said, helping Tyler finish securing his plate.

Nodding, Aiden pushed his way out of the tent and saw Eirian surrounded by her guards, some of them still pulling armor on. Celiaen's companions were there, Tara striding through the chaos with determination. She reached for Aiden, putting a hand on his arm while they shared a look of understanding. People ran, scrambling to help others trapped in tents and put out fires. Soldiers rushed to arm themselves, officers barking out orders to direct them toward the edge of the camp.

"He's right behind us."

Tara dropped her hand and started to the tent to collect Celiaen, saying over her shoulder, "Look after Ree and get her the fuck out of here. We need those trebuchets destroyed. I sent people to find Tessa and help her."

The telltale whistle of another object caught their attention, and Merle pushed Eirian in front of him, shouting, "Move your fucking asses."

Picking up the familiar brush of Tessa's power, Eirian said, "Follow me."

It was difficult not to run. Eirian knew her ability could take her to Tessa, but it would mean leaving the others behind. They were needed to help carry the clay and glass orbs. Several gasps told her the yellows were working to shield the camp against the great stones being flung their way. Ripples of magic filled the air. Letting her power see for her, Eirian watched as the wards stopped the objects.

Doing her best to lead the group along the quickest route, Eirian sensed Celiaen and his companions hurrying after them. Knowing he was following gave her a feeling of relief. As long as she could feel him close, she knew he was safe. Aiden was beside her, leaving only Fayleen and Galameyvin as her biggest concerns.

No one dared speak as they ran along the confusing pathways between tents. It was difficult as a large group to remain close, soldiers crashing through them in desperation to fight the enemy and help their fellows. People ran with buckets of water and dirt, trying to extinguish the spreading fires before the camp became an inferno.

"There!" Fox shouted, spotting Galameyvin in front of Tessa's tent.

Flinging herself at Galameyvin, Eirian hugged him. "I knew you were alive, but until I saw you, I didn't dare…"

He smiled tensely. "I know. Come on, Tessa has already sent a few ahead, including Fay. She's just grabbing the last of her tricks."

Striding out of the tent with her staff in hand, Tessa took them in. "Well, you look like it's the end of the world as we know it."

"This is hardly a time for jokes," Fionn muttered.

Slapping his back, Devin said, "Shut up, man, we're not here to speak."

Rolling her eyes as she pushed past them, Tessa wagged a finger. "That's right, you're here for decoration. Now, pick up those baskets and let's go save the day. The sooner we get done with this, the sooner you can start swinging your big manly swords around at other big manly swords."

Merle could not resist quipping. "You think we're big and manly? How sweet."

"I'm undecided. Let me inspect the goods first before I form an opinion." Tessa tossed her answer over her shoulder at him.

There were several awkward chuckles while people rushed to grab the baskets. Staying close to Tessa, Eirian squinted to take in what she was doing as they started walking. Focused on the staff in her hand, Tessa muttered quiet words that made little sense to Eirian. Celiaen had his hands on his swords, eyes sweeping the area. It would have been quicker to reach their destination with horses, but it was not worth the time it would take. A pang of regret hit Eirian. She would never see Halcyon again, and she hoped they would care for him.

"Over that way." Tessa pointed with the staff. "I had a few people search out the best spot once the sun went down."

Allowing her magic to search the area, Eirian picked up the handful of mages waiting for them. Fayleen stood at the edge of the group, her staff firmly grasped in front of her and magic ready if the Athnaralans noticed them. Wards were up, another yellow doing his best to hide their presence. She felt his power wavering, nerves and inexperience threatening to get the better of him. Barking orders to the guards carrying the last pitch-filled orbs, Tessa marched to over to stand beside Fayleen.

Joining them, Eirian stood on the other side and gazed into the expanse. "They've provided us with an easy target."

It was easy to spot the siege weapons, fires lit in rows so the Athnaralans could see what they were doing. Shadowy lines were between the edge of the camp and the fires, soldiers preparing to fight. Laying the clay and glass orbs out in front of the three women, those helping quickly got back behind the wards.

Before she began, she needed to feel where everything was and remind herself where the weak spots were. The whispers grew softer, encouraging the flow of power outwards with delight. Eirian knew better than to feel relief at their quiet. It would not be long before they began encouraging her to kill everyone. Taking a step forward, she spread her arms.

"And that's our cue to move," Fayleen said, waiting for the others to move back before she lowered her staff.

Tessa remained beside Eirian, facing her rather than their common enemy.

She wanted to return the encouragement she had given to her.

"You got this, Eirian. Remember, hit the weak spots as hard as you can."

"I know what I'm doing. Just keep everyone behind me." Eirian closed her eyes to shut out visual distractions.

"Don't worry, I will." Joining the others, Tessa shook her head at the watchers. "You heard her. No one goes past me."

Breathing in, Eirian relaxed into her magic and felt the sparks of life of the seeds embedded in the clay vessels. It took a great deal of concentration to lift a handful of them high enough to escape notice. She did not dare try to hit all six of the weapons. Instead, she worked as quickly as she could to spread what she had available one by one.

The Athnaralans did not take long to notice the trebuchets were under attack after the first few balls of pitch splattered over parts of the timber. If the noise of the clay breaking was not enough to alert them, the fragments raining down on the men below were. Horns blared, joining the symphony of noise coming from the camp.

Cursing, Galameyvin shook his head at Tessa. "They know we're attacking back. Won't be long before we're located."

Tessa pulled the hood of her tunic over her head and cackled. "Oh, don't worry, I have a plan."

"What plan?" There was a hint of apprehension in the voice of a yellow.

"Eirian isn't the only one full of surprises. Purples are the masters of keeping secrets."

Looking to Fayleen, Celiaen asked, "What about you?"

She cocked her head to the side with a wink. "I'm an open book, Celi, pretty sure you know all my tricks."

Pushing herself harder, Eirian kept carrying the objects over the great distance she needed to cover to hit her targets. She knew she was closer to completing the task with each batch. At the back of her mind, she was thankful they had attacked in the darkness, the lack of light hiding what she was doing before it was too late to stop them.

Eirian felt the scouting parties spreading out to locate where the attack was coming from, but there was nothing she could do about it while her job was incomplete. The whispers urged her to switch focus, but she clung to the plan. Upon striking the final trebuchet, she hesitated, debating if she could manage six glass orbs at once. It would be easier to light them all and use her magic to make the sparks jump, but the precision she needed to pull it off left her in doubt.

"Just do it." She breathed the words, gathering her focus as best she could.

Selecting six of the orbs, Eirian silently praised Tessa for attaching seeds to them as well. She did her best not to rush, fearful of wasting precious resources. Picturing a strand of power attached to each orb, she twitched her fingers, flinging them at the most significant weak spots coated in pitch. They struck, and the mixture of embedded wards and powder within ignited the pitch instantly while Eirian prepared to spread the flames.

"They found us!" Tessa cursed, her magic sensing the approaching enemy before the others did. "Fay, do what you can to shield them for as long as possible. The rest of you just do what you do best, but only if I fail. Which I won't."

Confusion rippled through the group as Tessa strode to stand in line with Eirian while maintaining a distance. The sky had lightened, signaling the approaching dawn, and providing them with the opportunity to make out what she was doing. Swirling the staff, Tessa slammed the butt into the ground and extended a hand forward. Then she let go, using her magic to see the particles.

Her power fanned out, focused through the wards carved into the wood to cause the ground to tremble outwards in waves. Shouts of fear rose as the Athnaralans discovered that the earth had become unstable beneath their feet. Horses reared and skittered sideways, fear filling them. Continuing to funnel her magic through the staff, Tessa grinned in delight. It was freeing to reveal what she could do.

Powerful enough to feel the emotions coming from the enemy, Galameyvin cast a glance at the others and said, "Sorry, but I can help."

Ducking around the grabbing hands, Galameyvin ran to join Tessa. Ignoring her confusion, he took a deep breath, relaxing the iron grip he held on his power. He was a fraction in front of the two women, hoping he could avoid affecting them. Concentrating on the fear and panic rolling off the soldiers, Galameyvin latched on to it and encouraged those emotions to grow.

Picturing chasms opening in the ground, he pushed the image at the soldiers, manipulating them into believing it was happening. Shouts of panic became screams of utter terror, the sound making Galameyvin's heart clench with conflict over his actions. Reminding himself what was at stake, he continued pushing the vision forward, chasing after Tessa's efforts to rip the ground apart. Fayleen and the other mages watched on in horror.

Not letting their actions distract her, Eirian focused on the seeds stuck to the pitch and drove her power into them. She had done her best to spread the sparks, but now she needed to make use of her other option. The seeds sprouted into vines, and directing them to entangle the trebuchets, she pulled the life from them. Drying and withering, they became fuel for the fires to spread and consume the weapons.

Knowing time was limited, the Athnaralans continued to load the slings, flinging several last boulders toward the camp. Task completed, Eirian's magic begged to be let loose, the whispers longing to destroy the men surrounding the weapons. She considered the option, lingering on the prospect of sucking the life from them. It would be easy to take the energy filling them and return it to the earth. Forcing the notion away, she refused to give in.

Withdrawing, Eirian opened her eyes to observe the towering infernos in relief. It had taken some of the pressure off, but the whispers continued to drag at her mind. Shadows danced, demanding attention while mocking her efforts to ignore their presence. They had become louder, no longer the flickering darkness at the edge of her vision. Clinging to what focus she had left, Eirian looked at the mages beside her.

Seeing her turn to Galameyvin and Tessa, Celiaen spoke to Fayleen, "Get these yellows out of here and back to the rest where you will be safe."

"I'm not leaving her!" Fayleen snapped, signaling to the tired yellow helping ward the group. "Jacob, you heard him."

Celiaen grabbed her arm, snarling, "You're not going out there."

Her magic flared, shoving him back abruptly. "Don't you fucking tell me what to do, Celi. Someone has to shield your asses, and there's no one better at it than me."

Ignoring their argument, Eirian spoke softly, "It's done. You can stop now."

Galameyvin stopped first, crumpling as guilt struck. "I'm sorry, I'm so sorry."

Tessa spun the staff around and gave it a delighted stroke, letting out a whoop. "You've got no idea how badly I wanted to do that. What a rush! Powers, Fay, you had a brilliant idea with these things. As for you, Galameyvin, now that was a surprise."

"I just broke so many laws," he whispered, and Eirian rushed to his side. "I raped their minds and twisted their perceptions...."

Gripping his shoulders, she shook her head. "It's war, Gal, you did what you had to, and you may need to do it again. If you don't think you can, then go back now."

"She's right."

Tara was there with Alyse. The two women propped him up as he sagged further, and Alyse spoke to him softly. Eirian recalled how she felt every time she used her powers to drain life from people. Brushing a hand over his face sympathetically, she kissed the top of his head.

"I understand, Gal."

He met her eyes, seeing a flicker of the earnest girl she used to be. "How do you live with the guilt?"

"You just do."

"It's different. Those men will remember what I did to them, and they will never forget that horror. They may never recover. You kill them." Pushing her hand away, Galameyvin bared his teeth.

Pursing her lips, Eirian took a deep breath to calm her irritation and made her words as a matter of fact as she could manage. "Okay, fine, you're right. Would it make you feel any better if I went and killed them right now? It wouldn't be hard to follow the lingering taste of your magic on their minds. It might even be rather delicious. The heightened fear as they wither into nothing after having thought the earth was opening to swallow them."

"Eirian!" Tara snapped. "That's not helpful."

Tara was wrong, Eirian's words striking a chord deep in Galameyvin's mind, and he recoiled from her further. "For all your ostentation, Eirian Altira, you and I know you'd never enjoy it. If you did, then we're doomed."

His response made her smile and turn to Tessa. "Nice move, Grand Mage."

"I told you, you're not the only one with a few secret tricks, Eirian. Now, shall we try to make it back to the rest? Because we're more than a little vulnerable here."

Striding past, Tessa pushed the hood back from her face and glanced at the dawning sun. Shading his eyes, Aiden looked around to make sense of the swarming lines of soldiers forming in various locations.

"We need to pull back. If we try to withdraw the way we came, we might find our people attacking us."

"Everyone will scramble to establish a front line and some sort of organization among the ranks. Chaotic pushbacks are ineffective, and considering the Athnaralans planned this, their lines will slaughter the small groups of prepared soldiers on our side." Shaking off his shock at seeing Galameyvin break down, Celiaen regained focus and pointed in a direction heading away from the camps. "If we go that way and turn westward to circle back, we should skirt the lines."

Turning her back on them, Eirian faced the dawn and stared at the sun peeking above the horizon. Clouds scattered across the sky caught the light, casting lines of color as far as the eye could see. She forgot the people behind her and lost track of the emerging battle for a moment. Instead, she breathed in the land's energy as it awakened with the light. Her power reveled in it. Spreading her arms, Eirian welcomed it and the sense of renewal it provided.

The breeze remained light, chasing away any smell of smoke headed her way. It was a moment of peace and a teasing of tranquility. But the shadows across her mind and vision quickly chased it away. They whispered and taunted, daring her to use her power, challenging her to prove she could do what she boasted she could. Digging claws into the walls Eirian struggled to prop up, they tore them further, letting memories spill through.

Swatting at the air, she growled at one of the dancing shadows she could see in the corner of her vision. They had become more persistent, and the lure of battle was an added strain. Eirian could barely hold on, magic spilling across the ground to add to the flowers her presence had grown. It oozed from her, a conflicting whisper of life and death, withered trails spreading through the growth.

"Leave me be!"

"Ree? Are you alright?" Fayleen approached tentatively, touching her shoulder.

"Fay?" Blinking, Eirian turned from the dawn to mumble, "Sorry, I was watching the sunrise. What's going on?"

Sharing glances of concern, the guards looked to Aiden for reassurance.

"Do you remember where we are, Eirian?" Aiden asked.

The whispers laughed, digging in further, and she nodded. "Yes, sorry, I do. I lost focus for a moment, but I'm here. It's fine. Let's go."

"Sir, she's not fine." Gabe stepped up to Aiden's shoulder and murmured, "I believe she's under attack."

Watching Eirian, he flicked his eyes to Gabe. "Why do you think that?"

"There's something dark in the corner of my eye. I can feel it. You're going to have to trust my instincts, Captain, but I think her fight has begun."

"I believe you, Gabe. You've always noticed things the rest of us don't. Tell everyone to keep a closer eye because we may not be safe from her."

Signaling to Celiaen, Aiden caught him before they all started moving.

"What? We're wasting time and putting ourselves at risk," Celiaen growled.

"Beware of Eirian. Something isn't right."

Celiaen's eyes narrowed, but there was no surprise in his expression. "You're right. If it comes to it, I'll do my best to distract her while you get your men away. I feel something over the bond, but she's trying to shut me out of it."

Huffing, Aiden shook his head. "If you think I'd abandon—"

"Do you want Ree to kill you? Would that prove something?"

Ending the conversation, Celiaen walked away to join Eirian, calling out instructions to his companions. The guards kept themselves in a neat group around Eirian, Fayleen, and Tessa without waiting to see if Aiden had anything different to order. Lending support to Galameyvin, Alyse and Ianto nervously watched the two powerful women in front.

Tara strode to the front of the group, her head held high and watching. She was the most experienced among them, her magic more than ready for a fight. A single hand rested easily on the hilt of a blade, nails scratching over the engravings. They had become accustomed to the horns, and the noise of the opposing armies was a buzz. Nothing had sounded closer, and with a pause, Aiden looked back at the burning trebuchets. He doubted they would pursue after what Tessa and Galameyvin had done.

Capturing Eirian's hand, Celiaen gave her a faint smile and squeezed. "I'm right here, dear heart. Just focus on me."

Scowling at him, she chanced a glance at the sky. "It looks like it'll be a fair day."

"Eirian, I know something is going on. We all do."

Dancing in the corners of her perception, the shadows laughed at her. They shifted between forms, drawing inspiration from the memories spilling through the cracks in her walls.

"Nothing is going on. We have the battle to deal with, and that should be your priority."

"My priority is getting you to safety so you can save yourself for when you're needed. There's more than enough able bodies to fight the battle. I'm not needed there." Squeezing her hand again, his mouth twisted wryly. "But you need us."

Tempted to yank her hand from his grip, she resisted. "At least we took care of the trebuchets."

Chuckling, Celiaen did not answer. Moving as quickly as possible, the group kept a watchful eye on the shifting battle lines. Banners fluttered in the breeze, helping those making their way to the front work out where they were going. The gleam of plate in the rising sunlight flashed as the red mages swarmed forward. It was easy to locate the camp, gray spirals of smoke drifting into the sky from the fires. Hooves beat like a drum, catching their attention, and they halted to watch a group of riderless horses headed toward them.

"Tharen," Eirian mumbled, her gaze locked on a silvery horse at the front. "So that's his form."

Tharen brought the animals to a standstill a short distance away, and it amazed them to find it was their horses. Rushing to Halcyon, Eirian pressed her face to the gelding's neck and watched as Tharen shifted back into his true form. He shone in the sunlight, arms crossed and an unimpressed look while he regarded them.

"Of all the stupid plans you lot could have come up with!" He huffed. "You're lucky I speak horse."

"We didn't have time," Celiaen said, hauling himself into the saddle.

Silvery eyes settled on Eirian, concern within them. "How long ago did it start?"

"What?" she asked, knowing exactly what he was referring to.

Every attempt to deny the mad god's whispering received further mocking. Eirian knew what her enemy was trying to do. Shadowy forms crossing her vision had become reminders of her past actions instead of figures from Shianeni's memories. The god intended to unnerve her, stir her anger and grief, unsettle her confidence, and inspire doubt.

She spent her control keeping the plan hidden behind shields, layers of power masking the tiny flutter of life Eirian carried within her. It wavered, the darker side of her magic rebelling against her refusal to fight at the urge of the whispers. It felt the call of battle and the prospect of slaughtering victims that would not stand a chance against her bloodlust.

"Oh, little queen, I need you to just hold on." Shaking his head, Tharen shifted back into his horse form and flicked his tail.

Hesitating, Eirian turned Halcyon toward the battle. Grabbing the reins, Aiden was not willing to risk her charging off. He spotted her fingers creeping toward her bow.

"Don't you fucking dare!"

"I was—"

"I don't care! You've said that before." He tugged at the horse, encouraging him to keep up. "Celiaen, you might need to put that hilt to use again."

Celiaen arched a brow and dropped a hand to a sword. "Sure, I can do that. Now shut up, Ree, and do what you're bloody told for a change. That is not our fight. Not unless you can tell me the darkness is walking among them, ready to face you."

She was not walking among the fighting soldiers. The dark god was taunting Eirian in her mind, but she did not dare utter the words out loud.

"No, she's not. She's drawing strength from the destruction and encouraging a frenzy."

The shadows mocked her, and Eirian clenched her jaw tight. Letting Aiden keep hold of her reins, she gripped tight to the saddle. No one wasted any time. The horses spurred into a gallop toward the illusion of safety behind the circling battle lines. Drawn swords and nervous soldiers greeted their arrival, taking a moment to realize who was among them. Telmians were waiting, Ilar holding clothes for Tharen once he transformed. Grabbing his arm, Tharen pointed at Eirian.

"Don't leave her side, and you know what to do. Tell Vartan when she prepares to enter the battle. Slow her down and give him as much time as you can," he said, tugging his clothes on quickly as he could.

The identical twin brothers that Aiden could never tell apart nodded, and Ilar hummed in agreement. "Of course."

His instructions angered Eirian, her focus shifting from the mocking shadow to Tharen as she snarled, "I do not require watching."

"Do you lie for your benefit or theirs?" Tharen stared at her coldly. "Hold on for as long as you can because you'll not go into your fight alone."

"I won't let any of you die for me."

"Who said anything about dying?" The first twin chuckled, a hand on his hip.

His brother grinned. "Faolan would come back from the dead to skin us alive if we let you go into battle without us."

Just the name was enough for her control to crack, and Eirian braced for the whispered accusations filling her mind. They were hard to deny, her guilt making her believe them. Slipping from the saddle, she elbowed her way through the crowd surrounding her. The rational part of her screamed a reminder they were trying to help, but she struggled to grasp on to it.

Lifting her hands to her ears, Eirian covered them, childishly hoping that it would block out the whispers. Squeezing her eyes shut, she shook her head in frustration, denying the press of memories crowding in. They were hers, but they were not. Flashes of Shianeni's life melding with her past. Feeling hands covering hers, Eirian opened her eyes to find Aiden staring in concern.

"Eirian, darling."

He gently pulled her hands away from the sides of her head. Feeling another hand on her back, she knew it was Celiaen.

"Ree, tell us what's going on. Please, we just want to help you."

"I think I can answer," Tessa spoke gently. "It's the mad god, isn't it? You're not invulnerable to her."

"How do you know?" Eirian whispered, turning to look at her.

Smiling grimly, she shrugged. "Let's say I had a suspicion."

They stared at each other in understanding, and for a moment, Eirian's mind went silent. "Thank you, Tessa."

"Hey, I just put the pieces together. You did the hard part, and you did it magnificently." Intentionally misunderstanding what Eirian was thanking her for, Tessa turned away and pulled the staff from where she had secured it across her back.

"You know that's not what I meant."

Glancing over her shoulder and leaning on the staff for support, Tessa winked. "Some things are best left unspoken, Eirian Altira. Now, I think everyone needs a drink and a rest before our turn comes."

"You're not a fighter, Tessa. Your part is over," Galameyvin said.

Flinching, Fayleen muttered, "Don't go there."

Striding over to Galameyvin, Tessa drew herself up to his height. "I might not be much good with a sword, but that doesn't make me less capable of holding my own in a battle. What I did out there wasn't the only trick I have."

"You're not Eirian. You can't fight with magic as she can." He regretted the words when he saw the fury appear in her stormy eyes.

"Tell me that again after the battle is over, blue."

With the power crackling around her, Galameyvin could not avoid seeing the similarities between her and Eirian. "Tessa… I didn't mean it like that."

"Didn't you, Galameyvin? Just another blue among other blues underestimating a purple. I think it's long overdue that you're reminded which order is at the top of the food chain." Tossing her head, Tessa spun on her heel and strode away.

Smiling in delight, Eirian chuckled at the stunned look on the faces of the others. "You asked for it. Honestly, Gal, do you think pissing off your future grand mage is a good idea?"

He turned his gaze to her and ran a hand through his messy blond curls. "I didn't mean it like it sounded. It's just… she's not you."

"No, she's not, but she's an incredibly powerful mage."

Focusing on what was happening around her, Eirian clung to anything that helped her mind stay clear. It was difficult. The constant barrage had worn her down, and it would take very little to push her over the edge.

Sensing her struggle, Aiden brushed a hand against her arm. "How can I help you, darling?"

It was something she felt, rather than heard, the whisper of her name repeated by the shadows. Eirian's vision clouded over with them. They crept over her skin, filling her with a revulsion so intense she wanted to vomit. Pushing Aiden and Celiaen away, she stumbled back and scratched at herself, trying to brush them away. Startled, the two warriors shared a look and attempted to grab hold of her again. Ducking around them, Eirian looked for a gap and halted at what she saw, allowing the two of them to catch her.

"*Eirian.*"

The shadowy figure laughed, beckoning her to follow as she turned and vanished.

TWENTY-SEVEN

"Let me go!"

Struggling against the hands grasping her, Eirian kept her eyes locked on where she had seen her enemy. She needed to end it before more people died.

Tightening his hold on her waist, Celiaen looked worriedly at Aiden and Merle. "What the fuck do we do?"

Signaling Merle to take his spot, Aiden got in front of Eirian, trying to force her to look at him. "Eirian! Darling, stop! Listen to me! There is nothing there."

Feeling the hands on her face, she snarled, "Get off me!"

"Sorry about this."

Slapping her, Aiden tensed and waited for the backlash. None came, Eirian going still and staring at him in surprise.

"You hit me!"

"I took a wild guess it might knock some sense into you," he replied, meeting Celiaen's gaze. "You need to get your focus back. Talk to us."

Shrugging Merle's grip off, she rubbed her stinging cheek. Reluctant to admit that Aiden was right, Eirian clung to the pain and the distraction it provided. It did not silence the whispers, but it was better than nothing.

"She's ready for me."

Celiaen scoffed. "I'd say she's more than ready, dear heart. Could Gal help?"

"No! No, no." Shaking her head, she whipped around to peer at him. "I can't risk it. She might tear his mind apart to hurt me."

"If we let go, will you try to run?"

Her guards formed a cluster of circles to shield her from watching eyes and to make a wall of bodies she had to get through. All of them looked worried, their eyes following her every movement. Fayleen and Galameyvin pushed in, looking grim. The shock of seeing Eirian start chasing after nothing had helped Galameyvin regain his composure. Confident she could not escape, Merle and Celiaen released their hold and stepped back to give her space to stand.

"Don't touch me," she said, recoiling from Galameyvin when he reached out. He gave her a patient look, brows raised, coaxing, "Ree, let me help you."

Switching focus to Aiden, Eirian pleaded, "Please don't let him touch me."

"Just him?" Aiden raised an arm in front of her and shook his head at Galameyvin. "Or do you mean all of us?"

"Him. Blues. Anyone that might touch my mind."

Realization dawned on Galameyvin, and he took a step back, almost knocking Fox over. He did not know why he had not seen it sooner. It had not occurred to him that the darkness would attack Eirian's mind.

"Oh powers, Ree. She's attacking your mind. That's why you're jumping at things we can't see. You're strong enough to shield your mind."

Opening her mouth, Eirian struggled with an answer. She knew she was shielding part of herself already from the attack, protecting something, but she could not recall what. Guarding it while she left areas of her mind intentionally vulnerable.

"I'm doing my best, Gal. Do you think I'd roll over and take what she's serving me?"

"It'd be a first," Aiden muttered, half smiling.

His attempt at a joke went over everyone's heads, and Ilar said, "It's only going to continue. What are we waiting for?"

They looked at him, and Tara agreed. "He's right. What are we waiting for exactly?"

"She's linked to someone. I need to find them." The explanation seemed simple enough, and Eirian hoped they would accept it.

Searching her face, Fayleen scowled. "There's more, but you won't tell us. Or you cannot. Either way, waiting is pointless, and you always knew it was."

Guilty, she looked at her feet, murmuring, "I hoped waiting would flush her out."

"Instead, it's weakening you."

"Fayle—"

Lifting her hands, Fayleen cut her off. "Save it. You told me enough already. How do we decide which front?"

Staring at Eirian's face, Aiden contemplated it before answering, "The one we're looking for is with the original legion. We saw her that day, and it was before these fresh ones arrived. I'd hazard a guess that Eirian has a powerful urge to go the wrong way."

"The mad one wants her weakened, possibly injured," Celiaen said. "Does anyone know for sure if they've entered the battle yet?"

"Our forces are fighting on two fronts. They coordinated the attack after the trebuchets started," Ilar replied.

Taking charge, Tara barked orders. "You heard them, mount up. We'll fight with the sun at our backs."

Hesitating, Merle looked around as his fellows started moving to their horses. "Where did Tessa go? She admitted to feeling something as well."

"I don't know, but you find her, Merle. We can't have her running loose if she's at risk." Aiden gave him a look that he understood. "As for you, darling, you can either ride with your prince or with me. There's no way we're letting you ride alone."

"I don't ne—"

"You can either mount willingly, or I'll toss you over the withers of a horse myself."

Rolling her shoulders, armor moving effortlessly with the motion, Eirian glared at him and crossed her arms. "What, no threat to spank me like a disobedient child?"

Celiaen choked back a snarl. "Powers, Eirian, can't you… just let us get you to where you need to be."

Glancing at his hands, Aiden arched a brow and smiled slowly. "Don't bloody tempt me. Now, my horse or his?"

Weighing up her options, Eirian looked between the two men before glancing at Galameyvin and Fayleen. She wanted to suggest riding with Fayleen to spite them, but knew it would not end well. Turning to Aiden, she nodded begrudgingly.

"I'll ride with you. Celi will be more useful in a fight."

"If I didn't know what you meant, it would hurt my feelings. Now get on."

He pushed her toward his horse, where Gabe was holding it, waiting for them. While she hoisted herself into the saddle, Celiaen stopped Aiden.

"Don't let go of her."

Smirking, he winked and said, "Don't worry, I won't take my hands off her."

"This is serious."

"You think I don't know that? If I don't lessen the severity of the situation for myself, I'm going to crack as surely as she is. Besides, this might be the last time I get to taunt you." Turning toward his horse, Aiden paused and looked back at Celiaen sadly. "This might be the last time we get to pretend things could have been different."

Letting him go, Celiaen's shoulders slumped, and he nodded. "I know. If I go down with her, I want you to know I don't hate you."

Pretending he did not catch the last few words Celiaen spoke, Aiden pulled himself into his saddle. Eirian had shifted forward, balancing carefully while she waited. They settled into as comfortable an arrangement as they could manage, Aiden wrapping a protective arm around her waist while his other accepted the reins. Shooting a wary look at Eirian, Gabe fingered the hilt of a dagger. His promises were at the forefront of his mind, and he wondered if it would be necessary.

Aiden could not help chuckling. Swords strapped to Eirian's back hindered his attempts to lean forward and peer over her shoulder. The quivers at her side sat awkwardly over their legs, further confirming why she chose him. If forced to defend themselves, it would be challenging to respond in a hurry. But Celiaen would be free to buy them time.

Twisting and craning, Aiden got his mouth close enough to her ear to murmur, "Of all the dreams I've had of taking you for a ride, this was not one of them."

He hoped to incense her enough to provide a distraction she could use. Tremors made her hands unsteady, and Aiden questioned how they would see her through a battlefield. Instead of letting his thoughts spiral around the fight, he focused on distracting both of them.

"For a start, you're wearing far too many weapons."

Eirian stiffened, glancing at him. "Do you think now is the time?"

"When is the time? When you're dead and can't bite back? You do like biting, and that delightful little whine—"

"I know what you're doing, Captain. Do you expect me to be appreciative?"

Desire to tell Aiden she appreciated his attempts fought with her wish to send him far away to a place where he would be safe. Safe from her. Safe from the fight. Stroking the leather covering Eirian, he felt the rough edges of the engravings.

"No, I know you better than that, and I know when you're putting on a front."

Her focus slipped again, and Eirian struggled against the barrage of whispers battering her mind. Sensing it, Aiden captured her hands, pushing the reins into her grasp, and curling his hand around them. Tightening his arm around her waist, he looked at Celiaen and shook his head in warning. Mouth twisting, Celiaen stretched up in his saddle, looking out past the heads of those in front.

There was no neat formation of lines on the Endaran side, ranks lost in desperation to prevent the enemy from breaking through. He did not know where to go, and a quick look at Eirian confirmed he would get no sense from her. Their bond was a turbulent river after heavy rain. He felt the fear and self-doubt overwhelming her, and it sent shivers down his spine. Fear at what might happen if she lost control entirely, fear that she might have been wrong the whole time, fears that she would fail and he could not save her.

"Captain!" Merle called from the outer edge of the group. "Tessa said to follow her."

"Tessa?" Galameyvin asked in surprise.

Not willing to hesitate and risk Eirian growing even more unstable, Aiden replied, "Fine, but you better know what you're doing."

Galameyvin still looked dubious. "You're going to trust Tessa?"

"Yep. The two of them have a plan. They've met a few times in private to make it." He kept his hand tightly over Eirian's, feeling the trembles worsen.

"Do you have a better idea, Gal?" Celiaen snapped in frustration.

Horses in front of them halted, and the sounds of battle echoed loudly. There were shouts, horns blaring as flustered officers recognized the Queen's guards. Familiar faces appeared, taking the horses away. Todd strode through the crowd, exchanging the odd greeting with the men. He took one look at his queen and cursed, shaking his head in concern.

"What the fuck happened to her?"

"Lieutenant, what a surprise to find you here." Aiden kept a tight grip on Eirian as she looked around wildly.

Todd said, "What can I say? I'm destined to hold the line for my queen. Speaking of, she does not look like she can grasp a sword right now, let alone fight."

Celiaen bristled, defensive even though the words rang true. "Eirian will be fine. She doesn't need to fight yet. We just have to get her where she needs to be."

"And where is that exactly?" Todd asked pointedly. "Because we'll do what we can to help, but it would be suicide to fight aimlessly out there."

"I know," Tessa said, the guards letting her pass without a word.

Her hand gripped her staff tightly, and Aiden took in the sight of her in amazement. He did not know if he simply had not noticed earlier or if she had changed her clothes at some point. Tessa wore no armor, a deep-red hooded tunic leading to plain black trousers and boots. A wide belt encased her waist and abdomen, the twin blades belonging to her brother hanging from it. Calmness surrounded her, the purple band on her finger gleaming in the sunlight. Her blue gaze took Eirian in, no surprise apparent in their depths.

"Everyone has asked me if I can kill people like she can." Shaking her head, her mouth twisted in annoyance as she added, "But no one, not one person, has asked what I can do."

"And what can you do?" Celiaen inquired.

Pointing with the staff, Tessa answered, "The one you're looking for is that way. I can feel the strength of the taint. It is a disruption of the particles."

Galameyvin's eyes narrowed. "Have you known the entire time?"

"Yes, and no. I didn't know what exactly I was feeling until today. After that, I put it all together. While you were arguing and struggling with Eirian, I tested it out, and it led me here. You headed this way when Merle found me."

"Do you know how to use those?" Holding Eirian up, Aiden nodded to the swords. "Because the longer we wait…"

His remark sparked a little of the snark they usually saw from her, and with a wink, Tessa turned. "Jaren kept my training up. Come on, this way."

"So, we're…" Todd waved at her back.

"Yes." Looking at Aiden and Eirian, Celiaen hesitated. "Do you need help with her?"

Huffing, Fayleen ushered him out of her way. "Don't worry, Celi. Captain Pretty and I have her."

Eirian muttered something, and Fayleen hushed her softly, slinging an arm around her waist. Nodding, Aiden signaled to his men to stay close, the guards keeping close ranks around their queen. Todd cleared the way, and many of his company were already engaged in battle with the Athnaralans. It was a close fight, and the line made no progress in either direction. The soldiers were primarily human, but there were elves and daoine scattered throughout, with the odd mage making quick work of anyone who got in their way.

Just the sight of the royal guards appeared to reinvigorate the Endarans. Their faith in their queen gave them the energy to push forward that they had been struggling to find. While erratic, the magic seeping off Eirian helped, washing away any signs of tiredness. Unfortunately, it affected the Athnaralans as well.

"We need her," Fayleen said, watching Aiden flinch from the corner of her eye. "There's no way we can get her anywhere safely without her help."

He agreed. "I know."

Her mind whirled with possibilities, and Fayleen made them halt. Moving in front of Eirian, she frowned anxiously and placed her hands on Eirian's face.

"Eirian? Ree, please, we need you to come back."

"That's not going to work," Aiden muttered.

Eyes darting wildly, Eirian did not respond, and Tessa asked, "Think hitting her will work again?"

"Let me." Ilar pushed her out of the way.

Magic swarmed around the Telmian, and remembering that he shared some similarities in his powers with Eirian, Aiden was unsure if it was a good idea. "What are you going to do?"

A smile appeared briefly before Ilar's mouth thinned. "What I was told to do. Vartan is coming."

"What's going on?" Doubling back, Celiaen took in Ilar with his hands on Eirian's face. "What happened?"

"Little queen, it's time." His magic felt like ice, and Aiden let go of Eirian, stumbling out of the way. "Time to stop chasing those shadows and let me have them."

Ilar's power drowned out the magic surrounding Eirian. Then something flickered in her eyes, and she tossed her head back in surprise. They watched in amazement as she recovered, and Ilar curled in on himself. She brushed a hand over his hair, a sad look on her face. Eirian turned to look around at the people surrounding her, and her gaze settled on Gabe, mouth set in a grim line.

"Take him away. This is no place for you."

Gabe arched a brow at her, his gaze flicking to Aiden briefly. "I disagree. If you're here, then it's the place for me."

"Gabe, that was an order. You and I know an open battle is not your forte. Take Ilar away. Protect him until he recovers. Think of it as protecting me." Brushing herself off, Eirian sighed. "He has taken a part of me to mislead her and buy me time."

The mages in the group shared looks, and Gabe reluctantly came forward to help Ilar. Not wholly convinced, Aiden regarded Eirian curiously. She seemed fine, and he felt the vibration of power as it surrounded her, but he was uncertain. There was still something subdued about her. A quick look at Celiaen told him he was unconvinced as well. The question was if they had the time to argue or take things as they appeared.

If Eirian sensed their hesitation, she did not acknowledge it and focused on checking her weapons. Her hands no longer trembled, flickers of her bloodlust hitting them like a scent in the wind. Ignoring the stares, she selected the weapons she would enter battle with. Holding the elegant recurve bow in one hand and several arrows in another, Eirian looked at Tessa.

"Well, then."

Tessa stared at her, fingers flexing on her staff. "About bloody time. I've been waiting for you."

"Gabe." She turned back to nod at him. "Thank you."

An arm was around Ilar's waist, and Gabe scowled. "Don't you fucking die out there, ma'am."

Half smiling, she replied, "No promises, Gabe."

Without speaking to anyone else, Eirian started after Tessa, the two purples slipping between Endaran soldiers. The ring of swords drew closer, the sharp clang of it making some of them flinch. Coppery, the smell of blood hit their noses before they caught sight of the first corpse. It was enough to fuel the leap to full raging lust for the red mages in the group. Swords appeared in hands before the non-mages could blink.

Galameyvin's performance had buoyed several of the blues with them, their willingness to blur lines of morality driving them to accompany the others into battle. Knowing they needed to keep the group together, Fayleen and the other yellows set to work, magic flaring into wards to deflect attacks. Their efforts lasted long enough to allow the group to drive into the fight, the twin daoine leading the way.

Catching the deadly focus on Eirian's face, Aiden felt his unease intensify. She moved with precision through the lines. Her bow made quick work of those she set her sights on, arrows doubling as makeshift daggers if anyone got close.

There was nothing of the warrior he had seen in previous fights, the lust-driven killer lost in her magic. It was with disdain that she yanked arrows from her kills when she went past them.

No raging power spread out from Eirian to drive the rest of them into a frenzy. Aiden was thankful for it, thankful that his men could keep their minds clear and focused on their tasks. Swinging her staff in one hand and a sword in the other, Tessa led the group, her magic the one he felt the most. He wondered what she was doing with it. The men she faced were leaping and hopping like something was biting at their feet. They did not raise their weapons to defend themselves before she made quick work of them with her sword.

Falling in line with Aiden, Merle said, "We're going to break through soon."

"I know," Aiden replied, lifting his sword to leap to Fayleen's defense when it looked like she was struggling.

Staff moving, Fayleen hit the Athnaralan in the face before Aiden ran him through. Winking, she brushed the loose hair out of her face.

"Well, this is fun."

He blinked at her. "You have an odd sense of fun, woman."

"Thanks for the save." Her eyes moved to her next target. "Keep moving, or we'll get left behind."

Before they reached the furthest point the Endaran forces had carved, Eirian slipped her bow into its quiver in favor of the twin blades. Hearing the ring of them, Aiden's eyes went wide as her bloodlust finally roared to life. It burst forth, an undeniable buzz of power that energized them. The call of it danced through their minds, encouraging them to kill any who opposed them.

Aiden was ashamed for doubting Eirian's ability to hold it together until she was at less risk of harming her people. Celiaen's power answered the call like a river welcoming the flood. He was a gleam of silver beside her darkness. The magic was powerful enough to send approaching Athnaralans scrambling backward in fear. On the other side of Eirian, Tessa twirled her staff and pushed forward with her magic. Aiden was close enough to see swirls of air shove the soldiers back and to feel the thud.

Moving like she was dancing, Tessa carved a path, and none of the warriors were stupid enough not to take advantage of the stumbling enemy. During the last battle, Aiden could not watch the pair fight together. But seeing how their movements mirrored each other, he understood why people viewed them as a match. Remaining as close as he could manage, Aiden monitored Fayleen whenever he got a chance. She was holding her own, her magic, and the staff she wielded as effective a shield as he had ever seen.

Her magic provided Eirian with a safe place to regain a sense of herself. She was thankful for what Ilar had done, and she hoped the exchange would not permanently change him. In the corner of her mind, the part Ilar had offered in return fought against her control. It wanted her to let go of it so it could return.

Eirian could not blame it. She had glimpsed the darkness within Ilar during their exchange and knew it paled compared to what she bore.

That darkness lurked around the outskirts of the circle of calm she had made. Lurked and waited. It offered reminders of how easily she could end all of those who opposed her, whispered of how good it felt to return their energy and their bodies to the earth. The whispers had changed. They did not mock and belittle or make her doubt every part of herself. There were no attempts to tear down the walls in her mind.

Instead, they were her voice, her power, the part of her she struggled with every day. Eirian hoped it would protect her for the time being and shield her from her enemy. Dropping the shields, she remembered the plan and the tiny flutter of life within her. It was a risk to release herself before the battle was upon her, but she could not help it. One last fight, that was all she had. One last time to feel the impact of blades vibrating up her arms. One last time when she could scent freshly spilt blood and feel it drip from the tip of her swords.

More than that, it was the last time she would get to dance with Celiaen. Their swords moved, mirrors of each other that did not miss a beat of the song their powers sang. It was an ancient song. Others shared it, but no two were ever the same, unlike Celiaen and Eirian. She knew they had intended it that way, another choice taken from them by the gods. Two lives entwined before they were born, and she would do anything to ensure his life did not end alongside hers.

Power rippled like a cold fury, tearing through the Athnaralans. It was ancient, and it smelled of blood and fur, with a hint of the forest. There was an answering rumble of power, so different and yet much the same. Burning brightly in its fury, it raged like a storm rolling in from the ocean. They were heading for Eirian, the release of her power drawing them like moths to a flame.

It attracted all those with magic, their powers turning to Eirian as though she were the sun. They wanted a taste of her power, to drink it in and feel it fuel them further than they could dream of going on their own. She gave them all they desired. Her power fueled them, driving their bloodlust as they drove their swords through the enemy. The well she had unlocked was deep enough to feed the world.

Tessa felt it, felt the swirl of power, and pushed it away, refusing the offering. "No, thank you, I've got enough of my own."

"What are you on about?" Tucked in close beside her, Merle yanked his sword free of a corpse, turning to look at Tessa.

"Your precious queen is doling out helpings of magic." Swinging the staff, she shielded herself from attack and allowed Merle to deal with the man. "I get she has so much to share, but time and place, time and place. Wouldn't you agree, honey?"

He blinked at her, the dead body between them. "Honey?"

Grinning, she winked. "You seem like the sweetest one, and I like honey. Plus, I've forgotten your name."

"I..." Merle continued to stare at her, flustered by her response.

"Behind you."

Raising her staff, Tessa prepared to shield him, but before either of them could do anything, Baenlin appeared behind the Athnaralan. With blood dripping from his swords, he stared at Tessa in surprise, and she leaned on the staff, mouth twitching in amusement. He turned to Merle, taking him in with a curious tilt of his head before turning back to Tessa.

"What are you doing?" he demanded.

Smirking, she pushed the hood back from her face and looked at the sun. "I'm playing my part. Don't worry, Archmage, I'm more than able to look after myself."

Eyes dropping to the swords she carried, Baenlin scowled. "You know he wouldn't want you out here taking stupid risks."

"He'd be the first to tell me I have a job to do. You'll understand when the time comes. Now, don't you think you should kill some poor fools rather than trying to lecture me?"

Tessa looked at the wall of soldiers and swallowed back her anxiety. She had not suffered another attack since the day Jaren died, but the fear of it crept over her mind. Whispers made her doubt and question why they were bothering to fight. It seemed impossible to stop the Athnaralans, the lines of men appearing endless. She knew it was not true, knew they had the advantage. Magic gave them the edge.

Madness drove the enemy. It made them more careless than they would have been if the ancient god had left them alone to fight. Their frenzy made them weaker, encouraged them to make mistakes. Rubbing her thumb against a ward carved into her staff, Tessa drew herself together and smiled at Baenlin. He frowned and moved to stop her, but Merle shook his head, putting a hand up to stop him.

"She doesn't need you, and she doesn't need me. Watch."

She felt it, the shadow she had been chasing. The shadow she had been leading them to. Letting her magic reach out to Eirian, Tessa reminded her of their plan, and the touch was enough to make her pause. It was a summons, a rope thrown to pull her from the murky waters of the battle. Knowing it was enough, Tessa finally let go.

Part of her was glad Baenlin was behind her, that he would witness what she was capable of. Sweeping her gaze across the lines, Tessa pinpointed her target and pushed her magic forward. The ground ripped, cracks appearing beneath their feet, causing the Athnaralans to panic. Deep-rooted fear of being swallowed by the earth overrode the frenzy the god drove them to.

Keeping it controlled, Tessa angled it away to give her allies an unobstructed view of what was happening and stop themselves before it caught them. As quickly as she pulled the earth apart, she slammed it back together. The impact vibrated through the ground at their feet, Baenlin grunting in surprise. With the ground healed, screams rose into the air from those who had gotten parts of themselves trapped.

Tara was the first to stride forward, slitting the throat of an Athnaralan and silencing his cries. Others followed, swords and knives making quick work of those unable to escape. Those who could, fled in different directions, terrified the ground would open up again. They left the lone figure standing at the furthest edge, sword held up as he watched the chaos in front of him.

"I thought you said you weren't capable of killing large numbers of people?" Baenlin muttered, unwilling to take part in the slaughter unfolding.

She screwed up her face. "I'm not. I can move the ground in ways that can help us. Not just the ground, I can manipulate water, fire, and air as well."

Dark eyes gleamed from beneath his helm. "You're as responsible for their deaths as those striking the killing blow."

"I can live with that. You seem to think that I have delicate sensibilities, Archmage. May I suggest you get over it before you find yourself at odds with your grand mage?"

Walking forward, Tessa left him behind. Standing at the edge of the killing field, Eirian turned to meet Tessa's eyes when she sensed her close.

"Impressive."

Hovering beside her, Vartan grunted. "It's been a long time since I witnessed someone do that."

"He's coming. He's waiting. Whichever suits," Tessa said, watching the lone figure in the distance.

Tightening his grip on his swords, Celiaen looked at Eirian. It was a long look, and Tessa suspected he was at war with his emotions.

"Do we wait and make him come to us?" he finally asked.

Wiping off her blades on the clothes of a dead soldier, Eirian slid them back into their scabbards. "I think we should move forward. Those who wish to remain back may do so, but the fright factor Tessa provided will not last for long."

Not waiting to hear any more of the discussion, Tessa stepped forward to pick her way through the sprawling dead. Tara and others were working their way through, dispatching anyone who could not get out of their way. Their faces, where visible, were grim and determined. They took no pleasure in killing men who could not fight back.

Careful not to put the butt of her staff down on a body, Tessa held her head high. She knew Baenlin had spoken the truth. Each one was dead because of her. As much as she did not want it to, it weighed on her, and Tessa wished she could ask Eirian how she coped with it. Not far behind, Eirian did not look at the bodies as she stepped around them. Glancing over her shoulder, Tessa could picture her walking over the stone floor of some great hall rather than the bloody dirt of a battlefield.

As though he took his cue from them, the faceless figure on the opposite side started picking his way forward. His sword rested on his shoulder, nothing in his posture suggesting anything bothered him. He stopped once or twice, swinging the great blade he carried and separating the heads from the men crying out for help. The blows were swift, remorseless, and the sword returned to his shoulder with no regard for the blood coating the blade.

Something about him made Aiden's blood run cold, and he was not the only one who felt it. It was as though darkness loomed behind him, casting a shadow over everything he passed. Aiden knew, deep down, without seeing the man's face, that it was Tomas. He knew he needed to kill him. A voice whispering across his mind urged him to do so, and he assured it he would as soon as the opportunity presented itself.

"It's Tomas," he murmured.

"That makes sense. It explains why he made my skin crawl. Aeyren was a puppet all along." Eirian glanced at Aiden thoughtfully. "How did you figure it out, Aiden?"

Staring at the approaching figure, Aiden gave the slightest of shrugs. "I just know."

Reaching out a hand, Fayleen touched his arm. "It sounds like you and this Tomas have something personal."

"I killed his son."

"That would do it," Baenlin grunted, giving Aiden a sideways look.

Holding up a hand, Tessa shook her head and said, "We stop here."

Looking around, Celiaen realized it was the clearest space. Endaran troops ringed the area, many battling with Athnaralans. Others watched their queen, knowing something was going on. They knew their job was to protect her and provide the space she needed.

Guards fanned out in a semicircle behind Eirian, with Celiaen's companions among them. Standing with Eirian and Celiaen in the middle of the line, Galameyvin, Fayleen, Aiden, Baenlin, and Vartan kept their weapons in hand. Tessa stood in front, the wind catching her loose hair as she leaned on her staff. Getting closer, the situation did not bother Tomas, and the shadows following him grew darker with each step he took.

"Poor little bitch." He sneered at the people surrounding Eirian. "You can't do anything without someone holding your hand."

Eirian smiled sadly, her eyes filled with pity as she replied, "They want to be here. I never asked them to be. They chose it for themselves. How long have you been her puppet? How long has it been since you had a choice?"

Stare settling on Tessa, his sneer grew. "You're a poor substitute. Why do you bother?"

"I'm sure that's what all the ladies say to you." Arching a brow, Tessa shifted her weight, angling so she could see both Tomas and Eirian.

"Do you think anyone here respects you? You try to hide your insecurities behind sarcastic comments and strange creations when you are another pathetic little girl. At least she has the power. Yours is still asleep, daughter of chaos."

Drawing herself together, Tessa grinned. "Thank you."

Her response confused Baenlin. "Why are you thanking him?"

"Well, clearly someone has noticed me, otherwise why would the puppet bother to address me?" She continued to grin, watching Tomas's sneer become a glare. "Isn't that right, Tomas? Why bother trying to unsettle me if I'm not important?"

Returning his focus to Eirian, Tomas laughed. "Do you think this mottled group you surround yourself with will defeat her? You'll fall, and she will drive the world."

"Yes, drive it to ruin. She'll see it burn. Tell me, Tomas, why you?" Eirian asked.

"Ignorant child, you're truly clueless. I've always served her, as my father and his father before him. As my son should have. She rewards those who serve her faithfully."

Aiden kept his eyes on Tomas. "I killed your son because I caught him raping and mutilating a family traveling to a market. The apple doesn't fall far from the tree."

There was the hint of a smile, and Tomas chuckled. "I've been angry for so long, but I understand now. My son had to die, and it had to be by the hand of one with Altira blood. She will return him to me, and together, we will lead the armies of the faithful across the lands."

"You can't bring back the dead," Vartan said.

"Perhaps you cannot, but she is our god. There are no limits to what a god can do."

The princes held their breath, eyes on Eirian in concern. They recalled her distressed suggestion that she try to bring Faolan back, and it crossed their minds that Tomas might have been trying to distract her. It occurred to Aiden and Fayleen, their attention shifting from Tomas to Eirian. Tessa studied him thoughtfully, fingers drumming against the staff she grasped. She was biding her time, waiting for her cue.

Ignoring the looks directed her way, Eirian started laughing with one hand on her hip and the other covering her mouth. Confused, the guards behind her shared looks before looking at Aiden for a hint of what they should do. Her laughter startled Tomas, and the shadows lurking behind him shrunk back.

"Oh, Tomas. Tomas. Tomas." Shaking her head, Eirian wiped a tear of laughter from her cheek. "You poor, poor fool. If you think she can bring your son back from the dead, you'll discover you're sorely mistaken. Even if she could, it would never serve her purpose. She has manipulated you for her use. She will leave you as nothing but a hollowed-out husk of the man you could have been. She will leave you babbling mess standing in the middle of a ruined, burning world, and your death will be your reward."

Her words and laughter incensed Tomas, his sword swinging away from his shoulder as he snarled. "I will kill you, bitch! In front of your pets, and she will be pleased."

Prompted by the same instinct that had told him he would need to kill Tomas, Aiden blocked the swing aimed at Eirian. "I don't think so."

Eyes flicking to Tessa, Eirian nodded, and the finger drumming ceased. "No, General, I don't think you will kill me."

He followed her look, turning toward Tessa as she lifted her staff, and said mockingly, "Do you think your silly little tricks will work on me?"

Tessa raised her eyebrows, grinning. "Why yes, yes I do."

Lifting his eyes to hers over Tomas's blade, Aiden understood Tessa was providing him with an opportunity. All he needed was for Tomas to slip, and he could strike a killing blow. Despite his focus, Aiden saw Celiaen and Baenlin creeping forward. He could not let them take the kill from him. He needed to do it. For himself. For Eirian. For all the people harmed because his actions had sent a man over the edge to madness.

The slip of the blade reached his ear before his eyes picked it up. It was the sound of his opportunity. Tessa saw it the exact moment as he did, her head cocking to the side as she swung the staff toward Tomas. Forgetting the man who had killed his son, Tomas turned to defend himself.

"Did you think you could hurt me, bitch?"

"Maybe a little, but it's not me you should be blocking."

Her eyes met Aiden's again, his sword raised high. No one moved. Every set of eyes on Aiden's sword driving through Tomas's back. With his face to Tessa, she was the only one who witnessed his surprise. A shock that faded to understanding and acceptance. He smiled, and it made her freeze. Shadows flickered over him, danced across his form, and reflected in his eyes.

Taking a step back, her hand tightening on her staff, Tessa turned to Eirian and shook her head. She doubted the plan they had, doubted everything Eirian had told her, doubted the power she knew the other woman held. But seeing the peaceful look on Eirian's face, Tessa pushed her doubts away and reminded herself to trust. Together they could do this, but only if they had faith in each other.

The shadows continued to grow, flickering around Tomas. Pulling his sword free, Aiden stumbled back, and Fayleen caught his arm, pulling him toward her. Shooting her a look, he did not speak when he saw the fearful expression on her face. Tip of his blade resting on the ground, he let her keep her hand wrapped around his arm and covered it with his own to reassure her. Eirian muttered something, waving at them to move, and took a step to stand next to Tessa.

They shared a look, Eirian reaching out to put a hand on the staff below Tessa's, and a ripple of magic flared out. Most of them shielded their eyes, the flare of Eirian's power bright against the darkness. Tomas was on the ground when it faded, and the shadows collapsed in on themselves until they formed the figure that had confronted Eirian so many weeks prior. Blinking at the two women, Aiden frowned. There was something different about them he could not quite figure out.

"Fayleen."

"What?" she muttered, not taking her eyes from what was unfolding.

"Does something seem off to you?"

Looking at him, Fayleen frowned. "What are you on about?"

"Eirian and Tessa. I can't explain it, but something seems off. I don't know. Maybe it's the darkness messing with my mind," he said, doubt filling him.

Narrowing her eyes, Fayleen turned to stare at the two purples, her head tilting to the side slightly. "If you feel something isn't right, Captain, I'd be a fool to dismiss your concerns."

Laughing, the figure raised a hand and pointed at the two women standing side by side. Shadows dripped from it, joining the swirling mass covering the ground. They crept out, seeking the opportunity to latch on to anyone.

"You can summon as many allies as you wish, my sweet life," she said, and Eirian arched a brow. "But I'll still win."

"We'll see about that, won't we, love?" Eirian replied with a knowing smile.

TWENTY-EIGHT

Vartan thought he was watching the past replay before his eyes. Two brown-haired women standing together in front of a god who wanted nothing more than to destroy them all. They had planned something that would hopefully give Eirian the advantage. Glancing at the people watching, Vartan suspected they needed more room than they had.

Aiden's words sat uneasily on his mind, but no one else had said anything similar, so Vartan attempted to brush them off. Sheathing his sword, he clicked his tongue at the others to get a little of their attention. Once he had, Vartan nodded away from where the fight would occur.

"If we're to help, she doesn't need to worry about us being too close," he said to Celiaen, knowing the others would hear. "There's nothing we can do, except keep out of the way."

Fayleen knew he was right. "We can't do anything unless she asks, and we don't need to be this close for Ree to pull power from us."

"Celi." Grabbing Celiaen's arm, Galameyvin tugged him. "Come on, you need to be sensible about this. She cannot fight if she's worried about hurting us."

The watching crowd of soldiers was far enough away, thanks to a combination of respect and fear, that they were not of concern. Helping Galameyvin usher Celiaen back a distance, Baenlin watched Tessa. He did not know what she was doing with Eirian, but he hoped she was not making a mistake. She had surprised him, so he suspected she had other surprises to fall back on. He simply was not sure she had enough power to keep herself alive.

They had moved back far enough to have room to stop Celiaen if he tried to involve himself in the fight. But they were still close enough to catch snippets of what they said. They heard the tormenting comments thrown at Eirian by the mad god. Glancing over at the guards dedicated to their queen, Baenlin saw the looks of confused uselessness they wore and the tight grips they had on their weapons. It was easy to understand what they were feeling. There was nothing they could do to protect the woman they served.

Giving silent thanks for their decision to move away, Eirian maintained a carefully blank expression as she stared at the god. The whispers had fallen silent, and for the first time in a while, she felt at peace. Silence was a strange sensation, but she embraced it.

"I believe words are all you have. What do you think, Tessa?"

"She talks a lot," Tessa replied.

Snarling, she raised her hands to either side of her, shadows trailing from her fingers like water. "Words are a far mightier weapon than men realize. Words turn the mind, and where the mind twists, the body will follow."

Watching the shadows flicker, Eirian let go of the staff and stepped closer. Her power danced around her, cutting through the shadows and sending them scattering. To those watching, she shone, flickers of light rippling over her.

"You're right. Words have so much impact. Is that why you choose to remain hidden behind them and your shadows? You're powerful enough to have this form while still imprisoned. Why not show me your true self?"

"Name me, and I will." The shadows laughed. "Surely you remember my name, my sweet life. Tell it to me, and I'll let you see me as I am in your memories."

It felt like her heart would beat out of her chest, and Tessa fought not to let her sudden panic show. She did not understand why Eirian would have memories of the god. But knowing she could not surrender to her doubt, Tessa kept a tight grip on her emotions.

"Why should we use your name? You abandoned this world, left us to do as we wish. Recalling your name suggests a respect for the gods that we do not possess and you do not deserve."

Chasing over the ground, shadows circled Tessa's feet. "Your fear is showing. Would you find respect before I choked you to death with my power? It is far greater than any you possess in this form, little chaos."

"You harbor so much hate for Shianeni. What did you do to make the Great Mother love others more than you?" Ignoring Tessa, Eirian kept her focus on the god.

"The Great Mother indeed," she said mockingly. "But are you asking the right question?"

Pursing her lips, Eirian arched her brows. "Quite sure. Once, so long ago, you were magnificent. You were beautiful, but your bitter jealousy twisted and warped you until you became a mere shadow of your former glory."

"Ignorant child."

"And I am sorry. Sorry for what drove you to that. I'm sorry Shianeni set you aside for others. I'm sorry they disagreed with you and did not support you. But, more than that, I'm sorry you were so absolutely abandoned that all they left you with was the burning desire to destroy what replaced you in her affection." Speaking over her snarls, Eirian smiled sadly.

Tightening the grip on her staff when the shadows grew larger, Tessa knew she could do nothing but wait for Eirian to need her. Her part of the plan fought with the desire to run, and she clung to her promise of helping save the world. It was what Jaren would have wanted, and she had no intention of disappointing his memory.

"I hope you know what you're doing, Eirian."

Glancing over her shoulder, Eirian continued to smile. "Have a little faith, Tessa. Just believe in me."

Hands outstretched, Eirian took another step. She continued to glow, a shimmer in the air that chased the growing shadows back. Lightning cut through them, the energy shattering the fog. Further back, where they stood watching and waiting, Vartan gasped. He recalled his suspicions about Shianeni. At that moment, he expected a gray mist to come rolling in across the land to overwhelm the shadows.

Nothing happened except that Eirian seemed brighter as she stood against the shadows that circled her. To the side, he heard Celiaen arguing with Galameyvin, expressing his desperation to stand by the side of the woman he loved. In the back of his mind, Vartan sensed Neriwyn panicking as he worked his way through battlefields to reach them. Refusing to cower before the battle of light and shadows, Tessa stood with her staff in front of her.

"How?" the darkness asked.

Cocking her head to the side, Eirian smiled. She was beginning to grasp the mess of memories leaking through the wall in her mind. It was more than simply Shianeni's past.

"I am the light in the dark, the light to guide my people through the mist and the storms. I am the fire to warm them when winter is bleak, and it feels like the day won't come again."

"Oh, sweet life, my darling."

"I am the earth. I nurture and give life. I am the water that feeds and washes the blood away. I am the air they breathe, the wind that blows across the land spreading seeds to new homes, and I am the storm."

Lifting her hands higher, Eirian felt the lightning surround her, the light she had found flickering in response against the shadows trying to get past.

Hissing, the god withdrew. "Everything was hidden when Shianeni passed over. How could you know? You haven't died. The memories are not yet yours."

"Yes, everything was hidden. But the thing is, once you know there's something hidden, it becomes easier to search for. Things slip through the cracks in the wall."

Power slipped through her fingers, dancing on strings of life. It was glorious, a beauty Eirian could control. The wall was crumbling, and she remembered drifting among the stars.

"Knowing it's there, you search for the edges of the veil drawn over the world and to grasp the memories slipping through your fingers. All it takes is a few bits of information, half dismissed rumors and thoughts, and that persistent suspicion something is waiting out of sight in the corner of your eye."

"You don't have the power to undo it yet, or you would have done so."

Nodding, Eirian admitted, "Perhaps you're right. However, let me tell you a story about a god who was special. A god so close to her queen that they had once been one. She felt everything so strongly. That was her power. So, she helped her queen and their fellows create creatures to worship them. She had such high hopes for these creatures, and she imbued her capacity for glorious feelings into them."

The mad god did not move as Eirian spoke. Mixed among the shadows and light, shapes twisted, fragments of memory playing out.

"Except she didn't realize she had great darkness within her, dark feelings that could twist and kill. Not until their creations showed signs, fed by her jealousy of their attention and the games her selfish queen played. The perfect little worshippers that they had hoped to make were not so perfect."

"It was not my intention." The words were barely a whisper, but Eirian heard them.

"No, it was not. You never intended for it. How could you when you had never had a reason to see your darkness? War and death were the dark ones. But that did not stop them from blaming you, from turning Shianeni against you."

"Their games can never be trusted!"

"They turned on you, and, in your grief and your anger, you turned on the unsuspecting creatures you helped create. You hid in the shadows, working and weaving, turning them against the other gods, but by the time they realized the truth, the games had gone too far. You and they had become a danger to her mortal toys, and so the great queen, the source of life, she hid them away. Then Shianeni drew her power across the world to make it appear the gods had left."

Listening to the story Eirian was telling, Tessa could not believe what she was hearing. It seemed too far-fetched to be true.

"Eirian, what are you saying?"

Glancing over her shoulder, Eirian shook her head. "Hush, Tessa, and listen."

"I am listening, and you sound crazy."

"Shianeni found the descendants of the first four mortal creatures you created in your image, the basis on which they built all the rest. Those four were special, weren't they? They were the ones you had all put parts of your power into, the ones who carried a drop of your blood. Your heirs. A human, two elves, and one duine."

Eirian shifted slightly, glancing back to locate Vartan among the watching crowd. Grief ripped through her. The memory of what they had done to him played out like a nightmare. She knew he did not remember, and she swore to fix it with her dying breath.

"The duine she changed. Shianeni took his place and throne, keeping him at her feet and in her bed. She continued to weave her power over Tir and through the minds of those living. With his help and his unwavering devotion to both her and her consort, the god of war."

"She blamed everything on me, but it was her fault! Everything was her fault! She grew bored, with us, with traveling the stars, bored with eternity. She wanted more! The darkness wasn't just in me. It was in her, just as it is in you. But no, she claimed it was I who corrupted her precious pets." There was more fury in her voice than Eirian expected, the shadows flaring to beat at the shield of light. "They weren't the first! We made others before elves, and humans, and daoine. She locked them away as well."

Eirian knew where the others had been locked away. She sensed the veil separating them from the rest of Tir. Shianeni had spun it from a mixture of her power and Gebael's, but she held the key to the prison.

"I am not my mother. The people of this world, of Tir, the people you helped create, they aren't to blame. Can you not find some consolation in the fact she's gone?"

Unable to resist asking, Tessa stared at the back of Eirian's head in shock. "Are you implying your mother was the queen of the gods?"

The shadowy god chuckled. "Gone? Are you sure about that? Her power exists, her memories. It's all in you, and her voice guides your hands. Even without being reborn, you dance the same steps that she did."

"Stop this war, and we can find out together how much influence over me she has. You can heal, Annawyn. You don't have to be this creature spreading madness to those she wrongfully blames for the mistakes of another." Extending her hand, Eirian waited patiently. "We can deal with this together. We can start over and return to the stars, seeking a fresh beginning far away from the memories of what happened."

Hearing her name spoken aloud for the first time by Eirian, Annawyn faltered. Eirian's words carried a sweetness she was unfamiliar with, a genuine desire to help that reminded her of what life had been like. It reminded her of the honey-laced way Shianeni had always spoken, words coated with poison that would twist and manipulate. Filled with fury, Annawyn released her power on the two women who dared stand in opposition.

Sensing the attack coming, Eirian spun around and leaped at Tessa to protect her. Cocooned in magic while shadows swirled around them, trying to find a crack, Tessa stared at Eirian in apprehension. Things barely made sense, but the gleam of power in Eirian's gaze offered some reassurance.

"Will it work?" Tessa asked softly, not fighting the way Eirian sheltered her.

Biting her lip, Eirian turned to peer out past the shimmer of her magic and the shadows where she could barely make out her friends watching them. She could not make out their faces, but she knew it terrified them. She saw the way Baenlin and Vartan struggled with Celiaen. She sensed his desperation over the bond. They were safe beyond her wards, protected from Annawyn.

Letting her power go, she felt the world around her one last time and let it replenish her desire to fight back. It was a reminder of why she was fighting and what was at risk if she failed. They had a narrow window to put their plan in motion, and she nodded once before turning to Tessa. There was determination written in every line on her face.

"It has to. I can't see how else I'm going to force Annawyn to strike me. I'm sorry, Tessa, so sorry to put you in this position. One day you'll understand that you're the only person who could have helped me."

Snorting, Tessa rolled her eyes, grumbling, "Don't get me killed, and you won't owe me anything more than you already agreed to. I just wish you had told someone else about this plan. They won't understand what is happening."

"You know I couldn't risk them knowing everything. Besides, how many people know about your little trick with the faces?" Eirian replied.

"Good point."

"Exactly. Now, I'm ready if you are."

Preparing, Tessa lifted a hand between them and said, "You better not fuck this up."

The surrounding magic intensified before Eirian stepped back from Tessa and turned to Annawyn. Gripped tightly in Tessa's hands was a knife that Fayleen had gifted her friend. She was sure the quaternary knots engraved into the hilt would leave marks on her skin long after the fight ended. Pulling the hood over her head, Tessa left her staff on the ground behind Eirian and waited for her chance to move.

Eyes locked on Eirian's back, Tessa watched her crouch and bury a hand in the dirt at her feet. Magic flared out, tendrils of vines shooting out of the ground to wrap around Annawyn, the god forced to battle them off as bright-yellow flowers surrounded her. Screams of rage left her mouth, and Eirian reached her free hand forward, twisting it to cause the vines to tighten. It was a temporary distraction.

"Go." The word was barely audible, but Tessa picked it up.

Keeping the knife tucked in close to her side, she crept slowly along the edge of the shadows swarming around Eirian and Annawyn. Swallowing back a pang of fear, she looked back at the group behind them. They watched the battle unfolding, Celiaen pinned between others to prevent him from rushing to Eirian's side. She wanted to pretend they were there for her, that just once, she would save everyone. A glance at the knife in her hand reminded her she was helping to do exactly that. Returning her focus to her task, she ground her teeth.

"What is Tessa doing?" Fayleen muttered, not expecting an answer. "She's going to get herself killed."

Shaking his head, Aiden could not shake the feeling something was not quite right when he looked at the two women. The voice told him he was right, and it coaxed him to focus on Tessa instead of Eirian.

"I don't know. She's not stupid, and Eirian wouldn't let her do something so foolish."

Eyes as blue as a summer sky turned his way before turning back to the battle. Her hands tightened on her staff, fear evident as Fayleen battled the desire to protect.

"Look at Ree! She's busy fighting. She might not know what Tessa is doing."

Knowing Fayleen had a point, Aiden watched shadows shred through the battling vines and flowers surrounding the god. Occasionally rippling light flashed through the shadows like lightning. They were the visible flashes of Eirian's power as she shielded herself from attack and did her best to fight back. Neither of them moved.

The only person moving was Tessa, her purposeful strides sidestepping the shadows on her way toward her target. Catching the sun, the knife gleamed in her grasp, and the watching warriors exchanged worried looks. It was clear what her intention was, and none of them expected it to lead to anything but her death. There was nothing they could do, the prickle of magic warning them of Tessa's shield that kept the battle from spilling over.

"We have to stop her!" Pleading with Aiden, Fayleen was not sure what they could do.

Helping hold Celiaen back, Baenlin echoed her sentiments. "Stupid girl is going to get herself killed. Surely one of you with a bow in their hand is a decent enough archer to give her a warning shot."

Hands on his bow, Fox stepped forward and asked, "Cap'n? Do you want me?"

Torn, Aiden looked between Eirian and Tessa. The voice told him they needed to keep out of the battle. He did not want to heed it, but the impulse was strong.

"No. I can't say what it is, but something is happening that we can't see. If we tried to stop Tessa…"

Shifting the knife in her grip, Tessa aligned herself behind Annawyn and took a deep breath before she started. She kept her steps as soft and steady as she could, careful not to make any sudden movements that would distract the god from her battle. The sheer amount of power surrounding the two fighting made every hair on her body stand on end. Tessa was glad she had pulled her hood back over her head, or she suspected her hair would float in the air. It was a storm of magic, lightning of power darting between them.

Almost in position, Tessa prepared to strike at the god with the knife. She knew this was her moment to make sure their plan went perfectly. Annawyn felt the movement and turned, catching her wrist, nails digging into the leather armor protecting the limb. Then, wrenching the knife from her grip, she drove it into the woman's stomach, feeling more resistance than she expected.

"Stupid girl, did you think you could hurt me?"

Witnessing the god stop Tessa, Baenlin saw the flash of the knife and shouted. Letting go of Celiaen, he ran toward them, screaming Tessa's name as he moved. Behind him, Fayleen followed, her power prepared to shield Baenlin as best as she could. With the two of them breaking the line, the others started forward, Celiaen determined to reach Eirian. They almost made it to the trio when they hit the wall.

There was nothing they could do as they watched Tessa drop to her knees with Annawyn standing over her. Eirian remained still, watching while the storm of magic continued. She knew what was happening, and power kept her frozen. It was the plan they had devised in the quiet of Tessa's tent. An exchange so perfectly executed that no one realized what they were doing.

Everything stopped. The magic that had been swirling between Eirian and Annawyn vanished the moment Tessa's knees hit the ground. Instead, power rippled and clicked into place, and Aiden understood why he had sensed something strange about Eirian and Tessa. It was not Tessa at Annawyn's feet. The woman standing by and watching was not Eirian. Somehow, they had swapped places.

Lifting her head to smile at Annawyn, Eirian ignored the warm blood coating her fingers. "Yes, I did."

"How?"

It startled Annawyn to see Eirian at her feet, blood running from the wound she had inflicted. A blow intended to kill. She grasped what was unfolding as she felt the pull of her chains.

"We always have tricks up our sleeves," Tessa answered, turning to pick up her staff from the ground behind her where Eirian had left it.

She could not bear to look at the woman she knew was about to die in front of her. Nor could she look at the men and women struggling against the shield, desperate to reach them. If she did, Tessa knew her resolve would shatter. Panic twisted her gut, the desire to vomit leaving a bitter taste at the back of her throat.

Everything felt strange, and Eirian struggled to keep her focus, her magic fighting against what was happening to her. There was a touch of coldness to the air, suggesting Gebael was close. She hoped her death would satisfy him.

"With our blood, Annawyn, I bind you. The blood on your hands will be your prison, and it will never fade so long as the earth remembers."

Annawyn screamed, long and loud, the shadows she surrounded herself with spread across the battlefields. Waiting patiently, Eirian tried not to notice how hard it was to breathe or how much it hurt. She sensed Celiaen's desperation, the shield of magic that Tessa had thrown up keeping him from her. He could not be close, not in these last moments.

When the sound coming from the god faded, she was a translucent shadow of herself as the chains of magic that bound her body tightened. As they drew closed, they pulled her power and form back to her prison. Exactly as had been intended. Eirian was thankful for it and knew her people would be safe.

"You're just like her!" Annawyn snarled. "She would have sacrificed another, just as she did a thousand times before. Just as you have."

It was difficult to speak, but Eirian knew she had one last thing she needed to do. "By our blood and our power, I release the veil and undo what Shianeni did to Tir."

She did not know if it was because her death was so close, but Eirian could see it. The veil shimmered like gossamer silk across the earth, drops of power woven into it like dew on the tip of a blade of grass. Using the last bit of her control, she reached out and drew it into her. Tugging at the strands of power, she felt it fill her like a deep breath and lifted her eyes to stare at the god as she faded away.

It gave Eirian enough strength to relish in the earth's beat waiting beneath her, the beating of the hearts that still lived. There was a breeze, cool air caressing her face as though to comfort her, but she knew death was coming for her. Gebael was a silent shadow slipping through the lines, his power a blanket offering comfort as her heart paused.

Satisfied that the plan had worked, Eirian smiled faintly at Tessa. Taking a step toward her, Tessa was not sure if she should drop the wards that she held around them. It seemed like the air shifted beside Eirian, a flicker of movement that her magic picked up like a disturbance in the particles.

"Eirian? Ree, hold on, help is coming. We can heal this."

"Thank you, Tessa. Tell them I love them."

A peaceful look appeared on Eirian's face before she slumped down on the ground, flowers spreading out like wildfire. Dropping her magic, Tessa rushed forward in a panic. She had made a mistake in keeping the wall up, and it was going to be too late to save Eirian.

"No! No, no, Eirian, please! Don't you dare die now!"

TWENTY-NINE

M agic hit Tessa like a wave of light, blinding her. She felt hands grab and turn her against their owner. Cold plate armor bit into her cheek as Baenlin did his best to shield them both. A voice screamed Eirian's name, desperate and filled with anguish, and she knew it was Celiaen. Her heart broke for him as she hoped he would survive the breaking of the bond that had linked him to Eirian.

Even with her eyes shut and face pressed to Baenlin's chest, Tessa knew when the light faded. Magic lingered everywhere, echoes of Eirian coating them and the ground. Traces fueling the flowers growing at their feet, joyful colored faces turned to the sky. Everything felt alive with energy. Her energy. A rich floral perfume blanketed them, so thick it made Tessa gag worse than the smoke from the funeral pyres had.

"You can let me go now, Archmage," she grumbled, struggling against his grip. "I don't think any of us are at risk of going blind."

Baenlin did not fight to keep her there, his eyes wide while he looked at where Eirian had been. Her body had vanished, no trace of it remaining except dandelions coated with blood. They were everywhere, mixed in with the other flowers.

"By the powers…"

Tessa shook her head. "She was the powers. You don't know the full extent of it."

Vartan was the only one who had closed the distance, and he stood in the middle of a spreading carpet of flowers, blood-soaked dandelions covering his feet. His face was pale, like the rich color of it had drained away. Turning in a circle, Vartan struggled with the memories that were flooding back to him with every passing moment. The connection between him and Neriwyn shattered, and he felt the presence vanish from his mind.

Horn blasts rose through the air, shouting louder than they had heard before. The haunting scream of a bird came from far above them, her eagle eyes following the spread of the flowers as they raced across the earth. Saoirse watched as the fight drained out of the Athnaralan army, the madness no longer pushing them to throw themselves at their enemy. Instead, they fell to their knees, dropping weapons in surrender while begging for mercy. Only the most battle driven continued to fight on, unwilling to admit the war had ended.

"What has she done…" Vartan trembled, a hand covering his mouth as he moaned, "Oh, Eirian, what have you done to us?"

Approaching Tessa, Aiden nodded to her. Only his iron will prevented him from wrapping his hands around her throat to demand an explanation of what had happened. It kept his grief at bay. He could not break in front of his men when they needed him to be a display of strength.

"How did you do it?"

"It was her idea. Eirian thought if the mad one was so focused on who she thought was her, she could trick her into a killing blow. I agreed to help spin an illusion that made her think I was Eirian and she was me. We'd done it before, years ago. She helped Jaren get me out of Riane before my father had me killed. Though that time she wore my mother's appearance."

Baenlin remembered Tessa's demonstration when he discovered her presence in his army. She had told him it was the face only, but what she had done with Eirian proved otherwise. Between that and the revelation she could shift the elements, Baenlin realized Tessa was far more powerful than any of them had given her credit for. He knew she would be a grand mage to fear, which made him more determined to become the one she answered to.

"Even with Eirian's help, tricking a god would have been an arduous task," Baenlin commented.

Shaking her head, Tessa felt exhaustion creeping in and said, "No, it wasn't easy to keep it up, but I did. I did exactly what she asked of me. It had to be her blood, and it had to be Annawyn's hand. It was difficult. We were inside each other's minds and the things in…"

"I knew something was strange about the two of you!" Aiden growled.

He turned to stare at Vartan, pacing in circles among the flowers. Placing a hand on Tessa's shoulder, Baenlin also stared.

"What do you think is going on with him?"

"I don't know." Tessa looked at Celiaen cradled in Galameyvin's arms while Fayleen hovered beside them and asked, "What about him?"

"Well, at least he's not dead. I don't fancy having that conversation with my sister. Galameyvin is there. He'll help Celiaen."

Giving Baenlin a horrified look, Aiden arched his brows. "He's your nephew, and he just lost the woman he loved… a woman that many of us loved!"

Rolling her eyes, Tessa forced her feelings aside and stepped away from Baenlin, turning to face him. Anxiety was tugging at her mind. The urge to curl up in a ball and cry was strong. She refused to surrender to it. It could wait until after they claimed control over the day.

"Archmage, I suggest you find the other commanders and take control of the armies. The battle appears over, but we don't need Paienven taking advantage of the situation."

"Are you giving me orders, Tessa?" His eyes narrowed at her.

"Yes. Do you feel like arguing with me right now? Especially since you know I'm right about the King of Ensaycal."

Huffing, he sneered. "Fine. But only because you make a valid point."

Watching Baenlin turn on his heel and storm off through the dead, Aiden looked at the stunned faces of his men. He knew exactly how each of them was feeling.

"Let me talk to the princeling. I know what to say."

"Captain." Tessa stopped him before he moved toward the princes. "She wanted me to tell you she loved you. All of you."

She could not bring herself to tell him what else she knew. The thoughts that had been on Eirian's mind before the end were something Tessa would take to her own grave.

"I know," Aiden muttered, walking toward the trio of friends.

Fayleen looked at him, her eyes rimmed with tears. "Aiden, I don't think you should be here."

Ignoring her, he crouched in front of Celiaen. The confused and devastated look he wore matched how Aiden felt. He wanted to gather Celiaen in his arms and assure him it would be fine, but he could not.

"I need you to pull yourself together right now."

"How dare you speak to me! You were supposed to protect her!" Celiaen snarled, hands reaching for his weapons. "You failed her! I should kill you."

"Celiaen, focus and look inside yourself. What do you feel? Because it doesn't feel like she's dead to me."

Frowning, Galameyvin shook his head, muttering, "I don't think that's wise to suggest."

"You as well. Look deep inside. You know exactly what I'm talking about. That spot where she lingered, that's still there."

Cocking his head, Aiden's eyes flicked between them thoughtfully. Eirian might not have said anything to him, but he had felt it for a long time. The thread between them remained intact. Closing his eyes, Celiaen reached for the bond and discovered Aiden was right. It was still there, though he could not feel Eirian anymore. The bond remained.

"But we saw her stabbed. We saw her die. I felt her die!"

"So did I," Aiden replied. "I can't explain it, but somehow, she's still with us."

Not sure if she should believe them, Fayleen pursed her lips. "Alright, if she's still alive, then where is she? How do we find her?"

"You don't," Tessa informed them, leaning heavily on her staff.

"What do you mean, we don't?" Galameyvin demanded.

Her eyes turned to the sky, and she scowled. Dark clouds had formed the threat of a storm that had not existed earlier. Tessa wondered if they were because of Eirian.

"You don't find her. Eirian was not half duine. Her mother was never one of the daoine. If she is alive, you may not like what she is. I saw inside her mind toward the end and the memories, the power…"

Frowning, Aiden glanced at Vartan and took in how he was sitting on the ground with his head in his hands. "I'll bite. What is she?"

"Her mother was the queen of the gods. The god who created everything. I mean, I didn't take in everything, but from what I understood, Shianeni was a manipulative bitch who treated everyone and everything as playthings," Tessa explained.

"A god?" Fayleen spluttered.

"Now, I don't know a lot about the gods. None of us does, but I can't imagine that one little knife in the gut would be enough to kill one. There is always the chance a half-god could survive it." Shrugging, Tessa looked at Vartan. "However, I suspect he might have some answers for us."

"He doesn't strike me as being in the most helpful state right now," Galameyvin commented, screwing up his nose.

Rubbing his face to get rid of the tears, Celiaen glared at Vartan. "I need answers, and if he has them, he will give them."

Giving him a hand to stand, Aiden nodded to Celiaen. "She's out there. Even if we can't find her right now, she's not dead, and there is hope."

"You're right." He nodded back, ignoring the concerned looks shared between Fayleen and Galameyvin. "I have years in which to locate her. I'll find her."

Fayleen glanced at the flowers, murmuring, "What if she isn't alive? What if she redirected your bonds and what you three think you can feel isn't her?"

Eyes narrowing, Celiaen turned first to Aiden before shifting to stare at Galameyvin. His grief remained, but it was tinged with curiousness and a touch of fury. There was a hint of guilt on their faces, making him realize that the other two men knew something he did not.

"That's a point. How is it you both can sense Ree?"

"Eirian unintentionally bound them to her, not quite the same as you, but enough that she could feel it. It's not relevant right now. You can thump it out of each other some other time," Fayleen explained and lifted her staff to give each man a quick whack to the arm, intended to scold them.

Falling silent, they followed Tessa over to Vartan. She dawdled, leaning on her staff for support. It was clear she was exhausted, but she had enough strength left to hold herself together, enough to ask questions in the middle of the chaos. All around, Athnaralans were withdrawing in surrender while the allies watched in a mixture of confusion and suspicion. Those in command were hurrying to take Athnaralan officers into custody. The fight had left them, and no one was going to let the opportunity pass by.

News of Eirian's death traveled almost faster than the continuing spread of flowers, and soldiers surrounded the area. None of them dared come close. Countless sets of eyes watched the royal guards and the mages. It provided the guards with something to focus on, and they formed a circle that faced outwards, hands on their weapons.

Lifting his face to regard the three men and two women staring at him, Vartan took a deep breath before saying, "I know what you want, and I can't give it to you. I don't know."

"You're taking this very hard," Tessa observed.

His eyes settled on her. "You do not know what it feels like for all of us right now. Eirian filled me with memories of things taken by the woman I thought I loved. Things only some of my people will remember. Eirian has changed the world, and I don't know how to explain it to you."

Galameyvin asked, "Changed it for the better?"

"No," he replied bitterly. "Not for the better. Things will change. I cannot say how long it will take, but the gods banished others, and Eirian may have freed them. They are things we cannot fight."

Dread filled Tessa, and she looked at the sky, taking in all the birds circling overhead. His words confirmed the feeling at the edge of her mind. A strange shift in the balance of everything. Particles were changing, her magic allowing her to witness it.

"What sort of things?"

"The sort of things that make you bar your windows and doors at night. The sort of things you fear will steal into your homes and eat your children. Because they will. We called them the Unseelie."

Speaking slowly, Vartan could not remember the last time he had uttered that name. It was a word he had forgotten for so long that it surprised him he could recall it. They were the first people of the gods, true immortals no blade could harm. His mind scolded him, reminding Vartan that there had been one with the ability to kill them. She had been his sister. A duine created by the god of death for one purpose.

Suspecting she was the one most familiar with old stories told by parents to scare their children into behaving, Fayleen ran a hand over her hair. They were tales she had shared with Eirian and the others, learning that most were not familiar with them.

"The monsters in the dark that will bite your ankles if you're naughty and sour the milk if you displease them."

"What are you on about, Fayleen?" Celiaen asked.

"I've told you the stories before, remember? Ma used to tell them when she put us to bed. They were often vague, but they were rarely pleasant. Stories about creatures with wings that would drink your blood. Others that would sit on your chest and crush you to death."

Galameyvin rubbed his face and said, "I do vaguely remember them."

"I used to wonder where they came from, even more so after they sent me to Riane. Ree would laugh because I'd get sudden urges to search through books for references."

Talking about it helped Fayleen hide from her feelings, the anger she felt toward Eirian, the grief over her death, and the confusion over whether she was dead at all. Looking at the surrounding people, she took in the flickers of emotion on their faces. Each of them was holding themselves in check.

The only one showing obvious signs of distress was Celiaen. He had never been the best at hiding his feelings for Eirian. Fayleen suspected his mind was replaying how it felt to see and feel his mate die, even if the bond had not shattered. She promised herself that she would be strong for her friends, and she intended to keep that promise no matter what. She could grieve in her own time, but until then, she had to keep herself intact.

"Yes, something like that," Vartan said and blinked at her. "It's amazing what they overlook. I can't imagine Shianeni thought to consider children's stories when she was hiding the truth."

"People in power overlook a lot of things about us common folk," she replied.

Growing serious, Vartan reached out to grab Tessa's arm. "You'll be the grand mage. You must lead these people through a great deal of change. But you cannot count on Telmia for help because there will be war among my people. I am the rightful king."

"If you're the rightful king, what about Neriwyn?" Galameyvin asked in confusion.

"Neriwyn is not a duine. Salt and iron will help you against the first people, though it will not kill them. It will only hurt them. Not all of them are Unseelie. I don't know if Eirian told you, but there are more lands out there, more people. Everyone has forgotten everyone else."

Gasps of surprise came from the others, but Tessa inclined her head. "She told me. I don't suppose you'd be interested in finding sanctuary in Riane? Our doors will be open to any who would."

She did not mention her mysterious assistant. Part of her hoped he would be interested in the offer and come to Riane with her.

"There may be one or two. We won't stay the night because we must return home. Already chaos is erupting there, and I must reclaim my throne." His hand dropped, and Vartan shook his head. "Salt and iron."

"Is Eirian alive?" Celiaen demanded.

"I told you, I don't know. But, if she is, she is the only one who can fix what she has done. Annawyn was not the only god still walking among us. Shianeni imprisoned the lesser gods, but not the other two. They've been pulling our strings the whole time."

Celiaen snarled. "How can I find her?"

Vartan arched his brows at Celiaen and said, "You're her mate. You figure it out. Right now, I need to contain the disaster she has unleashed upon my people."

He pushed past, but stopped to look at each of them. There was a rage in his magic, and flickers of hate appeared on his face.

"Perhaps you should forget she might be alive and focus on your people. All of you are responsible for the lives of others, so look to the living and protect them."

Letting him go, they stared at each other, and Tessa was the first to speak. "I'm struggling, and there's little else I can do here. Others will interrogate us, and I suggest we agree to let people think Eirian is dead. Who is going to believe the word of three men known to love her claiming she lives when so many saw her vanish?"

"You want us to say she is dead? Do you believe it?" Galameyvin asked.

Sucking in her cheeks, Tessa took a deep breath and tried to sort through the fragments of thought lingering in her mind. She could not explain it, and she had no intention of trying.

"No, I don't. Someone died to that knife blow, but it was not Eirian. However, if we are all wrong because we're so desperately hoping…"

"You're concerned about how people will react if they believe she is still alive."

Aiden shifted, a hand going to the hilt of his sword. "If people think she's still alive, it will make things harder for Everett. How can he take the throne if half his army believes their queen lives on? Better they think she is dead and accept him as king. Endara does not need a civil war."

Rubbing her face, Fayleen offered Celiaen and Galameyvin an apologetic look before bowing respectfully to Tessa. Face blanching, Tessa knew what she would ask and desperately wished she could deny the request.

"I request your blessing to remain in Endara, Grand Mage. I promised my sister I'd help her family, that I would protect them, and I intend to remain here to do just that."

"Of course." Tessa knew what Eirian had done, but she dared not say it. "You can be my official ambassador to Endara. I suspect whatever Lord Vartan was warning of will force the mages to leave Riane a lot more."

Eyes downcast, Celiaen glanced at Galameyvin and said, "I need to find my mother and reassure her. Besides, it's time I informed my king that I will not be returning to Ensaycal."

Slinging an arm around his shoulders, Galameyvin nodded. "And afterward, I have several bottles of good Telmian wine that need to be drunk."

Aiden muttered, "I thought we drank them all last night?"

"No. I kept the best just in case we survived."

"There is just one more thing," Tessa said.

Her words stopped them before they could start picking their way back over the battlefield. Eyes settling on her, they waited to hear what else she had to say.

"Her last words were to ask me to tell you she loved all of you. You were on her mind constantly, her driving force. Everything she did was to save you. Everybody else was extra."

Celiaen's eyes dropped before he returned them to her, murmuring, "Thank you, Tessa."

Watching them walk away with Tara and the other elves surrounding them quickly, Aiden scowled. He knew what he needed to do, but the prospect of facing the Endaran nobles and officers was daunting. There would be accusations of failure thrown at him and his men.

"I should find my brother. He needs to be told the truth of what happened here and not some diluted and twisted version that has been through a hundred mouths before it reached him."

"I'll come with you," Fayleen said.

He looked at her, hair gleaming gold in the sunlight and blue eyes suggesting she would not tolerate any arguments. There was blood on her face, reminding him of what she could do. Aiden considered arguing anyway, but remembering the conversation between the three of them, he respected Eirian's request.

"As you wish."

Shrugging, Tessa rolled her eyes to look up at the sky and grumbled, "That's quite alright. I think I should make it somewhere on my own. I'm not exhausted in the slightest from helping Eirian fight a god."

"I had no intention of abandoning you." Her attitude prompted a smile, and Aiden called out to Merle. "Help this silly woman back to her tent, would you? Since you seem so fond of her."

Offering Aiden her arm, Fayleen kept her other hand on her staff. She told herself it was just in case they needed it. It had nothing to do with the weariness seeping through her bones as the rush of battle left her.

"I don't know about you, but this feels somewhat..."

"Anticlimactic," he said.

"Yes. Everyone came for a great battle, and I know it was happening all around us. So many people have died today, and I just... I don't know. I suppose

I expected it to take more to end it than Eirian being stabbed by a god."

"I know what you mean."

"She told me it had to end this way, but I kept hoping."

Aiden sighed. "We all did."

As they walked with his men surrounding them and Merle helping Tessa, Aiden looked at the watching lines of soldiers. None of them dared approach the site where Eirian had fought. He doubted they felt the same way about the battle, and he wondered if they would have felt the same if they had been busy fighting for their lives, sword to sword, while Eirian had been fighting with magic. If they had not been standing there as witnesses.

Each of the surrounding men had sworn their lives to protect Eirian, and Aiden promised them silently that he would take the time to remind them they had not failed in their duty. Even though they would face that accusation for the rest of their lives. They had gotten Eirian where she needed to be. Almost as if he sensed Aiden had looked at him, Fionn tossed a wry smile over his shoulder.

"So, Captain, do we have to call you lord now? You are the new Earl of Tamantal."

"Our queen just died," Zack grumbled. "Do you think now is the time to be asking questions like that?"

Smacking him in the arm, Lyle said, "I think the question is if we're supposed to be protecting the Captain now. He might cop some slack over what happened and all."

Fayleen squeezed Aiden's arm. "They'll cope better if they have a job to do. We all will."

"I know," Aiden replied quietly.

It would be a long time before they felt like themselves again. Fayleen hoped they could forge something out of what Eirian had left behind.

"You know, Ree always leaves a big mess for others to clean up. This was no exception."

Feeling a flicker of affection toward her that took him by surprise, Aiden agreed. "Well, this is one mess I suspect will take a long time to clean up."

"Don't worry, Aiden, you've got an amazing mage to give you a hand."

"I have a feeling you're going to be good for Endara."

Remembering Everett's offer the day the army from Riane had arrived in Kelsby, Fayleen was glad she had not taken him seriously. Lifting her gaze to the growing storm clouds, she smiled faintly.

"Maybe I will be. I'm a crafter after all, and there is a lot that we could build out of this."

THIRTY

Paienven stood under the awning with Darragh and Sannaeh. Officers dragged prisoners before him, Athnaralan commanders bound in chains and stripped of their weapons. He wore a delighted smirk, the news of Eirian's death having reached him quickly. With each defeated human brought before him, Paienven felt a growing triumph. He was on top again, the mighty king that no one would dare stand against.

All he needed was to make an example of King Aeyren in front of the weak man assuming the Endaran throne and remind his wayward son of who he answered to. Then he could focus on Riane and the upstart girl who thought herself the future grand mage. She would learn that not even the high council could stand against him.

Pursing her lips, Sannaeh watched out of the corner of her eye. She felt concerned by the delight on his face and the glee he exhibited over the news regarding Eirian. Hearing that Celiaen still lived had barely received a quarter of the response. Watching the carpet of flowers roll past, Sannaeh had waited for Baenlin, but he had not appeared. Every time Paienven's excitement grew as he commanded another execution, her blood ran cold.

Sannaeh worried his ambition was driving Paienven to turn against those who should be their allies. All she could do was try to guide him, to soften the impact of his desire for supremacy. To protect her son. Already she sensed the devotion Darragh held for Paienven wavering. He had given up trying to stop the executions when Paienven had threatened him with his own. Doubts had begun in his mind weeks before, and Sannaeh suspected something had changed his expectations after meeting Eirian.

Trying her best not to think of the dead queen and the impact it would have on Celiaen, Sannaeh kept her mouth in a thin line. She watched another Athnaralan dragged before Paienven. Word had not come of Aeyren's location, and she hoped to the powers that he had either escaped or the Endarans had him.

No one was sure what was happening with the Telmian forces, but messengers had reported they were busy packing their camp. That news had pleased Paienven, but Sannaeh could not help but wonder what had the daoine running from the battle. It made her nervous. She had never pegged Neriwyn as a man to flee before the dust had settled, and they had expected him to remain to help the Endarans.

Spotting Tynan and Tara to the side, Sannaeh cleared her throat softly. "Please excuse me, Your Majesty. Something requires my attention."

He barely glanced at her, replying, "Tell your brother his reds did good work today."

"Of course."

She did not bother to correct his assumption and met Darragh's gaze behind his back. Slipping through the crowd of soldiers, Tara and Tynan waited for her to join them, each offering a quick bow. Tara carefully looked around to observe their surroundings, waving at Tynan. He scowled, arms crossed. The determination in his stare reminded Sannaeh of why he had replaced Galameyvin when Celiaen had let his jealousy get the better of him.

"He's safe," Tara said. "Well, he's as good as we could expect, given the circumstances. He's so good he's packing."

"Packing?" Arching a brow, Sannaeh did not let her dread show.

Coughing nervously, Tynan replied, "As is Prince Galameyvin. Neither of them has any intention of returning to Ensaycal. Or Riane."

"Are they running away to Telmia?"

"No. They're going on a hunt."

Tara huffed. "Tynan."

"What, Tara? Am I supposed to lie to her?" He dropped his arms, hands spread. "She's his mother! Besides, we know Celi has no intention of sticking to the whole 'she's dead' story. He's too fucking stubborn."

There was only one woman that could refer to, and Sannaeh pursed her lips. "She's not dead? All the reports... people witnessed her fall even if there was no corpse to recover."

"He doesn't believe so. According to him, he can still feel the bond, which means she can't be dead. We're all supposed to say she is, though," Tara explained.

"Because of the concern that it could cause civil war in Endara if half the people believe their queen still lives. But you're right. Celiaen is far too stubborn to keep his mouth shut. He'll want to throw it in Paienven's face as a parting shot." Looking around at the people surrounding them, Sannaeh nodded slowly. "We let him because Paienven won't believe him. If he believes Celiaen is running away from his duty for a foolish search, then he might let him go without a fight. However…"

Tara's eyes narrowed. "Yes, ma'am?"

"I'm quietly suggesting that I'd prevent none of you from going with your prince if your loyalty to him was so great."

Sannaeh did not dare say more than that. She could not trust any ears that might be listening. Sharing a look with Tara, Tynan shrugged.

"I'm sure we will consider our options appropriately."

"When does my son intend to leave?"

"As soon as possible. You can't blame Celi for wanting to get away from the place where his mate died. He's heartbroken. I suspect he and Gal will find someplace that suits them, hole up for a while, and drink themselves into a stupor."

Inclining her head, Sannaeh met Tara's stern gaze. "Look after him. Make sure he knows his mother loves him."

"Yes, ma'am." Tara saluted before frowning. "The daoine…"

"What about them?" she asked.

Rolling her shoulders, Tara stepped closer, leaning in so she could whisper, "Vartan fears something Eirian did will cause a civil war in Telmia."

"What did she do?"

"She undid what her mother had done. I'm not privy to everything, but from what I overheard, there may be worse to come." Stepping back, Tara warned, "Just be aware."

Glancing at her hands, Sannaeh longed for years gone by. "I will. Thank you, Tara. You've always served me well, my friend. Take care of my son for me."

"I've been doing it since before he was born, and I intend to continue doing it for at least another hundred years. Unless the stupid boy gets himself killed doing something I tried to stop him from doing."

Moving away from them, Sannaeh paused and gave them a curious look. "You were both familiar with Eirian Altira. Do you not grieve her?"

Snorting, Tynan winked. "Grieving her would require us to believe she's dead."

"Indeed."

Parting with them, Sannaeh picked her way back to Paienven's side. She did not dare to leave him for long. The opportunity to mull over her thoughts did not last, and she soon realized Tara and Tynan had come ahead as a warning. Parting crowds let Celiaen stride through, his dark eyes locked on Sannaeh. Darragh muttered something under his breath that Paienven ignored, the king eager to remind his son of his place. She stepped away from him, hoping Celiaen would understand the unspoken message.

Standing side by side with Celiaen, Galameyvin looked like he was enjoying the prospect of what was about to unfold. It bothered Sannaeh more than she expected. He had always been a favorite of Paienven. Keeping his eyes on her, Celiaen had a hand resting on the hilt of one of his swords and his mouth set in a grim line. He had seen the prisoners and wondered when Baenlin or the Endarans would step in to stop it.

Arching a brow, Paienven smiled cruelly. "So, I see you survived."

"I'd say the same to you, but I doubt you entered the battle," Celiaen replied, barely bothering to glance at him. "Mother, I'm pleased you're well."

She wanted to reach out and offer him comfort. "I'm sorry to hear about Queen Eirian. We owe her more than we can express."

There was a flicker of amusement in his eyes, lips curling briefly as Galameyvin made a noise beside him. "Yes, you do. Every person here owes her their life. Perhaps you should hope she never wants to collect on that debt."

"And how would a dead woman collect on a life debt?" Laughing, Paienven stepped forward. "You sound foolish, boy, don't embarrass me."

"Eirian Altira is not dead."

"Celiaen," Galameyvin murmured.

Suspecting what was coming, Paienven reached out and grabbed a handful of the tunic Celiaen wore. No one moved to intervene.

"Don't be fucking fool, boy. Countless watched her die in battle. The Queen of Endara is dead. Long live whatever his name is. You can grieve as long as you need, but you have a duty to your king and kingdom."

Lifting his free hand, Celiaen wrapped it around Paienven's wrist tightly. His magic thrummed with his anger, reminding Paienven which one of them was more powerful.

"I can't believe it has taken me so long to do this, but I'm finally telling you no. I'm giving up my right to the crown."

"You should watch your words, Your Highness. You wouldn't want to make a mistake."

"My mistake was not doing it years ago. I have no desire to be the next King of Ensaycal."

Fury poured off Paienven, and despite Celiaen's hand on his wrist, he yanked his son toward him. "You will shut your mouth and behave as befitting the Crown Prince of Ensaycal. I will not tolerate such dissent from you, especially today after such a victory."

Eyes flicking over to Sannaeh, Celiaen laughed. "You mean after her victory? The battle is only over because of Eirian Altira. This victory is not yours to celebrate! Those Athnaralan were not yours to condemn."

There were murmurs of shock. It stunned many of the soldiers that Celiaen behaved the way he was. They viewed him as the finest example of both prince and red, a warrior regarded as the best, a man worthy of their respect. Officers glanced at each other in confusion before looking to Darragh, waiting for some signal, a hint of an order to follow.

General Darragh stood taciturn, a hand on the hilt of a sword, and his eyes locked on the King and Prince. Sighing heavily, Sannaeh shook her head and stepped up to Paienven. Without looking at Celiaen, she placed a hand on Paienven's arm and gently squeezed. He bared his teeth, glancing at her angrily.

"My king, please, think about where we are. Think about what this is showing your loyal subjects. Let the boy go. If he wants to turn his back on his family and people, that's his decision. He'll have no support from us."

It was a lie, and Celiaen knew it, but Paienven's eyes gleamed at the suggestion.

Pushing Celiaen away, Paienven replied, "You're right, my love. Awena has always been the more grateful child."

Galameyvin studied his aunt and uncle, his power picking up the concern for Celiaen that was underlying Sannaeh's words. "I suggest we leave while we can, Celi."

"If you go with him, Galameyvin, you're giving up everything." Paienven said, "No more money, no more entitlements, you'd have to make your own way."

Grinning, Celiaen turned to Sannaeh and bowed his head in respect. They stared at each other, unspoken words of love passing between them.

"Good luck, Mother. I suspect you will need it."

Nodding, Sannaeh was unwilling to speak out of fear that her voice would betray her. Filled with pride, she watched Celiaen turn his back on Paienven and take his first free step. She knew he would return for the throne when the time came, even if he had to go to war for it. Ensaycal needed him, and the unity that he represented. If Eirian lived, she hoped he found her sooner rather than later. But either way, his journey would only help him grow.

At the end of the lines of soldiers, Tara waited with the rest of his companions, the older red smiling. They would protect him, and Galameyvin would keep him sane. Sannaeh was confident in that. Pausing before he disappeared completely, Celiaen turned back with a smug smile.

"By the way, if you thought you could get King Aeyren, you'd be wrong. King Everett has him."

Biting back a chuckle, Darragh bowed stiffly to Paienven. "Sire, would you like me to find out if that is true?"

"It's true, or the whelp wouldn't have said anything." Snarling with anger, Paienven rounded on Sannaeh. "No doubt your fucking brother is with them."

Celiaen could not believe how much lighter he felt as he walked away and said, "Come on, we have one last stop to make before we leave."

"Enjoyed that, didn't you?" Tynan chuckled, sharing a look with Galameyvin.

"I'm sorry I couldn't say goodbye to my mother properly. She was alright when you spoke to her, wasn't she?"

Nodding, Tara linked her arm with Alyse. "She was, and she gave her blessings in a roundabout way. So where are we going first?"

Looking at the sky, Galameyvin said, "North. I think the Indari might have some information we could use."

Soldiers were everywhere, helping the wounded and trying to clean up the damage. Others were resting, taking any chance presented to them. No one was certain if the battle was truly over, despite the obvious signs it was. Those with the stomach for it were dealing with the dead. While Paienven had chosen an open and obvious spot to set up his command, the Endarans gathered outside the walls of Kelsby.

The only elves among them were those loyal to Riane, reds guarding against any attempt by the King of Ensaycal to take the prisoners the Endarans possessed. They hesitated to let the group pass through, unaware of what Celiaen had done and fearful Paienven had sent him.

"It's fine. Let them through," Fayleen said as she appeared, staff in her hand and a faint smile. "I wasn't sure if you would say goodbye."

"You know?" Celiaen replied, taking the arm she offered.

Shrugging, she watched him from the corner of her eye. "You're predictable to those who know you, Celi. You're going to go search for Ree, and I wouldn't expect anything less."

"Are you coming with us? I'd like it if you did."

Catching sight of Aiden next to Everett, she shook her head. "No, I have a promise to keep. My path lies here in Endara."

Eyes narrowing, Celiaen's mouth twisted in annoyance. "With the Captain? He's a good man, I know that. Just don't fall for him and expect him to love you back."

"We all love the same woman, Celi. You have your grand quest to drive you and Gal to keep you going, but Ree knew I'd need something, and she knew he would as well. So, I'll remain in Endara where I can help Aiden, and Everett, and I'll keep my promise to share my grief with someone who understands it." Before she parted from him, Fayleen turned to look Celiaen in the eye, instructing, "Just bring her home."

Letting Fayleen pull away, Celiaen watched her walk over to Aiden and Everett. There was no anger, no bitterness that she would remain instead of joining the search to find Eirian. He understood her desire to keep her promise. They had been friends before he had met them. Shifting his focus to the group of men surrounded by drawn weapons, Celiaen waited with his companions to witness the outcome.

It was obvious which one was Aeyren, the defeated king on his knees before Everett and the Endaran nobles. He was speaking, offering apologies repeatedly, and begging for mercy on behalf of his people. Celiaen pitied the man, and judging by the pained expression on Everett's face, he could tell he did as well.

"Please." Aeyren spread his hands, pleading, "Please, do what you must to me, but do not blame the men who followed my orders."

Unable to resist speaking, Celiaen stepped forward. "You take the blame for what General Tomas did?"

"I do. I was his king. I allowed him to lead me down a path of madness that would have ended us all. All the deaths that resulted are on my hands as surely as if I had delivered the blow myself. My weakness allowed this to happen, and there is nothing I can do to change that or to make it better."

Marcellus leaned in closer to Everett, saying, "You know what you have to do."

"His Grace is correct," Cameron said, staring at Aeyren.

Lips thinning, Everett looked to Celiaen. "She would do it without hesitation, wouldn't she?"

"You know the answer," he replied.

"I want to hear it from you, Prince Celiaen."

Nodding slowly, Celiaen gave him what he wanted. "Her blade would severe his head faster than you can blink."

His hand tightened around the hilt of his sword, and Everett clenched his jaw. He had fought in battles, had taken lives, but the situation he found himself in was different. An execution was far more personal. Part of him wanted to ask someone else to do it, but he could not shirk the responsibility. He could not risk them thinking he was incapable of doing everything necessary. Looking over at the watching Athnaralans, he decided and crouched in front of Aeyren.

"I'll make it as quick as I can manage, but first, you will surrender Athnaral to me."

Aeyren's eyes went wide, and he choked. "What?"

"I will marry your sister and unite our families. Together, we will rule Endara and Athnaral as one. No more divided human kingdoms, no more war between our families. You told Eirian you wished for it to happen, and it will. But not with you as king."

Heart sinking, Celiaen's mouth parted, and he met Aiden's gaze across the space between them. They understood what it meant and the reaction it would garner from Paienven. Aeyren looked at the men behind him. They were the lords of his land and the officers of his army. Men who had served him well even when they grew fearful of what was going on. Some who had risked their necks speaking against Tomas.

Nodding to them, Aeyren turned back to Everett and carefully pulled the royal seal from his finger. Holding it out as an offering, he stared into Everett's eyes to get a measure of what sort of man he was. There was a flicker of grief in the brown depths, a sympathy that spoke of understanding. Accepting the ring, Everett slid it onto a finger beside the Endaran seal Eirian had given him and stood.

"For your crimes against all those living, I sentence you to death. May the powers have mercy on you, Aeyren."

Before Everett drew his sword, Aeyren smiled thankfully. "Look after my sister. You'll be a far better king for Athnaral than I was."

"I'll do my best."

The sword was heavier in his grasp than usual, and Everett thought he was going to struggle to lift it. Placing her hand on the inside of Aiden's elbow, Fayleen watched his face flicker through emotions. She had seen enough deaths that she felt no need to watch Everett lift his blade high, a powerful swing severing Aeyren's head from his body. The sound of it made her flinch, the thud of head and body hitting the ground.

Tilting his head, Aiden glanced at her with a hint of annoyance that faded when he saw her concern. Everett had not questioned her presence, and Aiden wondered what it was about Fayleen that made her fit in. Dropping his gaze, he noticed there were splatters of blood from the battle on her armor. A scattering of fresh drops from the execution joined them.

Everett took a deep breath and held his sword in front of him with the tip facing the ground. Blood dripped from it, joining the pool spreading through the dirt and flowers. His eyes caught on a white bloom nearby, several petals stained red, and it felt like a portent of what was to come. Lifting his head high, he regarded the Athnaralans coldly before looking at his people. Bowing his head in respect, Celiaen was the first to kneel, and quickly others followed.

"Hail King Everett," an Athnaralan lord spoke, those around him lending their voices in affirmation.

Unable to find reassurance in the voices echoing the sentiment, Everett felt a doubt that he could do what they expected of him. They had raised him to be a king, prepared him in case Eirian had refused, but that moment of acknowledgment filled Everett with doubt. It made him look to Aiden like a child desperate for the approval of an older sibling they worshipped.

He looked around, hoping in vain that Eirian was going to walk through the crowd with her confident swagger and amused smile. Everett wanted to hear her laugh at him, her voice telling him that everything was fine, and he did not have to unite two kingdoms that had been at war on and off for a thousand years. Gathering himself, he signaled an officer and waved at Aeyren's corpse.

"We will treat him with the respect owed to a king, and his body will return to Athnaral so that we can lay it to rest with his ancestors in Mirrenel. We will accompany him." He looked at the kneeling Athnaralans and said, "Pick yourselves up. We have work to do, and we had best get on with it before Ensaycal attempts anything."

The one who had hailed him first lifted his head and blinked in surprise. "Are we not prisoners?"

"No, you serve me now. However, for your protection, the Earl of Tamantal will arrange for an Endaran guard until we're certain no one will try to kill anyone else."

"Of course, Your Majesty." Aiden bowed slightly, uncomfortable with his title.

Settling his gaze on Celiaen, Everett cocked a finger to summon him. "Tell me, Prince Celiaen, how far away is your king?"

Blowing his breath out through his lips, Celiaen shrugged. "The King of Ensaycal does what he wants, but I told him about this. I'm surprised he's not here already. Granted, he may have dismissed my comment as the spiteful parting shot of a former prince."

"You did it then?" Aiden grinned. "Good for you."

Seeing the opportunity, Everett said, "Well then, if you have no more ties to Ensaycal, we can always use your insight. Unfortunately, I suspect peace will be a long time coming."

"On the contrary, you have the support of Riane. Paienven isn't stupid. He wouldn't attack you without the backing of the high council." Galameyvin nodded at Fayleen. "You have a mage at your side who is friends with the future grand mage. I'd say that counts for more than you realize."

"If I were free to remain, I'd gladly do so. Our horses are waiting for us," Celiaen informed them.

"Mostly to piss off your father?" Reminded of his father and the relationship between him and Aiden, Everett chuckled. "I can appreciate that."

Feeling the prickle of magic, Celiaen glanced over his shoulder. "Beware King Paienven. My father is many things, but he isn't forgiving. He'll feel cheated by this."

Striding over to him, Everett offered him his hand, and Celiaen clasped it. "Thank you for everything you've done, Celiaen. I mean it, everything. You'll always be welcome here."

"I suppose you could say I was almost your king," Celiaen said and let his grief show.

"I suppose you were. Look after yourself, and I wish you luck with whatever you feel you must do. We won't forget that you were there for Eirian until the very end."

Returning the nod, Celiaen let go of his hand so he could leave. "Long may you reign, King Everett Altira."

"And congratulations on your future marriage. May it be a fruitful union that brings peace," Galameyvin said with a bow.

"Thank you, I certainly hope so."

Everett watched the two men leave and wondered if he would ever see them again. Debating his options, Aiden scolded himself and stepped forward.

"Your Majesty, by your leave, I'd like to escort Celiaen to his horses. We wouldn't want anything to happen before he could get away from his father."

Everett nodded his approval, expecting it was less concern for Celiaen's welfare and more a desire to exchange last words. "Of course, return as soon as you are able."

Following Aiden, Fayleen smiled. She was proud of him for finding closure between them. Leading the group in a different direction through the crowds of soldiers, Tara pointed to the waiting horses loaded with their gear and the provisions they had scrounged. Among them, Halcyon waited, unaware that his rider was not coming for him. It was the sight of a naked Saoirse leaning against her horse that startled the group, and she smirked at them.

"You're stuck with me," she said. "She's out there somewhere, and it would disappoint Faolan if I didn't help you."

"What about... you know?" Galameyvin reminded her of the chaos unfolding among her people.

Mouth twisting, Saoirse flicked a strand of red hair over her shoulder. She remembered everything. Those memories were the reason she needed to help find Eirian.

"I'm not the only one who has no desire to return to that mess. I believe a handful of others are in conference with the mages for permission to join them in Riane. You're going to need our help, and some of us aren't stupid about it."

Curious, Aiden could not take his eyes off Halcyon. "Will there be a civil war? Vartan seemed sure of it."

"He's sure, because he will be the one leading it. Neriwyn betrayed us. He's one of them. He's the god of war, in fact." Eyes flicking between Aiden and Fayleen, she smirked at them. "Curious."

Knowing Saoirse probably sensed the link Eirian had forged without their knowledge, Galameyvin looked at Fayleen seriously. "I suppose now is as good a time as any to tell them about Ree."

Her brows shot up in confusion. "I'm sorry, what are you talking about?"

"You know..." He waved a hand at his stomach, looking uncomfortable.

"Oh. Of course, she told you. I doubt Celi could feel any worse than he already does. So go for it. Best to get it out in the open before you go any further."

Scratching an eye, Fayleen refused to look at either of the men staring at her. Breathing in deeply, Galameyvin let it out slowly before he spoke. It took him a moment to decide how to break the news, opting for a direct approach.

"Eirian was pregnant."

Silence fell, and the elves that had been busying themselves with their horses stopped to stare. Face blank, Aiden recalled the fireside conversation when Eirian had told him mages had ways of preventing unwanted pregnancy. The thought that she had done it on purpose made him go cold, and shaking his head to chase the idea away, he decided he would rather believe she had been careless. Lifting his eyes to stare at Celiaen, he knew he was debating the same thing.

"That's not possible. Eirian would never be so careless."

"She wasn't careless," Fayleen muttered. "Quite the opposite. It was deliberate and calculated to increase her chances of victory."

Celiaen's face filled with horror, his anguish prominent. "She conceived my child as a sacrifice. After everything she went through, everything they did to us, she turned around and did the same thing."

While the revelation surprised her, Saoirse was more pragmatic. "What if she hadn't and today ended differently? Would you be here saying, 'why didn't she do everything she could have done'?"

Selecting his words carefully, Aiden spoke softly, "What if the reason we feel like she is still alive is because of the baby?"

"What?" Fayleen asked.

"Well, she was stabbed in the stomach. What if she used the baby instead of herself?"

Wanting to defend Eirian, Fayleen said, "No, she expected to die as well. There was no intention of trading one life for another. She needed the baby to be of all the bloodlines, for what little truth there is to that."

"She used the blood of the babe and threw in her own to reinforce it?" Saoirse cocked her head to the side and looked at the flowers stretching as far as the eye could see. "Risky, but it worked."

"Why didn't you tell me before?" Celiaen's voice was icy, anger and hurt on his face as he looked between the two people he had counted as friends.

Aiden knew. "Another one of her fucking promises."

"It's a good thing she isn't dead because when we find her, she's going to bloody well wish she was." Dark eyes darted to Saoirse as Celiaen said, "And then she's going to fix whatever the fuck she broke. After that, I don't care."

"You don't mean that, Celi." Taking a step toward him, Fayleen held out a hand.

He snarled, "You don't get to call me Celi anymore, Fayleen! If you were truly my friend, you would have told me. You should have told me."

"She wouldn't have told me about it if I hadn't known the moment I touched her. Don't forget what I can do, Celiaen," she replied. "And don't for a moment think I approve of what she did. Do you know how much it hurt keeping it from you? How much I desperately wanted to tell you? I couldn't, though, because I understood she was doing everything she could to make sure every one of us standing here right now lived!"

"Fay—"

"Shut the fuck up, Gal! Just shut up! I know what she did! All of it. I've always known. You all overlook me, just like you used to overlook Tessa. Poor little Fayleen stuck in Eirian's shadow. Poor little Fayleen, clinging to the most powerful mage that would have her because she's not that strong. Well, guess what? I've never lacked power. You all lacked vision. I know she bound Aiden and I together to drive me to keep my promise to help him."

They stared at her, and Aiden scratched his chin. "She did what now?"

Her eyes narrowed, and pointing at Celiaen, her top lip curled in disgust. "You don't get to behave like she set out to hurt you. That's a downright lie! She was trying to protect you from your own bloody stupidity. We know what would have happened if you'd known. You would have done everything you could to stop her fighting, and in doing so, you would have doomed us all. So get that through your thick fucking skull, you stupid brat."

Power was rolling off her in angry swirls, and Saoirse laughed. "I did not see that coming."

"Not helping," Cai muttered.

Breath whistling through his teeth, Tynan held his hands up to call for calm. "This is not the way you wish to part with each other. Celi is right to be upset, but everyone has powerful emotions today. After everything that has happened, it's understandable."

"She bound us together?" Aiden asked Fayleen.

Glancing at him, Fayleen nodded. "We weren't to know. Ree had concerns you might not survive when she died. She hoped linking us would be enough to keep you among the living. Everything she did, she did out of love for us."

"Right down to her last words asking Tessa to tell us she loved us." Sighing, Galameyvin looked at Celiaen and waited.

Fayleen's tirade had taken the drive out of his anger, and, mulling over her words, Celiaen could not argue she was wrong. "I'm sorry, Fay. Tynan is right. We're all emotional right now. But he's also right that this isn't how we want to part."

"We've been friends for a very long time, by my standards. I know it's been a drop in the ocean for you, but it's been most of my life for me. I love you, Celi. You and Gal are my brothers."

Her staff fell to the ground as Celiaen pulled her in for a hug. "I love you too, straw head."

"Hey!" Laughing, she clung to him and blinked back tears. "You better bloody find her and bring her back. Then we can all kick her ass together."

Wrapping his arms around her from behind, Galameyvin joined the hug. "You can still come with us, Fay. It won't be right without you."

Observing the three of them hugging, Aiden had never felt as left out as he did then. It felt wrong to be jealous, but he was. He did not want them to go; he needed them to stay. Part of him felt like they were abandoning him.

"Fayleen, I don't need you to look after me. Go with them. They're your family."

She whipped around to peer at him, and Fayleen snapped, "Don't be stupid, Aiden. I'm not going anywhere! You're stuck with me, so you better get used to it. I won't hesitate to kick your ass if I need to."

Snorting back laughter, Merle started choking, and Fox slapped his back as he said, "I'll pay to see that."

"Me too." Tara winked at Aiden.

"Fine. Obviously, you're too stubborn to argue with." Crossing his arms, he pretended her response had annoyed him.

Arms slung around the necks of the two princes, Fayleen said, "Do you think it's the right thing to do? You know, searching for her. Tessa seemed to think it wasn't."

"Of course it's not," Saoirse grumbled, running fingers through her hair. "But that doesn't mean we shouldn't try. You don't fathom how bad things will get. I mean, it feels foolish scaremongering but better to be forewarned and disappointed than not forewarned at all."

"Why isn't it the right thing? She's out there somewhere, alone. She'd come for us," Galameyvin replied.

Turning her green eyes skywards, Saoirse said, "You don't know what the gods were like. What the world was like before things went to shit, and Shianeni did what she did. Eirian opened herself to that side of her, the god part. She may very well be nothing like the woman you knew this morning."

"Eirian..." Galameyvin fell silent when she looked at him.

"Isn't immune to change. We don't know what Eirian is going through. We don't know where she is. You're lucky I'm old enough to remember things, so I have ideas of where to look."

Rubbing his face, Tynan nodded. "I think what she's trying to say is we shouldn't get our hopes up for finding Ree. We might find her, but she might not be the person we wanted to find."

"We will find her," Celiaen stated clearly. "And we will bring her home."

Fionn shrugged. "I mean, I had to fetch her a few times, so I know what it's like trying to find her. This means I'll be the one to state the obvious. What if she doesn't want to be found? You could spend the rest of your lives trying."

"He's right." Agreeing, Tara crossed her arms and looked at Celiaen. "Celi, do you expect us to never stop searching for Ree? Be reasonable and limit the search because you have people who care for you here. People who'd like to see you again in their lifetimes."

Kissing each of their cheeks, Fayleen pulled away. "Like me, for example. Your mothers. Siblings. Other friends and family. Go with Saoirse, search the most likely places, but I want you both home within ten years."

"Ten years is not long enough," Celiaen replied.

"Ten years, Celiaen. If I die without seeing you again, I'm going to come back, hunt you down, and kill you."

He arched his brows, reluctantly agreeing. "Ten years, but I reserve the right to leave again after that. Even if I have to go it alone. So long as I can feel the bond, I'm going to search for her."

Touching a hand to his cheek, she nodded. "You can, but I expect you back every ten years until I die."

"Die? You're stubborn enough to outlive all of us to prove a point." Covering her hand with his own, Celiaen smiled in affection.

"Damn right I am!"

It felt wrong to be the one to point it out, but Aiden glanced at the position of the sun. "You had best get started before night finds us."

Walking over to him, Celiaen held out his hand. "Thank you, Aiden."

"Bring her back, you hear me? Bring her back."

They clasped hands, gazes locked. A request for them to stay was on the tip of Aiden's tongue. Searching Celiaen's eyes, he swallowed the words.

"I plan to. You better look after my Fay."

Glancing at her, Aiden promised, "You know I will."

Letting go of his hand, Celiaen turned to Fayleen and kissed her cheek before moving to the horses. "Come on, while we have sunlight."

Winking at Aiden, Saoirse spread her arms and transformed into her eagle form, taking a few bounding steps before her massive wings lifted her into the air. Aiden and Fayleen watched the elves mount with the rest of Eirian's guards behind them. Raising a hand to his chest, Aiden saluted the princes out of respect. They returned the motion, nodding to those watching their departure. When they finally disappeared from view, Fayleen sighed and turned to pick up her staff from where it had fallen.

"Are you alright?" Aiden asked with concern.

She looked at him and nodded slowly. "It feels rather final to watch them leave. I want to believe that he'll be back, and he'll have her with him, but…"

"But you can't help feeling some doubt."

"Yeah, exactly." Running a hand over the carved wood, Fayleen smiled sadly. "But it's not the end. We know that."

Offering her his arm, he agreed. "Not while we're still breathing."

Ignoring his offering, she slung her free arm around his shoulders instead. "You know, Captain, I think we're going to be fine."

"It's not captain anymore," he said.

Her smile turned mischievous, and she replied, "You'll always be captain to me."

EPILOGUE

Everything was silent. Nothing moved. Not even the wind dared rustle the leaves of the trees surrounding the mounds. But beneath the grassy coverings, the sleepers stirred as the magic holding them trapped crumbled. It would be a slow process. There were so many layers, each needing the previous to fade away before the next could begin.

The world of Tir froze while it waited.

It did not wait for the slumbering gods to awaken. No, Tir waited for her to take her first breath. Adorned in the weapons and armor she wore into the battle at Kelsby, she lay on the grass where Gebael had placed her. Blood covered her. The blood of the men she had killed in the fight. Her blood.

Gasping, she rolled onto her side and curled into a ball. Her hands found the hole in her armor where she remembered the knife piercing. Fingers dug between the layers, finding her skin beneath where the knitted flesh formed a scar. Eyes opening, she stared at the green and unfamiliar land.

Blinking, she felt the memories crowding in. They were finally free of the wall that had held them back all her life. She felt the press of power filling her. Her power. She pulled her hands away from her stomach and covered her ears, hoping it would block out the sounds assailing her. Heartbeats. The heartbeats of everything that lived. The heartbeat of Tir itself.

"No," she whimpered.

The ground gave way to new growth, brightly colored flowers surrounding her. In front of her eyes, a dandelion faced her, the yellow flowers oblivious to the torment she felt. Uncurling, she forced herself to sit and look around. Memories whispered of what the place was. They told her the mounds contained other gods. Feeling the decaying wards imprisoning them, she panicked and lashed out, her power scrambling to hold them together. Forcing them to remain trapped. She could not let them be free.

Thinking of the gods brought her mind to the others. She remembered Neriwyn, and a hand covered her mouth in disgust. Then it took her to Gebael, and her disgust became betrayal. She remembered the months he had been by her side, all the times he could have told her the truth. Screaming in anger, her hands returned to her stomach, and she doubled over. Everything she had done in what she thought was her last breaths came back, and she knew she had made a terrible mistake.

Annawyn was free.

Huddled over, hands pressed to her stomach where a tiny life no longer flickered, she sobbed and tore at herself in despair. She felt the thin threads of magic still connected to the ones she loved and clung tight. The power whispered in her mind that if she let go of the wards imprisoning the other gods, she could go to them.

For a moment, she let herself consider it. Let herself imagine throwing herself at Celiaen, of Galameyvin's arms holding her while her heart continued to break, the gentle way Aiden would stroke her hair. Tears ran freely down her cheeks, and struggling, she forced herself to remove the weapons secured to her.

When her hand closed around the hilts of her swords, revulsion filled her, and she vomited. The feeling only faded when she flung the weapons away. It returned when she freed herself of the knives on her belt and thighs. Spotting her bow quivers nearby, she wondered who had removed them. It made her question how she was in the mounds when they were so far away from the battlefield she had died upon. She could not remember everything that happened between feeling her life draining away and the moment the pain took over before she opened her eyes.

And it had been painful. Being reborn was painful.

Pulling the armor from her body, she finally saw the black lines on her arms where her sleeves had ridden up. They swirled and twisted over her skin, fracture marks where the four of them had divided. Shaking her head, she corrected herself. It had been Shianeni, not her, who split the gods. The memories were not hers, though they crowded her mind. She had to cling to her memories, to her mind, to anything Shianeni had not tainted. It was difficult when the power whispered. The bonds connecting her to the other three gods pulled incessantly, demanding she go to them.

Demanding to be whole.

Scrambling for one of her knives, she did not hesitate and drove it into her heart. For a moment, she felt a flicker of pain, but nothing happened. She did not die. She barely bled. Her flesh healed without leaving a mark. Throwing the knife away, she brought up more bile. Retching into the flowers, she felt nothing but hate. Hate for herself, her mother, Annawyn, and the two men who could have saved her from making so many mistakes. She hoped they could feel how much she hated them and how much she hated the power that made her exist.

She had expected to die. She had made her peace with it.

"Great Majesty?"

It broke through her spiral of thoughts and made her realize the creations Shianeni had locked away surrounded her. Lifting her eyes, she looked at the hopeful faces and kneeling people. Looked at the wings, the fangs, the claws, felt the eagerness to resume their predatory ways on those they viewed as lesser. Memories told her what they could and would do, and she clenched her fists in a fury. Shadows danced, screams of terror bouncing off the mounds.

The god of life hated, and she grieved.

END OF BOOK THREE

Thank you for reading! If you enjoyed this book, please review it!

Go to 5310PUBLISHING.COM
for more great books you can read today!

READ THE NEXT BOOK IN THIS SERIES:
SHADOWS OF LIFE

Careful; this blurb contains spoilers! If you haven't read the first three books of The Altira Series—*Magic of Lies, Blood of Husks,* and *Grave of Dandelions*—don't read this blurb!

For six years, Eirian has hidden from the world of Tir, letting her friends, family, and kingdom believe she is dead. Eirian realizes the mistakes she made. The mad god Annawyn is free to terrorize the world of Tir, and with her, the immortals previously imprisoned by Eirian's mother. Punishing herself for her choices, Eirian keeps the other gods locked away in the tombs where they had slumbered for more than a thousand years.

Celiaen and Galameyvin are faced with a different woman from the one they watched die. Tormented by her mother's memories, Eirian fears what she will become if she accepts her duty to the world of Tir. The gods of Death and War have waited patiently for Eirian to make her move. Willing to do whatever they must to ensure Annawyn is destroyed and reborn, the gods of War and Death must risk Eirian turning Tir into dust to keep her on their path.

"I died that day on the battlefield."

Six years after the war ended, the ripples of Eirian's death continue to affect her kingdom. The Unseelie army she released harasses small communities, killing indiscriminately. Now married, Aiden and Fayleen seek ways to stop the attacks, while Tessa and the mages do the same. With the treaty broken between Endara and Ensaycal upon Eirian's death and Celiaen's departure, King Everett faces mounting tensions amid the chaos of uniting the two human kingdoms under his rule.

Far from the lands they called home, Celiaen and Galameyvin seek Eirian. Whisked from the battlefield by the god of Death, Eirian has spent years struggling with her rebirth as the god of Life and her mother's legacy. Confronted by their reunion, she is forced to face the consequences of her choices and return to the land she left behind.

But there is more at stake than they realized: Eirian's return means a new war. This time, the enemy is the immortal Unseelie army that answers to the mad god who wants to destroy the world of Tir. To defeat them, Celiaen and Galameyvin must ask Eirian to risk crossing a line she might not be able to come back from.

Go to 5310publishing.com to get a copy now!
Scan the QR Code for more information and stores.

A Spellbinding Romantic Fantasy: AMONG STARS AND SHADOWS

Kayla Winters is no stranger to struggling, but the past year was too much, even for her. Kayla knows she needs to reclaim her life, but when she gets stranded in a world of magic and living myths, she realises two things: One, closure is the last thing she's going to get, and two, every fairy tale does indeed have a villain.

Desperate to return home as quickly as she can, the last thing she needs is her overwhelming attraction for the gorgeous Prince Declan getting in the way. Especially when his father has the power to control minds and is obsessed with gaining entrance to the human realm. When she has no choice but to seek refuge inside the castle, Kayla has every intention to stay away from its overbearing ruler and his son... until that plan backfires too.

Mind-bound, unable to escape, and forced into silence by a king who thinks her ancestry might be the key to his dreams of taking over the world, Kayla has until the next Winter Solstice for her true lineage—and her fate—to be determined. Between captivity at the hands of the king or certain doom, her options do not look so good. As the King's cruelty escalates, her potential magical heritage might be the one thing that can save her.

A Magical Romantic Fantasy:
TOUCH OF KINDNESS by R. Loomis

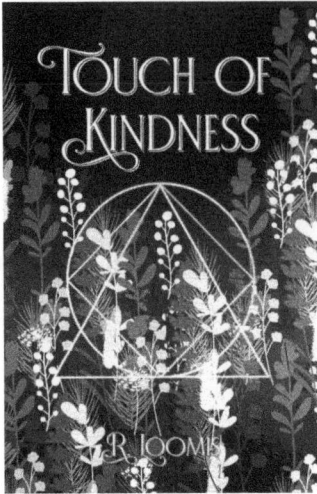

"Magical and entertaining!"
—*Early Reader Review*

Dori Livingston doesn't want to be anything special. She's fine staying in the background, helping her friends, and supporting her single mom any way she can while living in her small Texas town. That all changes when she meets a strange girl at school who is running away. In true Dori fashion, she welcomes the girl into her home without hesitation. Little does Dori know that in helping this girl she'll spark a chain of events that will change her life.

After showing Dori her ability to influence people with a single touch, Dori is left with more questions than answers. The next day, Dori is captured and taken to the Otherworld, a place full of magic and fantastical creatures. She learns the girl she helped was betrothed to a prince, and now Dori must fill the void, marrying His Highness in the girl's stead. Dori's mission becomes clear: get back home no matter what. However, getting back to the Mortal-world will be harder than she could have ever expected.

Milton Keynes UK
Ingram Content Group UK Ltd.
UKHW010756130624
444148UK00002B/13

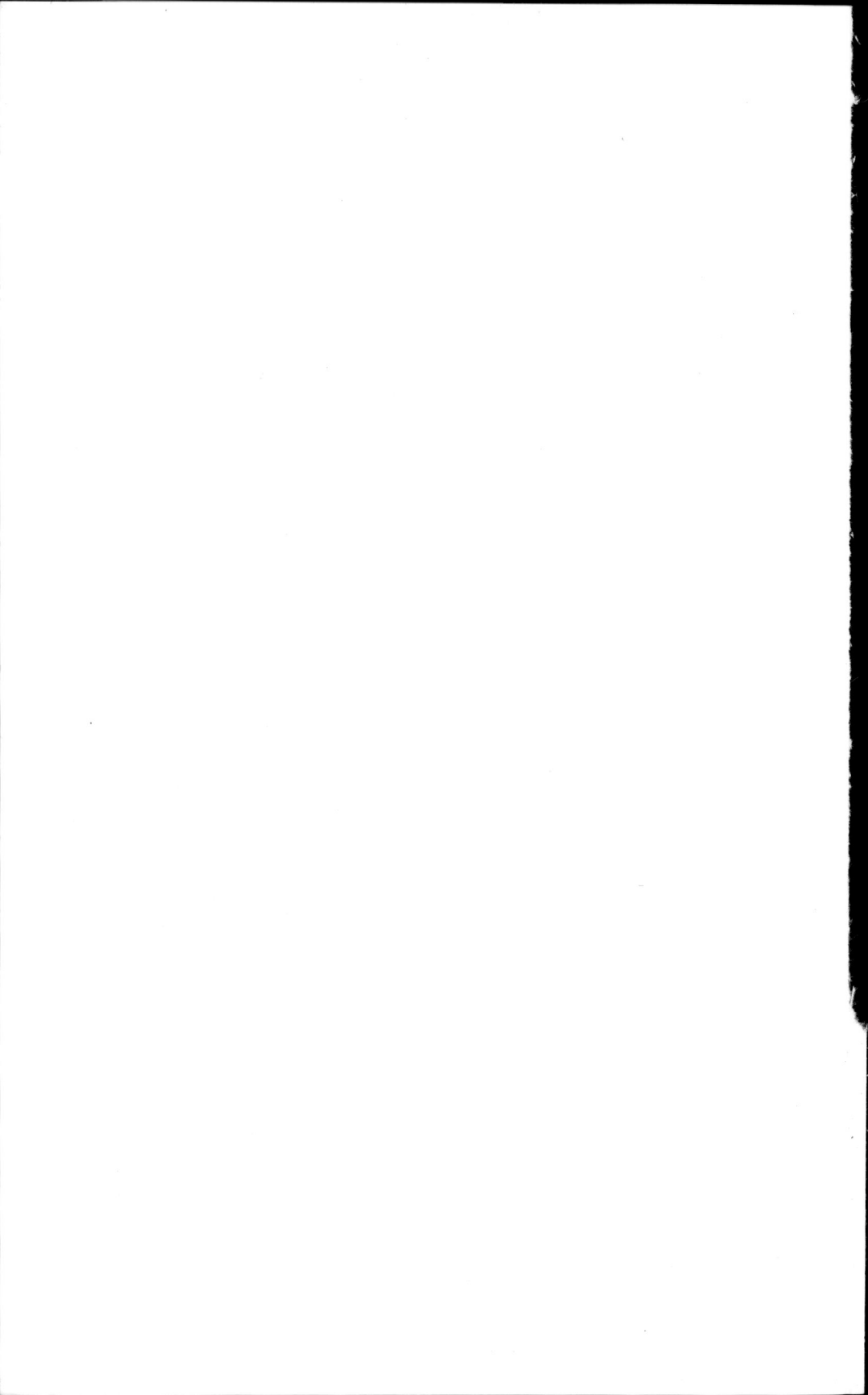